Earthly Remains

PETER HERNON

Earthly Remains

A NOVEL

A BIRCH LANE PRESS BOOK
PUBLISHED BY CAROL PUBLISHING GROUP

Library of Congress Cataloging-in-Publication Data

Hernon, Peter.
    Earthly remains : a novel / Peter Hernon.
       p.   cm.
    "A Birch Lane Press book."
    ISBN 1-55972-010-7 : $18.95
    I. Title.
PS3558.E69E37   1989
813'.54--dc20   89-15127
                                   CIP

To my wife, Janice

Earthly Remains

CHAPTER 1

THE FLOOR SHIVERED as the first shell exploded. It had hit somewhere close, probably near the Commercial District. I could often get a fair idea of the location from how violently the floor pitched or from how much broken plaster fell. It was just after three o'clock.

"Right on time," said Mike Weil, not looking up from his typewriter.

With unusual punctuality, the Arab batteries that had fanned out on the Mount of Olives had been lobbing 5-millimeter shells into Jerusalem between three and five every afternoon. One of their favorite targets was the blockhouse-shaped building on King George V Avenue, where the Jewish Agency had its headquarters. A few months earlier the place had been car bombed in broad daylight—a neat job that killed thirteen Israelis.

It was one of the first stories I'd covered since joining the AP bureau in Jerusalem. An easy one to write—but not to look at. The Arabs had managed to steal a Ford sedan from the United States consulate; they packed the trunk with TNT and parked directly in front of the wing where the Haganah had its command post. A sharp-eyed guard noticed the car, realized something was wrong and was driving it toward the gate when it blew.

Built like a fortress, the cementblock building had been severely damaged. The exterior wall was scorched black and there was a jagged hole big enough to drive a truck through.

Our bureau was only a few blocks away, and when I got there they had just started moving out the wounded. I helped them carry a young woman to an ambulance. I remembered that she had blond hair; most of her face was missing.

I wasn't looking forward to going back, but Weil had asked me to cover a press conference there at four o'clock. The Arabs, notorious fumblers with artillery, would just be getting their range by then, so I wasn't pleased—especially considering the subject. An archeologist from Hebrew University was going to talk about an "important discovery" he had made.

Another shell hit. This time the floor, our crude seismograph, didn't shake at all. The shell had exploded a few blocks farther away, probably near the Jewish Quarter in the Old City, another preferred target.

"You're sure about this?" I asked.

Weil, the bureau chief, kept pounding on his ancient Royal.

"It stinks, but you can be sure UP and Reuters will staff it. This kind of thing is right up their alley."

"Who the hell is this guy?"

"He's the head of the archeology department. His name is Glasner. And, brother, that's all I know."

"I don't mind risking my neck for the good of the team, but I've got to tell you, Mike, this one sounds like a loser."

The bell rang on the Royal's carriage return, then rang again. Weil, tall, moonfaced and wearing glasses with thick round lenses, had just signed off on yet another follow-up story that tried to explain, in 300 words or less, why the Irgun had wiped out 142 women, children and elderly men in the Arab village of Deir Yassin. The massacre had already become a worldwide cause célèbre. The other shoe had fallen a few days later when a truck convoy loaded with medical supplies was ambushed on its way to the Jewish Hospital atop Mount Scopus. The slaughter occurred in full view of the city's rooftops. Most of the passengers were doctors and nurses; the lucky ones were killed by snipers, but most burned to death when their trucks were fire bombed. It was that kind of war—an eye for an eye, an innocent for an innocent.

"You want out?"

Weil looked at me through a blue haze of cigarette smoke.

"No need," I said. "I just want to warn you in advance the story might be about a lynching if this doesn't amount to anything."

"So much the better," Weil said, smiling.

We got along well considering we were working seventeen-hour days and didn't get a chance to bathe regularly. I'd first met Weil three years earlier when I joined the AP in Paris. He'd been covering the worsening situation in the Holy Land for over a year—since early 1946. I owed him a lot; he had approved my transfer to Jerusalem.

I left him alone with the telephone as he tried to get an overseas line to Rome, the wire's hub bureau for the Middle East. It was always a crapshoot, and I didn't want to be around when he started dictating his story and the connection went dead.

Our office—a small room with two desks and two typewriters—was in the basement of an apartment building on Ben Yehuda Street. We'd moved twice in the last two weeks to get out of the line of fire. I had a few minutes, and so I climbed up to the roof, which offered a good view of the Jerusalem skyline with its spires, bell towers, minarets, and gleaming domes. The gray walls of the Old City rose and fell with the high ground to the north. I could just make out the leaden dome of the Haram-esh-Sharif. I counted three fires burning, the smoke billowing high in black clouds.

I looked up Ben Yehuda toward Zion Square. The street was deserted. Yarden's Coffee Shop, a favorite watering hole for newsmen covering the fighting, was just up the block. It was one of the few places where you could still get decent wine; at this time of the day, its metal shutters would be lowered. Somewhere to the north, toward the Old City, sirens wailed.

Almost four months had passed since I had arrived in the country aboard a British transport that had landed at Jaffa. We'd come up the Mediterranean Coast in a thunderstorm—three reporters and about thirty paratroopers assigned to the British forces in Palestine, the Mandatory Army as it was called.

Events had begun to move quickly by then. The United Nations had passed a partition resolution in late November of 1947. The British mandate was scheduled to end on May 15th, which was just over two weeks away. Everybody knew what was going to happen after the English troops pulled out—all-out fighting.

I'd worked for the AP long enough to know what war was like, particularly war against the Jews. I was there when Patton's Third Army went into Buchenwald. I'll never forget seeing a small boy, perhaps nine or ten, walking alone along a road lined with withered bodies stacked like cordwood. The child didn't seem to notice or mind the sight, which was hard enough to take, or the smell, which was worse. He was eating a piece of C-ration cheese.

He wore shorts and big heavy boots with open laces that came almost to his knees. I had watched him remove them from a dead man.

The next morning, Patton ordered 1,000 German civilians out to the camp to see firsthand what their leaders had been up to with their "final solution." They were led past the corpses. There were hundreds of them arranged in neat piles in front of the crematorium. Some of the men and women were crying. Not all, not even most. I had expected more tears.

Somewhere around that time I decided to put in for assignment in Palestine. My reasons were pretty simple: I wanted to see how the Jews were going to fight their way back from the Holocaust. I made two trips to New York on my nickel to push for the job. By then I'd become a partisan of what was happening in the Holy Land. I had never been one for causes. But after Buchenwald and Warsaw and Treblinka, after the ache in the soul, I'd found something to believe in again. I wanted to be there to report how a handful of men and women were building a state with little more than courage and cool intelligence. How they were coming back from the abyss. It took nearly a year of letter writing, of phone calls, of pulling strings, but finally I was sent over.

Crouched behind the chimney on the roof, I scanned the Mount of Olives for the muzzle flashes of Arab artillery until it was time to get going. Weil was on the telephone when I got downstairs. I pointed to my watch and went out into the street. I didn't have far to go, six or seven blocks.

For the moment the barrage had fallen off, but I heard the rattle of small arms fire in the distance. The neighborhood near the bureau, the Shaarei Hessed District, was in Jewish hands, but you could never be sure it wouldn't be infiltrated.

Most of the shops and houses that fronted the curving, narrow street had escaped damage. The one glaring exception was a two-story building, a private home, that had taken a direct hit a day earlier. The façade lay in an ugly pile of smashed stone and broken timber in the middle of the street; the second story had collapsed into the first. When I passed, four or five men and women were digging in the rubble.

A Jewish soldier, a member of the Haganah, stood in the street, holding a sign printed in Hebrew. I asked him what it meant. Slender and bearded, he looked very young. He frowned and in broken English explained that the sign asked for silence. They were trying to hear the cries of the wounded lying pinned beneath the debris.

I kept going and caught up with two men I recognized. One worked for the *Herald Tribune;* the other was with United Press.

"Let me guess," I said. "You're on your way to cover a little talk on archeology."

"I just want to lay eyes on the crazy bastard who set this up," said the man from the *Trib*. He wore an ill-fitting suit and a hat with the brim turned down over his eyes. "What kind of an ass would call a press conference in the middle of a bombardment?"

"The same kind who'd send asses like us out to listen to him," said the UP reporter.

I started to say something just as a shell landed with a wrenching blast a few streets over. The Arabs were back at it. We flattened ourselves against a wall. We could see the Jewish Agency across the next intersection. A flag with the blue and white Star of David was flying on the roof.

"That looks like Lottman," said the UP man. "Christ, he's frozen stiff."

Lottman, bald and overweight, worked for a large newspaper on the West Coast. He was lying face down on the sidewalk.

We shouted to him but he didn't move. Then the shells really started pouring in. We couldn't see where they were coming down, but it was very close. The ground heaved and smoke drifted toward us.

I made up my mind to run for it. I figured I'd have a better chance inside the Jewish Agency than out in the open.

I sprinted for the intersection with the two others right behind me.

We stopped for Lottman. I grabbed him around the waist and the *Trib* man took his legs and we carried him, arms and legs flopping, through the agency's gate. The courtyard was enclosed by a high, thick wall topped with barbed wire. Soldiers were crouched behind sandbags; two of them ran over to help us. We dropped Lottman on the brick pavement and sat down, our chests heaving.

"How bad's he hurt?" I asked.

One of the soldiers examining Lottman grinned. "He has fainted."

The shelling had veered off in another direction like rolling thunder. The soldiers helped us carry Lottman inside. The news conference was to be held in a basement office. Three or four reporters were already sitting on folding chairs near a wooden table. A single light bulb dangled from the ceiling. We deposited Lottman on the floor and a soldier gave him a dose of smelling salts which brought him around. He sat up and got sick.

It wasn't a pleasant gathering. After running a gauntlet to get there, all of us were in the same angry, jittery mood.

"If the rest of you bastards weren't so eager to cover this idiocy, I wouldn't have to be here," said the reporter from the *Trib*.

"Why don't we leave? All of us," said another man. "That way no one would get in trouble."

A nice thought, but none of us were willing to take the gamble. You could always count on at least one rat.

There was some more beefing, the mean, vicious kind, and then a short, round-shouldered man in a rumpled suit entered the room. He placed a worn briefcase on the table. He wore glasses and had thick black hair that touched the tops of his ears and was flecked with gray.

"My name is David R. Glasner," he said, facing us. "I want to thank you for coming here this afternoon. I am sure there are places you would much rather be at this moment."

"You've got that right, professor," someone said.

Glasner explained that he was the chairman of Hebrew University's archeology department. He'd spent much of the preceding year in the United States on a sabbatical. He said the events he wanted to talk to us about had started to unfold two months earlier, shortly after he had returned to Jerusalem.

In heavily accented but precise English, he began to describe how he had acquired three ancient Hebrew parchments. He called them "scrolls."

I could tell from the uneasy glances and nervous coughing that some of the boys were beginning to wonder what this was all about. A couple of the guys finally blew.

"Are these scrolls the big discovery?" asked the man from UP, anger lacing his voice. "Is this why we risked our collective butts?"

Another man, in a tone only slightly less hostile, asked Glasner why he had picked one of the Arabs' favorite targets in which to make his announcement.

The scholar took it all in silence. He laid some papers on the table.

"Forgive me," Glasner said finally. "It is so important, so extremely important that you understand. It is my conviction that these scrolls are among the greatest treasures ever found in the Holy Land."

He leaned against the table as if to steady himself.

"You asked why I chose the Jewish Agency for such a purpose," he continued. "The answer is simple. This small building will soon be the capitol of our state, the symbol of our independence. There could be no better place to report the discovery of these scrolls. I firmly believe they are a profound gift to our Jewish heritage."

I couldn't be sure because I was in the back of the room and it was dimly lit, but I thought his eyes were moist. There was no mistaking the emotion in his voice.

No one said a word. In spite of ourselves, we were all moved by the man's sincerity.

Finally someone said, "OK, professor, you win. Would you mind taking it again from the top?"

Glasner nodded in gratitude and I started scribbling notes. His story was that some Bedouin tribesmen had originally found the scrolls. They were tending their sheep out in the Judean desert not far from the Dead Sea when one of them threw a stone into a small entrance of a cave and was startled to hear something break. He and another man crawled into the cave, which was high up a cliff, and found some clay jars. The scrolls were inside one of the jars.

The Bedouin discovered five scrolls in all. After wandering in the desert with their small herd of sheep for a few weeks, they came to Bethlehem, where they sold the scrolls to an Arab antiquities dealer whom Glasner chose not to identify. The dealer had sent a message to Glasner through a mutual acquaintance that he had something he thought the professor might want to take a look at.

Glasner told us he had hesitated. Bethlehem was in Arab territory; a trip there would be dangerous for a Jew. He had bought several pieces of valuable statuary from the dealer in the past, so with considerable misgivings he boarded one of the few buses that still ran between Jerusalem and Bethlehem, and made the journey without incident. After examining the scrolls, he purchased three of them on the spot in the name of Hebrew University. He didn't have enough money to buy the other two and was still trying to raise it. He wanted to return to Bethlehem to continue negotiating with the dealer, but with the fighting that was out of the question.

"Where did you say that cave was?" someone asked.

"By the Dead Sea. I am told it was several miles south of Jericho."

He opened his briefcase and took out a small bundle wrapped in newspapers. He gently peeled away the husk of paper and held up a brown, brittle looking roll of leather badly torn at the edges.

"This," he said, "is the book of the prophet Isaiah. As you can see, the scroll has been damaged. I am convinced that it may be one of the oldest books of the Old Testament ever found."

At that moment a shell exploded nearby. Plaster fell from the ceiling and the light blinked off and on. I threw myself belly-flat on the floor like everyone else. When I looked up again, Glasner was still standing there, holding the scroll.

He went on as if nothing had happened. I don't think he even noticed.

"The oldest complete book in biblical Hebrew previously known to exist dates to the early 11th century. I haven't finished my examination yet, but this scroll is in a script that suggests it could be much older."

"You're sure it isn't a forgery?"

Glasner shook his head. "There can be no question of that. The script itself is the best proof of its authenticity. It resembles the markings made on burial ossuaries that are believed to date to the late 9th century. I should think it would be most unlikely for a forger to even be aware of that script, much less duplicate it in such a wonderful way. The writing is quite beautiful."

He explained that he himself had done work on several of these ancient ossuaries, burial crypts for bones that had been discovered within the last few years in Jerusalem. They had been chiseled with words written in a similar style. The similarity, he said, immediately came to mind when he first examined the scrolls.

"I can assure you that my hands were shaking when I started to read."

For the next fifteen or twenty minutes he continued to discuss the scrolls, which he also called "leathers." In addition to the Isaiah, he had acquired a nearly complete book of the Psalms and a work which he hadn't yet identified. He knew only that it wasn't a biblical text.

As he said this, another shell burst somewhere close to the agency. This time none of us ducked. We were too busy taking notes, swept along by the force of the man's narrative.

Someone asked who Glasner thought had written the scrolls.

After a long pause, he said, "I can't answer that. My guess would be they may have some connection with a group well outside the traditional Jewish mainstream. The Essenes come to mind."

The Essenes, he explained quickly, were an obscure Jewish sect that was thought to have first existed in Palestine some two hundred years before Christ.

"This is all conjecture," Glasner said. "The leathers were found in a region that may have been inhabited by the sect. The desert south of Jericho near the Dead Sea. We know very little about them—hardly anything at all. Ancient sources tell us that they apparently lived a monastic life. I will admit their connection with the scrolls is tenuous at best. But it's something that will have to be explored." He came to a full stop. Then with some hesitancy, he said, "The one thing I can say with conviction is that these scrolls will almost certainly require us to reexamine the authorship of many sacred writings."

By then it was well after five o'clock. The fireworks outside had ended. For the time being, the Arabs had moved from their guns to their prayer rugs. We asked a few more questions. None of us thought we had a page one story—nothing to file a bulletin over. And yet there was something to it. "Mysterious Archeological Find in the Midst of the Shooting." I figured a headline like that would play pretty well in the Sunday feature sections back home.

Glasner stood at the door and shook our hands as we filed out of the basement. I asked him what he planned to do next with the scrolls. He wished to finish translating them so that they could be published.

"This is only the first step of a journey that will take many years."

At the time I didn't realize how right he was or how much my life was going to change as a result of what he had told us. I just wanted to get back to the bureau and file two or three hundred words before the opposition beat me to the punch.

The sky was turning dark. It wouldn't be long before prayers were finished and the real fun in the streets started—the bushwhacking, sniping, no-holds-barred house-to-house guerrilla fighting that had transformed the Holy City into a war zone.

"What did you make of all that?" I heard one reporter ask another as we headed back into Ben Yehuda Street.

"A nice story," the man answered. "But not worth getting killed over."

CHAPTER 2

I GOT BACK TO THE OFFICE and somehow got a clear line to Rome. Weil listened as I dictated. He wasn't overjoyed but I didn't get any complaints. It wasn't until later that night as I lay in bed in my dark one-room apartment in the American Colony Hotel that I realized how much Glasner's compelling sincerity had impressed me. I would have liked to do a few follow up pieces.

But during those last grim days in April, the fighting really took off and I was lucky to keep my head above water. The Jews and Arabs were slugging it out as they jockeyed for position on the eve of the British pullout. Jerusalem was in a bad way. Bread was rationed and kerosene for cooking and heat was so scarce you could smell the smoke of charcoal fires all over the city. The water had been shut off for weeks, ever since the Arabs had blown the main aqueduct that ran to the wells in Ras el Ein. The emergency reserves in the city's cisterns provided four pints a day for each resident. Four pints for drinking, washing, and cooking. Long lines of people with buckets waited for water trucks to appear on the streets.

I was also out in the country for a few days, visiting key Jewish kibbutzim that were under constant Arab attack. Fighting raged almost every night around these farming settlements, and I always made sure to leave well before sundown. I was more convinced than ever that the Jews weren't going to roll over. Their backs-to-the-wall resourcefulness was remarkable. I'd seen how they had bolted steel plate onto war surplus jeeps, turning them into armored cars, and how they used Piper Cubs—an improvised air force—to bomb enemy troop positions with hand grenades and sticks of dynamite. It all made good copy, and I did several long color pieces, which seemed to please the boys back on the foreign desk in New York.

About this time I got a call from an Arab I knew who had operated a fleet of broken down cabs before they were seized by the Arabs. Now he sold information. He wanted to meet me a few hours later in the Old City.

Normally, I would have said no. I'd been to the Old City on business two or three times, enough to know that it was no place for a casual visit. The Arabs and Jews were fighting hand-to-hand for control of the district. At night the narrow, medieval streets that curved, climbed and twisted around the souks and holy places were a no-man's land. I almost decided not to go, but the Arab had provided some good tips in the past. I didn't want to discourage him. Against my better judgment, I heard myself asking where I should meet him.

"I will be at David's Tower," he said.

"This better be worth it."

"You do me an injustice," he said, hanging up.

David's Tower, also called the Citadel, was close to the Jaffa Gate. It was just inside the walls on King David Street.

Weil was out on assignment so I left a message and started walking. A few buses were still running but you could age badly waiting for one. It was a warm, clear spring afternoon. The Arabs had suspended their daily bombardment for the past few days, and there were a lot of people in the streets. I passed a bakery; the line extended around the block.

As I neared Allenby Square I met a burial detail—two men and a woman struggling with a pine casket. The cemeteries in the Hinnon Valley to the south of the city and in the Sanhedrin to the north were under Arab guns, and so the dead were buried in backyards, in vegetable gardens, in broken sewers.

The square was deserted. On a better day, before the shooting started, the Fellahin would have been in from the country to do their marketing. But the metal shutters were drawn on the shops, and most of the buildings had been scarred by bullets and shell fragments. A few of them had been smashed; a handful of Jews and Arabs were still searching the rubble.

I descended a steep flight of steps. I'd taken the Jaffa Road. A longer way, it had the advantage of avoiding Mamellah Cemetery. The open ground of the cemetery offered a clear field of fire to

Arab snipers who had been playing bullet tag for days; five or six people died there every week, and a few reporters had had close calls.

I was in the ruins of the Commercial District now; most of the shops and houses there had been burned out when an Arab mob rioted to protest the U.N. partition vote. The British had stood by and watched indifferently as Jewish merchants were clubbed to death in their stalls. A day later the Haganah retaliated by blowing up an Arab bus right in front of the Jaffa Gate. I'd covered that story, and when I saw the tall arched gate flanked by palm trees and the walls of the Old City, it all came back to me. That's how I had got to know Jerusalem, running with notebook and pencil in hand from one horror to the next.

I stopped and took a long look at the massive gate built by Suleiman the Magnificent in the 16th century. He would have been appalled by its present appearance. Part of the towering entrance-way was bricked over and an unsightly entanglement of barbed wire and concrete barriers blocked its approach.

Behind the gate's turreted walls, about 1,700 Jews, many of them elderly rabbis and Yeshiva students living in the Jewish Quarter, were being defended by a couple hundred well-trained Irgun soldiers. When the mandate ended, they were sure to be cut off. The Old City was controlled by partisans of the Mufti of Jerusalem, an Arab hardliner named Muhammad Said Haj Amin el Husseini.

A rifle cracked somewhere inside the walls. I began to have serious second thoughts about what I was doing. I hoped my friend had something good.

A group of Arabs carrying bundles of firewood approached the gate and I fell in behind them. I showed my pass to a sullen-looking Arab soldier, who eyed me suspiciously, but let me by. He had held my press card upside down as he examined it.

Fortunately, I didn't have far to go. David's Tower, with its minaret and decorative wall, was just inside the gate. I walked half a block down a cobbled street and saw my man leaning in a doorway.

He was behind a garbage cart, a small, light-skinned Arab with thinning red hair and blue eyes—features he said he had inherited from Crusader ancestors. He wore a baggy jacket speckled with plaster dust. His name was Rachid.

"I have heard something remarkable," he said, smiling nervously after greeting me.

"Don't expect to be remarkably paid."

Rachid's many contacts in the Arab community had made him a valuable tipster. To his credit, his requirements weren't lavish—a few English pounds and cigarettes that could be hawked on the black market.

From the way he was grinning at me, I got the idea that this time it was going to be different. He had turned greedy.

"For this, I would like ten pounds."

"That's pretty steep, Rachid."

The Arab continued to show me all of his bad teeth.

"I would not ask for so much if it were not worth it."

"What do you have?"

"Then you agree to the price?"

"Come on, Rachid. That's not how the game's played. First you tell me what you've got. Then we talk price."

The smile faded. I knew what he was thinking—should he try someone else. I wasn't the only reporter on his list of preferred clients.

After some hesitation, he said, "I have heard about Glasner and the rouleaux." He used the French word.

"You mean the scrolls?" He had thrown me a curve with that one. I was betting he had something on the military picture. I hadn't thought about the scrolls in a couple of days.

"These scrolls as you call them...are they important?"

"Glasner thinks so."

"So does someone else," Rachid said.

He asked for a cigarette, which was part of the ritual. I gave him the pack, hoping it would prime the pump.

"There is an American staying at the Hotel Luxor," he continued. "He is said to be offering great sums of money for these ancient scrolls from the desert. Is such information of interest?"

I'll admit that he had piqued my curiosity. If an American was involved in a setup like that it might make a good sequel to the

earlier story. The only problem would be finding a few hours to
write it.

I had just under six pounds. I crumpled the bills into his hand
and promised to make up the rest in cigarettes. We agreed on two
cartons.

"His name is May," Rachid said. "He is going to much trouble to
acquire these scrolls. He has already purchased one in Bethlehem
from the same man Glasner did business with."

I remembered that Glasner hadn't revealed the identity of this
merchant. Rachid said he was named Aqui.

"I do not know him personally," Rachid went on, "but for many
years he has traded with Bedouin. He is a shoemaker by trade. A
most crafty fellow."

Glasner had said he had purchased three of the five scrolls that
had been found in the desert. He'd been trying to scrape the money
together to buy the other two; but now this guy May had got in
ahead of him and bought one of them for himself. Rachid said the
American was also negotiating for the remaining scroll.

"How do you know this?" I asked.

"I have many friends among the tribes."

It was interesting, but not to the point that I was sure my money
had been wisely spent. There were too many loose ends for a quick
score. Finding May or running down the Bethlehem connection
wouldn't be easy. I wasn't sure it was worth sticking my neck out
for. Then Rachid said something that made the difference.

May, he said, was trying to organize an expedition to travel into
the desert. He planned to look for the cave where the scrolls had
been found. His hope, apparently, was that the Bedouin may have
missed something.

"He does this in great secrecy," Rachid said. "A strange thing to
do during a war, wouldn't you say?"

CHAPTER 3

I DIDN'T HAVE A CHANCE to talk to Weil about it until late in the afternoon. By then he had some news of his own, a bombshell. It wasn't for attribution, but he had been told that King Abdullah of the Transjordan was going to commit the crack Arab Legion to the coming battle.

"He's finally decided to pitch his tent with his Arab brethren," Weil said. He was already at work on the story, an exclusive.

For weeks Abdullah had sat on the fence. He had held secret parleys with Ben-Gurion, whom he regarded as a close friend. The Jews had hoped he would stay out of the fight. With good reason. His Legion, commanded by former British officers, included 20,000 seasoned, well-drilled troops. Equipped with tanks and heavy artillery, they were the best soldiers the Arabs had, men you could count on under fire. If the king was finally committing himself to the Arab cause, it meant the scales had tipped sharply away from the Jews.

"Glubb isn't happy about it, but there's nothing he can do," Weil said. "There's been too much blood over the dam. The Syrians have really been leaning on Abdullah to come in with them."

Colonel John Glubb, the English commander of the Legion, had said repeatedly that he wanted to keep his men neutral.

Weil had found out from a source that Glubb's soldiers were pouring across the Allenby Bridge over the Jordan River. They were setting up camp near Bethlehem.

I helped pin down a few details on the story, which meant calling the Jewish Agency to try to get comment on the report. The Jews had been badly shaken but they weren't talking, at least not for the record.

When I finished these chores, I called the Hotel Luxor. May was out. I left a message to have him call me. I knew the deskman, a young German, because I'd stayed at the hotel for a couple weeks when I had first arrived in Jerusalem. I had tipped him fairly well and figured he owed me one. I asked him about May, but he wasn't much help. May rarely stayed at the hotel. But there was this detail: the deskman had seen him with a young woman and another man.

Almost as an afterthought I mentioned that I'd been told he recently had gone to Bethlehem. That's when I got lucky. The deskman told me that May planned to go there again early in the morning. He knew that because he'd made the arrangements to rent a car for him.

It was late in the evening before the story on Abdullah was written and transmitted and I was able to bring up what Rachid had told me.

"It's worth checking out," I said. "If this guy May is willing to nose around in a war zone to try to track down some old scrolls, it should make for a good feature profile. You've got to admit he's taking some big chances. He must think there's something important out there."

Weil wasn't excited.

"I've got more copy now than I know what to do with," he said, reading over his notes again. "I could use four more reporters."

I argued that the story would be an offbeat change of pace from the daily drumbeat of violence. It was a cinch to get excellent play. Weil frowned.

"I've been told he'll be in Bethlehem tomorrow," I said. "Why not let me drive down there. While I'm at it, I can try to get a handle on the Legion's troop buildup. I might be able to knock off a couple of leads at the same time."

I didn't think it would work, but Weil bought it.

"Just make sure you're back here by nightfall," he said. "You can use my car."

The next morning, I called the Hotel Luxor. May hadn't checked in that evening.

I picked up Weil's late-model Ford at the King David Hotel, the seat of the British mandate authority in Jerusalem. It was parked in a guarded motor compound, the only sure way to prevent it from being stolen.

By ten o'clock I was on the Hebron Road. Bethlehem, six miles to the south, was in the Judean hills. In Hebrew, its name meant "the house of bread," a description inspired by the lush fertility of the land. But the war had ruined the farming and the pastures were empty of sheep or goats. The road ran through the Arab village of Sur Bahir. The soldiers there wore checked kaffiyeh and British khaki, the uniform of the Arab Legion. I was stopped and briefly questioned by an Arab who spoke perfect English. After examining my press credentials, he gave me a crisp salute and let me pass.

I would have had a tougher time with Arab irregulars. The legionnaires, thanks to their British discipline, didn't go in for massacres or mutilating the dead. Of more immediate concern, they didn't go in for roughing up newsmen.

A mile or so outside the village I got my first look at Bethlehem; lying across a valley, the ancient town was spread out on the cone of a hill. White clouds rose up behind it like smoke. The red tile roofs of the houses sparkled in the sunlight and there were many spires and minarets. In the distance church bells were ringing.

I started down the hill, following a stone wall. There were tread ruts in the road and the olive trees behind the wall were powdered with dust. Tanks had passed that way and not long ago. I saw them a little later pulled off to the side of the road, two olive-colored tanks of British make. The stubby gun barrels and turrets were draped with tan camouflage netting. The crews were sitting around a fire, boiling water for coffee. They waved when I went by.

When I got to Bethlehem, I parked the car and started walking. Rachid had told me the antiquities dealer, Aqui, had a shop on Manger Square. I stopped five or six people before I found one who spoke English and got directions. On the way I passed through the marketplace. The souk was jammed with stalls, jostling Arabs and pilgrims. Braying sheep competed with shrieking merchants. The air reeked of dung and urine. I elbowed my way past a butcher's stall and stepped in something liquid. Bloody slabs of meat crusted black with flies hung from the rafters under a sagging canvas awning.

I bumped into an Arab who grabbed me by the arm. He lifted his hand to his mouth as if eating. He smiled and pulled me to another stall, where two Arabs were bent over a charcoal fire cooking small chunks of meat on skewers. Two young lambs quivered in a pen. The Arab said something and one of the men got up from the fire. He raised one of the lambs by its hind feet and severed its head with a single blow of a long, curved knife.

"One pound English," said my captor in rough English.

Someone else stuck a block of goat cheese in my face. I pushed away from them. An old woman wearing a yellow bandana tried to sell me a rosary and when I refused she offered some candles. An Arab came by with a brass water jug strapped to his back; brass cups dangled from a chain around his neck. I bought a cup of sweetened water mixed with lemon and started walking again.

Manger Square faced the fortress-like Basilica of the Nativity. Two armored cars mounted with .50-caliber machine guns were parked in front of the church. The square was enclosed on three sides by shops, cafes, and, directly across from the church, a small hotel with a pink façade that flew the Arab Legion's crescent flag. Some nuns in white habits were sitting by a fountain sunning themselves. A line of pilgrims was filing into the dark, low doorway of the basilica.

Aqui was supposed to be a cobbler. A flaking blue sign shaped like a shoe hung from chains over the doorway of a two-story building. The building, like most in Bethlehem, was made of rough blocks of red granite. The door was barred and curtains were drawn over the windows. A dirt-caked automobile was parked next to the building on a side street. It looked like an old Dodge.

I sat down on a bench and lit a cigarette. I didn't want to barge into the place. I smoked and waited for ten or fifteen minutes. Just when I figured I'd have to take my chances, the door of the shop opened. Two men and a woman stepped out. One of the men was tall and heavyset; the other was of medium height and compact build. Both wore short-sleeved shirts and walking shorts. The woman wore a denim jacket and twill pants and had long black hair. The three walked to the car. The woman was talking excitedly to the tall, older man, who I figured had to be May. The other man wasn't participating in the conversation, which looked heated. He picked me right up when I started walking toward them.

I called out May's name.

The tall man and the woman stopped and stared. Until then, they hadn't noticed me.

"That's far enough," said the shorter man who had been watching me. He sounded English.

The tall man asked what I wanted. He was an American all right. The accent was pure Middle West.

"I'm a reporter," I said. "If you're John May, I left a message at your hotel to call me."

The other man walked up to me. He had a thick neck and broad chest. I guessed he was in his mid-thirties. His eyes looked like pieces of blue glass.

"Do you want me to send this fellow on his way?" he said, glancing back at the other man.

"Sure, you can run me off," I said. "But if you're May, I'll be waiting when you get back to the Hotel Luxor."

"I'm May," the tall man said. "Who are you?"

"The name is Davoren, Paul Davoren."

I handed my press card to the bodyguard who passed it to May without looking at it.

May was about fifty, maybe a little older. His broad face was deeply creased. The flat nose may have been broken and looked propped up by his upper lip. His gray hair was cut short. He had a thick salt-and-pepper beard.

The woman was angry. She didn't like the interruption and it showed.

"I'm still waiting to hear what you want," May said.

I couldn't help the rocky beginning. I had to jump in fast.

"I understand you want to look for the cave where the Bedouin found those scrolls in the desert."

Without mentioning Rachid, I also told him I'd been told he had already bought one of the scrolls from Aqui and that he wanted to buy another.

The woman's face tightened. May's expression didn't change, but I knew I had jolted him. Without saying a word, he put his hand on my shoulder and gently, but very firmly led me to the side of the building. The woman and the other man stayed behind.

"Who told you all that," May asked quietly. He kept his hand on my shoulder and I didn't try to do anything about it.

"Let's just say that when an American comes to Jerusalem in the middle of a shooting war and throws money around, people are going to notice."

"I asked who told you?"

"These scrolls aren't exactly a secret," I continued. "A man named Glasner told some reporters how the Bedouin found them in a cave out by the Dead Sea near Jericho. He bought three of them from the same man you're seeing. He thought they were important."

May lowered his hand. "I know about Glasner. But that's not what I asked you, Mister Davoren. I asked how you found out about me."

"I can't tell you."

"Who else knows what you do?"

"Maybe no one. But I can't guarantee that the guy who tipped me off won't go to someone else. If I was interested in this desert expedition you're planning, the chances are somebody else could be, too."

"How much have you been told?" May asked, watching my eyes.

"No more than what I just said. That you wanted to look for that cave. I drove out here to find out if it was true."

"What would you do if I told you to get lost?"

"It wouldn't be easy to conceal a trip like that, especially from someone who already knows about it."

"And who's a reporter."

"I wouldn't like it if someone else got the story."

"I don't give a damn about that."

He was mad all right, but I kept coming.

"The way I see it, you can either talk to me now or talk to a dozen guys like me later on." I was laying it on thick there. "A pack of news hounds can be hard to handle."

"Is that a threat?" May asked.

"It's whatever you want to call it."

I hadn't planned on getting that rough, which wasn't my style. I usually preferred to play the diplomat; the results were better. But there wasn't any other way. I was getting more and more interested in May and in whatever he was trying to keep under wraps. I also wanted to know about the woman. Who was she? I hadn't expected a woman to be in on this. Whoever she was, she was attractive enough to make me self-conscious. And who was the bodyguard? He hadn't taken his eyes off me. I was sure he was as tough as he looked.

"We'll take this up again later," May said. "I have some business to finish."

"Mind if I tag along? I wouldn't mind seeing one of those scrolls up close."

May motioned for his mascot, who came over at a trot.

"I won't say or write a word about whatever it is you're doing here," I said, trying to think fast. "You've got my word on that." I didn't expect him to go for it, but I didn't have anything to lose.

May didn't say a word.

"I'm willing to gamble you'll want to talk to me later when you've thought it over. I'll even give you a couple days."

"You're becoming a problem, my friend. Mister Benteen here is an expert at dealing with problems."

"I don't doubt it, but reporters have a way of coming back and sometimes they bring along friends. Once a story gets out, it can be hard to keep the heat off. And just for the record, I've already got enough to have something on the wire by this evening."

May's expression didn't change. He walked over to the woman. They spoke quietly for a few moments. I heard him call her Sara. I couldn't hear much more than that, but I knew what they were discussing. The woman didn't look like she was buying any of it.

When they finished, May motioned for me to join them.

"If I let you come with us, you won't write anything?"

"I gave you my word. Nothing that happens today goes into print."

"I don't know whether you keep your word."

"Call my boss. Tell him what I just told you. He'll have my ass for promising to keep any of this out of print."

May hesitated. Then he said, "We better be going now. We've kept Aqui waiting long enough as it is. He won't like that." He turned, standing so close to me I could feel his breath on my face. "I don't want you to say a word in there. The lady and I will do all the talking. Is that understood?"

"What's her name?"

"Sara Garner."

I followed them into the narrow doorway of the shop. A bell jingled when May opened the door. Benteen was behind me. He didn't look any happier than Sara.

The shop smelled of leather. It consisted of two small rooms streaked with dusty bars of light that filtered through the window shutters. A long workbench was piled with shoes; an ancient sewing machine was on another bench. Hammers and other tools were in wooden racks on the walls.

A young Arab was waiting for us. He was surprised when he saw me, but said nothing as he led us up a short flight of steps to the living quarters upstairs. A beaded curtain was drawn and we were ushered into a dark room with a low ceiling. A shaded oil lamp provided a feeble light.

The man I took to be Aqui greeted us. He was a short, fleshy Arab in his mid- to late sixties with a neatly trimmed white mustache. He wore a dark, loose-fitting jacket over his robes. Another man stood in a corner and was about the same age as the Arab who had met us downstairs. They looked like brothers.

Aqui frowned when he saw me.

"Who is this?"

"A friend," May said. "He was late getting here. Have you settled on a price?"

Now I understood why they had come outside earlier. It was a strategy session. I saw coffee cups and saucers. Coffee was always served before any serious negotiations in the Middle East. The preliminaries were over.

As my eyes adjusted to the darkness, I noticed that the walls were hung with exquisitely woven carpets the color of burgundy wine. There were also some fine looking pieces of statuary displayed on stands and tables. It was like an antique shop. The cobbler had a nice black-market side line.

"I find it hard to come up with a suitable figure," Aqui said, deciding for the moment to ignore me. "The Bedouin have put their trust in me in this matter. I do not wish to disappoint them."

"What will you give them for all that trust, five percent?"

Aqui smiled at May's blunt question. The gloves had come off.

I stood next to Sara Garner. Her slacks showed off a fine figure. Her hair was brushed straight back from her forehead and tied in the back with a leather cord. I guessed she was twenty-seven or twenty-eight. Wonderfully tanned, she had high cheekbones, a full mouth with finely shaped lips and dark brown eyes. She paid no attention to me at all. That was too bad, because she interested me a great deal.

"I'd like to see the scroll now," May said.

Aqui bowed and disappeared into another room. The other two Arabs kept their eyes on us. I wondered if they were his sons.

The dealer soon returned with a newspaper-sized bundle wrapped in scraps of cloth. He slowly unraveled the coverings. The mud-colored scroll was crusted with what looked like tar. Larger than the scroll Glasner had shown us in Jerusalem, it was tightly rolled, about a foot long, and four or five inches in diameter.

Aqui placed the scroll on a reed mat on a table and stood back.

Sara Garner gently started to unroll it. The material was fairly pliable and looked like a tanned hide.

She examined the script with a magnifying lens for five to ten long minutes. Then she took May aside, and speaking very softly said, "It's ancient Hebrew, far older than anything I've ever seen before. It's not biblical. I don't even want to guess what it might be."

I was impressed. She was obviously a scholar of some talent. I wondered when and where May had hired her.

Aqui's smile broadened.

"What's your price?" May asked.

"It would be more charitable for you to begin," Aqui said expansively. "Perhaps you need more time. Would you like some coffee?

"I don't want coffee. Just a price."

A single blue vein stood out on May's forehead.

"This is not the way to haggle," Aqui said gloomily.

May burst out laughing. "All right. Have it your own way. I'll pay $1,500."

Aqui hesitated. "A fine price. But unfortunately my costs have gone up since our last transaction." Stroking his mustache with the delicacy of a cat licking its paws, he sounded almost apologetic.

"A few days ago I purchased a scroll from Mister Aqui," May

said apparently for my benefit. "I paid $1,000. That's almost twice the amount Glasner paid for three scrolls. This is the last of the five that were found in the cave by the Bedouin, and so Mister Aqui hopes to extract an even better price. That's why his 'costs' have suddenly risen."

Aqui seemed to pout. Then he smiled, becoming light, almost buoyant.

"It is true what you say. The market has changed."

Now, suddenly, Sara Garner, who had been slowly unrolling the scroll, stood up like a shot.

"It's been cut," she said in disbelief. "A piece is missing!" She turned to Aqui. "You've mutilated it!"

Even I could see the neat clean line where the manuscript had been severed.

"What do you know about this," May said. He was furious. I thought he was going to strike the dealer. So did the other two Arabs, who put their hands on the knives in their belts.

"It was done by the Bedouin," Aqui said with composure. "It was very stupid of them, but what can one do? They are simple people."

"Where's the rest of it?" May said angrily.

Aqui said nothing; he looked perfectly at ease. To his mind cutting an ancient document in pieces in the hope of selling them off for greater profit was a normal business procedure. I doubted the Bedouin had done it.

Benteen, who stood behind me, now said something in fluent Arabic. Aqui's complacent expression changed dramatically; he looked as if he had been slapped. The two Arabs drew their knives. Benteen pulled out a .45-caliber automatic that was tucked under his shirt.

"Enough of this!" May shouted. "Put your gun away, now!" Benteen obeyed, but took his time about it. Aqui said something and the Arabs slowly put away their knives.

"I'll pay $2,000 for the scroll and I want all of it," May said. "You've got one minute to think it over."

"Two thousand five-hundred," Aqui said, his voice hard and insolent. He had managed to come up with a price after all.

"I want to see the other part."

Aqui went into the other room and returned with another small bundle. Sara opened the cloth wrappings that covered the second half of the scroll; the sections fit together perfectly.

May agreed to Aqui's price and paid him. For a moment I thought the Arab was going to ask for more, but decided against it. Sara rewrapped the two pieces and put them into a canvas bag.

"I hope we can do business again," May said sarcastically.

"I do not think so," Aqui said stiffly. "This was badly done."

When we got outside, I asked May when I could talk to him for an on-the-record interview. He suggested that I meet him the next afternoon at his hotel. He was in a good mood, and so I didn't remind him that we had a deal and that I wouldn't appreciate a doublecross.

The three of them got into their car, and I headed back toward Manger Square in sunlight so bright I had to squint. I still had some work to do. I'd promised Weil I'd scout out the Arab troop positions around Bethlehem. I had it in mind to try to find some of the Legion's British officers and see if I could talk to them.

I was walking away when the Dodge pulled next to me. May sat next to Benteen, who was driving. Sara Garner was in the back seat holding the canvas satchel on her lap.

Benteen leaned out the window and said, "I wouldn't stick around here, not unless reporters have started carrying guns."

"Why's that?"

"Those two boys with the knives aren't very happy."

CHAPTER 4

THE ONLY Legion officer I tracked down wouldn't talk on or off the record about their mobilization. But I could see enough troop trucks moving in the dusty hills south of the town to know the Arabs were bringing up reinforcements. On the way back to Jerusalem, I saw more tanks draped with camouflage netting pulled off the road near those I had noticed earlier. I wasn't an expert, but it looked like a heavy buildup.

Weil was out when I got back, but had left a message. The Foreign Desk in New York wanted another piece on whether the Jews could hang onto Jerusalem when the British withdrew. They wanted it the day after tomorrow. Weil wanted it tomorrow. I thought I could throw something together, fashioning a lead on what I had seen around Bethlehem.

I made a few calls on the story. Then I telephoned one of my sources, a press officer on the British High Commissioner's staff. I asked him if he could find out anything about May, Sara Garner and their Englishman. He didn't like it, but he said he'd see what he could do.

I'll confess that Sara Garner interested me more than May. I wondered whether they shared only a working relationship. I wondered about that one a good deal.

The next morning, I finished up the article, wrote a sidebar on the food shortages in Jerusalem, and, later that afternoon, went to meet May at the Hotel Luxor. When I arrived, I discovered there'd been a change of plans. Benteen was waiting in front of the building in the Dodge. He opened the passenger door.

"Mister May sent me to pick you up," he said. "He sends his apologies. He thought it would be better to meet you at Miss Garner's apartment."

I hesitated, but got inside. Benteen reached under the seat and pulled out an automatic rifle. He set the rifle on his lap with the muzzle pointed away from me.

"You never know when someone might try to borrow your car," he said.

I asked where Sara Garner lived.

"In the Mekor Barlich District."

I knew that was in the Jewish New City just off the Geula Road. It wasn't far.

Benteen drove fast and skillfully. The best way to avoid being ambushed was to keep moving, no matter what. He didn't even stop when he had to bump up on the curb several times to get around the rubble of shell-damaged buildings.

"How long have you worked for May?" I asked.

"Why don't you ask him that yourself," he said. "If he wants to tell you, it's fine with me."

"Do you like working for him?"

"I've got no complaints. He pays well."

I drew blanks when I asked other questions about May. How long had he been in the country? When did he plan to leave? Benteen wouldn't bite.

I remembered that he spoke Arabic. I asked where he had learned the language. This time he surprised me with an answer. "I picked it up in the Arab Legion. All the officers had to speak Arabic."

"How long were you in the Legion?"

"Two years."

"Why did you leave?"

Benteen glanced at me. "Don't take this personally, but I don't like reporters."

"Have you known many?"

"You're the first."

"I see."

"I hope so."

We reached the Geula Road and drove a few blocks and then Benteen turned onto a street that was lined with modern-looking apartment buildings and shops—most of them vacant. It was a newer part of the city. I saw little damage—just some broken windows. Benteen parked and got out of the car, carrying his rifle. He opened the hood and disconnected the ignition, a precaution against theft. I followed him into a three-story building with a stucco front. May met us in the hallway.

"Sara wanted to get right to work after we got back," he said. "I thought it would be easier if you came here instead."

He showed me into the first-floor apartment. Benteen locked and bolted the door. The tables and chairs were piled with books, scholarly journals and papers. Still more books were stacked in the corners and on the floor. Kerosene lamps had been set out in case the power failed. The place smelled of cooking oil.

We sat down. Benteen put the rifle in the corner by the door and lit a cigarette.

May said, "I'm still not sure I want to talk to you."

"If you're worried about what I said in Bethlehem, forget it. I already told you that was off the record."

"The last thing we need right now is publicity."

"You might not be able to avoid it. Those scrolls are a decent story. Guys like me are going to start asking questions."

"So I've learned," May said. "Another reporter called the hotel yesterday."

I sat up. I knew at once that Rachid had sold his information somewhere else. It was too good for him not to try to cash in twice. I told Benteen about Rachid and what had probably happened. I didn't mention his name.

"This is causing me more trouble than I need," May said. "I don't like that."

I repeated what I said earlier; I didn't mind holding off on the story as long as I could be sure I wouldn't get beaten. I told him he'd be better off working with me; that way he'd have some control. Changing the subject, I asked him about his assistant.

"I'd hardly call her an assistant," May said. "If anything, it's the other way around."

He told me that Sara Garner had received a doctorate in biblical archeology from the University of Chicago. For the last two years, she had lived in the Holy Land. She had done research at the American School of Oriental Research and had participated in several important digs, one of them at Jericho with a French team from the Dominican Ecole Biblique, a center of archeological research in Old Jerusalem.

I tried a few more questions. May answered, but not in great detail. He was still playing close to the vest with me. He said he was a businessman who lived in Chicago and had some oil interests and real estate holdings. He was fifty-two years old and unmarried.

I asked him how he got interested in scrolls.

"I collect ancient art. You might say it's a hobby."

It was some hobby. He said that he had several well-connected dealers in the Middle East who worked for him. One of them was in Palestine. A few weeks earlier, May had received a cable from this man, describing reports of ancient writings being circulated by the Bedouin.

"I wired back at once, telling him to buy as many as he could get his hands on," May said. "Unfortunately, the fighting broke out and the Bedouin dropped from sight. I decided to come myself."

"And that's when you met Miss Garner?"

"I knew I needed help with this. I've got a couple friends at the University of Chicago, who found out about Sara. They gave me her name. I looked her up as soon as I arrived."

Taking advantage of May's apparent willingness to talk, I asked him about the cave he wanted to find. "You're running a big risk going out into the desert, but I guess you know that."

"Wouldn't you say the scrolls are worth it?"

"What makes you think any are left? Wouldn't the Bedouin have cleaned that cave out by now?"

Before May could answer, Sara Garner entered the room.

"Mister Davoren was just asking..."

"I heard him," Sara Garner said, frowning. "He was wondering if we're planning to go on a wild goose chase."

She wasn't pleased to see me. Looking at her I felt a thickness in my throat. I started to ask a question, but she interrupted.

"It's true the Bedouin may have removed all of the scrolls," she said. "It's also probably true the cave is in shambles. But there's no telling what they might have missed through carelessness. Other sites scavenged for centuries by Arabs have yielded treasures to trained archeologists. The trick is knowing where and how to look and then make a systematic search."

She thought that pottery or other artifacts might still be hidden in the cave. If scrolls had been stored inside, the possibility always existed other items may have been stashed there as well. Considering the importance of what already had been found, any additional discoveries could prove extremely valuable.

"We've been told the floor of the cave is littered with small fragments of scrolls—dozens of them," May said. "The Bedouin must not think they're worth much. They haven't even bothered picking them up."

"How do you know that?"

May glanced at the Englishman, who was still smoking his cigarette. He hadn't said a word.

"Mister Benteen has a friend, who served under him in the Arab Legion. The guy's also a member of the Ta'amia. The Bedouin who found the scrolls belong to the same tribe. We've hired him as a guide. He's heard some interesting stories about the cave."

The fragments, Sara said, led her to believe the cave may have been the depository for more than the five scrolls already recovered, the three sold to Glasner and the two bought by May in Bethlehem.

"Are you sure you can even find the place? The location was pretty vague if I recall. South of Jericho near the Dead Sea."

"We're still working on that," May said. "We've made it known we'll pay well for accurate information."

"What about Professor Glasner?" I asked. "Wouldn't he want to find this cave as much as you do?"

"I'm sure he does, but I don't think there's much the old boy can do until the fighting dies down," May said. "A Jew could never get into that part of the country right now—even if he had enough money to bribe people. And Glasner doesn't have the money. Otherwise, he would have bought all of the scrolls, not just three of them."

I realized he was right. Glasner had said at his press conference that he was trying to raise the money to purchase the two remaining scrolls.

For the time being, May had said as much as he cared to about the cave or their trip. He stood and asked that I follow him. We went into a small dining room, where two tables had been placed end to end.

The scroll they had bought from the Arab lay on one of the tables in two rolled pieces. The exterior surface of the leather darkened toward the middle. I asked about the strips of cloth that lay in a pile on the other table.

"The Bedouin said the scrolls were wrapped like mummies

when they found them," May said. "Now we know what they meant."

I noticed a bell jar on the desk. It contained a scroll. "That's the first one we bought," May said.

Several moist sponges had been placed in the jar to increase the humidity, May said. The hope was they would make the scroll more pliable and easier to unravel. So far, Sara Garner hadn't attempted to work with it.

"If we tried to open it now, it would break into pieces like the pages of an old book," she said. "It was far more brittle than the scroll we bought yesterday."

Sara Garner slowly unrolled the larger of the two pieces. "This is an almost complete text of the Book of Kings," she said. "I haven't finished reading it."

The scroll was divided into sheets of cream-colored leather that had been stitched together with what looked like strands of linen. Stitch holes ran down the sides of the sheets, which were just over a foot long and eight inches wide. Some of the threads had disintegrated. Stitch holes also perforated the outer edge of the first sheet, which indicated another sheet might have been attached there. Each sheet was divided into two columns of script; the writing seemed to hang suspended from crease marks the ancient scribes apparently had used as guidelines. The bottom of the first two sheets was badly scalloped with tears, which in a few places had cut into the last two or three lines of script.

Sara Garner showed where she had patched several of the tears with clear adhesive tape, cautiously applying it to the back of the leather sheets. Badly worn in places, the scroll showed signs of hard use. Some of the letters had been obliterated through handling.

The script was written in dark ink which contrasted sharply with the lighter color of the leather.

"What beautiful work," I said.

"I've never seen such writing," Sara Garner said. "Look at these letters." She pointed to a line of script with a pencil. "Each letter is almost a perfect square. I'm not familiar with such archaic Hebrew."

She unraveled the scroll to where it had been cut.

"You can see how it's already been patched."

Turning the scroll over, she showed where a narrow strip of leather had been carefully sewn over a tear; the job had been done so skillfully that the stitching hadn't interfered with the writing on the other side.

"How old is it?" I asked.

Sara turned to May.

"Go on, tell him," he said.

I could sense their excitement. They could no longer conceal it. Sara had lost some of her reserve.

"It possibly dates to the first century before Christ."

I let that sink in for a while. "Two thousand years," I said softly.

"Sara worked on it all last night," May said. "I don't think she slept two hours."

She took a metal box from a desk drawer. About the size of a shoe box, it contained neatly arranged rows of color slides. The slides, she explained, were of various biblical texts. She said she had established an approximate age for the scroll by comparing its script with the slides, which showed passages from ancient Hebrew texts—texts that already had been dated.

After sorting through the slides, she placed one of them under a large magnifying lens directly beneath her desk lamp.

It was nearly dark by then. For the past few days the Arabs had held off on their daily, late-afternoon bombardment. I hoped the luck would hold.

As if reading my mind, Benteen said, "It's too quiet out there." He had gone to the window. "Something's coming. You can almost smell it."

"This is the Nash Papyrus," Sara Garner said. "It was found in Egypt just before the turn of the century." The fragment measured only three by five inches and contained the Ten Commandments and part of the Shema—the Book of Deuteronomy. The oldest scrap of ancient Hebrew known to exist, scholars believed it dated to the first or second century before Christ.

"The letters are very similar to the scroll," Sara Garner said.

She pointed to a letter on the scroll. Pronounced aloud, it sounded like she was saying "mem." Then she indicated a similar letter on the magnified slide of the Nash Papyrus. Even I could see the close resemblence. She did the same with several other letters, which also matched.

"I can't be completely sure, not yet," she said. "But there's certainly strong paleographic evidence they're from the same period."

Even Benteen was interested.

"How important is all that?" he asked.

"It could be priceless," Sara Garner said. "This isn't simply a fragment like the Nash Papyrus. It's an entire book of the Bible."

"I want to do a story on this," I said, turning to May.

He didn't answer.

Much less reluctant to speak her mind, Sara Garner came down hard on the idea.

"An article now could compromise everything. It would be foolish. I haven't even begun to complete an analysis."

"I agree, but we've already had two reporters call us," May said.

"Then cut your losses," I said. "Let me have it as an exclusive and I'll give you as much time as you need to get your work done."

I usually didn't like to make deals like that. But after everything I'd seen and heard, I knew it was a remarkable story. I was willing to bend the rules.

"It would be easier just to tell you all to go to hell," May said.

"Sure, you could do that. But like I said, I've already got more than enough to write something."

"I thought this was supposed to be off the record," May snapped.

"That was yesterday," I said, trying to stay calm. "I didn't make any promises about today."

May started to tell me not to press my luck when Benteen called us all to the window.

"Look at this!"

Green flares hung in the black sky. They were drifting down over the city from Mount Scopus, where the Arabs had some gun batteries. Firing could be heard in the distance, the sound gradually becoming louder. Machine guns and small arms.

I couldn't stick around much longer. From the intensity of the gunfire, something was up. Weil was going to need me at the bureau. With only a few days before the British pullout, the Arabs were probably making another big push to drive the Jews out of the Old City.

I started for the door. May followed me into the hallway. He came quickly to the point. If I would postpone writing anything until they had a chance to look for the cave where the scrolls had been found, he'd let me have an exclusive. He'd also pay me $4,000.

"I'm just asking you to wait for a while," he said.

Everything was happening much too quickly. I suddenly realized that I was facing a professional crisis, a thought which would have seemed preposterous a few hours earlier. I'd never been offered that much money in my life.

"I'll have to think this over," I stammered.

May went with me into the street. The firing now was very heavy and the sky had an orange glow, but I hardly noticed.

"You can find me here," May said. "I'll be waiting for you."

CHAPTER 5

I GOT BACK to the bureau about half an hour later after some hard walking. The gunfire had continued, a steady spatting of small arms. There were more flares, which descended slowly over the walls of the Old City. I reached the office just as an ambulance from the Magan David Odom, the Jewish Red Cross, came hurtling down the street with its lights off. It was heading away from the firing.

Weil looked mad when I walked in.

"That story you're working on better be good," he snapped.

The trouble was I had been gone most of the day and something had broken. It would have been a lot worse if I hadn't stopped by earlier and finished that piece for the Foreign Desk in New York.

"What the hell's going on?" I asked.

Weil gave me the details in a rush: the Jews had made an all-out effort to break into the Old City at the Jaffa Gate. They were trying to reinforce their men in the besieged Jewish Quarter. There'd been a sharp battle outside the walls.

"The British have sent up some soldiers to try to shut it off," Weil said. "I found that much out before the line went dead."

The last thing I wanted was to walk the dark streets with bullets flying.

"You want me to go have a look?"

I tried to sound eager.

"No, I'll handle that," Weil said. "You stay here and try to get an open line to Tel Aviv or Rome. Tell them what's happening and that I'll file something as soon as I can."

I spent the next few hours trying without luck to get a connection. I smoked a few cigarettes and thought about May's offer. Four thousand dollars was nearly half a year's salary, and I'd still get to write the story. All I had to do was wait until they looked for that cave. I wasn't sure whether I could believe him. I didn't think May was giving me a con, but I figured there had to be a catch.

I was still thinking it through when Weil returned well after midnight. The story was simple enough: the Jews had tried to force their way into the Old City and the attack had turned into a fiasco. Most of the shooting had been a diversion by the Irgun and Palmach; their men had opened up on Arab positions in the Sheikh Jarrah at the same moment the Haganah rushed the Jaffa Gate. An excellent strategy, but things went badly when the Jews tried to blow up an iron gate in the Citadel; the charge didn't work and the Arabs started pouring down fire from the stone towers. The Jews were shot to pieces and had to fall back, carrying their dead and wounded.

The phone was still down and we wound up sending the story out in the morning on a British convoy to Tel Aviv. We spent the night hunkered in our chairs, trying to sleep.

The next two days passed in a haze of work and anxiety. The city was turning into a shooting gallery. But I did manage to get in touch with my source at the British High Commissioner's Office, who had some information on May, Sara Garner and Benteen— not much, but helpful.

John May evidently had made a fortune speculating in Louisiana offshore oil leases. He had many business interests in Chicago, but spent most of his time collecting and selling art. He was considered an authority on Middle Eastern painting and sculpture—an interest he had acquired as a student at the University of Illinois. He had lived most of his life in Chicago and had worked hard for his money; his parents had been poor.

Sketchy stuff at best, and the information on Sara Garner was even less satisfying. She had been an outstanding student at the University of Chicago; her doctoral dissertation on Myceanean pottery had been published by a well-known university press. She'd been raised in New York City, but there was no information on her family. She wasn't married. Her passport said she was twenty-eight.

The report on Benteen was that he'd served with the British Army in Africa during the war and had been decorated in the campaign against Rommel. He had joined the Arab Legion as an

45

officer at the personal request of Col. John Glubb. He was thirty-two. He'd been born in Birmingham. Divorced. No children.

Unsure what to make of all this, I knew enough to realize that I was becoming more and more interested in the scrolls. It was a fine story and it would get even better if they went hunting for that cave in the desert. There was something else, too. Sara Garner. I wondered why she wasn't married. Anyone with her brains who looked like she did must have had a lot of chances. She was Jewish and lovely and had dark brown eyes and I knew I wanted to see her again even if she'd made it clear that I wasn't her favorite reporter.

CHAPTER 6

I SAW May again a few days later at Sara Garner's apartment. By now the sniping was going on almost round the clock. At night the Arabs had resumed their helter-skelter gunnery from the heights of the Mount of Olives and Mount Scopus. I didn't like being out on the streets then, but it was the only time I could get away.

May was waiting for me on the landing with a flashlight. The electricity was out.

"I'm glad you could come," he said.

Quickly getting down to business, I said, "I haven't decided what to do about your offer. I'd be lying if I said it didn't interest me. But I've got some problems we need to talk about."

"Sara has something I want you to see first," May said. "Maybe it'll help you make up your mind."

The apartment was lit by gas lanterns, which cast dim shadows on the walls. Benteen was out, which suited me fine. Sara was seated at her desk in the cluttered dining room. I saw that she had reattached the two pieces of the scroll they had bought in Bethlehem, the Book of Kings, I recalled. The manuscript, rolled open to its full length and held down by several narrow plates of glass, was a good five feet long. The buttermilk-colored leather with its strikingly bold script was an undeniably beautiful work of art. I was reminded of the illuminated manuscripts of the Middle Ages.

May said, "Sara, why don't you tell him what you know."

I asked whether I could take notes. May agreed, but it didn't please Sara.

"Mister Davoren, have you ever heard of the Essenes?"

Her voice was tense.

I told her that Professor Glasner had used the word during his press conference. Until she mentioned it, I had forgotten the name. "They were some kind of religious sect. He thought they might have been involved with the scrolls."

"Glasner may have been on the right track."

She explained that the Essenes were a community of Jews who lived together in the Judean wilderness. "The sect was probably founded in the first or second century before the birth of Christ."

"About the same time you think the scroll might have been written?"

Sara nodded. "We also know the members opposed the Pharisees and Saducees. The Essenes thought the priests had turned away from the law and had become too worldly. So they set up their settlement far from the towns, which they considered corrupt. They moved to the western shore of the Dead Sea, the area roughly where the Bedouin found the scrolls in a cave. We don't know what happened to the Essenes, but it's likely their community broke up during the first Jewish revolt against the Romans sometime between 67 and 70 A.D. That we know anything about them at all is mainly due to the writings of Pliny the Elder and the Jewish historian Josephus."

"At least until now," May said.

I could sense they were both keyed up, but were trying hard not to show it.

Sara had managed to read a small portion of the other scroll May had bought, the one they had kept under a glass cover.

She had only begun to unravel it, opening the outer fold. The painstaking process required cleaning centuries of dirt and grime from the brittle leather with alcohol. Working an inch at a time, she had gently brushed the surface with a sable brush after it had dried, a tricky procedure in which several pieces had broken off. She had read enough to realize that it wasn't a biblical text.

Sara turned to the scroll and pointed out two words that appeared slightly above the first line and a little off center—Serek Hayyahad. She translated them to mean "Manual of Discipline."

"This is only a first impression, but this scroll may be a kind of Benedictine Rule for a Jewish sect that vanished nearly two thousand years ago," she said. "It's completely out of the mainstream of Jewish thought. The Essenes came to mind immediately because they had a strictly regulated monastic community. If they weren't responsible, it had to be a group very similar to them. We still need to develop that theory. Right now, we've barely begun."

Bending over the scroll, she slowly translated: "These are the regulations for the way of the wise man in these times."

The first unraveled sheet described how members of the sect were expected to work outdoors. It also mentioned how they rose and retired with the rising and setting of the sun. Morning prayers were just after sunrise. Meals were taken in common.

That was as far as she had progressed. The inner folds of the tightly wound scroll remained stuck together. A great deal of work still needed to be done.

"Are you going to talk to Glasner about this?" I asked when she finished reading. "Maybe you could work together."

May didn't like that idea. I realized as he spoke that I had touched the raw nerve of a fiercely competitive collector.

"I want to get there first."

He had reason to be optimistic. The Bedouin who had served with Benteen in the Arab Legion had come up with precise directions to the cave.

"It's seven miles south of Jericho in a limestone cliff that borders the western shore of the Dead Sea," May said. "The cliff is set back from the water in a deep ravine. There's a spring that flows into the Dead Sea about half a mile away. The Arab is sure he can find the place."

"When do you leave?"

"As soon as we can arrange the transportation." He said Benteen was working on that detail as well.

They wanted to start for the desert in two days, but some details still needed to be settled. Among them, Sara hoped to discuss the scrolls with a former professor of hers at the University of Chicago, a man named Elton Parker. He was now in Jerusalem, where he had been named director of the American School of Oriental Research.

The problem was that the school was in the Arab zone. Jews couldn't enter without a special pass and even with Benteen's connections, Sara hadn't been able to get one. It was impossible to telephone; the service had been out for days.

"I think I might be able to help you," I said. "Maybe I can get you some press credentials. If they take the time to examine them, we'll be sunk, but I've never met an Arab guard yet who could read

English. The big problem will be getting past the British checkpoint."

"I'd love to try," Sara said quickly.

It was good to see her smile. Her teeth were white against her sun-browned face. Standing there by a glowing lantern, she was a striking woman.

May wasn't happy. He didn't think it was worth the risk.

"It's too dangerous now for a Jew to try to get into the Arab zone."

"He's right about that," I agreed. The Arabs weren't reluctant to kill Jews these days—even Jewish women.

"Doctor Parker could help us," she insisted. "He knows the Dead Sea region as well as anyone. There isn't a finer biblical scholar in the Holy Land. He might have some suggestions that could save us time."

May didn't press the issue.

I asked him whether the reporter who had called earlier at his hotel had followed up.

"He left several messages," May said. "I haven't answered them. What about you? You said you were interested, but that you had some problems."

"The big problem is the money," I said. "I don't mind holding off as long as I get the story when you get back, but I don't want to be paid. That kind of thing is frowned on."

I had struggled to make the decision, but the words seemed very natural and logical when I heard myself say them.

"I figured you might say that," May said. "I'd like to make a counter proposal. I want you to come along with us."

He had decided to increase his offer. "I'll pay you $10,000. Perhaps that way you could afford to take a leave of absence."

"This is starting to get a little crazy," I said. Ten thousand dollars was almost as much money as I could make in a year with the wire service.

May smiled and said, "I've been thinking it might be a good idea to have a reporter along. When the time comes to get the story out, I'd rather trust someone I know."

"You mean you'd rather have someone on your payroll," I said. "For ten grand, I'd say you'd fairly well control me. If I had wanted to get into the public relations business, I wouldn't be here right now."

"I'd be paying you to write as objectively as you can."

"What if you don't like what I write? What if you want to change it? Reporters can be pretty thin skinned. They get touchy about things like that."

The conversation no longer seemed real. But May kept talking and I kept listening.

"The writing will be your affair, Mister Davoren," he said. "We can draw up a contract if you like."

"Hold on, it's not that simple," I said. "This fight in the Holy Land is the biggest story I've ever covered, bigger even than the war in Europe. I did everything I could to get here. I begged for the assignment. I almost got down on my knees. It wouldn't be easy just to walk away, not even for ten thousand bucks."

"All I ask is that you think it over," May said. "You've got two days."

I wondered what Sara Garner thought about all this. It was strange that she hadn't objected as before. I couldn't believe that she'd suddenly changed her mind; she didn't seem like the kind.

CHAPTER 7

THE HILLS OF THE CITY were hazy in the sunlight of a fine spring morning. I watched yet another military convoy head down Ben Yahuda Street past the bureau. The heavy trucks with their brown canvas tops were performing the last rites of a thirty-year British rule in the Holy Land. Intermittent gunfire cracked in the distance as the convoy rumbled along the street. There had been shooting all morning. The date was May 12th, a Wednesday—three days and counting to the final British pullout.

I was waiting for Sara Garner. I'd sent a messenger, a young Jew, to her apartment with a note, asking her to meet me at ten o'clock.

Weil and I had had some hot words before I left. I told him that I wanted some time to work on the scroll story. Weil wasn't pleased.

He'd sat there at his beat-up typewriter, staring at me through the cigarette smoke.

"It must be damn important to you," he said.

"Yeah, I guess it is."

"Then go do it, but don't bother coming back if all hell breaks out while you're gone."

Sara Garner arrived a few minutes after ten. She was wearing a dark blue skirt and a white blouse. She carried the two scrolls in a large leather handbag; they were in a shoebox. She looked as nervous as I was.

"Thanks again for offering to do this," she said, shaking my hand. "I want to apologize."

"For what?"

"That's kind, but I've been rude and you know it. I've acted badly. I still think John's made a mistake talking to you."

"I understand how you feel," I said. "If I were in your place, I'd probably agree. The truth is I haven't figured out what I'm going to do, so why don't we declare a cease fire—at least for today."

"I'd rather call it a truce," she said.

I much preferred to see her smiling as she was now. I gave her a camera and the press pass; they were for an AP photographer we were expecting from New York. I'd forged her name on the pass, typing over the name that was already printed on the card. I told her to flash it if we were stopped and to let me do the talking.

The American School of Oriental Research was on Saladin Road in the Arab Musrara Quarter, a relatively new section of Jerusalem. A residential district, it lay in a shallow valley almost at the foot of Mount Scopus.

Even though there was firing in the hills above the city, the streets were as crowded as I had seen them in weeks. Everyone was out looking for food, water—anything they could find. The faces were grim and taut. The children looked hungry. There was intense haggling on every corner and a few fights.

We squeezed through a line that had formed by a water wagon.

A young girl—she couldn't have been older than ten or eleven— had tripped after filling her bucket. The water spilled onto the pavement, splashing onto her shoes and dress. She began to cry. Her face and dress were dirty.

Several women refilled the girl's bucket from their own.

"You've got to admire them," I said.

"They have nothing else to lose," Sara Garner said. "They know what this war means."

We soon arrived at Queen Melisande's Way, which came to a dead end at the perimeter of the Bevingrad, the "Green Line" that separated the Jewish and Arab parts of the city. The Central Police Headquarters and a row of buildings, their facades marked with bullet holes, were behind coils of barbed wire. Some Arabs were waiting for one of the decrepit buses.

We stood in a doorway, facing the street.

"Why did you come here?" I asked.

"I got a fellowship to do post-graduate work in archeology two years ago. I just stayed on."

She said that she had been hooked from the first moment she saw the Holy Land's ancient cities perched on their lonely hills. Since then, she had worked on digs in the Judean wilderness at Megiddo and Gezer, fortresses built by Solomon. She had written several papers on the pottery that had been found, which helped date the two sites. As she told me of long days spent on her knees under an unforgiving sun, her eyes lit up. Her ambition was to find Hazor—the third of Solomon's lost cities. She had been doing research on the subject when she met May.

I tried not to stare at her legs; they were long and slender.

She told me that she had been born in Brooklyn and that her father was dead. He had been a lawyer. Her mother did volunteer work in a New York City hospital.

"What do you think of May?" I asked.

"How do you mean that?"

She had quickly gone on guard.

I saw the green roof of the bus moving slowly down the street and dropped the subject. We hurried toward the Police Headquarters, the camera swinging from Sara's neck. At the barbed wire, we showed the British sentry our passes. The sentry, a young soldier wearing a bulletproof vest, hardly looked at them. It was the same with the Arab guard who stood a few feet away. We boarded the bus and sat in the rear. All the passengers appeared to be Arabs. The bus, one of few still operating, was packed.

A few of the younger Arabs were staring at us. They were sullen and silent.

When we halted at the market at the Damascus gate, some more Arabs boarded. Two lanky men stood next to our seats. They watched us steadily. One of them was wearing western clothing and a white kaffiyeh.

"No doubt the pictures you take of the Arabs are great amusement back in your country," he said in husky English to Sara when the bus began moving again.

"The pictures we take are for the newspapers," I said, trying to be courteous.

"You are American?"

"That's right." I smiled.

"There are too many Jews in America."

The bus stopped, and I pulled Sara Garner up by her arm and got off fast.

We reached the iron gates of the American School without any problem. The square, two-story building had gray stone walls and a tiled roof. Tall pine trees concealed most of the front from the street. I followed Sara Garner up the short walkway. It was cool in the shade of the trees.

She rang the bell and the door was opened by the man we'd come to see, Doctor Parker. About sixty and wearing a worn tweed suit and vest, he was portly with bushy white hair and dark brown eyes that were magnified behind his glasses.

Parker greeted Sara Garner, his former student, with affection. After she introduced me we went into a sitting room.

"We're quite alone," Parker said. "All the students have left. Only two of the fellows remain, Doctor Selinger and Professor Harvey Jones. Both of them have gone to Egypt on vacation, and I've cabled them not to return. The situation here is much too unsettled."

"Don't you have anyone to help you?"

"Two of the servants have remained. We get along splendidly now that they have no work to do."

Parker planned to stay on awhile longer to try, as he put it, "to keep up the appearance of scholarship."

I would have cleared out weeks ago. Stragetically located between the hills of the Sheikh Jarah and the Old City, the school was sure to be caught in a nasty crossfire when the real shooting started.

Sara had been a regular visitor to the school until the Musrara District was closed to Jews. When Parker asked what she had been doing for the past weeks, she told him about John May and the scrolls and what they contained.

Parker's jovial demeanor changed abruptly.

"Yes, I've heard about Glasner and some ancient manuscripts," he said with interest. His eyes shifted rapidly between Sara Garner and the leather bag she had placed on the table.

"Professor Glasner bought three scrolls from a dealer in Bethlehem, the same man who sold two of them to us," Sara said. "I wanted you to examine them."

"You do me an honor," Parker said gravely.

We followed him to the school's library. He locked the door behind him and we sat at a long conference table piled with books and papers.

Showing him the scroll of the Book of Kings, Sara took out the manuscript she had only partly opened, the one she called the Manual of Discipline. Parker studied the scrolls intently as she spoke. He used a magnifying lens to read the script.

For the next few minutes, the professor read in silence, hardly aware of us. He was concentrating on the Book of Kings.

"What an incredible find," he said finally. "My congratulations. This is certainly the oldest manuscript I have ever seen."

He took Sara's hand and shook it warmly. She hugged him.

"I wasn't really sure until I compared it with the Nash Papyrus."

Parker agreed that the scripts closely resembled each other.

"I'd give a date no later than accession of Herod the Great," he said. "Certainly no later than 100 B.C."

Sara told him that the manuscript was among a cache of five scrolls the Bedouin had uncovered in a cave south of Jericho.

"Where?"

"On the western shore of the Dead Sea. It's up in a cliff set back from the water in a deep ravine."

"How far south of Jericho?" Parker said. "Can you be more specific?"

"Seven miles we're told," Sara said.

"There's something else very near there," Parker said slowly.

He went to a bookshelf, got down another thick volume, and rapidly located the passage he was looking for. The author was one Charles Clermont-Ganneau, a Frenchman who had explored the Holy Land in the 1870s.

"This is what I was looking for," he said. "This passage mentions some ancient ruins that lie near the Dead Sea about seven miles south of Jericho. Clermont-Ganneau says seven and a half miles to be precise. They're located on a cliff that overlooks what the Arabs call the Wadi Qumran. It's thought to be the remains of an old Roman fort. The most interesting feature are some graves. They number over a thousand. Early explorers like Clermont-Ganneau couldn't figure them out. They certainly aren't Roman. The Romans would have cremated their dead. So how do you explain such a strange cemetery right next to a Roman fort? That question has always bothered me a little. But then controversy over the site isn't anything new. Although it's been thoroughly disproven, there was a time when some scholars even thought it was the ruins of ancient Gomorrah." He paused a moment before he said, "After what you've just told me about the scrolls and the cave, which has to be very close, I wonder if there isn't another explanation."

He retrieved a book. I noticed the title—Pliny's *Naturalis Historia*. Parker rifled the pages and, finding what he wanted, read to himself.

"Here, this is it," he said. "Pliny says, and I'm quoting, 'On the western shore of the Dead Sea, the Essenes have withdrawn to a sufficient distance to avoid its noxious effects. They are a lonely people, the most extraordinary of the world, who live without women, without love, without money, with the palm trees for their only companions.'" Skipping some paragraphs, he continued. "'Above them the town of Engadda once stood—in its palm groves and general fertility second only to Jericho but now a heap of ashes like it. Beyond this is Masada, a fortress on a rock and itself not far from the Dead Sea. To this point Judea extends.'"

"I'm familiar with that passage," Sara said. "That area isn't far from the cave. It's one of the reasons I thought of the Essenes."

The professor looked at Sara Garner. "This is only a deduction—and a hasty one at that. But what if Pliny was in error? What if the Essene settlement wasn't below Engadda but rather somewhere to the north, much closer to the cave? Pliny never visited the site. He might easily have made a mistake about its location. A very simple, understandable mistake. There might even have been an error in translation. What if it's possible these strange ruins are the remains of the long-lost Essene monastery? Or if not that, perhaps a kind of satellite community?"

Sara sat in a chair, listening intently. She'd been struck by Parker's suggestion.

"Those scrolls most likely would have been hidden in the cave by people who lived nearby," the professor said.

I asked a question. Assuming everything he said was true, why would the Essenes or any other sect have gone to the great risk of stashing their valuable writings in a cave?

The professor smiled and said, "The answer to that will take a good bit of field work and luck. It may be that the scrolls were placed in hiding during a time of danger. Perhaps during one of the many revolts against the Romans."

When Sara told Parker that she and May planned to visit the cave and search for any artifacts or scroll fragments the Bedouin may have left behind, he went to a desk and got out a geological survey map of the western shore of the Dead Sea.

"We have an excellent collection of these," he said, giving it to Sara. "Keep this. It might help."

He cautioned us that any archeological trip into the Judean hill country would require a permit from the Department of Antiquities of the Transjordanian government.

"So what would you suggest?" I asked.

"Don't tell anyone."

Sara looked surprised. She hadn't expected him to say anything like that.

Sensing this, Parker said, "Of course, I'll deny ever giving you that advice."

After they examined the scrolls a while longer, it was Sara's turn to startle the professor. She asked him to keep them. Taking them into the desert was out of the question, and she didn't want to run the risk they might be stolen from her apartment while she was gone. She'd already discussed this with May.

The professor looked flustered. At first he didn't want to accept the responsibility and agreed only reluctantly. The school, he said, had a hidden safe. He would keep the scrolls there.

"I hope you'll continue to study them," Sara said.

"You'd let me do that?" Parker sounded incredulous.

"We need all the help we can get," Sara said, smiling. "I just hope you'll have the time."

"The time? My god, I'll have the time for nothing else." Parker pulled himself to his feet. "I don't know what to say."

We were interrupted by the doorbell. Parker went to answer it. I looked down the hallway from the library. Two English officers stood on the porch. In clipped tones they said that heavy fighting was expected within hours in the district. They suggested that he evacuate as soon as possible.

The soldiers hurried off and Parker returned to the library.

"What are you going to do?" Sara asked.

"I'll be staying," he said cheerfully. "I've got some good friends among the Arabs. I should be all right."

I didn't share his optimism; neither did Sara.

CHAPTER 8

THERE WAS NO POINT in trying to catch a bus. We started walking the deserted streets. I followed Sara, who knew the quarter like a native. We went quickly down sloping, cobbled streets that rose, fell and twisted at sharp angles. Turning a corner, we came out at a broken wall at Jeremiah's Grotto; a paper-littered courtyard opened onto the sunken chamber where the prophet Jeremiah was said to have been imprisoned. A few blocks later, I noticed that we were being followed. There were two of them. Arabs in white head-dress, they were hugging the walls of the buildings, keeping a safe distance behind us.

We crossed a small square and headed south toward the Old City. I dropped behind and took cover in a doorway so that I could watch the square. I wanted a better look at the Arabs. My breath was short and I could feel the tightness in my chest. The Arabs were still coming, walking steadily, neither fast nor slow. When they crossed the square, I recognized one of them: he'd been with the antiquities dealer in Bethlehem. I remembered how it had been with Aqui and felt a spasm of fear.

There was no telling how long they'd been following us. I cursed under my breath and ran to catch up with Sara who had waited down the street. I told her about the Arabs.

"I don't think they're out to invite us back to Bethlehem."

"Here, take this," she said. She reached into her bag and handed me a snub-nosed automatic pistol. I couldn't tell the caliber. English made, it felt small and cold in my hand.

"Benteen gave it to me when he found out where we were going. I tried to refuse, but he insisted."

"I wish he were here to use it," I said, slipping the pistol in to my pocket.

I slung the camera over my shoulder and we started running. We were close to the Old City and I could catch glimpses between the overhanging roofs of the spires of Notre Dame de France.

Sara was in front of me when I heard the shot, the sound like a motorcycle backfire. I looked behind and saw the Arab leaning against a wall to steady himself. He fired again and I heard the flat whine of the bullet. I shouted to Sara to keep running. I dropped to my knee behind a mail box, braced my right wrist and fired over their heads. The Arabs flopped onto the pavement.

We ran hard, arms pumping, and almost stumbled down a steep flight of steps cut between the close-fronted buildings. The street was barely wide enough for a cart. There was more rifle fire; it was in front of us, the echo of the shots smashing back along the walls.

It took over an hour for us to shake off the Arabs and work our way back to Sara's apartment. On the way we encountered the same crowds we had seen earlier in the Musrara District. Stunned, frightened-looking people bent over with sacks or cardboard boxes. Most were on foot. Some had bicycles. There were even a few cars, with furniture, bedding and other belongings lashed to their roofs. Like their Arab neighbors, these Jews had waited to the very eve of invasion before they could bring themselves to evacuate. They moved along as if drugged. The elderly were the most pitiful—brittle-looking men and women who walked side by side, or alone, their heads bowed, not talking.

"I know women younger than me who are fighting with the Haganah," Sara said, watching them. She sounded bitter.

"I'd say you're doing something damned important yourself," I said.

She frowned and said, "I was born Jewish, but my father and mother weren't very religious, not even on the high holy days. I wound up going to private schools, where there weren't many Jews. I didn't consider myself Jewish. I didn't have Jewish friends. I knew next to nothing of the Talmud. Right now that makes me very ashamed."

I wanted to say something to let her know I understood. Instead, I blurted out that I was going to accept May's offer.

Sara looked at me. "I'm not surprised," she said.

"For taking the money?"

"Is that the reason you're doing it—for the money?"

"What do you think?"

"I wish you'd tell me."

"Sure, the money has something to do with it," I said. "Ten thousand bucks isn't easy to turn down. But that's not the only reason. The way I see it, I've got a chance to write a story that's going to make people talk. And I'll have it all to myself. No, I wouldn't miss your trip into the desert, lady. I want to do it so much I'm ready to walk away from a job that's been good to me."

That was most of the truth anyway. I couldn't tell her that she had something to do with it, too.

She smiled. It was time for her to go and I had to get back to the bureau.

Before we left, she told me that May planned to leave for the Dead Sea early in the morning.

"Tell him I'll be there," I said. "I hope his offer still stands, because after this evening, I'll be out of work."

The real shooting started after dark. The Arabs and Jews apparently had decided to wait until sundown before they started playing for keeps. Automatic weapons were popping like firecrackers, vicious, sustained firing.

When I got back to the bureau, Weil was slumped at his desk. He looked like hell. His suit was covered with dust and he was bleeding slightly from a cut over his left eyebrow. He said he had slipped in the street.

"The Arab Legion is moving up men," he said quietly. "It's finally started."

I told him I was resigning.

"I can give you a letter if you'd like."

Weil sagged back into his chair.

"I was expecting it," he said. "I've already sent word to Rome to get a replacement in here." He lit a cigarette and took a deep pull, letting the smoke fill his lungs. "You know you'll never work for us again. You might not work for anybody again."

I nodded.

"This business about the scrolls. You're sure it's that big a story?"

"I'm quitting, Mike. I guess I do."

When I left the bureau and started walking up Ben Yehuda, the sky over the Old City was lit by red, spidery lines of tracers. Fires were burning in the Sheikh Jarrah District. People were still out in the streets, carrying their bundles and boxes and small children. The hour of exodus had begun for all of us.

CHAPTER 9

I REACHED Sara's apartment just after six o'clock. I carried a haversack that bulged out with clothing. A much-traveled Ford station wagon and a dusty, olive-colored jeep were parked outside the building. The jeep had British markings that had only partially been struck out with black paint. The back end of the jeep was lashed down with a tarp. Benteen came out of the building with two five-gallon water cans; he carried them easily and set them down next to the station wagon.

"A word to the wise," he said, seeing me. He loaded the cans in the back of the car. "I'm paid to protect the man and the woman. I'm not paid to protect the reporter. Clear?"

"Very."

"Then we shouldn't have any problems."

He was wearing a khaki shirt, shorts, leggings and heavy boots. He looked fit. He asked me about the Arabs that had chased us yesterday.

"What did they look like?"

I told him I thought I recognized one of the men.

"I'd say the shoemaker sent them to settle accounts," Benteen said, tying the water cans in the back of the station wagon. "You were lucky."

I went into the apartment. May and Sara were packing some cardboard boxes with canned food. I knew that food and water must have cost a small fortune on the black market.

"I'm glad you decided to join us," May said, shaking my hand. "Sara told me you resigned."

"I just want to be sure we still have a deal."

"I'll put it in writing if you like."

I said that wouldn't be necessary.

"Let's keep our truce in effect a while longer," Sara said to me, smiling.

"That could be dangerous," I said. "Some truces have lasted for years."

She was in good spirits. Despite breaking the ice the day before, I had wondered how it was going to be with her; this was a better beginning than I had hoped for. She almost looked happy to see me.

The arrangements had gone well, May said. The necessary safe conduct papers had been acquired—for a hefty price. Benteen had worked hard the past few days setting all this up with his former military friends in the Legion. He had also managed to buy the jeep and station wagon.

Benteen carried the food down to the car, then came back and took a look at the large survey map that Professor Parker had given to Sara.

He described the route, which wouldn't be easy. We'd take the Jerusalem-Jericho road out into the Jordan Valley, turn onto a trail that ran due east to the northern end of the Dead Sea and follow it almost to the water. After that, we'd have to pick our way south along the shoreline any way we could.

"How long is this going to take?" May asked.

"That's hard to say. There's going to be a lot of military traffic on the main road. The Legion is moving into position around Jerusalem. You can be sure we're going to be stopped and questioned. That's always chancy, even with our papers. I'd be happy to get out to that cave before nightfall."

We carried the remaining supplies down to the cars. Benteen would go in the jeep; the rest of us would follow in the station wagon.

"Try not to stop, and stay close to me," he said. "And keep an eye out for snipers. Watch the roofs and upper windows."

Sara sat next to May in the front seat. I got into the back. The rear of the car was filled with food boxes, shovels, picks, water-cans, climbing gear, and other equipment.

We drove quickly down Geula Road, taking a serpentine route

toward the Mea Shearim. The road was jammed with traffic—British trucks moving in convoy and heavily laden automobiles well down on their axles that were also heading out of the city. The refugees were more numerous in the Arab District, which we entered at an unmanned British checkpoint near the Italian Hospital. They were walking north toward Nablus. It took nearly an hour fighting the foot traffic for us to reach the eastern wall of the Old City. From there the road descended from the Wadi el Joz and then climbed again as it passed the Garden of Gethsemane.

Sara pointed out the ruins of an ancient chapel that stood on a low hill covered with pine trees. The site had a Latin name, she said. Dominus Flevit, meaning "the lord wept."

"It was built as a reminder that when Jesus came to Jerusalem for the last time, he wept over its future."

"He'd weep again now," May said, working the gears smoothly as he hugged the bumper of Benteen's jeep. "You can almost hear the bells tolling for what's going to happen tomorrow when the mandate ends."

We drove through the rocky foothills that rose in terraces to the Mount of Olives. The road skirted the Valley of Kidron, where a few thin rows of pine trees and countless broken headstones covered the eroded slopes. We weren't stopped until we turned onto the Jericho Road; three soldiers wearing the checked headdress and khaki uniforms of the Arab Legion ordered us to pull over. Benteen handed them our papers.

"They say there's a lot of traffic up ahead," he called back to us.

The soldiers let us pass, and we were soon into the hills. Benteen increased his speed, driving straight into the morning sun. The heat already rose in glassy waves off the macadamized road. You had to scour the horizon hard to spot even a stunted olive tree.

A few miles outside Jerusalem the country became even more rugged. Shapeless hills, hazy blue in the sun's glare, were sprinkled about and a line of steep ridges, toothed and serrated like a saw blade, rose in the distance.

We soon started running into convoys carrying Legion soldiers toward the Arab positions outside Jerusalem. The soldiers, riding in the back of the trucks on benches, looked in good spirits.

Armored cars, light trucks pulling artillery, and, later, a string of tanks also passed us on the narrow road. We pulled over to the shoulder and let the tanks clank by in a great cloud of dust.

Benteen stopped again at a place where the road dipped into a ravine that had been carved out of the rocks by a prehistoric stream. The Bedouin guide that Benteen had hired was sitting there in the shade of a boulder. His name was Juma. He rose and stood motionless as Benteen pulled up next to him.

"Ahlah wa-sahlan," Benteen said, greeting him with the traditional words of welcome.

The Arab was young, well made and very dark. He wore a kaffiyeh and army trousers and boots. A bandolier was slung over his shoulder. His rifle was wrapped in a blanket to protect the barrel from sand. He nervously looked back at us and silently swung into the front seat of the jeep.

"He isn't overjoyed to see us," Sara said when we started moving again.

May said, "Benteen trusts him. He said the Arab really wanted to do this. His family has feuded for years with the people who found the scrolls. They're members of the same tribe but blood enemies. That cave was on land Juma's relatives claim as their own. They want a piece of the action."

May drove with his left arm resting on the open window. I took advantage of his good mood and asked some questions about his oil business back in the states. He told me he had invested in oil leases off the Louisiana coast; he also had some leases in downstate Illinois.

At my prompting, he offered a short biography. After he had got out of high school, he spent two years in the Army. He was sent to France with the American Expeditionary Force. Nothing heroic there. He was a clerk-typist and not a very good one. His camp was shelled once, and so he could say without stretching it too much that he had been under fire. The truth was he'd slept right through the bombardment. When he was mustered out after the armistice, he did what his father had always wanted him to do—he went to college. His high school grades were all right and he got into Northwestern. He finally graduated with a degree in business administration and a minor in art history. That worried his old man. Why so much art? And Oriental art at that. What the hell good was it? When he started working for a real estate company in Chicago, everyone breathed a lot easier. After a few years he got into oil and started collecting paintings with the money he made.

"What do you hope to get out of all this?" I asked.

"At first just the scrolls, but now I couldn't tell you," he said. "The whole picture has changed. All this has taken on a life of its own." He laughed. "The beauty of it is I used to think I was in a rut."

CHAPTER 10

"THAT'S THE MOUNTAIN where the devil tempted Jesus."

Sara was describing a jagged, sinister-looking hill in the dun-colored distance.

"He wandered forty days and nights in this wilderness," she continued, shading her eyes with her hands as she scanned the stark landscape.

We had crested a rocky plateau from which we could survey the sharp-pointed hills and flat ridges that ran in choppy waves to the Dead Sea, a blue-gray line on the horizon. Clouds rose like smoke over the summits of the treeless, naked hills. It was nearly three hours since we had left Jerusalem.

May asked Sara whether the land—dead, hot, silent—had always looked so bleakly inhospitable.

"Only monotheism could have come out of a barren place like this," he said. "The Roman and Greek gods would never have had anything to do with it."

"I'd say it's fit enough for vipers and scorpions," I said.

"A great and terrible wilderness," Sara said, quoting Deuteronomy. "Moses speaks of the 'fiery serpents and thirsty ground.'"

More than terrible, I thought. It was like being buried alive. There was no sense of shadow, depth, or color—only an almost black and white sameness. Although it was still spring, the sparse, wiry grass was already dying on the few places that held moisture and looked like flecks of green mold sprinkled on the sunbaked rock. The undulating hills resembled the humps of camels. There were Bedouin about; we had passed a few of their goatskin tents, which looked old and patched enough to have been handed down from Abraham. In the distance, visible through the binoculars May had bought, an Arab woman squatted atop a ravine, watching a few shaggy, black-haired sheep.

Benteen halted on a ridge beyond which the road descended into a shallow plain. "Get ready," he warned. "It'll be rough from here on."

He put the jeep back into gear and we followed him down the slope of a hill that bottomed out in a rock-strewn valley. A few miles distant, the valley opened like a channel into a littoral of the Dead Sea.

I felt the pressure building on my eardrums; it was like a fast descent in an airplane. We were on our way to the lowest point on earth—1,300 feet below sea level.

The path—the road itself had long since played out—was little more than a faint tracing in the rocks. We were jolted and pitched about in our seats despite the slow, creeping speed.

The mid-day sun was blinding. A hawk or crow—I couldn't tell which—wheeled high overhead. When we finally reached the floor of the valley, we drove east for several miles until we came to a fantastic spire of limestone with two lower shoulders that folded out like wings in front of us, blocking our view of the sea. I could smell the water, the salty sea smell. The towering vertical face of the rock was streaked with veins of black basalt. It was like a fortress gate and when we got around it, I had my first look at the dull, pale-blue water of the Dead Sea.

My immediate thought was of the Great Salt Lake. The sea, smaller and narrower than I had imagined, reminded me more of a wide, deep-flowing river. The surface of the water was choppy in the wind; out toward the middle the color was a harder blue. Hills of drab browns and purple lined the far shore.

Reaching smoother ground, Benteen stopped on a low rise that offered a view of the curving shoreline. We all got out. Benteen and the Bedouin guide opened a canteen. The rest of us did the same. There was no shade anywhere. My hair felt as if it were going to ignite as I stared out at the Dead Sea.

"You'd never believe anything dramatic could have happened out here," May said. "It all looks...so lifeless."

"Ten or fifteen miles to the north where the Jordan flows into the Dead Sea, Jesus was baptized by John," Sara said. "Is that dramatic enough?"

"Where's Masada?" I asked.

"About twenty miles south," Sara said. "It looks like one of those buttes you see out in Arizona."

"I've heard of that place," Benteen said. "It's where the Jews slit their throats rather than let the Romans capture them. If I had two hundred men like that I'd own Palestine."

Juma was giving directions now; we were heading toward a wall of cliffs that loomed a few miles in the distance and rose in gradual stages to a high plateau. Tapered like the prow of a masted ship, a terrace jutted out midway up these cliffs. It was set in about a quarter mile from the beach.

When we reached the base of the terrace, Benteen forced the jeep up a narrow, washed-out trail. The steep climb was treacherous and even with its four-wheel drive, the jeep slid dangerously backward, the tires spinning in the gravel. Unable to come up in the station wagon, May parked at the foot of the cliffs. Following the trail, which switched back and forth through the rocks and ledges, we eventually reached the terrace after some hard climbing. Several hundreds yards wide at its bulging center, it projected like a spur from the backdrop of cliffs that soared another 500 or 600 feet behind us. We were overlooking the Dead Sea. The view of the water and the hills beyond it was spectacular. A strong breeze stung my sweaty face.

Benteen and Juma were waiting for us. Climbing out of the jeep, Benteen made an expansive gesture with his hands and said, "This is it. The Wadi Qumran."

The wadi, or ravine, was cut like a gorge into the cliffs and fell away sharply to the southern side of the terrace. The sheer walls of limestone that lined the wadi were scoured with fissures and crevices and pitted with caves.

At the far end of the terrace, clustered on the prowlike formation I had noticed earlier, stood the ruins that Professor Parker had mentioned back in Jerusalem.

Only the foundations and parts of the walls were left. The leveled buildings that had once stood there had been constructed of rough blocks of thick gray stone. Piles of the round-edged stone and the remains of a broken wall littered the ground. The site was dominated by a solid-looking but truncated tower made of solid rock.

The cemetery that we also had been told to look for started almost at the fringe of the Qumran settlement and extended back nearly 100 yards to the cliffs that hemmed in the terrace. Roughly triangular in shape, the area was crisscrossed by two sunbleached paths. There were no headstones; most of the graves were covered by a layer of stones with a larger stone erected vertically at each end.

Below us, half a mile to the south, a small oasis with a thin covering of grass was wedged between the plunging cliffs and beach.

The setting was everything I had imagined—desolate, abandoned, haunted.

The plan was to go to the cave and make a preliminary inspection while there was still light. It wasn't supposed to be far, just 1,000 yards or so up the wadi, according to Juma's information. We would come back later and set up camp on the Qumran terrace.

Benteen sent the Bedouin on ahead to reconnoiter. Juma crossed the terrace and descended through the rocks, carrying his rifle.

As we waited in the late afternoon sun, I asked Sara how she planned to excavate the cave in our search for artifacts and scroll fragments.

"I'm not sure yet," she said. "I'll have to see how much damage has been done."

"How bad do you think it's going to be?" I asked.

"The Bedouin will have had plenty of time to work the place over. I'm almost afraid to see it. . . . Whatever we do, we don't want to make it any worse. A false start could be a disaster. You don't often get a second chance on a dig. Even an innocent mistake can wipe out something forever."

I was thinking about how miserable it would be digging inside a cave in this heat when Juma ran back. His face didn't show anything at all, but he spoke rapidly to Benteen.

"Some Arabs are in the cave," Benteen said. "Four, maybe five. They've set up a camp."

"We're bitched," May said angrily. "The bastards have come back for seconds."

"I was afraid of that," Sara said. She looked just as upset.

72

"So what do we do?" I asked.

"We convince them it's in their best interest to leave," Benteen said.

His idea was to go up to the cave and have a talk with them—all of us but Sara. He wanted her to stay behind. She didn't argue about it; she just said that she was coming. Benteen shrugged and said, "Have it your way."

"I don't want any trouble," May cautioned. "Offer them whatever you have to. Make it a good price. We've come too far to screw it up now."

"Sure, maybe we'll get lucky," Benteen said.

I didn't like the way he said that; neither did May, who probably remembered what had happened in Bethlehem when Benteen pulled a gun.

Benteen checked his carbine. He told May to bring the pistol he had given him when we left Jerusalem. Sara and I carried canteens. She also brought a trowel for digging. Even with the breeze off the water, the heat was explosive. My eyes ached in the sunlight, which struck up from the hard marly surface of the terrace.

"Watch for scorpions," Benteen warned.

That's wonderful, I thought. Arabs and scorpions. We were off to a fine start.

We descended from the terrace single file and proceeded up the wadi. Juma was in front; Benteen brought up the rear. The path between the limestone cliffs was incredibly rough—broken rocks, boulders that had to be climbed over, soft gravel that could turn an ankle. Not a flower or blade of grass or scrub bush in sight. Nothing to soothe the eye. Nothing but sand and stone—all of it neutral and colorless. The only sound, a howling wind.

I followed May and Sara up the ravine. Fortunately we didn't have far to go. After a couple hundred yards, the wadi widened out into a narrow valley.

We reached the cave after twenty minutes of backbreaking walking. At first I didn't see the entrance, which was halfway up a cliff about 80 feet high. Then an Arab emerged from a dark crevice in the rocks; he saw us immediately and ducked back into the hole, shouting shrilly. There were two other caves, one 15 or 20 feet higher up the cliff; the other, much smaller, a little below and to the right of the slit where I had seen the Arab. The cliff, with its many recesses and outcroppings, was dented with openings.

Benteen cautioned us to stay behind cover. "If anything happens, come up fast with that gun," he told May. Then he and Juma walked out into the open. They held their rifles in front of them, the muzzles pointed down. Benteen shouted in Arabic. Three heads appeared at the entrance of the first cave I had noticed, the largest of the three; two more popped up from the opening above it. One of the Arabs, balancing on a ledge, stood up cautiously with a rifle.

The parley began with Benteen and Juma shouting back and forth with this man, who was apparently the leader. I counted four others. Several of them were boys. The Arab cut a dramatic figure standing up there with his white headdress, robes and long-barreled rifle.

After a few minutes, two more Arabs we hadn't seen before emerged from the third cave, the one closest to the ground.

"Christ," said May. "How many of them are up there? They're like ferrets."

"I hate to think what they've done to those caves," Sara said grimly. "Thank god none of them have picks and shovels."

If the Arabs had been tempted to try anything, they must have dropped the idea when they saw Benteen and Juma's automatic weapons. They sat on the rocks in sullen silence while their chief negotiated.

A deal was quickly arranged. After ten minutes or so, the Bedouin began to file down from the cliffs. Some carried water bags; others had coils of rope looped around their shoulders; a few had baskets. They had set up a small campsite at the base of the cliff; it consisted of a single, low-slung tent and a campfire.

Benteen told May the particulars: he had promised them five English pounds a man if they left peacefully, an offer they had accepted with only a minimum of haggling. The Arabs insisted they hadn't found any scrolls; instead they had some fragments, which they displayed on a dirty scrap of cloth. There must have been a dozen pieces—none larger than a playing card. Brown, with curled edges, they reminded me of dead leaves. These were sold for ten pounds.

Another ten pounds was paid for the fragments of a clay jar and a small, intact lid with chipped edges. The Bedouin said that the scrolls had originally been found in old water jars.

At one point, May told Benteen to offer the Arabs more money. "You give them too much, they'll come back later and try to cut our throats," he snapped back. "We're paying enough as it is now."

Benteen and Juma kept their rifles leveled as the Arabs broke camp. The Bedouin worked swiftly, but even though they had been paid in cash and the deal concluded, the tension was thick enough to cut. I could guess the reason. A single thought must have been gnawing at them: maybe they could have got more for their loot from their friend in Bethlehem.

Juma didn't help; he had been enjoying himself immensely throughout the proceedings. His family's sworn enemies had been bested and he had played a part in it. Some sharp words were exchanged between himself and several of the Arabs, especially with the head man, who up close was much older than I had thought when I first saw him perched on the cliff. His dark face was cracked like worn leather; he looked at least seventy, but his hard, erect body was that of a much younger man.

Benteen finally intervened. He made a great show of chastising Juma. Then he had a few softly spoken words with the Bedouin leader. The Bedouin grimly stared at the ground, not answering.

"What did you tell him?" May asked when the conversation had ended.

"It was just a friendly warning," Benteen said.

"I want to know," May insisted.

"I said I'd shoot them if they came back or tried anything."

The Arabs left swiftly, moving off down the wadi and heading west, away from the Dead Sea.

The Arabs weren't out of sight when Sara started up the cliff. I watched her work her way up through the rocks toward the larger of the caves. She climbed easily, expertly, without any effort.

"A nice piece there, you've got to admit," Benteen said. He had set his rifle down and was taking a drink from a canteen.

"What did you say?" I said.

"You can't take your eyes off that fine tight ass, can you?"

I hit him without thinking. I hit him as hard as I could, throwing straight from the shoulder with as much weight as I could get into it. I knew I was in trouble when he didn't go down.

He came at me with his head, butting me in the chest. We went down and rolled over and he got in several sharp punches before May pulled him off me. May was as strong as he looked. He took Benteen around the chest, lifted him so that his legs went off the ground, and dropped him hard.

"You crazy bastard," he said, breathing heavily. "What in the hell are you trying to do?"

Benteen sat up and shook his head. He pushed his hands through his dark hair. "This guy wasn't in our agreement," he said coldly.

The calculating anger I had seen in his eyes when I hit him was still there. He rubbed the back of his neck where he had hit the ground.

"Then we'll change the agreement," May said. "I promise you, Benteen. You pull this kind of stunt again, you're going to be out some money, a lot of it. You were paid to get us here and get us back—all of us. It's going to be very much worth your while to do that. If that's no good, you better leave. Now."

Benteen got up and dusted himself off. I did the same, still aching in the side.

"I get the picture," he said.

May said he was glad to hear that. He looked up at Sara, who had reached the cave. Its entrance looked like a wound.

CHAPTER 11

The sky was already turning a fiery orange in the west as the sun dropped on the horizon. Sara didn't spend much time up at the cave, the largest of the three the Bedouin had abandoned. It was too late in the day to go inside, and she didn't have a flashlight. During her brief inspection she saw enough to rule out the two smaller caves for serious investigation. Little more than recesses in the limestone, they were extremely shallow.

After hiking back to the terrace, we set up our camp near the ruins. If we hadn't been running out of daylight, I would have liked to explore the place, especially the watchtower. A good ten feet high, it reminded me of the stone grain silos I had seen in Normandy during the war.

We pitched three tents of heavy canvas, pegging them down in the hard ground. One was for Sara, May and I were to share another, and Benteen and Juma were in the third. They were all British army issue and smelled of mildew. We arranged them so they faced the Dead Sea, which had turned from blue to murky gray as the sky darkened.

Warming some soup cans on a portable gas stove, we ate our dinner seated on the ground in front of the tents. If Sara had seen my fight with Benteen, she didn't mention it. Neither did Benteen. I hadn't meant to hit him until it happened. We were out of our corners now and face to face. Maybe it would clear the air, but I had my doubts.

When we finished eating, the air had already cooled. The Southern Cross, the stars pale in the sky, was almost straight overhead; the early moon cast a rippling dagger on the water. We all turned in early. Juma and Benteen split the guard detail between them. After what had happened with the Bedouin, we would have a guard posted every night.

In the morning, we headed back to the cave shortly before sunup. It was already hot. In addition to the shovels and other tools, Sara had brought a wiremesh screen to sift the loose soil for artifacts; the screen's wood frame was about a foot square and was fairly heavy. She also had a large canvas bag filled with containers of assorted sizes and a bundle of loose rags to wrap and protect any fragments we found. May and I were going to help in the cave, and so we had trowels and flashlights. I carried the screen, May had two shovels. Juma brought a lantern and climbing rope. Everyone carried water.

May and Juma also lugged two pieces of rolled tarpaulin, which they strung up at the base of the cliff for shade.

Before we started climbing, Sara explained what she wanted to do. She was professional to the point of crispness. She wore faded wool pants with scuffed knees, boots and a cloth cap with a brim she pulled low over her eyes.

"If this were a regular dig, I'd want to get some elevations and then lay out a proper gridwork," she said. "But we don't have time for that and you're not familiar with the procedure, so I'll try to keep it simple. We'll dig sections two-feet square. Work slowly and carefully. I can't emphasize that enough. Use the edge of your trowel like a scalpel. The idea is to peel the soil back in layers. Don't chop at the ground; it's the easiest way to damage or miss something."

I asked about the screen.

"We'll sift the loose dirt. Maybe we'll catch some fragments."

It was just after six o'clock when we started climbing for the cave, but the sun had already run up into the sky like a red flag. I followed Sara and May. Every muscle in my back and legs ached. I played out rope as we ascended the cliff, so that we could hoist up the shovels and the screen. There was absolutely no shade.

As I struggled up the rocks, sweating, dry-mouthed, my chest heaving, I wondered what the cave was going to be like. Ever since reading Tom Sawyer as a kid, I'd been afraid of caves with their damp walls, mud and pitch darkness.

When we got to the entrance, Sara shined a flashlight inside. The opening sloped down to what appeared to be a larger chamber. Sara threw a rock inside to scare off any snakes that might have been curled up there to get out of the heat.

Following her and May, I slipped through the entrance and, bent over at the waist, edged down a narrow passageway. Light filtered into the inner chamber from a saucer-sized hole higher up the cliff. The air was thick with dust. The chamber had a dome-like ceiling that was just high enough so we could stand up.

Sara had been right about the Arabs. The dirt floor of the cave had been badly churned and was riddled with small craters apparently scooped out by hand. The Bedouin had dug dozens of them. In the dusty light, we could see that the powdered soil was littered with pottery shards. If there had been any unbroken jars they had been either removed or smashed.

"All the strata have been obliterated," she said, surveying the damage. "The surface, middle layers... it's like a mixing bowl in here." She shook her head. "There's no telling how much has been destroyed."

We had brought a camera with us and she took several pictures, the flash attachment popping loudly as she pressed the shutter. May and I stayed near the entrance as she used a tape measure to check the dimensions of the floor; she took great care where she stepped. The tapering chamber was roughly eight feet deep and seven feet wide.

"We'll start near the back."

Sara marked off three two-by-two-foot sections with twine, pegging down the edges of the squares with sticks. We would dig only within the borders of the twine. As for the holes the Bedouin had dug, she told us to scrape away at their sides, carefully enlarging them.

She repeated her instructions for using the trowels.

"They aren't shovels. Probe gently. Don't go any deeper than an inch at a time."

That was the program for the next several hours as we squatted in the dirt, using the trowels like chisels.

It was soon apparent that although the Arabs may have made off with the better pieces, they had left plenty behind. We uncovered dozens of scroll fragments and bits of pottery, which we placed in

Sara's cloth-padded containers. She sifted the loose soil through the screen. This usually resulted in a few more fragments. The pieces of scroll were often imprinted with letters, sometimes several words. Sara couldn't read them in the dim light.

The shards of pottery resembled the pieces of a jigsaw puzzle. A few seemed to fit together. Most were the color of clay.

"What are you going to do with all of this?" May asked.

"Try to reassemble them."

She hoped there would be enough fragments to reconstruct at least partially one of the jars.

I asked whether she could date any of the pieces.

"The best clue is the lid we bought from the Bedouin yesterday. It's a Greek design that was fairly common during the late Roman period. A number of these jars are on display in the Rockefeller Museum in Jerusalem. They were in use all over the Holy Land. For that matter, throughout the entire Mediterranean basin. It's an ordinary example of domestic pottery. Nothing special at all, but of great use to archeologists trying to date the past. If we can restore just one of the jars it would be a big help."

"What were they used for?" May asked.

"Usually for storing water or wine," Sara said.

"Or scrolls?" I asked.

Sara said, "The Talmud mentions that the son of Jacob ordered that scrolls of the law should be placed in earthen vessels. But the practice wasn't common. I think the scrolls in this cave were put in jars to try to protect them. It was probably done in a hurry."

I was surprised the scrolls hadn't rotted away.

"This is the driest region in the Holy Land," Sara said. "The climate's a lot like the Egyptian desert. There's very little rain or humidity even during the short rainy season. The conditions are perfect for preservation."

"It's amazing none have been found before," May said.

"They have been," Sara said. "In the 8th century, the patriarch of Seleucia, a man named Timotheus, wrote a letter to a friend in Palestine. The letter mentions scrolls that had been discovered in a cave near Jericho. They included a number of books from the Old Testament."

Timotheus, she explained, was eager to get more information about the strange documents. He especially wanted to find out whether any of them included certain Old Testament passages referred to in the New Testament—passages he couldn't find in his own version of the Old Testament. They were extremely important verses because they prophesied the coming of Jesus Christ. One passage in particular troubled him: "He shall be called a Nazarene." There was nothing like it in the patriarch's copy of the Old Testament.

Sara said, "These passages—they're sometimes called proof texts—have always been an embarrassment for Christians. They aren't found in the Hebrew Old Testament or if they do occur they're in much different form. They've been a thorny problem for centuries."

I asked how it had worked out for Timotheus.

"It didn't. He never found the solution to his dilemma. The scrolls that were uncovered near Jericho were of no help at all."

We worked until ten o'clock. By then, we had found perhaps twenty fragments of scrolls in the loose soil, most of them less than an inch square. It had been nearly four hours since we had started. The heat inside the cave was worse than outside. May and I took off our shirts as we scraped at the dirt. Sweat poured down our faces and chests and we tied handkerchiefs around our foreheads. We had cut out six neat squares two feet deep but had hardly dented the floor. There was no evidence at all that the cave had been inhabited; we didn't find any trace of charred firewood or utensils or any other personal objects that would have been proof that people once had lived there.

"How much of this do you want to clear?" May asked.

"We could spend a week here and not do a thorough job," Sara said in frustration.

We all knew that was out of the question. We didn't have the time. There was enough food and water to last three, maybe four days at most. After the water went, we'd have to get out fast.

May suggested taking a break. Sara didn't want to stop, but it was fine with me. Benteen and Juma were waiting for us when we climbed down; they were sitting under the tarp in a patch of shade. We opened some cans of fruit and cheese and had lunch.

"How's it going?" Benteen asked. He sat against a flat rock with his carbine resting on his lap.

May told him what we had found.

"The Arabs made off with the good stuff, assuming there was any," Benteen said. "I wouldn't be sure they sold you everything they found yesterday. They might have been holding back."

May said, "Maybe we'd do better if you came up and helped us." He sounded irritated.

"I wouldn't count on it," Benteen said. "If I were you, I'd write this cave off and try to find one the Bedouin haven't mucked up."

"There are caves all up and down this valley," May said in annoyance. Benteen's tone had angered him. "Where would you suggest starting?"

Ready for the question, Benteen said, "Juma has some thoughts on that." He spoke to the guide who chatted away excitedly, pointing back up the wadi toward the Qumran terrace.

Translating, Benteen said, "His grandfather used to tell a story about a cave he discovered when he was a young man. It was high up a cliff back near those ruins. He saw a partridge fly into the entrance and went in after it. He was looking for dinner, but Juma says he found an old lamp inside and a few pieces of jewelry. The tribe used the lamp until a few years ago. It was stolen during a raid."

"Can he find this cave?" May asked.

Benteen smiled. "If Allah wills it."

May, disappointed with what the cave had yielded so far, thought it was worth trying. Sara wanted to stay where we were; she was pleased by what we had uncovered.

"I say we move on," May snapped, making it clear he was paying for this trip.

An argument broke out fueled by the heat. May wouldn't budge. Sara reluctantly agreed to look for the cave Juma had mentioned, but first she wanted to explore the Qumran ruins. I remembered that Professor Parker had suggested we take a look at them to see if there might be some link to the Essenes.

May agreed with the plan. In a better mood, he changed his mind about the cave, deciding we'd work there a while longer. It was early in the day. We could put in a few more hours and still devote most of the afternoon to the abandoned settlement. The next morning, we'd look for the cave Juma was talking about. If that didn't pan out, we could always come back here.

Later, after returning to the cave, we continued excavating the earthen floor. Using the blades of our trowels like knives, we carved away at the sides of the cup-shaped indentations the Bedouin had made. We worked more rapidly than Sara would have liked, but there wasn't any alternative. We were sacrificing archeological technique for speed, trying, in the process, to do as little damage as possible.

About an hour after we resumed work, May uncovered a coin with his trowel. It lay buried in the loose soil close to the surface. One side of the coin was inscribed with what looked like a palm tree and some words that had been effaced. The other carried the Hebrew inscription, "Leherut Yerushalayim" and the Roman numeral II. Badly tarnished, the coin was made of copper. Sara was able to remove some of the tarnish with a cloth.

The words meant "For the Freedom of Jerusalem." Sara read them without hesitating.

The coin was about the size of an American quarter. The edges were roughly squared. The Roman numeral, Sara thought, meant that it dated to the second year of the First Jewish Revolt. Ruthlessly put down by the Romans, the revolt lasted from 66 A.D. to 70 A.D. and ended with the destruction of Jerusalem and the burning of the temple. The fighting occured during the reign of Herod Agrippa II, a non-Jewish puppet who had been put on the throne by the Romans.

Sara's excitement was contagious. The coin offered a clue as to when the scrolls might have been hidden in the cave.

"I wasn't expecting this kind of luck," she said happily. She turned to May. "And you wanted to leave here!"

CHAPTER 12

THE SUN BEAT DOWN over the brown shoulders of the cliffs. Shadowless and foreboding in the exhausted air, they rose above the terrace where we had set up our camp. As I studied them after our return from the cave, I felt as if I were standing on the far side of the moon.

Sara suggested we start our inspection of the ruins and adjoining cemetery by taking a look at the collapsed tower that dominated the site.

"What do you think it was for?" I asked. The tower was stone-belted with an arched opening at the base.

"The design certainly looks Roman," Sara said. "It might have been a kind of blockhouse or storage room. Notice how it faces the northeast, toward Jerusalem and Jericho? An attack probably would have come from that direction...let's take a look."

Impetuously, without hesitating, she scrambled up on the tower, working her way along the rim of the curving wall with sure steps. May and I reluctantly followed. It made me giddy to perch there on top, sitting on the wall with my legs dangling over the edge. But the height offered a bird's-eye view; the sweep of the Dead Sea stretching away from us in a wide blue band only increased the sense of exhilaration.

I noticed how the cemetery was separated from the rest of the settlement by a crumbling stone wall and by an open space about ten feet wide that resembled an esplanade. All of the graves, obviously arranged with great care, were close together.

"The Jews always used a wall to separate a cemetery from the dwellings of a town or village," Sara said as she surveyed the ground. "It was meant to represent the division of the living and the dead—the unclean from the clean."

"Then you think Jews were buried here," May said.

"It's possible," she said hesitantly.

She took some pictures, taking advantage of the elevation; then we climbed down off the tower and began to explore the settlement while Benteen and Juma set up their tarp and got out of the sun.

The area occupied by the strange cluster of destroyed buildings stood near the tapering point of the terrace and was about half the size of a football field. Only parts of the exterior walls and the stone floors remained, the roofs having disappeared long ago. The largest of these ruins was adjacent to the tower. Sara stepped off the dimensions, which she carefully recorded in her notebook. The structure was approximately 30 x 37 meters. The walls had been skillfully plastered and there were openings for windows.

The most striking feature of the compound was the intricate network of cisterns, some with steps leading down into them. A broken aqueduct of Roman design trailed off toward the hills in a crooked white line. Two of these pools looked fairly deep and were plastered. There were six cisterns in all; most of them were partially filled with stones.

"There certainly isn't much rainfall out here," Sara said. "They would have tried to save every drop they could during the short rainy season."

As she examined one of these pools, Sara noticed a long crack that ran up the steps. The line, which cut through several of the collapsed buildings, had opened wide breaches in the stone foundations and apparently had pulled apart sections of wall. The crack swept across the entire settlement on a diagonal path.

"That's an earthquake fissure," she said, studying the gaping rent. "It's recorded that a tremendous earthquake struck Judea in 31 or 32 B.C. The heaviest destruction was out here in the desert and in the Jordan Valley. I wonder if this damage might have occurred then."

We inspected the remains of several other buildings that were attached to the larger structure. The walls suggested that the buildings once had been honeycombed with cell-like rooms.

It didn't take much longer for Sara to agree with Professor Parker; his intuition had been on the money. She was increasingly convinced that the site most probably had been occupied by an ancient sect like the Essenes.

"This wasn't a town or village," she said. "Everything here indicates the place was laid out like a monastery."

I found it incredible that anyone could have lived in such a setting—or would have wanted to. Only the hardest of men, fanatics, could have made their home in a land so grotesque and unforgiving. I couldn't help but admire their audacity. Qumran was a sunbaked hell.

I remembered what Parker had said about Pliny, how he might have made a simple error in locating the site for the Essene community farther to the south. I mentioned this to Sara.

"From what I see here that sounds like a real possibility," she said. "Everyone assumed their settlement had vanished, but maybe it was at Qumran all along. The traces of Roman construction might have thrown people off. The Romans certainly occupied the site, but someone else may have been here long before them. Until those scrolls were found, no one made the connection."

As we continued to search the ruins, or to use Juma's Arab word, Khirbet, it became apparent that the settlement had been systematically burned. We noticed signs of charring and in several places carbonized ash showed through the layers of dust.

Sara thought the ash might cover the original flooring. She suggested digging down through it with our trowels in the hope we might uncover pieces of pottery or other artifacts.

The ash was thickest in two small adjoining rooms. Sara and I worked in one of them while May dug alone in the other. Before we did anything she photographed both sites.

She knelt next to me. She had tied the ends of her shirt in a knot, exposing her slender waist. I looked at her admiringly. There was a faint line of beaded sweat just over her upper lip. As she concentrated on her digging, I felt the familiar dryness in my throat. I couldn't recall what it was like the last time I'd had a woman. No, that was wrong. The last time was just like all the others; I had them and then I was through with them or they were through with me. I didn't want anything steady in those days and walked out once or twice when I should have stuck around. I'd stick around with Sara, I thought. I'd stick as long as she let me.

She delicately jabbed the trowel into the ash.

"It could take months to clear away these foundations and walls and do a proper excavation out here," she said gloomily.

"We can always come back."

"That might not be easy. In case you forgot, there's a war on."

I had all but forgotten the fighting. It was May 15th, the long-awaited day when the mandate ended and the British officially pulled out of the Holy Land. By now Israel would have declared her independence. That had been a foregone conclusion for months. I had talked to enough well-placed Israelis to know that Ben-Gurion would make the announcement as quickly as possible. The hope was that the United States would immediately recognize the government and sent military equipment before the Arabs could deliver a knockout blow. I wondered what Truman had done on that score. It was probably getting rough back in Jerusalem. I thought about Weil. I'd left him in a bad scrape. I felt rotten about that.

We continued working on our knees, digging with the trowels near one of the walls. The layer of ash was nearly a foot deep.

May called us. He had hit something with his trowel in the adjoining room; the room had a shallow, trough-like hollow at one of its ends, where he was kneeling.

"Something's down there," he said as Sara crouched next to him.

The three of us began to scrape away the covering of ash. After digging down eight or nine inches, we uncovered a stack of bowls, one piled atop the other. All of them were shattered. We removed some more ash and found more bowls of similar design. They apparently had been neatly stacked. Sara probed the ash with her trowel, trying to gauge the dimensions of the space; she gradually outlined a section of floor about five feet square.

"This might have been some kind of pantry," she said. "The pieces were probably smashed when the roof collapsed."

One of the bowls was scratched with a name. The square, blockish script, Sara said, was similar to that used on the scrolls, but much cruder.

The words, Yohanan ha-taleh, she translated to mean John the Younger.

From the number of bowls, the pantry must have supplied a large community.

Another discovery came to light as we continued digging in the ash. We found two arrowheads. Made of iron, each of the heads had three winged-edges tapering to a point.

"Those look like they may be Roman," Sara said immediately.

The Roman Legions commonly used arrows with such lethal-looking tips, she said.

May later found another arrowhead embedded in the stone frame of a doorway.

The discoveries convinced Sara that the Romans probably had put the torch to the settlement. From the presence of the arrowheads, she speculated they may have encountered resistance. She thought the destruction most likely had occurred during the First Jewish Revolt. The coin May had found in the cave as well as the paleographic evidence of the name scratched on the bowl nudged her in this direction. The Romans had come with fire and the inhabitants of the settlement had evacuated, hiding the scrolls—their most precious possessions—in the nearby caves. At least that was her theory.

"The Romans may have occupied the monastery long after everyone was driven away," she said. "That might account for the tower. How long they were here is anyone's guess right now. This might have been a major outpost for several centuries."

The evidence—Sara was almost certain of this—suggested that the scrolls and pottery fragments found in the cave came from the settlement at Qumran. She found another clue in one of the ash piles, which were proving fertile ground.

In the corner of one of the small rooms, she uncovered an empty jar. Intact except for a missing lid, it was about two feet tall.

"That lid the Bedouin found in the cave might fit a jar like this," Sara said.

She thought that if a jar could later be reconstructed from the clay fragments we had dug up in the cave, it would closely resemble the one from the monastery.

By mid-afternoon, we finally got out to the cemetery. The sun had long since burned off the few clouds. This time Juma and Benteen joined us. Juma came very reluctantly; he didn't like the place.

The ground was littered with burial mounds covered with piles of loose stone. I walked to the edge of the terrace and looked at some low hills, which sloped down to level ground. I saw more graves there, concealed behind a humpbacked ridgeline that faced the Dead Sea. The faint outline of a trail wound down the face of the cliff to the graves. We hadn't noticed them before.

"That might be a secondary cemetery to handle the overflow," Sara said. "The graves down there are probably more recent."

"Parker was right," I said, studying the ground. "There must be a thousand people buried out here."

"This had to have been a large settlement," Sara said. "How else would you account for all these graves?"

She walked about the neatly laid out cemetery, stopping frequently to jot her observations in her notebook. We also took photographs of the site, which was set between the precipice and the cliffs.

Sara said, "The Essenes preached that all men were equal before God. There was even equality in death. Look at these graves. Each is exactly like the next. None of them are set apart for special recognition. There aren't any unusual markings, or unusual headstones or tumuli—nothing."

"Whoever's responsible for this certainly did it with care," May agreed. "They didn't waste an inch of ground."

Juma stood nearby shaking his head, muttering to himself.

"He says these are the tombs of Kuffar—unbelievers," Benteen said.

Mussulman graves, he explained, always pointed east and west. All these graves, he said, were arranged on a distinct north-south axis.

"The Arabs have never liked to come to this place," Benteen said. "They believe infidels are buried here."

It was very late in the day by then—too late to continue our exploration of the ruins and cemetery. Sara asked me if I wanted to go swimming.

CHAPTER 13

"I NEED TO COOL OFF," she said. "It will help me think."

"I'm game," I said. "But there's something you ought to know. I can't swim."

Sara laughed.

"That's one of the advantages of the Dead Sea. You don't have to worry about that."

She said that when the Tenth Legion was camped at Caesarea on the Mediterranean, Vespasian decided to visit the Dead Sea because he had heard reports about its mysterious heavy water. If Josephus is to be believed, the emperor had several of his soldiers who couldn't swim a stroke thrown in with their hands tied behind their backs. He was amused and pleased, she said, when they bobbed to the surface and floated.

May said, "So were they, I'll bet."

All of us laughed at that. I was glad to see it. We had all become a little tense.

Benteen, who didn't want to go swimming, went back to the camp to get something to eat. But not before he smiled at me. I knew what it meant. Sooner or later he and I were going to settle up.

May declined Sara's invitation to join us. He wanted to rest and returned to his tent.

The sun had almost set, but we had some twilight left as we descended the path that wound down in corkscrew stages from the terrace. The rocky trail, washed out and broken in places, looked ancient and I wondered how many men had passed over it during the centuries.

After stopping to check the station wagon, which we had left parked at the base of the cliff, we walked toward the shore. It wasn't far, less than a quarter mile. White birds were making short, diving sweeps over the water. We crossed the edge of what once must have been a flourishing oasis. It extended south, ending abruptly at a sheer wall of rock that plunged straight into the sea. Reeds and rushes were plentiful in the marshy ground, and as we walked we flushed two coneys from their cover. They skittered away, their wings flapping loudly.

"This must have been alive with flowers in the spring," Sara said. "I've read there were gazelles and wild boar here as recently as fifty years ago. Even cattle."

That sounded hard to believe. It was like imagining cattle grazing in the middle of the Mojave.

The inhabitants of the monastery, Sara said, probably used the oasis for much of their water and food. Yet the area was only several acres at most. I told her it wasn't much bigger than a small truck farm—hardly enough ground to feed a large community.

"The Dead Sea is at least 20 feet higher than it was several hundred years ago," she said. "Most of the oasis is under water. It was much larger in the days of the Essenes."

We were out on the ash-colored sand of the beach, which smelled of sulphur. Sara took off her boots and, without hesitating, unbuttoned her shirt. She wasn't wearing a bra; her small breasts were firm and uptilted and I had trouble not staring. I took off my shirt and followed her out into the surprisingly cool water.

Wearing only our shorts, we waded out until we were in up to our waists. I could see far down the coast. The cliffs of the Qumran wadi, in evening shadows now, rose sharply in front of us.

"Just let yourself go," Sara said. She pushed backward and floated, lifting her arms and feet to show that she wasn't treading water.

I followed her example and was amazed when the water held me up. We floated like that for a while. I couldn't take my eyes off her. I had never seen a more beautiful woman—her fine body moving gracefully in the water. We went out 40 or 50 yards, rocking in the gentle waves that lapped over us, bobbing like corks on a line. I tried to touch bottom and couldn't. At any other time or place, I

91

would have panicked, but I was enjoying myself; kicking my feet I could go wherever I wanted, supported by the salty, buoyant water.

"You're doing fine," Sara shouted as I dogpaddled after her. She floated on her back, her black hair an open fan.

"I should have had swimming lessons here instead of at the YMCA," I said. "I might have learned something."

"I learned at a community center in New York. We had to swim in the nude."

I whistled and said, "I would have given blood to have been a lifeguard at that pool."

Sara laughed and headed back for shore. I followed her, swimming easily. It was all so wonderfully crazy. I experienced something that had been missing for a long time in my life— something akin to joy.

When we came out of the water, Sara put her shirt back on and lay down on the beach. The moon was high by now, but the stones were still warm from the sun. I lay next to her, our wet bodies almost touching. She closed her eyes and put her arm under her head. She lay still as if asleep.

"I feel so much better," she said. "Thanks for coming with me."

We lay there a long time without speaking, the salt drying to a white powder on our skin. I finally worked up the nerve to ask her a question I'd kept bottled up for days.

"How is it a woman like you isn't married?"

Sara rolled over and faced me. At first I thought the question had upset her, but it was pain, not anger I saw in her eyes.

She told me that the man she had loved, a graduate student in archeology at Hebrew University, had been killed in a parachuting accident. She had known him less than six months.

"He was being trained by the Haganah," she said. "They went out on maneuvers in the Negev. It was his second jump. Somehow his chute got tangled and didn't open. He was twenty-six."

That was all she said, and I didn't press her for more. She turned over on her back and shut her eyes and I bent over and kissed her softly on the lips. Her hands touched my shoulders lightly and then she pressed against me, our arms entwined. We kissed until we were gasping for breath.

"I kept waiting for you to do that," she said. "Why did you keep me waiting? It was so foolish."

"I'll never make you wait again."

I kissed her and she returned it, digging her fingers into my back until it hurt. I kissed her breasts through her shirt as she held my head against her, stroking my hair.

"I didn't want to think this could happen," I said, watching her smile up at me. "I wanted it too much."

I kissed her again, and she held me tightly around the waist. When we got up and started back to camp, both of us knew how much we were risking.

CHAPTER 14

WE WERE UP BEFORE SUNRISE. The full moon looked like a white hole punched into the sky. The air was still, almost cool. We were going to look for Juma's cave and wanted to get going before the sun came. The Bedouin had told Benteen the cave was high in the limestone cliffs that fronted the Dead Sea. Fortunately we didn't have far to go—no more than an hour's hike north of the Qumran ruins.

I carried a coil of rope slung over my shoulder. May and Benteen were also carrying rope. Juma had a heavy waterbag and shovel. Trim and dark-eyed, he looked almost frail in his British khaki and headdress.

Sara and I had sat outside her tent talking until very late and now in the morning she kissed me on the cheek before we started. She made no effort to hide it. May saw this and smiled; he must have had a good idea all along what was going to happen.

Dawn came quickly as we reached the bottom of the trail that wound down off the terrace. Following Juma, we headed up into the low hills that ran along the shoreline. As the sun edged over the horizon we were in the shadows of the fretted bluffs. We climbed steadily, moving higher in the cliffs as if working our way up a flight of steps. We finally came to a place where the wall was less sheer.

Juma studied the ridgeline. Even in the shadows, you could see the openings of three or four caves in the rockface. He pointed to one of them and spoke rapidly.

"That's it, up there," Benteen said.

Midway up the cliff, the entrance was a gash in the limestone. Getting there wasn't going to be easy.

Sara wasn't optimistic. She thought that if Juma's grandfather had been inside, other Bedouin almost certainly had explored it.

We climbed single file, trailing behind Juma, who scrambled through the rocks like an Alpine guide. The first half wasn't bad, but then the path got steeper and footholds were harder to find. My legs started cramping and I was gasping for breath long before we reached the entrance. The cave was small and shallow.

Sara and Juma went in with flashlights. May followed.

I stayed by the entrance, looking back at the ruins perched on the edge of the terrace not a mile to the south. The Dead Sea had changed color, turning from milky gray to soft blue in the early light.

"What do you think?" May asked when they emerged from the cave.

"It's going to take a lot of digging," Sara said. "And I still have my doubts we'll find anything."

After talking it over, they decided to try several of the other caves that cut into the cliffs. Two of them were especially tempting. Their inaccessibility would have made it difficult for the Bedouin to enter.

One of the caves was just below the rim of the cliff, which rose over 100 feet from where we were standing. The other, lower on the rockwall, was 50 or 60 yards away. Sara studied their entrances with binoculars; they were large enough for a man and the ledges in front of them appeared to have eroded. There was no way to approach from below; the only possibility would be a rope descent.

We spent what seemed like an eternity scaling the cliff. I was the last to reach the top and had to sit down until I got my wind back.

"Who's going first?" Benteen asked. We had laid the rope down flat on the rocks, about 150 feet of one-inch hemp.

Sara volunteered, but May vetoed that idea.

"Let me do it," he said.

"No offense, but you're too heavy," Benteen said. "We're going to have to lower someone by hand. I don't think we could hold you."

I made some quick body comparisons. I was taller but lighter than Benteen, and Juma had already made it clear that he wasn't about to dangle over the side of the cliff.

"I guess it's me."

Benteen said, "I was hoping you'd see it that way."

We walked along the uneven crest of the bluff until we were directly above the cave. I looked over the edge. It was a 50-foot drop to where the wall flanged out into boulders and rocks. The narrow ledge in front of the cave's entrance was about 15 feet below the summit.

Benteen had brought two steel spikes with him. He hammered these into the ground with the blade of the shovel. When the spikes were deep and secure, he wrapped the rope around and between them, so they would serve as a brake. I'd be lowered as May, Benteen and Juma slowly played out the rope, keeping it taut around the spikes.

"You sure you want to do this?" May asked.

"Are you sure you want to hold onto that rope?"

Benteen fashioned a loop and I slipped it over my shoulders and under my arms and pulled it tight.

"Brace your feet against the side of the cliff as you go down," he said. "We'll play out the rope nice and easy."

I smiled at Sara, but inside myself I wasn't smiling at all. I went over the side with my back to the ground, both hands gripping the rope, using my feet as if I were trying to walk down the face of the cliff. I didn't look down until I could feel the ledge.

It was difficult to get a toe hold. Pushing off, I had to swing like a weight on a pendulum until I had enough momentum to carry me into the entrance. I landed hard and rolled over on my back. The sloping floor of the cave was sticky. Guano. I played the flashlight beam on the ceiling. It was covered with bats, their folded wings shiny in the light. Some of the wings opened and closed.

I reported what I saw. May finally called for me to come up; he wanted to try the other cave. I was getting ready to slip into the looped end of the rope when I noticed a small jar with curved handles. Half buried in the dirt, it was just a few feet inside the entrance. I was surprised I hadn't seen it earlier.

"I've got something here!" I shouted.

Kneeling down, I lifted the jar from the soil. The size of a large soup bowl, it was filled with caked dirt and bat droppings. Something else was underneath. I brushed away some of the loose dirt and uncovered a pair of sandals that were wrapped in what looked like leather. The sandals still had their straps; the leather was stiff, but not brittle.

I leaned out the entrance and told Sara what I had found. She lowered a haversack by rope and told me to wrap the pieces in the cloth inside the sack. When I sent the bag back up, they hoisted me to the top.

Sara had the jar out of the bag. Made of bronze or copper, it had three short legs; she gently rubbed the sides with a damp rag.

"This looks Roman," she said. "It might be some kind of ritual vessel."

She cleaned more of the dirty surface.

"You can see where it's been defaced." The curved exterior of the bowl had been deeply gouged. I could make out the shape of a woman etched into the surface. Sara thought the figure represented a Roman goddess.

"They probably scratched out the image so they could use this for cooking without giving offense."

"Who do you mean?" May asked.

"Jews. There's no telling how they got it. Maybe it was stolen or captured from Roman soldiers during a raid. It's been well used."

Sara couldn't date the piece accurately without checking some references. But based on what we had already uncovered—the coin, arrowheads and pottery—she thought the bowl likely dated to the first century A.D.

The sandals, she said, were of a type commonly worn in the country for centuries. The piece of leather that wrapped them turned out to be a short jacket, which closed in the front with leather lacings.

The discoveries pleased May, who decided to make a quick check of the other cave, which was nearby. If it proved to be a bust, we'd come back here and do some digging.

While we were coiling up the ropes and working the spikes out of the ground, Juma thought he saw a reflection. Something had caught the sunlight in the hills far up the coast. Benteen checked the area with his binoculars but saw nothing. Juma wanted to go off at once to investigate; so did Benteen, but May overruled them. He didn't want to waste any more time. The decision left Juma irritable and sulky, which disturbed me; I didn't want to worry about an irritable, sulky man holding onto a rope while I dangled from the end.

We followed the edge of the bluff 30 or 40 yards to a point where the wall was very sheer. The next cave, located midway between the summit and ground, was about 20 feet down. I didn't see how anyone could have got in or out of it. There wasn't even a trace of a ledge. Sara thought ladders and scaffolding might have been used to reach the entrance. Other cliff dwellers had done that, she reminded us. The Zuni and Hopi Indians for example.

The stakes were again driven into the ground, and with the rope tied around me, I went over the edge and down the side of the cliff. They let me out with a jerk. I dropped five feet before the rope went taut, snapping me hard. When I got my heart out of my mouth, I started using my feet.

The recessed mouth of the cave was almost a perfect rectangle. There was something odd about it; the top and sides appeared to have been scraped out by hand.

I decided on another swinging approach. Dangling above the opening, I pushed off. When I had enough momentum, I swung inside, pitching over on my back and elbows. I shined my flashlight at the vaulted ceiling. At least there weren't any bats.

Slipping out of the rope, I could see that this was a much larger cave. A draft was blowing down from the ceiling. There were at least two grotto-like chambers, one smaller than the other; the walls and ceiling were scorched from camp fires. There was enough room to stand. I played the flashlight on one of the walls and froze. Three skeletons were lying there next to a small pile of bones—tibias, forearms, a rib cage, and on top—two skulls. They were propped against the wall, two with their legs drawn up in fetal position.

I shouted the news. Sara said she'd be right down. I sent up the rope and a few minutes later I heard her coming down the side of the cliff, her boots scraping on the rock as Benteen told her to lean back and use her legs. When she was near the entrance, I pulled her into the cave.

Speechless, she stared at the skeletons. The bones were covered with dust and guano. One of the skeletons was much smaller than the others. I wondered if it were a child.

As shaken as I was, Sara knelt by the skeletons, examining them with her flashlight. The bones and skulls looked the color of bleached flour.

"What do you think happened to them?" I asked.

"It looks like they just decided to lie down and die."

I remembered how it had ended at Masada. But there were no swords or knives near them. They could have taken poison, Sara said, but she wasn't sure. They could have starved or died of thirst. The one certainty was that these poor bastards hadn't had an easy death.

We explored the cave. The smaller chamber was connected to the room in which the bodies lay. From the stones piled in the passageway between them, Sara thought part of the ceiling might have caved in. We both felt the strong flow of air I had noticed earlier. I lit a match; the flame danced and went out. The draft was coming from above us. We went as far back into the large chamber as possible; it was almost 15 feet deep. Sara shined her flashlight on the ceiling and saw the opening. Footholds had been carved into the rock—the entrance to yet another chamber. The cave apparently had two levels.

"Give me a boost," Sara said.

She climbed up, using the steps while I steadied her. I followed, placing my feet into the cuts in the wall and pulling myself up. The upper chamber was wide, but the ceiling was low and I had to bend over. The air current was stronger. I lit another match, which flared. There was a hole in the ceiling. I looked up a shaft and saw a sliver of light.

Sara said, "That has to be another entrance."

She called out to May, who answered, his voice clear and close.

During the next several hours, May and the others worked to pry loose the rocks that blocked the opening. Sara thought it probably had been the main entrance. Juma returned to the jeep to get a crowbar; eventually they opened a breech large enough for a man to get through. The shaft, notched from top to bottom with footholds, was about eight feet long.

While they were working on this, Sara and I did some preliminary digging in the cave's main chamber. We used trowels and a spade lowered by rope. From the scrape marks on the walls, Sara was sure the cave had been enlarged; it probably had been occupied for a long time.

We dug along the wall near where the skeletons lay, trying not to mind the stench from the guano. The floor was covered with a four- or five-inch layer of dust, guano and loose soil; but the ground beneath was firm like clay. We started to find pottery shards and animal bones. Sara also uncovered fragments of leather and parchment. She thought they might be the remains of a phylactery. The writing appeared to be Aramaic.

May eventually joined us, climbing down through the newly opened entrance, after lowering a lantern. The shaft was just wide enough for his shoulders. We now had an easy way to get in and out of the cave, which pleased me greatly. I hadn't looked forward to another rope ascent.

As soon as May was inside, Benteen and Juma hurried off to investigate the reflection Juma had noticed earlier. It was like a piece of polished glass catching the sunlight, May told us. They had seen the flashes several times again while they were digging— always from the same place in the hills. Before he left, Benteen had warned May to get us out of the cave fast if there was trouble.

We tried to prepare May for the skeletons, but he was still startled.

"What are they doing up here?" he asked Sara. "Were they killed?"

"They might have hidden in the cave when the Romans attacked the monastery. They might have been trapped. There's no sign of a struggle."

We worked well into the afternoon. The main chamber, which proved rich in artifacts, provided fragments of pottery of a kind similar to what we already had discovered. Sara uncovered an ax hidden in a crevice in the wall. Wedged behind a stone, the short wooden haft was still in one piece. We looked for other crevices and, in the rear of the cave, Sara found a reed basket that contained fragments of parchment. They were in a thick bundle wrapped in a gummy, partially disintegrated scrap of linen. The linen was stuck fast to the parchment.

Sara pried loose the basket, working at the edges with her trowel.

"There's something else here," she said.

The basket lay over a waterskin. Sara eased the skin out of the ground. It folded over another basket similar to the first, which held a thick scroll.

Patting Sara on the back, May looked happily excited. "This is the best day of my life," he said. "Better than my first gusher."

Sara, trying not to show her agitation, took the basket to the entrance of the cave and examined the scroll in the sunlight.

"This isn't made of leather," she said, sounding puzzled. "I think it's copper." The rolled metal was badly oxidized and had a sea-green patina.

May was grinning. I was feeling good, too. We were back in business. First the parchments and now another scroll. The cave was proving to be a gold mine and we hadn't even begun to clear the floor.

"Some words are carved on the surface," Sara said, slowly turning the scroll in the light.

"Can you read any of it?" May asked.

Sara continued to study the cylinder, brushing the dust from the metal exterior.

"This is Hebrew," she said, a tremor in her voice. "It's a very old script."

She looked transfixed. Something extraordinary was happening to her. She suddenly said she wanted to get back to camp. She wanted to work on the scroll right away. There were more words. They had to be translated.

"I think these are directions."

CHAPTER 15

WE CLIMBED OUT OF THE CAVE into the beating sunlight. Sara came last after sending up the scroll and parchment in her haversack. I carried some of the pottery fragments and May had the ax; we also brought the Roman bowl I had found in the other cave. It was well into the afternoon by the time we climbed down off the bluff and hiked back to our camp at the Wadi Qumran. Juma and Benteen were still gone when we got back.

Sara sat down in the shade under the tarp and began to reexamine the writing on the exterior of the scroll.

May asked, "Can you open it?"

Sara shook her head. "I'm not sure. The metal is badly oxidized. It might fall to pieces if we tried to use too much force."

The writing, she said, was in an archaic Hebrew similar to that of the other scrolls. The letters apparently had been beaten into the copper with a stylus or some other sharp instrument.

Sara said, "I can read part of the third line." She looked at us, her face tense. "It says 'from the second go six cubits.'"

"From the second what?" May asked. "What's that supposed to mean?"

"I wish I knew."

Kneeling next to her, May watched impatiently as she tried to translate the writing.

"The rest of the third line is obliterated. But the next line begins, 'from this side walk five cubits.' Then I lose it again." She continued studying the letters, rotating the scroll, slowly, carefully, as she tried to find something legible. Minutes passed. She pieced together some more of the writing. "The fifth line says, 'in the pit nearby, a vessel of incense in cassia wood.'"

"It sounds like a treasure map," I said.

May looked at me. He'd had the same thought.

Sara translated the following line as, 'At the cistern below the wall..."

She had placed the scroll on a folded blanket and was examining it with a magnifying lens. She got a bottle of rubbing alcohol from her tent.

"I need some gasoline. Not much. Just a few drops."

May went to the jeep and opened one of the five-gallon petrol cans. He poured some gas into a cup and brought it to Sara who emptied most of it onto the dirt then added alcohol to what remained. She dipped a piece of cotton into the amber solution and gently rubbed the surface of the scroll. Seven lines were scratched into the exterior of the cylinder, which appeared to be in two pieces, one rolled inside the other. Both were stuck fast. The entire document must have been fairly long. The scroll was just over eleven inches high from end to end.

"I still can't read all of this," Sara said. She had cleaned away some of the greenish overlay that obscured the lines.

"Why do you think they used copper?" May asked.

"It would last longer than leather or parchment," Sara said. "They must have considered this a valuable document."

I realized how keyed up I had become. It was like finding the scroll in the cave all over again.

"The line that mentions the cistern below the wall—could that be the cemetery wall?"

May asked the question as Sara continued trying to decipher the illegible words and letters. The only wall on the Qumran plateau separated the cemetery from the monastery dwellings.

"There could have been other walls when this was written," she said skeptically. "Right now we don't even know if this was the work of the Essenes. It doesn't resemble anything I'm even remotely familiar with. The style. The form of the composition. It's all a mystery to me."

"But there's a cistern out at the edge of the cemetery and it's below the wall," May said, pressing her. "At least that much fits with what you've read."

Sara, delicately wiping the scroll with the alcohol-soaked cotton, translated a few more words, a phrase: "on the east side."

She was still hard at it when Juma and Benteen returned. Their dust coated faces and arms were muddy with sweat.

"Someone's been watching us," Benteen announced. "Two, maybe three of them. They must have cleared out when they saw us coming."

Juma had located their hiding place high up in the cliffs about a mile north of the cave where we had found the copper scroll. They had left plenty of footprints behind as well as an empty food tin, which could have accounted for the reflection. The can might have caught the sunlight.

May asked, "Who do you think it was, Bedouin?"

Benteen nodded. "Maybe the same ones we chased off, or someone sent by that sonofabitch in Bethlehem. We didn't get a look at them. From the way they disappeared into thin air, they were Arabs all right. They're staying in the neighborhood to see what we're up to."

He repeated his fear of running into a band of Arab irregulars. He bore down hard; he wanted to clear out before we were trapped.

May told him about the scroll.

"Then why don't we get out of here," Benteen said. "You've found something big. Take it and run. We may not have that much time."

"We've got enough water for two or three more days," May said. "There's plenty of food. I don't see the hurry to get back."

"You hired me to protect you," Benteen said. "My advice is don't stick your neck out."

May said he had had no plans to leave, especially now.

Benteen's face hardened.

"Let me know if you change your mind."

He leaned his carbine against a rock and lit a cigarette. Juma also started to smoke. Sitting on the fender of the jeep, he looked upset after Benteen explained things.

Sara, who had kept working with the scroll, managed to translate nearly two complete lines.

"I think this says, 'At the cistern below the wall, on the side facing east, go 70 cubits.'" A cubit, she explained, was an ancient unit of measurement, meaning roughly 18 to 22 inches. It was the length of the arm from the tip of the middle finger to the elbow.

"There are some more words after that, but I can't read them." She looked up. "The next line mentions a grave."

That one caught May's attention. Mine, too.

"What's that?" May said. "Whose grave? Does it say any more?"

The poor condition of the copper made it impossible for her to read the last line, which might have offered an answer.

She wasn't sure of her translation about "seventy cubits." The faint letters were extremely difficult to make out.

"The language is very terse and business like," she said. "It almost reminds me of a list."

The next question that came to mind was whether the rest of the scroll contained more of the strange, almost unintelligible writing. We knew it mentioned a vessel of incense and now a grave. But would there be anything else? It was easy to get carried away with possibilities even when you knew better.

May still wanted to check whether the reference points cited on the scroll corresponded to the cemetery. Sara agreed it was worth a try. Benteen wasn't excited about the idea, but at May's direction, he got a length of climbing rope and began marking it off in cubits. The idea was to lay the rope out from the cistern's eastern wall and see if it led to anything.

While he was working on this, we walked to the broken stone wall. The scroll had mentioned a cistern "below the wall." There were actually two cisterns—part of the elaborate aqueduct system that had carried water to the settlement. Both fed off a shallow, stone-lined canal that ran down from the bluffs. One of the cisterns was near the edge of the plateau; its eastern side faced the wadi. Seventy, even 17 cubits would have taken you over the edge.

The larger cistern was about ten yards from the wall and almost filled with stones. Its eastern side faced the cemetery.

Benteen brought a length of rope 128 feet long, roughly 70 cubits with a cubit measuring 22 inches. May held one end down at the mid-point of the cistern's eastern side while Sara walked out into the cemetery, carrying the other. The rope stretched across one of the paths that bisected the burial field. It just touched one of the graves. Similar to the others, the grave was piled with stones with two larger stones standing upright at each end.

May suggested opening it.

Nearly five o'clock, the late afternoon heat was as murderous as ever; the sun looked eight feet away and there wasn't a cloud in the sky. I realized we hadn't eaten anything since early that morning.

Juma said something, his voice sharp and angry.

"He doesn't like this," Benteen said.

"Then tell him not to watch," May said. "This whole thing could be a wild goose chase anyway."

Benteen shrugged and walked back to the camp, returning with two shovels. Sara photographed the grave before May and I carefully removed the covering of stones. Sara had already measured the dimensions—six feet by three.

May and Benteen began to dig into the low mound of earth. They worked slowly, carefully. Benteen stopped to take off his shirt. It wasn't going to be an easy job; their shovels bit into stone on every turn of the blade.

They took nearly an hour to dig down three feet.

"Maybe it's empty," I said.

Sara said, "You never know what you'll find until you start excavating. The important thing is to be sure you go far enough. I'd hate to guess how many discoveries have been missed because someone gave up and stopped digging too early."

I offered to help May, who looked winded.

"No thanks," he said. "This is one job I want to finish myself. I'm to blame for this."

He was breathing heavily; the tendons in his neck looked like wires, but he kept digging, trying to keep up with Benteen, who was handling his shovel with skill, bending to make a short stab at the earth and then pivoting to empty it, all in one easy motion. The sun didn't seem to bother him at all.

Benteen and May had dug down to their waists when one of their shovels struck brick.

"That's far enough," Sara said.

The remaining dirt was loosened by trowel and scooped out by hand; when the bricks that sealed the crypt were finally exposed, Sara photographed them and then got down into the grave for a closer look. The layered brickwork was solidly constructed. She dusted off the bricks. There was no inscription or symbol, nothing.

Sara proceeded very deliberately, stopping often to take measurements and record them in her notebook.

Benteen was starting to get impatient.

"This isn't the time to be writing a bloody book," he snapped, jabbing his shovel into the ground.

Ignoring him, Sara started to remove the bricks. They had to be pried out one at a time. Chipping the mortar loose with a trowel, Sara worked steadily, handing the bricks up to us. After an opening was made, we saw that the burial vault was also lined with brick.

"Give me a flashlight," she said.

Benteen fetched one and Sara shined it into the sunken chamber.

"The skeleton is lying on its back."

She pulled out the remaining bricks. The bones lay on a niche. A complete skeleton. Except for the remains, the burial pit was empty. There were no distinguishing features, nothing out of the ordinary at all.

"Well, that's that," May said. He was disappointed. We all were. The treasure hunt had ended as most treasure hunts do.

"It's unusual for a Jewish grave not to contain any pottery or jewelry," Sara said.

"Could it be Christian?" May asked.

Sara didn't think so. "In that case there probably would have been some mark or symbol. A fish or a cross."

"I can't believe the bones haven't turned to dust," I said.

"It's amazing what can happen in a dry climate like this," Sara said.

She told the story of "Ginger," a corpse found in the Egyptian desert and put on display in the British Museum. Far older than any mummy, he got his nickname from his reddish hair, which was still attached to the skull. Even more surprising, loose folds of skin adhered to the bones. Found lying on his side in a shallow grave, he looked poignantly lifelike.

"Ginger is over 5,000 years old," Sara said. "But he's not a mummy. In those days, the Egyptians simply wrapped their dead in animal skins or linen and buried them deep in the sand."

Many of these primitive graves had been uncovered, she said. The bodies were often well preserved. The hot sand sucked every drop of moisture out, leaving the skin like jerky or tanned leather.

I suggested digging into the floor of the tomb to see whether anything was buried there. Sara didn't like that idea. She wanted to recheck the distance from the cistern. A cubit was an imprecise measurement, even in biblical times, she said. We had between 105 and 128 feet to work with, assuming she had properly translated what could be read of the scroll.

"What do you think of this," Benteen said. He'd been examining the ground near the opened tomb. He stood by another grave. There were no marker stones and only the slightest burial mound. I was surprised he'd even noticed it.

The grave was about 20 feet to the side of the extended rope and maybe four or five yards closer to the cistern.

"See anything unusual?" Benteen asked. Without waiting for an answer, he said, "Look how it's pointing. It runs east and west."

The idea hit each of us at the same time. All the other graves in the cemetery seemed to have a north-south axis, a detail we had observed earlier. This one, clearly an exception, didn't fit that pattern.

"Well done, man," May said. "I must have walked right over it without noticing that."

He moved the rope so that it touched the edge of the grave. It was 110 feet from the cistern, within the distance cited in the scroll.

"It's the only place where the symmetry of the burial pattern is disturbed," Sara said.

She knelt down to inspect the almost imperceptible rise in the earth. "This grave was meant to stand apart but not be too noticeable. You had to know where to look."

"Or how to read a scroll," I said.

Benteen and May started to dig. The sun was starting to set when they got down to the bricks that sealed the burial chamber. As before, Sara cleared off the layer of brick and photographed the tomb, which was similar to the other one.

Juma came over for a look as she loosened the bricks, his curiosity getting the better of his scruples. We stood there, not talking, waiting, the suspense building. Digging up the bones of the ancient dead because of a scroll we couldn't open and could barely read wasn't what I had expected when I had signed on with May. I wondered what I would write about all this.

When Sara removed enough of the brick covering so that we could see into the crypt, the payoff wasn't easy to look at. A skeleton in superb condition lay there bent over as if in prayer, the arms and rib cage supported by a block of smooth stone. Its head was missing.

"What the hell do you make of that?" Benteen said.

Juma burst into a shrill staccato and hurried away from the grave.

Sara removed some more bricks from the ceiling of the vault. The burial chamber was also lined in brick, but of a darker shade; the bricks apparently had been oven-fired.

"This was probably a middle-aged male," she said, studying the skeleton. "You can tell by the pelvis and the sacrum." She showed where the pelvis formed an almost perfect V. It would have been more U-shaped if it had been a woman. The sacrum, she said, was an even better indicator of sex; it was high and narrow. A woman's sacrum would have been broader.

"How do you know all that?" May asked.

"I had two years of anatomy."

I kept telling myself that this was really happening. There she was, a woman I was falling in love with, kneeling in the desert under a merciless sun, studying the earthly remains of a headless corpse. I felt as if I were walking through a dream.

The femur and fibula had become detached from the hip socket and lay on the brick floor of the crypt.

Sara examined the skeleton's truncated neck bone, which was scarred by deep gashes.

"I think his head was cut off," she said at length. "From the marks, it must have taken several blows to get the job done."

CHAPTER 16

"THERE'S SOMETHING ELSE DOWN HERE."

Sara found a cup fashioned from black stone lying to the side of the body near the wall of the crypt. The surface of the cup looked polished. There were no other funerary objects.

"I'd give a year of my life to know who he was," May said.

He stood at the edge of the grave, staring at the remains. The neckbone had been hacked like wood splintered by a dull ax. The cuts in the bone were deep and wide. If an execution had finished him, the job had been badly bungled.

"I saw a man lose his head once," Benteen said. "It wasn't very pretty. They might as well have been trying to kill a pig."

Arab justice, the incident had happened during the war in North Africa. A Tunisian merchant had been caught buying liquor from the Germans and selling it on the black market. The use of alcohol of any kind was a serious offense against Allah, and so they cut off his head in a public square in Medina. After chopping away at the victim with a long sword, spilling gouts of blood but not severing the neck, the headsman lost his nerve. He threw down the sword and ran away.

"They had to force another man to take over," Benteen said. "Held a gun on him and damn near caused a riot until he got the job done." He looked down at the corpse. "Somebody mucked this up the same way."

Sara had continued examining the cup, which had a wide flanging lip. She found both the design and shape curious.

"This looks like soapstone."

"Can you date it?" I asked.

"If I had to guess, I'd pick sometime during the reign of the Herods."

The piece, roughly carved and finished, wasn't the work of a skilled artisan, she said. It had been meant for everyday use.

110

We still weren't certain that this was the grave described in the copper scroll, or, for matter, whether we had properly followed the vague, largely illegible directions. At Sara's suggestion, Benteen and May stretched out the rope from several other points along the cistern's eastern side. The tomb remained the most likely candidate.

No one doubted that we had to open the scroll if we hoped to learn the identity of the corpse. There might be a name or a clue or some other detail. But for the moment, considering the poor condition of the metal, there seemed little chance of that.

"He must have been someone important," Sara said. "I wish I could read more of this."

We worked into the twilight with lanterns, replacing the bricks and refilling the first of the two graves we had opened. We covered the other crypt with a piece of canvas until we could figure out our next move.

Benteen opened more cans for dinner. Corned beef and tomatoes warmed on the gas stove. Sara hardly touched her food. Juma, meanwhile, went off alone into the hills to do some reconnoitering. It was Benteen's idea; he wanted to keep our guard up after what had happened in the morning. If someone had been watching us, there was always the chance they might return.

We were sitting around the cook stove. The night was cool, almost cold. I regretted I hadn't brought a sweater. The moon and stars blazed in the clear sky. The Dead Sea was still, and high over the water and the ridge of the cliffs, birds or bats darted.

Breaking her silence, Sara speculated that the scroll, at least the part that could be read, might have been an inventory of the monastery's most valuable possessions. Perhaps the Essenes' treasurer had beaten the list into the copper when danger first threatened, she suggested. That would explain the crudeness and illegibility of some of the writing. The work probably had been done in a rush.

"Is there any way you can open that scroll?" May asked.

"I've been asking myself the same thing," Sara said. "It might be possible to loosen the outer sheets." She spoke reluctantly as if uncertain of herself. "I'll need some more light."

We went to her tent. Benteen carried over two lanterns and set them on the floor. Sara spread out a blanket and sat down. The safest way, perhaps the only way, she said, would be to cut the sheets into vertical strips. The cuts would have to be made with great care between the lines of writing.

"If this is a treasure list, to lose a single direction..." She didn't complete the sentence. She looked at May. "I'm not sure I trust myself to try this."

Closely inspecting the copper cylinder, Sara eventually hit on the idea of inserting a slender but stiff wire into the narrow gap between the exterior sheet and the one it overlapped. The wire—Benteen cut a piece from the jeep's radio antenna—was wrapped with cotton, and it took some experimentation before she was able to wedge it securely in place. Her plan was to work the wire back and forth and hope she could pry loose the outer sheet so that it could be cut away.

The process took several hours; working with the wire, Sara managed to loosen the two outer folds of copper. Then, using a magnifying lens, she carefully cut the exterior sheet vertically with a pair of snippers. She stopped often to wipe her face with a handkerchief as she cut the sheet of copper into ten strips; each strip was about an inch wide and carefully sliced so that no words were obliterated.

She repeated the process with the next sheet. When she had peeled away the last of the strips, she lay them on a folded cloth and gently flattened them out. She had gone as far as she could; the remaining sections of the scroll were rolled too tightly.

"I can't do any more," she said. "I don't dare."

After cleaning the strips of copper, Sara tried to translate them. She also examined the scroll; with the removal of the two outer sheets, it now had a new exterior.

Whatever she was reading had brought a pallor to her face.

"Another grave is mentioned," she said.

"What's that," May said, sitting up. He had been hunched over, watching Sara.

"It calls him the Teacher of Righteousness." She looked at May, then at me.

"What are you talking about?" May asked.

Sara continued studying the copper fragments. Finally, she said, "I may be wrong, but the location of his grave appears to be given in relation to the tomb we've already found."

She slowly read out the words. "His body...has been hidden..." It took a few moments before she was able to translate the next phrase: "...from the wicked priest...who has profaned his flesh."

The man whose body we had exhumed was referred to as the "prophet." The sentence, the first on the second sheet of copper, appeared to flow directly from the final, partially illegible line on the exterior of the scroll—the one that had described his tomb.

The grave of the Teacher of Righteousness was north of the prophet's tomb. But the scroll didn't say how far north. The directions were maddeningly vague.

Sara translated them out loud: "Toward the north, near the face of the cliff, in a place cut out of the rock."

No distances were mentioned.

Sara said, "Whoever composed this scroll must have feared there was a chance they wouldn't survive and that they needed to tell others where to find the body. They left this record in the hope the location of the grave wouldn't be lost forever."

"It's almost like a time capsule," I said.

"Is there anything more," May asked.

No such luck. Large sections of the copper strips still couldn't be read. It was impossible to read the three bottom lines on the second sheet because the faded, square-shaped letters weren't as deeply etched as the others.

May wondered whether the Teacher might have been a general name given to the leader of the community.

Sara doubted that, arguing the name more likely referred to a specific person, someone who had suffered for his beliefs. The scroll specifically mentioned that his flesh had been "profaned."

"What do you think of that?" May asked.

"I have no idea, but it sounds like violence was done to him in some way," Sara said.

"Tomorrow we're going to look for that grave," May said.

We talked it over until Juma returned. He had seen nothing

down in the wadi or in the hills. He lit a cigarette, the red ash burning in the darkness.

"I'd give 20 pounds to know who those bastards were," Benteen said irritably.

He was worried they were still in the area.

"Keep your eyes open tonight," he warned us. "I don't like the smell of this."

I was still thinking about the strange details on the scroll when Sara said she was tired. When I got up to leave, she asked me to stay. She spoke the words simply and quietly.

Startled, I felt the blood rush to my face. May and Benteen stared at me.

"I'll let you explain the facts of life to the boy," Benteen said. He stood up, stretched, and disappeared into the darkness.

"You're a lucky guy," May said, smiling. He followed Benteen.

When we were alone Sara closed the tent flap. After carefully wrapping the scroll and putting it away in her pack, she spread the blankets and bedding out on the ground so that there would be room for both of us.

The flame of the lantern was turned low. I knelt down and kissed her, which was like entering a new wonderful land. She clung to me, our kiss lingering and I knew a desire so urgent and aching that I trembled.

"Let me get out of these," she said, unfastening the snaps of her shorts and kicking them away. I unbuttoned her shirt and slipped my hand inside. I touched the smooth hollow of her back.

"Sara, my Sara. I hope you know how much I love you."

I held her close. How could she understand that when she kissed me, nuzzling my chest and then moving lower that she was carrying me beyond everything I had ever known or felt or wanted? How long had I waited for her? Five years? Ten? Did she know that? How could she. She was touching me now with her lips.

I turned on my side and held her tightly, cradling her head as I kissed the curve of her neck and her breasts and then we were moving on the blanket, her long legs up against me, still moving, touching and kissing her everywhere until, breathless, I was inside her and she was holding herself up for me, cupping her waist with her hands.

"You need me. You know that, don't you," she said, throwing her head back.

I kissed her soft hair.

"I want us to be happy." She looked up at me. "Tell me you love me...please."

"Don't you feel it? Don't you feel how much I love you? How much I've always loved you? It's why I'm here now. It's the only reason."

And then, afterward, I was no longer with her. I was lying beside her, but I was outside, walking in the cemetery and wondering who it was who lay there in the open tomb. I could still see the shattered neck. It wasn't the kind of memory you could shake off. It left me uneasy—more so than with the skeletons we had found in the cave, more than anything I could remember; and I could remember a great deal from the butcherfields of France and Germany. I wondered why it had been placed in a kneeling position. And why was the head missing? The image carried me away from her, but when I returned and felt sleep coming, I knew that whatever we had to face in the morning or in the days to come would be worth it.

CHAPTER 17

SARA WAS ALREADY DRESSED and I rolled out of the blankets and slipped on my trousers and boots, and we went outside as it became daylight. I had always loved this hour with the play of color that comes with the rising sun. But this morning as the cliffs became sharp and clear in the soft light I was too busy thinking to appreciate it. If that body was out there, we had to work fast to find it. Our food and water wouldn't last for more than a few days.

We were eating our breakfast when the Arabs walked into camp. There were three of them with Juma close behind as they came up the steep trail from the beach. He was carrying his rifle and an ancient looking breechloader, which he had apparently taken from the men. He also had three knives stuck down in his belt.

"These boys belong to his tribe," Benteen said, translating what Juma told him. "They say they're looking for work."

They were the ones who had been watching us. Juma had noticed them earlier coming up the shoreline and had gone out to intercept them. Their story was that it had taken them a while to work up the nerve to come down from the hills and ask for a job.

May wasn't pleased, but he decided to let them stay. He thought we could use the extra help when we started digging for the other grave.

"We don't want them going back and getting their friends. We could have the whole tribe out here. At least this way, we can keep an eye on them."

"There's also the problem of what Juma would do if we sent them away," Benteen said. "He knows these men; he's related to them by blood. If we told them to clear out now, he might take it as an insult."

One of them could speak broken English. He was called Muhammad the Goat. Older than the others, he had a compressed serious face and a long neck. His waxed mustache curled at the ends. The other two looked in their early twenties.

"We help dig," Muhammad said. "Dollar a day, each man."

May had Benteen tell them he would pay them ten dollars a day. I thought Muhammad was going to fall to the ground and kiss his feet. When his companions learned the news, they grinned broadly.

"He's sorry this happened," Benteen said after talking to Juma. "He says it wasn't his idea they come here and that he doesn't know how they found out about us. He'll take responsibility for them."

I knew enough about the Bedouin to realize a pledge like that had the same force as an oath.

After making sure they were unarmed, Benteen got them started by telling them to bring out the shovels and water cans from the station wagon. He went with them, cradling his rifle over his left forearm. He didn't take his eyes off them, reminding me of a guard on a chain gang. They were nimble, dark-skinned men who moved in their dirty robes with the grace of athletes.

Sara said she wanted to go up in the cliffs to get an overview of the cemetery.

While Benteen stayed below with Juma and his Arab brothers, we climbed into the rocks. The creviced, weather-beaten wall of limestone formed a backdrop to the ruins. Sara sat on a boulder and stared down at the cemetery, studying the ground. We were up about 30 feet.

"Maybe the grave is somewhere in the cliffs," May said.

"Just like Queen Hatshepsut," Sara said.

The queen's tomb, she said, had been carved several hundred feet up the side of a rock wall in the Valley of Kings. The entrance was cunningly hidden so that it couldn't be seen from below. But once inside, the tomb quickly widened into a tunnel 90 feet long; the burial chamber, cut into solid rock, was 18 feet high. The tomb, never occupied, had been built for the wife of King Thothmes II. It was a marvel of engineering and showed the lengths the pharaohs went to frustrate grave robbers.

"Couldn't they have done the same thing here?" May asked. "What if they sealed the body in a cave?"

"The scroll says the tomb was near the face of the cliff, not in it," Sara said.

She restudied her handcopied translation of the copper scroll's directions. The site, she reminded us, was supposed to be north of the grave we had already opened in a place hollowed out of rock.

Calling down to Benteen, she asked him to run some rope out from the tomb to the cliff. He pegged down the rope, using a compass, as she directed, to sight it due north. Sara wanted him to walk along the marker line, pacing off the distance several times slowly.

"It's got to be out there," she said, standing up on a ledge.

When Benteen finished his task—she had seen nothing to catch her attention—we climbed down from our perch. By now the sun was far up in the sky. Sara repeatedly walked over the area near the base of the cliff. Benteen joined us, all of us straining our eyes in the harsh light, looking for anything unusual in the lay of the ground. Only the Arabs and Juma stayed out of the sun, sitting in the shade of the stone wall that separated the cemetery from the ruins of the settlement.

A cup-shaped swale about 20 yards beyond the last grave we had opened was the only thing even remotely out of the ordinary. Deciding to excavate, Sara asked the Arabs to dig there. Muhammad led the work with the shovels. After two hours of difficult labor, they had found only a few shards of pottery.

Late in the morning, kneeling in the dust, Sara made yet another sighting down the rope, which ran out from the grave of the "prophet."

"What do you make of that?" she asked May. She pointed to an outcropping of rock at the base of the cliff.

"It stands out a little," May said.

"That's what I thought, too."

The rock formation, its vertical face notched like the edges of a leaf, was slightly off true north. The outcropping was about ten feet high and nearly as wide and was pressed into the slope of rocks and loose gravel like a retaining wall. We'd climbed around it earlier on our way up the cliff.

We walked over for a closer look.

"The ground may have settled here," Sara said thoughtfully. Her figure cast a slender shadow.

There was a definite sag in the rocky soil; the impression was roughly 12 feet across.

Sara looked at May. "It might be worth a try to clear away some of these stones."

The Bedouin stood at the edge of the shallow indentation, looking back at Juma as if waiting for an explanation.

"We dig there?" Muhammad asked, leaning against his shovel, his dark, too-long face beaded with sweat.

Sara gave the go-ahead, but told them not to hurry.

The Arabs moved the larger stones out of the way by hand. Some were heavy and hard to lift and had to be rolled. We all helped them. Sara picked up one of the smooth egg-sized rocks when they started using shovels.

"This looks like flint," she said. She seemed puzzled. "I don't see anything like it around here. It's all limestone."

Benteen handed me a canteen. I took a long drink and offered the canteen to Muhammed who was standing next to me. He smiled and shook his head and kept on digging, bending low and putting his back to the shovel.

"They can work in this heat for hours," Benteen said in grudging admiration. "They're born to it."

The sun was straight overhead. The Arabs had cleared out a six-by-six foot square roughly two-feet deep.

The Bedouin heard the sound first, then Benteen lifted his head.

I heard it now, the high-pitched drone of an engine.

"That's a patrol boat," Benteen said.

He told Juma to take the Bedouin into the cliffs and wait there. The Arabs scurried into the rocks and were quickly out of sight.

"Let's see what we've got," Benteen said. We hurried back to the ruins on the far end of the terrace, where we'd have an unobstructed view of the Dead Sea. The engine was much louder.

We lay down behind some low rocks. Benteen had binoculars. Moving slowly along the western shore, a motor boat was chugging out on the water.

"There's four of them," Benteen said. "They're Arabs."

"I wonder if that's the Transjordanian navy," May said.

"If it is, it's no joke for us," Benteen said.

The patrol boat, he said, had probably put in at Kallia at the northern tip of the Dead Sea. That was close to the Allenby Bridge over the Jordan. An Arab strongpoint, there was a big potash plant there and some fortifications.

"They could be swinging down the coast for a look at En Gedi," he said.

I suddenly remembered the station wagon. It was parked near the base of the Qumran plateau behind some rocks. I hoped it couldn't be spotted from the water.

The boat moved closer to shore, a low-slung inboard with cowling at the bow and some benches in the open stern. The men sitting on the benches were holding rifles.

Just keep going, baby, I thought as the boat went by, slowly heading south.

"You think they'll be back?" May asked.

Benteen smiled. "I wouldn't want to bet against it."

The patrol boat was farther down the coast, still hugging the shoreline.

The Bedouin came down from the hills. We went back to the cliff and continued digging. The Arabs worked hard; the deeper they dug, the more tightly packed were the pieces of flint that filled the depression.

"Those stones must have been brought here from somewhere else," Sara said. "It almost looks like they were used for fill."

She asked the Bedouin to expand the area of digging. They were down about three feet by then. May and Juma joined in the work. I think we were all starting to wonder whether we should give up and try elsewhere. Only the Arabs still looked enthusiastic.

They had cleared away another half-foot of loose stone when one of the shovels hit something hard. Sara called a halt. She motioned for the Bedouin to get out of the way and climbed down into the hole. Using her hands, she uncovered a step cut into the limestone bedrock.

May let out a shout. "This is it!" he said. "This has to be it."

He was about to jump down next to her when Sara stopped him.

"We don't know that yet," she said. "Stay back until we have more room."

She soon uncovered another step. About two feet long and six inches high, they reminded me at once of the steps carved into the cisterns back at the monastery.

"It may be a tomb entrance," Sara said.

The Bedouin watched from the sides of the hole. We all knew that something out of the ordinary had been found. May finally stepped into the depression and helped Sara dig. They removed the loose rock until they had revealed three more descending steps, one following the other; they were cut into the ground at a sharp angle.

As she cleared the fourth step, Sara uncovered the upper part of a doorway.

"I think it's sealed," she said, for once unable to hide her excitement.

Working slowly, scooping out the stones by hand, they cleared three more steps and in the process slowly laid bare the doorway, inch by inch. The rectangular surface had been heavily plastered. The masonry was in excellent condition.

A waterskin was found lying on the seventh and last step up against the base of the door.

"This might have been used for water by the plasterers," Sara said.

She sent me back to the camp for the camera. I took some pictures of the steps and doorway. The last of the stones and dirt had been removed; the door was four feet high by three feet wide.

Sara recorded these details in a notebook and then rechecked the dimensions with a tape measure to make sure they were accurate. The delay got to Benteen.

"What are you waiting for," he blurted angrily. "Let's knock down that damn door and get this over with."

Sara glared at him.

"That's enough," she snapped. "We're going to do this properly. If you don't like that, you better leave now."

"Don't even say it," May said when Benteen started to open his mouth.

Sara knelt on the last step and examined the plasterwork on the door. "I don't see any inscriptions or graffiti."

"What's that at the top lefthand corner," May said, looking over her shoulder.

A piece of plaster was missing there, revealing a layer of wood

121

underneath. Sara scraped away another small fragment of plaster. It covered a lintel over the doorway.

She decided to make a peephole beneath the lintel to see what was behind the entrance; she also wanted to find out how the door had been constructed and how thick it was.

"Bring me a candle and a flashlight," she said.

May hurried back to the campsite and got both. When he returned, she chipped out a quarter-sized hole in the space just below the lintel, using a hammer and chisel. She stopped often to remove the fragments of plaster and stone by hand, taking care that nothing fell behind the door. She didn't want to damage anything on the other side.

When she'd finished the peephole, she lit the candle and held it to the opening.

"What's that for?" May asked.

"I want to see if there's any gas trapped inside."

The candle flickered in the cool air that escaped from the chamber. The air was safe enough.

"See if someone can find me a stick or piece of wire that will fit in here."

Benteen said something to the Arabs and Muhammad trotted off. He returned a few minutes later with a piece of kindling wood about a yard long. Sara inserted the stick as far as she could into the hole.

"Good, there's no resistance," she said.

She widened the opening slightly, then held the flashlight to the hole and peered inside. She knelt there for a long time, not speaking. Finally, unable to stand the suspense any longer, May asked whether she could see anything.

"It's a tomb," Sara said at length. "I can see the sarcophagus."

CHAPTER 18

MAY LOOKED THROUGH THE CRACK under the lintel. Then I took a turn. I felt the air on my cheek from inside the chamber and was aware of a strange, faintly pungent odor. Even with the light, it was hard to see clearly. I could just make out the dark shape Sara thought was the sarcophagus. The crypt wasn't large.

Sara took another look inside the tomb.

"It might only be a ledge or bench of some kind," she said.

We were at the threshold of a tomb that had been sealed, how many years ago? Twenty centuries? Twenty-one? And yet the wall might have been plastered yesterday, it was that smooth, the work that fresh looking. The waterskin only added to the sensation of the past suddenly made present. I could almost picture the workmen leaving it behind, forgetting it, their hands still caked white with plaster. It might have happened a week or a month ago—or two millennia. The concept of time had been annihilated.

I hadn't felt like this when we opened the other graves in the cemetery. For reasons I couldn't entirely explain or understand, I felt that way now.

Sara continued to examine the surface of the sealed entrance. She noticed a handprint low on the door.

"Someone might have leaned against the wet plaster by accident," she said.

That smudge was yet another link that brought the past into sharp focus, making it much more immediate and human. The passage of so many obscure centuries had been made meaningless.

There was a sudden coolness as a shadow passed over us. A large cloud with black edges covered the sun. The more clouds the better, I thought. Anything to provide a moment's shade in this sweatbox. We were in for some hard labor.

Sara began to chip away at the top of the doorway with the pointed end of a crowboar, carefully lifting out the broken plaster and stone. She worked across the width of the entrance, just below the lintel. After about half an hour's work, she had opened a space that offered a better view inside the chamber.

"It's a sarcophagus all right," she said. "Possibly some kind of arcosali tomb."

"What does that mean?" Benteen said. He was standing with the Bedouin at the top of the steps.

The word, Sara said, described a rock tomb in which a bench-like sarcophagus was carved into a wall.

"Tombs of that design generally date to the Christian era. They were fairly common in the Holy Land."

In the corner of the tomb, the sarcophagus looked as if it were one piece with the wall. The chamber was slightly arched and appeared to have been cut from a solid block of limestone. Except for the sarcophagus, the tomb appeared empty.

The Arabs stared down at the entrance, their curiosity, like ours, growing by the minute. Juma and Muhammad spoke together in rapid Arabic. From Muhammad's seious face, he was upset. His two friends, following his lead as always, also showed nervousness.

Sara chipped out some more of the plaster. The door was fashioned from irregularly shaped stones, some as large as cinderblocks. Worried that the stones might fall inside the tomb, Sara got a blanket from the camp and after enlarging the opening, suspended it on the inner side of the doorway. She did this by nailing the ends of the blanket into the wooden lintel. The idea was to form a protective backdrop.

When she finished, she went to work with the crowbar again, removing more plaster and loosening the mortar between the stones. She attacked the doorway stone by stone, carefully removing them one at a time, wedging the crowbar under them and lifting while May and I pulled them out.

After clearing away the top layer, it became apparent that the burial chamber was about two feet lower than the stairwell.

"This was skillfully done," Sara said. "This tomb was made as carefully as any I've seen in Palestine."

"It's sure not like any of the others," May agreed. "This had to have been built for someone special. What other explanation is there?"

The sky darkened as storm clouds built steadily in the west.

"We don't need any rain," Sara said, looking nervously at the threatening sky. "A heavy rainfall could be a disaster."

She was worried the tomb would flood in a downpour.

May took a turn with the crowbar, knocking loose the plaster and mortar in small pieces.

Sara pushed aside the blanket to look inside the tomb.

"There's something on the floor."

The doorway was half open. She pointed the flashlight near the base of the sarcophagus. Two small clay jars with sealed lids stood there.

"What are those for?" May asked.

"I don't know," Sara said. "They might have held spices or oil."

"Can you smell anything?" I asked.

The odor I had noticed earlier seeped from the tomb, stronger than before.

Sara and May also had smelled it.

We worked at clearing the doorway for several more hours. Sara stopped often to have photographs taken. The tension was greatest when only the last few stones remained; the temptation to step over them into the tomb was almost overpowering. Sara would have none of that. She kept working with the crowbar, never rushing, until the entrance was finally cleared. We removed the blanket curtain and then May took a number of photographs; the battery-powered flash cast a garish light on the stone walls of the burial chamber.

When he finished Sara said, "I think you should go first."

May frowned. "Nonsense." Sara started to object, but May stopped her.

"I don't want any arguments."

Sara smiled and entered the crypt, stooping through the entrance and cautiously stepping down into the chamber with a flashlight.

There wasn't enough room to stand up. The tomb, about seven feet long at its widest point, was slightly circular in shape. Sara knelt before the sarcophagus after moving the clay jars out of the way. Carved from a solid piece of limestone, it had been cut out of the wall.

She examined the lid. There was no inscription on the rough surface, no identifying marks of any kind. May joined her.

Muhammad approached the entrance and stared into the dim crypt. He leaned forward to see better.

"You find the dead man?" he asked as the two other Arabs came up behind him.

"We don't know," May said.

Muhammad studied the tomb in silence. Then he said, "It is not good here."

He muttered something in Arabic.

"He doesn't like this," Benteen said. He was standing next to the Bedouin.

The lid, made of a single, heavy-looking piece of limestone, fit firmly down on the sarcophagus. "Give us a hand," May said.

I stepped into the crypt; there was barely room for three of us.

We managed to slide the lid to the side with a crowbar until its edge rested on the floor.

I staggered backward, gasping for breath. The odor, the same one I had noticed earlier but now much stronger, hit us like tear gas. Scrambling out of the tomb, none of us had had a chance to look into the sarcophagus.

"What is that?" May said, coughing into a handkerchief.

"Probably natron," Sara said.

The fumes dissipated quickly. Natron, Sara said, was a naturally occurring salt, a mixture of sodium bicarbonate and sodium sulphate.

"The Egyptians used it for enbalming. It retards decomposition by absorbing moisture. A chemical reaction must have started when we exposed the inside of the sarcophagus to the air."

The salt was easy to find. "You can pick the crystals right off the shore of the Dead Sea."

"Are you saying a mummy's down there?" May said.

"I'm only saying the skills were available," Sara said. "We know from the Bible that at least two important Israelites were embalmed—Jacob and Joseph. The Jews didn't do it often. The practice was generally considered unclean."

After a few minutes we went back inside the crypt. Traces of the smell still lingered.

126

"It's natron all right," Sara said, peering into the sarcophagus.

A thin layer of whitish material covered whatever lay beneath it. The substance reminded me of bread dough.

"Well, what do you have?" Benteen shouted. "What's down there?"

"We don't know yet," I said, watching Sara. She knelt at the side of the sarcophagus. Her face changed. "There are flowers in here!"

A tiny wreath of withered flowers lay in the corner of the sarcophagus; the petals, still intact, were a faded red and yellow, the tinge of color amazingly preserved through the centuries.

I was moved by the touching simplicity of this final gesture of mourning. Who had done it, I wondered. What did he or she look like? Were they crying? The mysterious body in the sarcophagus— if there was a body there—suddenly became more real to me, more human. I was conscious again of how slender the barrier of time really is.

"If we can preserve those flowers they might tell us when the burial occurred," Sara said. "The blossoms would bloom at a certain season. We'd know what time of the year it was."

"They almost look too fragile to touch," May said.

"We'll coat them with paraffin wax. That should strengthen them enough to be moved."

Sara went back to the camp and returned with a bundle of cloth padding and a packing box. She wrapped the clay jars and placed them in the box. Then, with May and Juma's help, she set up our cook stove and melted a block of wax. When the wax turned liquid, she brushed it onto the wreath of flowers. The clear wax quickly hardened, protecting the flowers so that they could be lifted without danger of disintegration. She placed the wreath on a folded cloth in another small box.

The next step was to remove the natron from the sarcophagus. Most of the gummy coating came up easily in pieces and covered a sheet of darkened, much decayed linen.

"It's going to be hard to protect that," Sara said. "We don't have enough wax."

Sara began to roll back the linen, which was worn in places to the thinness of gossamer.

"The sheet has been doubled over," she said.

Near the top of the sarcophagus, the linen covering adhered to whatever lay underneath. Sara carefully loosened the cloth with a knife blade. Sections of the material tore and crumbled.

"There's a shroud under this."

Working with painstaking deliberation, Sara eventually peeled away the linen. The unmistakable shape of a body lay concealed under the cloth. The color of water-soaked canvas, the shroud bulged slightly where the head and feet were positioned.

"You can see how the arms have been folded over the chest," Sara said.

The shroud was stained in several places. The marks, which had seeped into the fabric, were riviting. One of the biggest discolorations was in the center of the cloth. There were others near both ends.

I had seen those kinds of stains before in battlefield first-aid stations in France.

May read my mind.

"That looks like blood."

CHAPTER 19

I LEFT THE CRYPT, pushed past the Arabs who blocked the entrance and sat down in the shade of the rock. I had to get out of there for a while. Shafts of sunlight bore down through the clouds like pillars. The clouds that had blown in from the west were fast breaking up.

I wondered if the body in the tomb were really the unnamed man mentioned in the scroll. There were so many questions I wanted answers to after seeing that stained shroud. One of the biggest: If that was really blood, what happened to him?

Muhammad joined me. He had taken a look inside the sarcophagus. His small, close-set eyes were bright, almost glowing.

"You take the dead man?" he asked in his halting English.

He looked at me, his eyes open wide and unwavering, his lips set in a tight line. I didn't answer.

"Better you leave this place."

He turned and shouted something and the other two Arabs joined him. They returned to their camp at the far end of the cemetery and sat with their backs against the wall, watching us. There would be no more work from them today.

I went back into the burial chamber without answering. May was taking photographs of the shrouded figure inside the sarcophagus.

"Are you going to try to open it?" I asked.

Sara shook her head. "We've got to get this back to Jerusalem. The sooner the better. The safest place would be the American School."

May wanted to know how she planned to move it.

Sara had been considering that problem. The best approach would be to slip a sheet or blanket under the body and try to lift it out.

She measured the shroud; doubled over at the ends, it was just over five-feet-ten-inches long. The cloth completely enclosed the body and was held in position by three bands woven of the same material or of thick linen. One crossed the center of the body at an angle; the other two ran down the sides. The wrappings that covered the feet looked frayed, as if they had rubbed against something.

Before we tried to lift it, Benteen fashioned a makeshift casket. He did this by taking apart three of the long wooden packing cases we had brought with us and, using the boards, nailed and lashed together a larger box.

Juma and May carried the casket to the tomb. Sara took some more measurements.

"It should just fit," she said. "There may be a problem at the shoulders." She placed blankets in the bottom of the case. "The tricky part will be working the sheet under the body without causing any damage. It's certain to be fragile."

When we were finally ready, she said, "Let's hope the body isn't stuck to the sarcophagus." She recalled how the corpse of King Tutankhamen had adhered to his coffin; over the centuries, the ceremonial unguents poured on the body had hardened; the thick crust had to be chipped loose, a process that was finally resolved by placing the gilded casket upside down over a portable stove and melting the substance.

While May pulled back the edge of the shroud, Sara slipped one end of a sheet underneath and delicately repeated the process on the other side.

"When I give the word, bring it up steadily," she said. "Don't let it sway."

The body came up easily on her signal, nestled in the sheet. It had almost no weight at all.

Moving slowly up the steps, we lowered it into the casket. The corpse fit with less than half an inch to spare.

Sweat running down my face, I took a deep breath. Sara packed the sides of the case with rolled blankets. She put more padding at both ends of the body. Then she closed the lid and fastened it with cord.

Two hours later, exhausted and still tense after placing the casket in May's tent, we were back at the camp planning our next move. Sara had opened one of the clay jars she had found in the tomb. The jar had a rounded lid and was nearly a foot tall. The lid of the other container was still sealed. The bottom of the opened jar was covered with a hard, amber-colored material that smelled like resin.

"That could be myrrh," Sara said.

She thought it was probably the congealed remains of an unguent or oil used to annoint the body.

The sun had started to set and there was a fresh breeze off the water of the Dead Sea. The horizon—all reds and orange—looked on fire.

"What are we going to do about them?"

Benteen took a pot of coffee off the stove. We knew who he was talking about.

The Bedouin were still sitting together in their camp. They had finished eating and were watching us as carefully as we were watching them.

"I'll pay them off in the morning," May said.

We were tired, but we had a great deal to talk about. There was no question of staying any longer at Qumran. The problem was where to go and how to get there. Jerusalem seemed the best, the only bet.

Sara thought we could do some preliminary work on the body at the American School and then perhaps move to a safer location.

"I want to leave the country," May said, lighting a cigar. "As soon as we can get out."

"What do you mean?" Sara said, looking at him.

"I'm not about to stay in Jerusalem. It's too dangerous. I don't even want to go back there, but I don't see that we've got much choice."

"We can't take these remains out of the Holy Land," Sara said. She brought up the antiquities laws.

May said, "Those laws don't mean a damn thing right now and you know it."

I remembered that Professor Parker had made much the same observation back in Jerusalem the first time I'd met him.

"This body, the copper scroll... they belong in Israel," Sara said firmly.

"Maybe they do, but you know as well as I do that they need to be examined. How in hell do that in the middle of a shooting war? I'm sorry, but I'm not about to risk losing this."

Sara started to object.

"I've made up my mind," May said. "We're leaving. We'll stop in Jerusalem for a while, but then we're going to drive to Tel Aviv and find a ship that will take us to Europe."

"It won't be any picnic getting through to Tel Aviv," Benteen said. "All those roads, even the bad ones, are going to be patrolled."

May said, "That's why I'm paying you. Figure it out, and do it fast. We're driving out of here tomorrow at first light. We can worry about the rest later."

"What about that other body?" I asked. "Are we going to leave it behind?"

Sara didn't want to do that. The skeleton was far too valuable. Swallowing back her anger, she thought we could wrap it in sleeping bags and blankets. Not an ideal solution, but at least there was a chance that way of getting it back safely.

It was soon twilight; the shadows touched the tops of the cliffs that hemmed in the plateau. The Dead Sea was a ribbon of dark blue in the fading light.

May drew the first watch. I got the second. Juma and Benteen, as usual, would split up the rest of the night.

Sara and I went to her tent and sat down on the bedrolls. I put my arm around her shoulder. She was very still as she leaned against me.

"I want to leave the Holy Land as much as John does," she said softly. "I didn't want to admit that. It doesn't make me very proud of myself."

She looked at me.

"I'd do almost anything to translate the scroll and examine that body. It's like I'm standing outside a room full of gold and silver and all I have to do is push open the door. I don't want to give it up or risk losing it."

I heard myself say, "I keep thinking about what the scroll said about the Teacher and the Wicked Priest. How the teacher somehow suffered."

"I've got to find out who it is," Sara said, her eyes flashing. "I want to know so badly I'm willing to go anywhere. We can't stay in this country—not now. I'll never be able to work here. May's right about that."

"You need to sleep."

I kissed her then. We lay down, holding each other, not talking.

A wind had blown up, breaking the stillness of the night. The walls of the tent rippled out in a sudden gust that came with a howling wail as if from far away. Another gust made the support pole sway.

"It's such a lonely sound," Sara said sleepily.

We lay there, listening to the wind and I felt her fall asleep next to me. I kissed her on the forehead and then I must have fallen asleep myself, for the next thing I knew I thought I heard something. It sounded like someone moving quickly. I looked at the luminous dial of my watch; it was three o'clock. May should have called me an hour ago. I pulled my boots on and staggered out into the cold air, shutting the tent flap behind me.

The wind still blew strongly from the west, but the sky had cleared and moonlight covered the ground. The ruins stood out against the cliffs.

I went over to the jeep. May was slumped behind the steering wheel; a rifle was across his lap. I touched his shoulder and he woke up. He sleepily rubbed his eyes. Then he realized what had happened.

"My god, I must have fallen asleep!"

I heard boots on stone. Benteen stepped out of the shadows. I knew something was wrong as soon as I saw his face.

"They've gone," he said.

I looked where the Arabs had been sleeping. They had vanished, taking their bedrolls with them. Only the ash of their fire remained. To get back to the path that led down from the plateau, they must have passed near the tents. That must have been what I had heard.

"You were lucky," Benteen said to May, speaking with the same flat voice. "They killed Juma."

CHAPTER 20

WIDE AWAKE NOW, I no longer felt the sting of the cold. Sara joined us. May kept staring at the black sky and shaking his head. No one said anything.

Juma was lying down by the broken wall; his throat had been cut. His rifle was missing.

"I should have seen this coming," Benteen said, angrily.

He figured the Arabs had been spooked by the body and had decided to steal something and clear out. Juma had probably been killed when he tried to stop them.

"No, it's my fault," May said miserably. "I fell asleep. I was the guy who decided to let them stay here in the first place."

"We better check the camp to see what's missing," Benteen said.

The results of the search were depressing: the Bedouin had taken a large canvas satchel that contained most of the artifacts we had found at Qumran. We had left it at the campfire when we turned in, forgetting to put it in one of the tents for safekeeping. They must have grabbed it on their way out.

"What's happening to me!" Sara broke out. The bag had been her responsibility. "I can't believe I was so careless."

"Where do you think they'll go?"

I asked the question as I stood beside Sara, who was leaning against the side of the jeep. A lantern was on the hood, the light casting up on Benteen's face.

"Masada."

"That's almost fifteen miles south of here," Sara said.

"I'm betting they'll head south for Bethlehem and try to make a fast sale on the blackmarket. That part of the country is in Arab hands. It wouldn't make sense for them to go north or west toward Jerusalem and run the risk of wandering into the fighting. They'd also figure we might come after them by car if they went that way. My guess is they'll move south, toward Masada."

"What should we do?" May said, sounding as if he were coming out of a heavy drunk.

"Go after the bastards," Benteen said sharply.

"What are you going to do if you catch up with them?" I asked.

"Juma was a friend. The Arabs have strict rules about avenging the deaths of friends. If I don't settle accounts, I might as well clear out of this country. My reputation wouldn't be worth sand. Juma's tribe is big and news travels fast in the desert. I'm going after them no matter what you decide. If I can bring them back, fine. I'll do that and let their brothers kill them. But I'm going after them. And if that means the deal's off with us, then it's off."

"I don't want any killing," May said.

Benteen slammed a fist on the hood of the jeep.

"You still don't get it, do you? What happens if those Arabs sell that stuff to some dealer and tell their story about what you've been up to out here? Your fine secret goes up in smoke. This place will be crawling with every Arab who can carry a shovel. Is that what you want? There wouldn't be much left of this place when they get through with it."

"I've thought about that before," May said.

"You better think about it again. That bastard in Bethlehem already has your number. What do you think he'll do if he finds out what you've been up to out here?"

Benteen had something there. The dealer Aqui was capable of anything. I was convinced he'd sent those two Arab thugs after us in Jerusalem.

May asked whether he thought he could find them; they already had a good head start.

"We've got a chance, no more than that."

"Chance? What chance?" said Sara, derisively. "How do you expect to find Bedouins in the desert?" She turned away from us, her folded arms clenched to her chest. "I can't believe this!"

"How long do you think it will take?" May asked.

"If we move fast, I might be able to run them down by morning.

My guess is they'll probably make camp around sunup and sleep through the heat."

"What if they don't?" Sara snapped.

"Look, dammit, this is a crapshoot. We might find them. We might not. You got any better ideas?"

May agreed to let him try, but he wanted me to go along on the theory I could move more quickly than he could in the desert. I didn't like that idea and neither did Benteen, but there wasn't much choice. The odds were bad enough as it was.

I tried to say something to Sara, but she hurried to her tent.

"You hear anything in those rocks tonight, you shoot first," Benteen told May.

The two of us started down the trail from the marl terrace. I had to take care to watch my footing in the darkness. My boots knocked loose stones that started small avalanches.

When we reached flat ground, Benteen said, "We're going to have to travel fast. If you can't keep up, it's your lookout."

We walked side by side, not speaking, following the shore of the Dead Sea. Benteen's carbine was slung over his shoulder. I was carrying a rifle. We both carried canteens. I hoped we wouldn't have to go as far as Masada. Fifteen miles in the desert was no joke, 30 when you considered the return trip.

I asked Benteen what he had in mind if we caught up with them.

"That depends."

"What can they do with one rifle?" They had Juma's weapon, but we still had their rifle and knives. The Arabs had made off without trying to get them back.

He laughed.

"They probably hid their guns before they ever climbed up to Qumran. They knew we were up there, and they wanted to bluff us. That's why they brought that old breechloader along and made a great show of letting Juma take it. That was part of the set up. I know Arabs. They'll steal, beg and kill to get the best rifles money can buy. They take pride in them like other men take pride in their women. Believe me, they're well armed right now."

"Then what do we do," I asked, fighting back a stab of panic.

"Try to ambush them."

"How do you ambush Bedouin?"

Benteen laughed again.

"With luck."

We walked for a long time without speaking. I didn't know how far we had gone. The sky was starting to lighten. There was a salty breeze off the water. The hills, rounded smooth like skulls, began to reveal themselves in the east. Farther down the shoreline and still out of sight rose the rock of Masada with the broken remains of Herod's pleasure palace perched on top. I'd always wanted to go there, but not like this. The thought of chasing three Arabs to the place where several hundred Jews had committed mass suicide wasn't reassuring.

"If and when the time comes, I want you to do exactly what I tell you," Benteen said, breaking his silence.

I didn't answer. I could see Benteen's face in the dim light; he had the intense look of a hunter walking through a cornfield where he knew there was quail to be flushed.

"I don't think they'll be expecting us," he said. "That's in our favor."

We continued for another mile or so and then Benteen stopped and pointed up ahead. The sky was clearing now. Sunrise was coming fast.

A thin trail of smoke drifted over a low hill.

"They're more careless than I thought. They've stopped to eat. They must be very sure of themselves."

"Why do you think they killed Juma?" I asked.

Benteen shrugged. "Maybe he knew they were planning to steal something. Whatever happened, they must have surprised him. He was a good man."

We moved away from the beach, heading for the cliffs that rose steeply from the shoreline. Benteen wanted to flank them, and so we started up into the foothills, taking care to stay behind the rocks. We crept forward over the rough, uneven ground; I fell hard, bruising my leg and elbow. Benteen didn't stop or turn around.

It took a while to work our way to the top without breaking cover. When we reached the summit, Benteen told me to stay behind while he went forward to make a reconnaissance. He returned a few minutes later, smiling with his lips, but not with his eyes.

"They're just over the next hill," he said, indicating the humpbacked rock ahead of us.

"Are they armed?"

He nodded. "Three rifles. Juma's and two Mausers."

Benteen checked his pistol, a heavy six-shot Welby.

Cold sweat was running into my eyes.

"We'll have the sun at our backs," Benteen said. "If they start shooting, squeeze the trigger. Don't pull it."

We crawled along the crest of the hill, going the last few yards on our bellies. Benteen raised his head for a look and ducked down.

"They're making coffee."

I had expected Benteen to call out to them. Instead, he braced his elbows, sighted quickly down the oiled barrel of his carbine and fired twice, the crack of the shots echoing loudly in the hills.

My god, what's he doing, I thought. I threw myself down next to him just as he fired again.

Two of the Arabs were lying face down on the ground. The third—it looked like Muhammad—had taken cover behind a rock. He raised his head and I saw the barrel of the rifle. The bullet passed over us with a dull whine.

Benteen fired a long burst, ejected the clip and shoved another into the magazine.

"What in hell are you waiting for!" he shouted. "Start shooting!"

When I saw the rifle come up again, I fired and felt the sharp, bone-wrenching recoil against my shoulder.

Benteen fired. Slivers of rock flew up from the boulder where the Arab was hiding.

Two more bullets hissed by, and then the Arab jumped to his feet and sprinted down the beach, carrying his rifle in a crouch. He was heading for some rocks that offered more cover. Benteen came up fast to a sitting position. He braced the stock against his cheek and shoulder, exhaled, and fired. The Arab staggered and pitched forward. He tried to pull himself up and fell backward.

"Let's go!" Benteen said, getting up.

We descended from the rocks. I stayed well behind, holding the rifle at my side. Benteen examined the two Arabs he had dropped with his first shots, rolling them over on their backs with his foot. Hit in the chest, both were dead.

The third man lay still. It was Muhammad. We approached him slowly. His rifle lay near his hand. He was breathing heavily, his chest heaving. He had been shot in the groin; a dark widening stain covered his robe.

I couldn't believe Benteen had fired without first trying to get them to surrender. We could have taken them prisoner.

"Now what do we do," I said. I felt as if I were sleepwalking.

"You must be crazy."

Benteen walked up behind the man, whose eyes were closed against the pain. He was biting his lower lip. I turned away when Benteen put the barrel against the back of Muhammad's head.

I winced at the shot and walked away without looking back. I picked up the canvas bag of artifacts that rested near the still burning fire. I slung the strap of the bag over my shoulder and started back along the beach. I wanted to get away from the dead men and I wanted to get away from Benteen.

I followed the shore of the Dead Sea for several hundred yards and then I heard him running after me. He grabbed me from behind and spun me around.

"They would have talked," he said. "Think about that, you damn fool. They would have talked like crazy and your fine secret would have been blown to kingdom come."

I looked at him and said, "You bastard."

He hit me in the jaw with his fist and I went down. I shook my head and got up. I blocked another punch with my left forearm, and clipped him hard in the face. Before I could land another blow, he hit me twice in the stomach and I sat down again, gasping for air. I stayed there until I caught my breath.

"Sure, I'm a bastard," he said, panting. "But the job's done."

I stood up stiffly and picked up the bag. Benteen watched me. He was only a foot away, his legs squarely braced. I noticed his eyes—there was something funny about them. They were dilated like the shutter of a camera set at slow speed.

"Have it your way," I said.

Benteen smiled and picked up his rifle.

I started walking again. The sun was half up, painting the cliffs red and gold. I took one last look behind. In the distance I could make out the towering shape of a square-shaped rock. Masada.

CHAPTER 21

WE MADE GOOD TIME on the walk back. Late in the morning, the fire was in the furnace again, the sunlight burning through banks of massed clouds. Puffs of sultry, hot wind scorched our faces.

When we reached our camp, I put the canvas bag down and leaned against a rock. We had walked hard for hours past cliffs with faces as sharp as knife blades. I felt as if someone had slid a file up under my ribs.

May and Sara were waiting for us. Sara looked at me. She saw something in my eyes that I didn't want her to see.

"I'm a little winded, but I'll live," I said.

May shook my hand. The wind blew back his beard, which, untrimmed for days, was thick and matted.

"What happened to the Bedouin?"

Benteen glanced at me but said nothing.

"There was some shooting," I said.

"Bad?"

"Bad enough."

May let the subject drop and Sara didn't ask any questions. I was glad of that. Four people were dead, but it was more than the killing. I would have had a hard time trying to describe or explain what I felt, yet it was just as real to me as the cool touch of the sea breeze. You can tell when things have gone bad. There'd been a change. It was that simple. Everything had been fine, and now wasn't.

"We buried Juma," May said.

They had dug the hole in the monastery cemetery, covering it with dirt and stones so that it looked like the other graves.

"If this place is as important as you say it is, he should be in good company," Benteen said.

May said, "I don't think any Arabs are buried here."

Benteen grinned. "I don't expect Juma will complain."

141

Sara and May had also removed the bones from the grave the copper scroll identified as the resting place of the prophet. They had wrapped them in blankets and placed them in a sleeping bag. When we arrived, they had just finished filling and covering the grave.

I asked if they planned to do the same with the opened tomb.

"We'll have to let it go," May said. "It would take all afternoon."

There was plenty of daylight left to get back to Jerusalem if nothing went wrong. Benteen didn't want to be out on the road after nightfall when nervous, trigger-happy soldiers might mistake us for the enemy. We packed the tents in the jeep, which Benteen drove down off the Qumran terrace. Then we carried down the casket, walking in short, careful steps to avoid jolting it on the rough trail. We padded it on the bottom and sides and lashed it in the back of the station wagon. We put the sleeping bag with the skeleton next to it.

"I guess it's time," May said when everything was ready.

Benteen and May got into the jeep. Sara and I would follow in the car. Sara reminded Benteen to drive slowly. She didn't want to damage the body.

When we started, the heat reflected up from the ground. Clouds of dust blew down from the Qumran plateau. We drove along the rocky shoreline at a crawl. I was glad we were finally on our way.

Unlike Sara, I had never come to love this country. The land remained as bleak and impersonal to me as it had from the first moment I saw it. How long ago was that? Six days? Seven? I'd lost track.

It was well into the afternoon when we finally reached the great cliff of limestone that marked the place where we turned inland. I took a last look at the Dead Sea. I wondered if I would ever see it again. I hoped not.

CHAPTER 22

WE HAD LUCK during the long, slow drive to Jerusalem. The hardest part was working our way back to the Jericho Road. We stopped often, getting out to carry the casket to avoid jarring the body on the steep, bouncing climbs through the wadis. We were halted once outside the city. Benteen arranged for an escort. Some Arab irregulars, followers of the Mufti, agreed to take us in for a fat fee. Shortly after midnight, we started into Jerusalem from the south, following two Arab jeeps down the dark, deserted streets. The Legion had pushed as far as the St. George Road, which meant their soldiers controlled a wide swath of territory from the Old City east to the Sheikh Jarrah and then north as far as Ramallah. With the Arabs in front of us, we made it to the American School without difficulty.

Professor Parker helped us carry the casket into the study. The electricity was off. A lantern burned in the hallway. After introducing May and Benteen, Sara got down to business, telling him what had happened at Qumran. Parker listened closely, rarely interrupting. Benteen had found a bottle of gin and had opened it without asking. Parker didn't notice. He was wearing the same pair of trousers and moth-eaten vest he'd had on the last time I'd seen him.

He didn't take his eyes off the casket, which we had placed on the conference table in the school's study.

We were all tired, having been up nearly 24 hours. But no one suggested sleeping. I even managed to forget for a while what had happened early that morning near Masada.

Sara and May removed the lid. The professor gazed down at the shrouded body.

"Finding something like this in Palestine...In this condition...It's unheard of."

He gently touched the shroud.

143

"That looks like linen. The tomb must have been extremely well sealed."

"It was tighter than a drum," May said.

"The dryness of the climate must have helped," Sara said. She also mentioned that natron had covered the shroud.

"Natron?"

Parker held a lantern over the casket.

"How extraordinary," he said. "That was an Egyptian burial procedure."

Sara pointed out the strange stains on the shroud.

"We think they could be blood."

"This has to be X-rayed," Parker said firmly.

He thought the technique could help us determine the body's condition and indicate how best to open the shroud. Archeologists had routinely X-rayed mummies before unwrapping them, he said. It was a useful, often revealing procedure.

May was immediately taken by the idea.

"I have a friend, an Arab doctor who runs a clinic in the Old City," Parker said. "I am sure he would have no objections if you used his machine."

"Sure, no problem," Benteen said derisively. "Just drive off and have the stiff X-rayed. It's a cinch."

The risks, Sara and May agreed, were worth the trip. Parker wrote a note to his friend, a man named Damelah, explaining what had happened and asking for his help.

Benteen wasn't happy, but May insisted; and so, shortly before dawn after we'd slept for a few hours, we loaded the casket back into the station wagon and drove to the Old City.

Before we left, Benteen tied an Arab Legion flag to the front bumper. The professor remained at the school. There was traffic in the streets, Arab troop trucks and jeeps. It was fortunate that the area was under the control of the Legion. We were stopped once without incident and entered the Old City through Herod's Gate.

The clinic was on the Via Dolorosa in the Moslem Quarter. We pulled into an alley-like street that climbed toward the Temple Mount. The Legion had set up its HQ a few blocks down from the clinic, a narrow, three-story building with iron balconies. Arab soldiers had taken over all the buildings along the street and we could smell their breakfast fires. The fighting in the Old City was over; the Jews had been forced out after a house-to-house battle that had raged along the Street of the Chain. The scars were everywhere—burnt houses and shops, shot up walls, broken furniture.

There was bedlam inside the clinic. The wounded were lying on the floors; most of them were bandaged in strips of torn sheeting. One soldier had his bloody leg up on a low bench. Benteen spoke to him in Arabic. They were preparing him for an amputation; he had been given a single shot of morphine.

A young, sleepy-looking orderly in a dirty white coat went off and returned a few minutes later with Doctor Damelah, an elderly, dark-skinned man in shirt-sleeves, wearing a tie. He looked surprised when we explained that we wanted to X-ray a corpse.

He read Parker's note. "I will do what I can," he said. "I am not sure we have much time. We are using an emergency generator for electricity and it is low on petrol."

We carried the casket into the X-ray room and placed it on a metal table. Sara opened the lid. An Arab medical attendant, a young woman, adjusted the machine, working quickly and efficiently. She didn't look happy, wondering no doubt why they were wasting time on a dead body when there were so many wounded to treat.

After the X-ray was taken and the film developed, Doctor Damelah examined it. He looked tired, but now he woke up. His face changed expression.

"What is this?"

Sara said that the body had been found in an old tomb in the desert.

The doctor, growing more interested, held the still wet film up to a light bulb that dangled from the ceiling. He studied it without speaking. Then he said it was the body of a male, who had what appeared to be a broken right wrist—the metacarpal bone. The small finger on the right hand was also fractured.

"The nose too is broken," he said, examining the film at arm's-length against the light. It showed only the upper torso.

The doctor checked the position of the arms again.

"The hands," he said, "are folded over the chest. The left arm is bent under the right. A dark area shows in the left wrist, but there is no indication of fracture."

Doctor Damelah agreed that the stains on the shroud were probably blood caused by a strong flow from a major artery. One of the stains appeared to match up with the fractures noticed in the right wrist.

"There was serious trauma to that area," he said. He watched us carefully. "This man, who was he?"

"We don't know," Sara said.

"He did not have a...good death," the doctor said solemnly.

I remembered the scroll's description of the Teacher of Righteousness—how he had somehow been made to suffer for his beliefs. There was no doubt at all: the extent of the injuries showed with dramatic clarity on the X-ray. Violence had been done to the man—a lot of it.

"I ask myself if there is not more here than you say," the doctor said. "I do not like this."

None of us answered. May asked the doctor whether his clinic could use a donation.

Damelah stood there, staring at him as if he didn't understand.

May took out his checkbook, wrote out a check and handed it to the doctor. It was for $1,000.

"If we can do more, tell Professor Parker. We're in your debt."

The doctor looked at May as if not believing what was happening. He started to say something, but was interrupted when two badly wounded soldiers were carried inside. We shut the coffin and left the clinic quickly. As we climbed into the station wagon, Sara pointed to a sign on one of the buildings just down the street. Made of glazed tile, it marked the fourth station of the cross—the place where Jesus was said to have fallen the first time. Someone screamed inside the clinic. Not much had changed over the centuries; it was still the Via Dolorosa.

All of this had taken most of the early morning. The streets were filled with Arab soldiers; there were delays, but we got back to the school without any trouble.

In our hurry to leave the clinic, we had forgotten the X-ray. We described the results for Parker, who was perplexed by the broken bones, especially the one in the right hand.

"You must leave here," he said abruptly, speaking to Sara. "As quickly as possible. It's your professional duty to get this body to a place of safety. It needs to be examined fully."

He spoke rapidly, emotionally. He meant every word.

"Couldn't we open it here?"

May asked the question. I'd been wondering the same thing.

"That would not be wise," Parker said.

"I'd just like to know a little more about what we've got in case something happens," May said.

"I don't want to do that," Sara said. "This isn't the time or place."

"I want it opened. Do I have to spell it out?"

May spoke loudly, angrily.

Sara bit back her own anger. She thought it might be possible to open the top fold—at least enough for a look at the face.

"That's as far as I'll go without a laboratory," she said. "I won't do anything else, John."

When May agreed, she examined the shroud. "We better strengthen it first with paraffin."

Although the shroud itself was in fairly good condition, she was afraid the linen bandages would crumble.

Parker still wasn't convinced. He thought it was a mistake.

"In normal times I'd agree with you," May said, becoming calmer. "But everything has changed. It won't be easy to get this out of Jerusalem. Something could happen. Wouldn't it be better to make a preliminary investigation now—just to be on the safe side? If something goes wrong, at least there'll be more of a permanent record that way."

Parker started to object again but not as strongly.

"Would you help us?" Sara asked.

Parker looked at her and said, "Of course."

It didn't take long to get ready. Sara heated some paraffin wax on the kitchen stove and painted the clear liquid onto the top fold of the shroud with a brush. She also coated the linen bandages that crossed the top of the shroud. The liquid hardened rapidly, forming a waxy coating on the fabric.

With May and Parker next to her, Sara made a shallow incision with a scalpel through the outer linen binding and down into the

147

shroud itself. Then she made another shallow cut along the top of the shroud so that the portion covering the face could be lifted away.

"There may be more natron inside," she said. She showed where the shroud bulged slightly at the chest.

Her hands steady, she made two more careful incisions. There was the faint seepage of that same strangely pungent odor we had noticed in the tomb at Qumran.

Benteen joined us. He thought we should have jumped at Parker's suggestion to clear out. But now he stood there, watching like the rest of us.

Sara lifted away the hardened pieces of linen and shroud, revealing the face.

I felt as if someone had kicked me. Revulsion swept over me when I saw that twisted face—revulsion, then pity. It was a tortured face broken by suffering—withered, the brittle skin shrunken and cracked like tanned leather, almost black and with a gaping rictus of a mouth, a mouth that seemed frozen in a scream. The man had died in agony, and staring down, transfixed, I was overwhelmed and terribly sorry.

"How he must have suffered," Sara whispered.

"What's that sticking from his eyelid?" May asked."

What looked like a splinter projected through the flap of brittle skin.

The right cheekbone appeared as if it had been broken. The nose, somewhat flattened, also looked broken, which corresponded with the X-ray. A deep gash plunged from the scalp to the eyes; what remained of the hair was long, the strands hanging down over the forehead. The scanty beard was forked. The head was propped on a wad of linen. The eye sockets were large and rounded, almost owlish.

"This must be photographed," Parker said, his voice hoarse and raspy.

I kept studying the head; hideous in death with its mummified, wasted skin, the face was still powerful. I was struck by its strength.

"The body has been crudely preserved," Sara said slowly, almost to herself.

"My dear child," Parker said after a long silence. "I don't trust myself to say this. But that broken bone in the wrist.... And that thorn."

I didn't understand he was driving at. Neither did May or the others.

"I recall a prophet who was put to death by a Wicked Priest... A Teacher of Righteousness, if you will," Parker continued. "A holy man."

No one said a word. I was aware of rifle fire.

Parker bent low and stared at the broken face. We were all waiting for him to speak. He was troubled about something, but found difficulty in expressing it.

"It's that thorn through the eyelid," he said.

"What are you talking about?" Benteen asked irritably. "I don't follow any of this crap."

The professor was hardly able to stand.

"I keep asking myself if this... if this could possibly be the body of Jesus of Nazareth."

The words seem to hang there.

Benteen laughed.

Sara looked at May, her face frozen.

"The broken wrist," Parker went on. "The stains that correspond with the position of the hands and feet. This must sound mad, but couldn't such injuries have been caused by crucifixion? A man nailed to a cross would have wounds like that."

"But the Romans must have executed hundreds by crucifixion," May said. His voice was strained, the words almost jeering. "If it was Christ, why would they have moved the body all the way out to Qumran? He was put to death in Jerusalem."

Parker slumped into a chair. He said, "You might make the case that his followers wanted to make sure his body wouldn't fall into the hands of his enemies." He suggested that perhaps they moved the corpse to Qumran, thinking it would be safer there. "The Essenes hated the Pharisees. They might have been the only ones the friends of the murdered Christ could have turned to without fear of betrayal."

"Christ was executed under the reign of Tiberius early in the first century A.D.," Sara said, recovering. "That would roughly fit with the likely age of the copper scroll."

"And it would correspond with the likely timeframe for the settlement of Qumran," Parker added.

I had begun to think it was all a monstrous joke. It certainly wasn't the handsome bearded face of the paintings and frescoes, the gentle face with the soulful eyes that beamed down in ruby and emerald light from the stained glass windows of cathedrals. The face was from hell.

Parker pointed out some small, dark marks around the top of the forehead just under the hair line. "Is it possible they might have been caused by other thorns?"

"A crown of thorns?" May asked skeptically.

I was transfixed by what Parker had suggested even though it was preposterous. Sure, maybe the man had been crucified, but that wasn't enough for me. Nowhere near enough. Like Benteen, I felt like laughing out loud, but I was afraid the laughter would turn to something I couldn't control.

May said, "It's madness to keep talking about this."

Parker lifted a hand to his brow. "I'm afraid we're all over-wrought," he said. "It's my fault. Forgive me. It was foolish speculation." He sat there breathing deeply. He looked at Sara and said, "But, dear god. Who is this?...Who?"

Sara had been very quiet through most of this discussion. But now, almost reluctantly, she mentioned the headless skeleton we had dug up at Qumran.

"I think I know now who that might be. At least I have a theory."

"Fine," Benteen said sarcastically. "Don't keep us in suspense."

Sara said, "We know how he died—the victim of a foolish promise."

"What are you leading up to?" May said. Sitting there, his shirtsleeves rolled to the elbows, his thick forearms propping his head, he was getting uneasy again. "What are you trying to say."

"He was beheaded," Sara said. "By orders of Herod Antipas, a man who feared and respected him."

I remembered the gruesome marks on the neck bone.

"What in hell are you talking about?" Benteen said.

"What if it was John," Sara said. "The one they called the Baptist."

She let that sink in and then mentioned the stone cup with the flanging lip she had found in the grave. She wondered if it might have been for pouring water.

"A lot of people believe that he was raised by the Essenes from childhood. It's certain that he spent most of his adult life preaching near the Dead Sea. The same area where the Essenes may have had their monastery. Much of his message seems to dovetail with the sect's deepest beliefs.

"He came," Parker said, slowly quoting the King James, "to prepare the way for another, one whose sandal he was not worthy to tie."

"What's that got to do with the poor bastard you've got lying here," Benteen said.

"He preached the arrival of Christ, the Messiah, the one who would baptize with the Holy Spirit and with fire," Sara said. "The two names have always been linked—John and Jesus."

She reminded us how the grave was situated, pointing toward the other tomb.

"I can't believe that's all a coincidence. In death, he may have served the same purpose he did in life." She started to say something else, then quickly stopped. "I don't know what I'm saying. I don't believe this is real anymore."

CHAPTER 23

WE STOOD in the middle of the room waiting for someone to say something. The body lay in shadows on the table.

"The copper scroll mentioned a prophet," May said, breaking the uncomfortable silence. He kept staring at the remains as if unable to turn away.

He was referring to the headless, mutilated skeleton we had brought back from Qumran wrapped in a sleeping bag.

"A prophet who disappeared in the wilderness after Christ appeared," Parker said just under his breath.

The sleeping bag was still in the station wagon. May suggested carrying it inside so the professor could have a look.

"To hell with that, let's take the bandages off," Benteen said sharply. He hadn't taken his eyes off the body.

I thought he was joking, but the hard set of his face indicated otherwise.

"If it's the right man, there should be holes where they nailed him to the cross."

"You must be insane," I said.

Benteen scowled. "I don't see it that way," he said, his voice bad-tempered. "Your friend here thinks this mummy or whatever it is could be the remains of Jesus Christ. Now maybe that's insane. But after everything that's been going on, we ought to talk about it some more. . . . I want to see what's under that shroud!"

The professor glanced at him nervously. "I should never have said that. It was inexcusable. I'm not sure what came over me."

"Uncovering the body is out of the question," Sara said heatedly. "We already went over this. We're not prepared to do that. You don't know what you're asking."

Benteen slammed his fist against the wall. "I want to see the hands and feet! I'd say I've got the bloody right after what I've done for you."

His right hand rested on his pistol belt. If he made a move, I didn't see how we could stop him.

"I'm paying you a great deal of money," May said. He spoke coolly, stepping closer to Benteen. They faced one another across the table. "As I see it, you've got two choices. You can take what you've earned and clear out—now. Or you can stay with us and stop acting like a fool. It's the only way you're going to find out what's under that shroud."

Benteen broke into a grin, but his unsmiling eyes remained riveted on May's face. "Right now I'd say you're not paying me enough, nowhere near it," he said.

"We can talk about that later," May said. "I'll decide when and where."

"I'll make sure you won't forget."

None of us trusted him. But for the time being, at least, the immediate danger seemed over. I sucked in a deep breath and let it out. We had edged very close to something that was sure to have turned out badly.

I took a final look at the bearded face with the haunting, empty eyes. Then Sara covered it with a layer of cotton and linen and put the burial cloth back in place. We refastened the lid on the casket.

Light gunfire had broken out again. Then the artillery opened up. After a quiet morning, the street fighting was starting another round late in the afternoon.

The shooting prompted May to renew our earlier discussion about leaving the country.

Parker encouraged us again to get out as soon as possible. The alternative was to run the risk of being trapped.

"You must leave the Holy Land," he insisted. "If you've got a chance to do that, you better take it. I'll help you any way I can."

May repeated his plan to head for a port like Tel Aviv or Jaffa.

Benteen thought it would be suicide to drive out of Jerusalem.

"We'd never make it five miles." Whatever he had been trying to do earlier had been carefully and conveniently laid aside; from the calm way he spoke now, it was as if nothing had happened. "You might as well try to drive through a shooting gallery. The Jewish irregulars would just want your car; the Arabs would want your life."

He mentioned a makeshift airstrip in the southern part of the city; it was in the Rehavia District just off the Gaza Road. The Jews, who had occupied the area after the English withdrawal, had bulldozed a crude runway into the middle of an old truck farm. The field was frequently bombed by Arab fighters, but a few supply planes managed to get in and out during lulls in the shelling.

"Maybe we can find a plane," he suggested. "It's a longshot, but I don't have any other bright ideas."

May thought it was worth a try. Benteen and I would visit the airfield and nose around; but first Benteen wanted to see what was happening in the streets. After making sure his carbine was loaded, he left through the garden for what he promised would only be a short reconnoiter.

The artillery fire had picked up; it sounded as if the guns were on Mount Scopus. A good fight was raging in the hills to the east. I was glad it was Benteen out there and not me.

"What if he talks," Sara said as soon as he was gone.

May said, "It wouldn't do him much good to tell the story here in Jerusalem—not with a war on. The time to worry about blackmail is later."

"If someone found out about your discovery before you've had a chance to draw any conclusions it would be most unfortunate," Parker said. "It might jeopardize everything. You'd be under tremendous pressure to complete your work quickly—perhaps too quickly."

"The trouble is we need the sonofabitch," May said.

Another problem remained: where to take the body, assuming we could leave Jerusalem and get across the border?

Parker thought we should try to reach Cairo. He had professional contacts at the British Museum who could help us.

Sara objected. She was afraid our discoveries would be confiscated by the Egyptian authorities. They'd be sure to question any recent arrivals from the war zone, especially if one of them was Jewish.

A better bet, she thought, would be to go to Paris. She knew several archeologists there who could provide access to a research laboratory. Parker immediately went for the idea. If we went to

Paris we could also look up Gabriel-Marie Bourgonne—the Dominican biblical scholar he had mentioned earlier. He repeated his argument that Bourgonne, an expert on ancient manuscripts, would be a good man to try to help us solve the mystery of the copper scroll.

May, who had listened to the discussion in silence, finally said, "No, we're not going to Paris." He stood at a shuttered window, arms folded.

"What do you have in mind?" I asked.

"We're going back to the United States—to Chicago."

He let that sink in for a moment. His blunt tone made it clear he wasn't in any mood to argue.

"I want to be damn sure everything we've got is safe," he said. "We can control things in Chicago. We can't do that in Paris or anywhere else I can think of."

After the initial shock wore off, Sara began to see some advantages to May's unexpected proposal. "I know several people at the University of Chicago, men I can trust," she said. "One of them works for the school's Oriental Institute. He could be of tremendous help."

"The university isn't a mile from my home," May said.

"There's just one little difficulty," I said. "How do we get there? Unless I've forgotten my geography, Chicago's a good 10,000 miles from here—give or take a couple thousand either way."

May thought that if we could reach a neutral port like Tunis or Algiers on the North African coast, we could find a liner or merchantman that took passengers. From there his plan was to head for Western Europe, preferably France or Italy, where we could book passage back to the States.

If we couldn't leave the country by plane, the only other alternative would be wait for a Jewish military convoy to reach Jerusalem and try to break out with it.

The suggestion was Parker's. Several small truck convoys loaded with food and weapons had already shot their way into the city; one had even managed to get back out. It was Parker's understanding the trucks had returned to Tel Aviv.

"For the right price we might be able to join one of those convoys," May said, picking up on the idea.

I whistled and said, "I don't like to be the gloom and doom guy here, but that sounds like a tall order."

"It might not be easy getting out of Tel Aviv," Parker added. "The British have the port under a blockade."

"We've got to take the chance," May snapped. "Somewhere on that goddamn coast we ought to find a ship. If anyone's got a better idea, I want to hear it now."

I didn't have any ideas at all, but I thought of another problem—getting the body through customs.

"What do we say if someone wants to know what's in that casket?"

Sara said, "We can tell them it's my brother... that he was a Jewish soldier who was killed in the fighting and that I'm taking his body to the United States for burial."

It wasn't a bad suggestion. That kind of thing had happened often enough after the war in Europe ended. I'd even written a couple of stories about parents who had gone to France and Germany to bring back the bodies of sons killed in action.

"What if they decide to open it?" I asked.

"Let them," Sara said. "They'll be looking for a dead man, and that's exactly what they'll find."

"Do you have a name for him?"

Sara looked at me. Then she understood. I was talking about her "brother."

"Why not Paul," she said, smiling. "I've always liked that name."

Benteen returned a short time later. He reported heavy skirmishing around the Green Line, but that he thought we could avoid it by cutting south near the Old City. We decided to leave for the airfield at once.

May's final instructions were to make whatever offer was necessary to any pilot we could find. Money was no object.

"We need that plane," he said.

156

CHAPTER 24

IT WAS A LONG HIKE out to the Rehavia District, but Benteen moved quickly. There were more people on the streets than I would have expected—Jews and Arabs alike, most of them women or old men, even children, all of them foraging for water and food. We crossed the Bevingrad without any trouble. There weren't any soldiers in sight, but the fighting had left scars on every block— ruined houses and the smell of ash and fire.

Once past the commercial district and Mamillah Cemetery, we cut over to the Gaza Road. An hour later we reached the airfield. A Romanesque chruch, the Monastery of the Cross, and a flanking row of desolate houses were just off the runway, a suicidally short strip of broken asphalt protected by a solitary anti-aircraft battery. The only plane I saw—a small, single engine job that looked like a Piper Cub—was on its side at the end of the field; the right wing was snapped off and the prop was gone.

Two trucks with canvas tops were parked near a metal quonset hut with a tall antenna attached to the side; banked high with sandbags, it served as a radio shack. Men and women with rifles and Stens were standing around. Except for their weapons, they might have been college students. I noticed how they hugged their fortified trenches and dugouts; more soldiers were positioned over by the monastery.

We walked to the front of the church. I showed my press credentials to a woman in baggy olive-drab trousers and boots and asked to see the officer in charge. A young man—he couldn't have been older than 20—came over, a submachine gun strapped across his shoulder. He wore a British field jacket with loose threads on the sleeves, where the insignia patches had been cut off.

I said I'd like to interview any pilots who might be available. I told him it would make a good story for the folks back in the States, who wanted to know how Jerusalem was managing to hold out. I played it up big. Maybe I could talk to the man who had flown the Piper Cub. I promised I wouldn't take much of his time or get in the way.

The soldier eyed me cautiously. I knew he had never talked to a reporter before. He was unsure what to do.

"Try around back," he said, struggling to sound decisive.

A man in his late twenties was sitting on a folding chair in the shade behind the church. Deeply tanned, he wore shorts and scuffed combat boots. His head was bandaged. I introduced myself as a reporter and asked whether we could talk to him.

"The name's Lawrence, Tom Lawrence," he said without looking up.

He sat there with his legs stretched out in front of him. Our faces were reflected in the silver lenses of his sunglasses.

I began by asking some general questions, suggesting that I was interested in writing a feature on his experiences in the war.

"How much you pay a guy for something like that?" he asked, cutting me off.

"About twenty dollars?"

Lawrence smiled and said, "Fire away."

He had come to the Holy Land as a freelance pilot, he explained. He'd been in the country six weeks, flying military cargo and food to kibbutzim near Haifa and Acre to the north. He was paid a flat fee for every trip, strictly a cash-and-carry arrangement.

"Why are you doing it?" I asked.

"I needed the money."

He had flown heavy bombers during the raids on Germany. A year after he was mustered out of the service, a friend told him the Jews were looking for experienced combat pilots so he had come over. He had paid $1,200 for an aging war surplus DC-3, which he had flown in from Biloxi. He started to explain how he had ferried the plane to the Holy Land when I interrupted him.

"You say you've got a DC-3?"

I looked at Benteen, trying not to show my surprise. His mouth opened. His reaction was the same as mine. If it was true about the plane, it was the best break we'd had in a long time.

"There must be four or five of us who flew over from the States in Gooney Birds," Lawrence said. "We all took the southern route. A couple more are supposed to be on the way."

"Where's your plane now?" Benteen asked, controlling his excitement.

"Back in Tel Aviv," Lawrence said in his rich Mississippi accent. "You might say it belongs to the bank and that I'm just borrowing it for a spell."

Provided his luck held, he figured that after expenses, he could recoup his investment in four or five months as a freelance.

"What brings you to Jerusalem?" I heard myself ask the question, but I was still thinking about the plane.

"They asked me to fly some radio equipment in here. It wasn't much of a load, so I took one of the Cubs. I lost oil pressure coming in. If we had some mechanics who knew what a sonofabitching wrench was for..." He spat a brown stream of tobacco juice that beaded in the dirt. "Shit, you can see what happened."

The wrecked plane was crumpled up at the far end of the runway.

"What did you mean about taking the southern route?" I asked.

"It's the way we ferried most of the planes over during the war," Lawrence explained. "You come across the Caribbean and down the coast of South America as far as Natal. It's right on the tip of Brazil. From there you head due east across the Atlantic 1,400 miles to the Ascension Islands. It's another 800 miles north to the Gold Coast. As soon as you hit Africa you're home free."

"That sounds like a long way around," I said.

"It's shorter to come over Newfoundland and the North Atlantic, but a hell of a lot more risky. You can never count on the weather. I'll go south every time. I've seen what ice can do to a plane."

Benteen asked about his bandaged head.

"Banged it on the windshield when she flipped over. No big deal. Just a few scratches and a mother of a headache."

I glanced around to make sure no one was near us.

"We want to charter your plane," I said.

Lawrence broke into a broad grin.

"To hell you say."

I stood there, staring at him.

"You're serious?"

"Very."

"Where will you fly?" Benteen asked. "How far?"

"Wherever you want, friend—just as long as you put your money up front."

"What about Tunis?"

Lawrence's brow furrowed.

"Boys, I hate to tell you, but there's some mighty tough, well-defended air down along the coast," he said.

I asked how much he charged.

"Two hundred bucks a trip, cash in advance. You pay for the fuel."

"We'll pay you two thousand plus a thousand dollar bonus if we get there in one piece," I said.

Lawrence stood up.

"What did you say your name was, mister?"

He held out his hand and both of us shook it. I could sense that he still had his doubts.

There was another detail that needed to be settled. I told him he'd have to pick us up here, in Jerusalem.

"Not good," he said, frowning. "Not good at all. Putting a DC down on this runway would be like landing on a postage stamp. And even if I could do it, I'd be asking to get my ass blown out of the sky. These hills are thick with A-rab guns and every once in a while they actually hit what they're aiming at."

"That's why we're offering you $3,000," Benteen said.

"I haven't seen any of that yet."

I took out a wad of bills May had given me before we'd left for the airfield. There was just over $600. I counted it out and handed all of it to Lawrence.

"Consider that a downpayment. You'll get the rest when you land. Do we have a deal?"

Lawrence hesitated. "It's going to be tight, damn tight, but all right—I'm game."

He stuffed the bills into his shirt pocket without bothering to recount them. "Now who's going on this little junket."

"The two of us and a man and woman."

"Any cargo?"

"A casket."

I watched to see how Lawrence would react. He said nothing.

"It's the body of an American who was killed fighting for the Israelis."

"It can happen," Lawrence said. "A friend of yours?"

"The brother of the woman."

"If you don't mind me asking, when do you want to leave?"

"As soon as you can get back here."

"A couple of Cubs are going to try to get in tomorrow morning, early. I'm supposed to fly out on one of them. I'll have to refuel in Tel Aviv." He was thinking. "Be here ready to go around sundown tomorrow. I'll have my best shot then. The darkness will help. We might pull a surprise."

"What about the Jews," Benteen said. "You're supposed to be working for them."

"I work for myself, friend," Lawrence said, smiling.

"But they might not understand if somebody makes an unannounced landing right in their backyard."

"He's right about that," I said. "They might have their own ideas about how they want to use your plane."

We talked it over and decided that Lawrence would land and keep the engines revving. Our job would be to get through the cordon of soldiers and out to the plane. We wouldn't waste any time trying to get permission; I didn't think that would work, not for a minute. They'd be sure to stop us. We'd make a run for it and take our chances.

"Sounds like a snap," Benteen said. I could tell that he knew better.

"What if you don't show up," I asked.

"Then something went wrong. I'll try for the following night, the same time. I'm not giving you any guarantees. If I'm not there, you'll have to wait it out."

"What's to keep you from hanging onto the money and forgetting about us," Benteen said. "For all we know, we might never see you again."

Lawrence gave him a steady look. "I shook your hand, mister," he said quietly. "You say something like that again, I might get angry."

On the way back, I thought about stopping at the Associated Press bureau on Ben Yehuda Street, but finally decided against it. They probably would have evacuated the office weeks ago. It would have been nice to see Weil before we left, but I didn't have the time to hunt him up. Besides, he would have been sure to ask questions, and I didn't want to stonewall him about what had happened in the desert. I owed him too much for that kind of treatment. Better just to let it alone.

As things turned out, I was grateful we didn't make the detour.

When we got back to the school and opened the gate, Benteen grabbed my arm and pulled me back.

I started to say something when the door slammed open. I saw an Arab with a rifle, one of Aqui's men. I recognized him immediately.

At the first shots, Benteen dived behind one of the trees that flanked the walkway. I threw myself down behind the iron gate and hugged the ground.

The Arab fired again, the rifle jerking spasmodically in his hands. The bullets made a pinging sound when they ricocheted off the bars of the fence.

"Stay down!" Benteen shouted. I didn't lift my head to look at him, but I heard his carbine cut loose and glass shatter and then the door bang shut.

"He's got an automatic!" Benteen hollered.

Another burst of gunfire came from inside the school. I sprinted for the door. I didn't stop to think. Sara was in there.

Benteen pushed me out of the way, butting me hard with his shoulder. He kicked in the door, let it swing wide and went in with his weapon up. I followed right behind him. May and the Arab were struggling in the hallway. He had the Arab pinned from behind; kicking savagely, the man broke free. He had dropped his rifle. Before he could grab it again, Benteen shot him dead. He slid forward to his knees, his forehead striking the floor.

That's when I saw the other Arab. He was young, almost a boy. I'd never seen him before. He was standing just inside the study, holding a pistol at his side, the muzzle pointed down. Sara was next to him.

"No, don't!" she screamed when Benteen turned on him with his carbine.

He shouted something in Arabic and the boy dropped the weapon.

Sara was all right. I took in the rest of the room. Parker was backed up against a wall; he slowly wiped a handkerchief across his forehead.

"What in hell happened?" Benteen said.

May, still winded, tried to explain. The boy had knocked on the front door a couple of hours earlier; he said in stammering English that he was frightened and lost. Parker was talking to him when the older Arab, who'd been hiding on the porch, forced his way inside. He had kept them covered while he waited for Benteen and me to return. He had probably seen us leave. I didn't doubt for a moment that Aqui had sent him to kill us and get the scrolls back.

"It's my fault," Parker said. "I wasn't ready. They caught me by surprise."

The dead Arab lay in the hallway, his blood soaking into the carpet. He'd been shot in the head and chest.

Benteen spoke to the boy in Arabic. At first the youth was too afraid to answer. He stood there in his dirty robes, shaking his head piteously; his cheeks were sunken from lack of food. Benteen slapped him across the mouth.

"Stop that!" Sara shouted.

His tongue suddenly loosened, the boy began chattering like a frightened monkey.

"He says he's a tribesman of the dead man," Benteen said coldly. "That he doesn't know anything about Aqui.... He's lying."

He raised his arm as if to strike him again, but Sara grabbed it. "I told you, don't!"

Benteen stared through her. He motioned to the door and the young Arab ran out like a shot, not looking back.

Later, we carried the Arab's body into the garden in the back of the school. We dug a shallow grave and buried it there, wrapped in a blanket.

May decided to leave for the airfield early in the morning. Benteen thought it would be safer to be out on the streets then. We'd have to hide near the runway and wait for the plane, an unpleasant prospect but there wasn't any other alternative. There was always the chance Jewish soldiers would try to stop and question us before we could get out to the field.

It was almost dark. The hills of Jerusalem had a wine-red glow as the sun set. An ugly smudge of black smoke hung over the New City; some buildings had been hit by artillery earlier in the day and were still burning.

Sara and I slept together that night. She was still upset by what had happened.

"It was horrible this afternoon," she said quietly, holding me close. "There's been so much killing."

"Try to forget it," I said. "It's over."

"He enjoyed shooting that man."

"We'll be all right," I said, trying to shake off my own apprehension. "A few more days and we'll never see him again."

I tilted her head back and kissed her lips.

Her fingers found me, softly touching, caressing. I gently pressed her shoulders down into the blankets and kissed her breasts. She wanted me and I entered her quickly, her black hair pouring over the pillow.

I closed my eyes, unable to hold back the spasms.

"Thank god you're with me."

I held her all night, held her until my arms went numb from her weight, not daring to move.

CHAPTER 25

STILL DARK with a crescent moon falling lower in the sky, the morning was cool and damp. We drank some weak tea by lamplight. Benteen wanted to drive to the airstrip before the sun was up and the fighting broke out again. His plan was a gamble: stay off the main roads, cut south through the Mea Shearim District and hope we didn't run into a Haganah patrol.

"I'm not stopping for anyone," Benteen said. "There may be shooting, so be ready for that. Keep your heads down and hold on."

The station wagon was already loaded. Sara and Parker had packed the skeleton in a plywood box, lashing it down on top of the casket. The scrolls, wrapped in cloth, were stored in a leather briefcase. Two canvas bags contained the artifacts from Qumran.

When Sara slid into the front seat, Parker kissed her on the cheek.

"I promised I wouldn't get sentimental, but I can't help it," he said, smiling. "I suppose I should have known better."

There was nothing sentimental about his parting advice. It was direct and concise, a warning not to be rushed into publishing the news of our finds at Qumran.

"No one's going to be ready for anything like this," he said. "There's going to be a furor of the kind not seen in archeology since Tutankhamen's grave was opened. You're sure to be accused of fraud, invention, lying—who knows what else. Be precise in your analysis and skeptically cautious. I'm afraid they're going to come at you with knives. Of course, I'll support you any way I can. So will others. But the attack will be ruthless. You must be prepared for that."

Sara leaned out the window and hugged him.

"My dear girl, I'm afraid you're about to become famous," he said. "I'll be able to write in my memories that I knew you."

We left soon after that. May was in the front with Sara and

165

Benteen. I sat in the back, wedged in next to the caskets. Benteen drove, as always, with his carbine on his lap.

Despite a few detours to skirt some blocked roads, it didn't take long to get out to the airfield. Benteen pulled in between two abandoned houses several hundred yards back from the runway. When the time came, we would have to cross a shallow ravine, but it was a straight shot to where we expected to meet the plane. More trucks were down there now and more soldiers. The only thing to do was sit tight and hope that Lawrence had managed to get off safely in one of the Piper Cubs. Two of them landed and took off again during the next three or four hours; they were on the ground only minutes. We were too far away to see who was on board.

There was sporadic shooting throughout the day, mostly rifle and machine gun fire that flared first to the south from the direction of the Valley of Hinnom and then, later, in the hills that shadowed the New City to the north. The shelling didn't start until well into the afternoon. Typical Arab gunnery, a bombardment without specific targets, the unaimed shells dropped randomly at long intervals. I thought it was over when the ground rocked from a heavy explosion several blocks behind us.

We stayed in the car, straining to hear the first sound of an airplane.

While we ate the cheese and canned ham we had brought along, Sara raised a point Benteen and I had already discussed with Lawrence. She wanted to know whether we shouldn't try to smooth things out with the Jews.

"Why not talk to them?" she asked. "There'll be room on the plane for supplies or wounded. We could agree to fly to Tel Aviv before heading for Tunis."

May didn't like it.

"Cargo planes are worth their weight in gold to them right now," he said. "They'll stop us from leaving the country any way they can. As soon as we go down there and tell them what we're up to, it's over. We'll never get out of here."

I worried about how Lawrence was going to find scarce fuel and take off from Tel Aviv. I couldn't believe the Jews would let him leave voluntarily.

I was still thinking about it when we heard the engines—a faint, low-pitched throb that quickly grew louder.

"That may be him!" Benteen shouted.

The sun was almost down. I saw the plane, a speck over the hills. It grew steadily larger as I watched and then we were moving.

Benteen drove out from between the houses and crossed a grassy clearing. The station wagon pitched badly when we hit the ravine. The plane was already over the crest of the hills; its wheels were down. It seemed to hang there motionless, growing larger, coming closer and then touched the ground, bounced once, and hurtled along the runway.

We came onto the smooth ground as the plane slowed, almost stopped, and swung around in a tight circle for take off, its engines still pounding. Benteen drove right to the cargo hatch behind the starboard wing and slammed on the brakes.

I jumped out and glanced back toward the Jewish positions. Soldiers were standing there. Someone was waving at us and yelling shrilly in Hebrew.

"Move it, dammit!" Benteen shouted. His carbine was slung over his shoulder. He ran to the back of the station wagon with a knife in his hand and slashed at the ropes that secured the casket.

The hatch opened. Lawrence helped Sara on board. I followed with the box that contained the skeleton. I forgot how heavy it was and almost fell, trying to push it inside the plane, which shook from the idling engines.

Lawrence pulled me up by the shoulders.

"Nice to see you," he said, smiling.

Soldiers were running toward us now. The gunfire started as soon as May and Benteen headed for the plane with the casket. We had taken them by surprise, but that advantage was over now; they weren't going to waste time asking questions. Bullets slapped against the DC-3's mud-colored fuselage.

Benteen shouted for me. He'd put the casket down and un-strapped his rifle.

I jumped down from the hatch and ran over to them.

"I've got to slow them up."

He started firing at once, bracing his arms on the hood of the station wagon to steady his aim.

Five or six men were hurrying toward us. When Benteen opened up, they threw themselves down. He gave them two long bursts, shooting over their heads.

"Get going! Move it!" he yelled.

May picked up the casket, gripping it with his powerful arms. I took hold of the end and we staggered for the plane. Lawrence helped us slide it through the hatch. We were still struggling with it when Sara screamed.

I looked back at the station wagon. Benteen lay face down on the ground by the front fender. There was enough light left to see that he was missing the back of his head.

More bullets ripped into the car, smashing out the rear window.

May started to leave the plane, but Lawrence kicked his legs out from under him and slammed the hatch shut.

"He's dead, forget him! Get those goddamned caskets tied down!"

"It's the bags!" May cried out. "We forgot them!"

The canvas bags with the pottery shards, scroll fragments and other artifacts from Qumran were still in the back of the van.

"To hell with them!"

Lawrence threw himself into the pilot's seat. I fell hard on my back when the plane lurched forward, its twin engines roaring. Sara and May were trying to fasten the caskets with the web belting attached to the bulkhead when the bouncing plane nosed up. I rolled over May and managed to grab hold of a strap.

"We're in the air!" Lawrence shouted over the roar of the engines. "Hang on!"

CHAPTER 26

THE PLANE LEVELED OFF and I saw the gray horizon glint in the windows along the cargo bay as the wings dipped back to horizontal. May and Sara were sitting on the slatted metal floor, holding onto the straps to keep from tumbling forward.

Lawrence yelled to us from the cockpit. He wanted to know if we were all right. The plane, he said, had been hit a few times during takeoff, but no damage had been done. The words broke the trance; the shock of what had happened would settle in later, but right now there wasn't time to think about it. There were no seats; we hunkered down on folded blankets.

Lawrence banked to the west.

"We should be in Egyptian airspace in half an hour," he said. "But don't worry. Those boys never fly at night."

I got up and sat in the co-pilot's seat. The drone of the engines was ear-splitting. The plane banked again. There was a sprinkling of dim lights far to the north. We were flying away from them.

"Tel Aviv," Lawrence said. "It was blacked out last night."

I asked him how he had managed to get out of the city.

He grinned and said, "A damn fine piece of work if I do say so myself. I was supposed to fly some guns and ammunition up to Haifa. They wanted me to bring a load of food back down the coast, but I told them I had engine trouble, an oil leak. Spent most of the afternoon pretending to patch up a cylinder."

He had stalled until it was time to leave for Jerusalem.

"I gassed up and turned over the engines for a little test," he said. "The test sort of turned into an unscheduled takeoff. The cargo was still piled up in boxes out by the runway." He thought it over for a while. "I don't feel too great about not delivering those guns and ammo, but I guess I'll get over it."

Twenty minutes later we reached the coast, a strip of moonlit sand set off against the black water of the Mediterranean. Night had fallen and the sky was ablaze with stars.

169

Tunis, Lawrence said, was another 400 air miles down the coast. It had a good airport.

"Why don't you relax," he said. "Pretend this old crate is a Pan Am Clipper and you're on vacation."

We talked for a while. "What are you going to do with the money you make on this trip?" I asked.

"Get back to the Gulf Coast and start me a charter service," he said without hesitating. "The offshore oil business down there is going to take off. They'll need cargo planes, a lot of them. I thought I was going to have to spend a year over here raising the dough. But after this little junket, I might have enough to head home early."

He was facing me in the cockpit, his profile illuminated by the lights of the instrument panel. A scar ran down the bridge of his nose and across his right cheek; the nose, slightly off center, had been broken. It surprised me that I hadn't noticed it before.

I went back to the rear of the plane and stretched out on a blanket. Sara and May had already done the same. I let the steady pounding of the engines lull me to sleep. Two hours later I was awakened when the plane shuddered; Lawrence had lowered the landing gears. As I slept, we had crossed the bulge of Libya, flown over the Gulf of Sidra and made a wide arcing turn to the north at Tripoli. We were now approaching Tunis. The lights of the city gave the sky a white glow.

"What should we expect to run into down there?" May asked.

I told him it was a French colony, just like Morocco and Algeria. The French had had a heavy garrison in Tunis ever since the war ended; there were bound to be gendarmes and customs agents. We were going to have to answer some questions; and the always officious French—I'd seen them at work—could be difficult on that score.

"If there's something I ought to know, now's a real good time to cut me in," Lawrence said. He glanced back at us. "I don't mind driving a flying hearse. But if you folks got something else in those boxes, you better tell me now. I don't like last minute surprises, especially when my ass is on the line."

May told him not to worry.

Lawrence smiled. "Why did I keep telling myself that's what you were going to say?"

He got on the radio and, after giving the serial numbers of his plane and point of origin, requested permission to land. He had to repeat the message twice before a voice with a French accent told him that he was cleared to make his approach.

We made a pass over the airport and flew out across the bay, so that Lawrence could land into the wind. We were on the ground within minutes, the plane lurching on the scoured runway as Lawrence dropped his flaps and feathered the engines. He taxied over to a low-slung hangar at the far end of the field. Some military planes with French markings were parked there in a tight cluster.

When we rolled to a stop, a jeep drove over to meet us. Two men in uniform got out and walked up to the starboard wing. They wore kepis and white gloves.

"Those guys look serious," Lawrence said, taking off his headphones.

Sara went out first followed by May. The gendarmes didn't waste any time getting down to business; they wanted to know where we were from and what we were carrying. They also wanted to see our passports. One of them spoke English, badly.

While we were answering their questions, another jeep pulled up with four soldiers, military police. They checked the plane from tail to nose and asked about the caskets. Sara said they contained the bodies of two Americans killed in the fighting in Palestine. After a short conference, they marched us to a square, white-washed building set back from the runway. We were taken inside and told to sit on a bench. Eventually another soldier, an officer, arrived. Tall enough to remind me of De Gaulle, he wore a freshly starched khaki shirt and a Sam Browne belt. He motioned us into his office and after his men carried in the caskets, Sara repeated her story. Adding one embellishment, she started to cry softly when she mentioned that the dead man was her brother.

Nice job, Sara honey, I thought. You scored some points with that one.

"Is this really necessary," May said, feigning irritation. "We're American citizens after all. This is very hard for her. I wouldn't want to have to call our embassy."

The officer was all apologies, but he politely insisted that an inspection of the two caskets was *une necessité*. Arms smuggling had become a serious affair with the war on in the Holy Land.

171

They were under strict orders to look for guns as well as drugs and other contraband.

Sara asked to leave the room and the officer quickly obliged.

"I guess I'll go with her if nobody minds," Lawrence said. "I don't have the stomach for this."

He followed Sara into the hallway.

May and I unfastened the lid of the casket that contained the body. The faint odor of natron was still noticeable.

We pulled back the top fold of the shroud. The officer stared impassively at the withered face.

"He was in the desert for several months before they found him," May said. "The body was badly disfigured."

The officer was trying to hold a steady expression.

"Forgive me," he said at last. "It was my duty. My condolences to the lady."

He asked about the other box.

"Her brother had a friend who was also killed," I said. "We promised his mother we'd bring the remains back for burial. Would you like to take a look?"

"That won't be necessary."

"Then we can go?"

"If your papers are in order, of course."

We closed the casket. Trying not to let him see how relieved I was, I asked whether any passenger ships were in port. The officer, now very affable, wasn't sure. When May asked if he could suggest a hotel, we had better luck. A small hotel was near the airport, the Hotel Tunis.

An hour later after climbing steep, picturesque streets that offered magnificent views of the bay, we arrived at the hotel in a military jeep. The small pink building was built in the Moorish style with balconies and a veranda that overlooked a public square old enough to date to the crusades.

Lawrence, who had come with us, didn't plan to stay. He wanted to check his plane before he turned in. He would sleep on board with the caskets, which had been returned after the interview.

May said he would wire his bank in Chicago for some money first thing in the morning and settle accounts.

"You were magnificent," he said, shaking the pilot's hand. "We all owe you a big debt of thanks. You earned every penny."

"It was a pleasure doing business with you," Lawrence said. "Running into you folks was the best thing that's happened to me since my old man died."

Before leaving, he paused by the door.

"There aren't many people who'd go to all this trouble to bury a brother," he said to Sara. "He must have been some guy."

"He was," Sara said, watching him carefully. She wasn't sure if he was being ironic.

Lawrence stood there a moment, staring at her. Then he nodded and said, "I guess I'll see you in the morning."

CHAPTER 27

WE GOT THE BAD NEWS EARLY. Lawrence and May went out to the harbor, which was locked like a mountain pool between a rim of green hills, a place the French called La Goulette, and learned there weren't any ships taking passengers. Three or four merchantmen and a couple of rusty oilers out of Sicily were tied up at the wharves. But none of them were going anywhere soon—fallout from the war in Palestine. Ship traffic in the Mediterranean had been bottled up for weeks. British destroyers were patrolling the North African coast like wolf packs, and several merchantmen suspected of running arms to Israel had recently been fired on. Few captains were willing to risk their vessels on such troubled waters.

May suggested that we fly to another port, possibly Algiers. But there was no guarantee we'd make out any better.

A thought suddenly occurred to me. "What if Lawrence flew us to the States? He wants to go back anyway to start a charter service. So why not? He's taken us this far already."

"Hell yes," May said, jumping on the idea at once. He turned to Lawrence. "What do you say?"

"Slow it down, boys," the pilot said. "My plane's due for an annual."

"Would you do it for five thousand?"

Lawrence didn't hesitate. "I'd sure give it a try."

"When can we leave?"

May was driving hard.

"Two, maybe three days. At the least I'll need a compression check on the engines and new plugs."

"Have it done as fast as you can," May said.

"You better know this isn't going to be a breeze," Lawrence said. "I already told you what it's like to cross the South Atlantic. You're over the water a long time."

"You did it before, didn't you?" May asked.

"That was with a co-pilot. And we'll be bucking a headwind."

"Make whatever arrangements you have to," May said. "Take as much time as you need. We'll leave as soon as you say you're ready."

We took off three days later—a Sunday morning when the sky was like a mirror for the sea—and headed west to Casablanca. Lawrence's plan was to reverse the route he had taken on the way over; we'd fly down the western coast of Africa as far as Accra and then make for Ascension Island, a block of volcanic rock nearly midway between the African Coast and the bulge of South America. The jump to Natal, Brazil, would be the longest—1,400 miles he'd told us earlier. Mississippi was our final destination. Lawrence knew of an abandoned Army airfield there; we could land without worrying about a customs check.

The weather was good all the way to the Gold Coast. We spent a couple of days in Accra making our final preparations at a rundown airfield that had seen heavy duty during the war. The place was in shambles—piles of engine parts and other scrap rusting in the sunlight along the runway, beggars, roaming packs of dogs. We stayed close to the plane every minute we were there.

It was raining when we left for Ascension Island, but the sky cleared and we made the 800 mile jump in less than four hours. The roughest part of the trip home occurred when we were landing. Lawrence had to fly through a flock of birds that rose up from a field and crossed our path; the plane took a beating as the birds smashed against the engine cowlings and windshield.

"They called them 'wideawakes' during the war," Lawrence told us later. "It's some kind of tern and let me tell you, they kept you plenty awake during landings and takeoffs. The guys liked to joke they brought down more planes than the Germans."

After resting in a bug-ridden hotel run by a British telegraph company, we refueled and took off for Brazil the next morning. The plane performed wonderfully and three days later, after another layover at Natal on the Brazilian coast, we started the last leg, reaching Caracas and the Caribbean and then island hopping from Port au Prince to Havana. The Gulf of Mexico was the final hurdle.

Lawrence flew low enough to see the schools of fish moving in the Gulf Stream: sleek torpedo shapes silhouetted in blue water, flying fish by the thousands, and the unmistakable dorsal fins that knifed above the waves like scythes. There were a lot of sharks down there, swimming near the surface. We had an inflatable life raft big enough for four on board with food and water to last a week. The sharks made me think dark thoughts about what could happen if something went wrong.

Lawrence guessed what was on my mind. "Don't worry, old buddy. These Wright engines never let you down."

"Then I guess this is a hypothetical question," May said, "but what would we do if the impossible happened and one of them quit?"

"We'd have to make it in on one engine," Lawrence said. "She'd fly like a brick truck, but she'd stay up."

Three hours later we saw the first fishing boasts, shrimp trawlers with v-shaped booms for dragging nets. White boats churning white wakes. It wasn't much longer before we crossed the coast—Lawrence skimmed the water on the way in to avoid any radar that might have been aimed our way—and found the deserted military airstrip near Gulfport. The Army had used the field for training B-24 crews during the war; Lawrence had learned how to fly there. Three or four satellite fields just like it were scattered through southern Mississippi.

We made a pass, banked and came around again. The runway, carved into the green heart of a pine forest, was in bad shape— pitted, broken, and choked with weeds. It was a rough landing.

"I thought we'd blow a tire for sure," Lawrence said, switching off the power.

I got out of the plane and looked around. The airfield was like a ghost town; barracks with smashed windows and missing doors flanked the runway. The place was apparently still used by local pilots; two small single-engine planes were parked in front of a broken-down hangar. They looked like crop dusters.

It wasn't the kind of homecoming I'd always expected. Out of the country for over two years, I had planned to come back to a cushy writing job with the Associated Press or on one of the good papers in New York. Instead, I was mixed up in something that was as much a mystery to me now as it had been in the Holy Land.

I was also with a woman I loved. My life was starting over; another cycle had begun and the thought of what that meant, with all of its anxiety and anticipation, sobered me as I stood stretching my stiff back in the warm Mississippi sunshine.

Except for the French officer in Tunis and an official May had bought off for $200 in Port au Prince, we hadn't had any trouble with customs agents. By landing in the backwoods of Mississippi 20 miles from Gulfport, we'd managed to slip across the border through the backdoor. Lawrence had done everything we had hoped for and a good deal more. From here on out, we were on our own.

After making some plans, May and I hitchhiked into Gulfport. We bought a used panel truck for the trip north, a rusty, heavily dented Chevrolet with over 70,000 miles on the odometer. A gap-toothed salesman wearing suspenders made the deal as he swigged on a bottle of Coke. May didn't even bother to haggle. He telephoned his Chicago bank from a post office and had some money wired down to one of the local banks. A few hours later, we drove back out to the airfield on country roads dusty with red clay.

We loaded the caskets onto the truck. May settled up with Lawrence, handing him a cashier's check for $5,000.

"You're sure about this," the pilot said, swallowing hard as he held the check. "You could have bought two planes for a whole lot less money."

I could tell something was on Lawrence's mind, and when we shook hands and got ready to leave, he finally brought it out into the open. He wanted to know—as he had from the start—what we were carrying.

"After all this, I'd just like to find out what the score is."

"You still don't believe us," May said, smiling.

"I believe you got a body in that box. But if it's somebody's dead brother, I'll give you back your money no questions asked."

He promised he'd keep the secret—whatever it was—and I believed him. I wanted to set him straight. So did May and Sara. But it was out of the question.

We stood there in an uneasy silence. Lawrence finally shrugged and said, "Have it your way. What I don't know won't hurt me, right?"

What we know could hurt us a great deal, I thought.

For the first time since we had left the Middle East, the vague, yet palpable sense of foreboding had returned. I had hoped it would be different once we got back home, but the feeling was still there.

May promised to stay in touch. He wanted to know how the charter business turned out. "If you need any help with that, just call me," he said. "I'll be happy to give you a line of credit." He wrote down his address and telephone number in Chicago.

"Where can we find you?" Sara asked. She hugged him.

"Biloxi!" Lawrence said, grinning. "Just call the airport."

We left him standing by the plane, wearing his torn flying jacket. He took off his sunglasses and waved. I didn't think I'd ever see him again.

Two days later, we pulled into Chicago. We came in from the southwest just as the tall buildings along the lakefront caught the evening sunlight, thrusting up out of the flatlands like a forest of steel and stone.

The outlying fringe of the city looked weatherbeaten and run down. After passing a succession of factories and tenements, we arrived in the Loop just in time for rush hour. May handled the snarled traffic with the skill of a native, maneuvering around tracks of the El and onto Lake Shore Drive. We headed south past the switching yards of the Illinois Central. The city's dramatic skyline was behind us now, perched at the sandy edge of Lake Michigan. The waves curled against the seawall that paralleled the highway; white sails glided back and forth far out on the water.

May lived in Hyde Park not far from the University of Chicago. "You might call the place a feed-lot for intellectuals," he joked, turning off on an exit ramp.

I remembered reading that the first atomic chain reaction had been set off under some bleachers at the university's athletic field. The risky experiment had almost run out of control.

Reminding May of this, I said, "How does it feel knowing you and seven million other people came within a few seconds of going up in a mushroom cloud?"

May smiled and said, "I always thought eggheads were dull fellows. I've changed my mind since then."

We passed rows of handsome brownstones that lined the quiet residential streets; May's townhouse was at the end of a private cul-de-sac. After pulling into the driveway, he stopped and sat there, staring at the home.

"There were times the last few weeks when I didn't think I'd get back here in one piece," he said. "When I saw the lake, it was like crossing a finish line."

The house, as deep as it was tall, was fronted by trees and a lush row of manicured shrubbery that lined the walkway. It had a magnificent arched doorway and a turret made of rose-colored granite.

We drove around back and parked the truck in a basement garage. May and I carried the caskets upstairs to his library. As soon as we were inside, I could see why he needed all the room: the place was a museum. Art objects—carvings, busts, bronzes—were displayed in rooms filled with beautifully carved furniture from the Middle East. Oriental tapestries of ruby and gold weave hung on the walls. I wasn't a good judge of such things, but I thought I recognized a few paintings I'd seen in art books.

May put the three scrolls—the two from Bethlehem and the copper scroll we had found in Qumran—in a wall safe. Then he opened up a liquor cabinet and took out a bottle of scotch.

His first toast was to me.

"I'll admit I didn't want to have anything to do with you when we first met," he said, his thick beard framing a smile. "But we could never have done this without your help."

He mentioned my writing; we hadn't discussed that since Qumran. The plan was still to hold off releasing anything until Sara had completed a thorough analysis of the remains. She wanted to get to work on that as soon as the arrangements could be made. She had a friend she wanted to call, a former professor of hers she had mentioned earlier who worked at the Oriental Institute. His name was Jerome Edwards.

Part of the University of Chicago, the Institute conducted field operations throughout the Middle East, she explained. An Egyptologist who also had training in pathology, Edwards specialized in funerary rituals and had worked on a number of mummies from the Egyptian Royal House. He had published widely on techniques for preserving exhumed mummies; that had become a serious problem for museums, Sara said. Time had proven that the bodies didn't hold up well unless storage conditions were carefully controlled; many of them were in varying stages of decay.

"His work on Ram-menekh's mummy set new standards for preservation," she said. "He really is the best there is in the field."

Ram-menekh, she told us, was a high priest who served the god Chen in the fourth century B.C. On display for over 30 years at the institute's museum, his mummy had deteriorated until Edwards took charge of the remains.

Sara hoped the professor would help her examine the body in the shroud.

"Can he be trusted?" May asked.

"I'm sure of it. I'll call him tomorrow. I think he's still in the country. He spends most of his winters in Egypt."

The best approach, she thought, would be to do the work at the institute, which had several well-equipped laboratories. School was in summer recess, so we weren't likely to attract much attention, especially if we came at night.

The major steps involved opening the shroud without damaging the corpse and doing an autopsy.

"It won't be easy with a body this old," she said. "There's always the chance something could go wrong. A poorly preserved mummy can crumble like dust as soon as it's handled. If that tomb hadn't been so well sealed, we'd have a much harder time."

"What are we going to do about the copper scroll?" I asked. I recalled that Professor Parker had said we'd need a good metallurgist to finish opening it. And even then there weren't any guarantees.

Sara thought someone in the university's engineering school might be able to help. "I'll have to check on that."

Some big questions still needed to be addressed: was the Teacher of Righteousness, the mysterious prophet so tantalizingly described in the scroll, the same man whose body we had brought back from the Holy Land? Who was he and what had happened to him? Why was he killed, and when?

The fragile piece of copper and the brittle parchment that May had bought in Bethlehem, the one Sara called the "Manual of Discipline," were also our best bet at filling in the blanks about the elusive desert sect of Qumran, the Essenes. I wanted to open those scrolls as much as I wanted to get to work on the body.

All of us were worn out after the long drive from Mississippi. But Sara wanted to examine the remains before we turned in. May helped her open the casket. The head hadn't been damaged, and there was nothing to indicate that the rest of the body had suffered any harm during the trip.

"How are we going to explain this to your friend at the Oriental Institute?" I asked Sara, staring at the grotesque face. "What do we tell him?"

"We tell him the truth, that we don't know what we have here and need his help," May said.

CHAPTER 28

WE DROVE to the Oriental Institute at nine o'clock the following evening. Sara had called Professor Edwards earlier in the day; she told him that she had just returned from a dig in the Holy Land and had found something that she wanted to discuss with him in private. Edwards, happy to hear from his former student, was immediately interested. At Sara's suggestion, they had agreed to meet at night when other faculty members and the few graduate students attending summer classes had left.

"Are you ready for this?" May asked after we had loaded the caskets in the back of the truck.

Sara smiled and said, "It's almost a relief to get started."

The institute was across the street from one of the University of Chicago's main quadrangles, a short drive from May's house. It was a three-story, gray-stone building with casement windows and a large stone frieze carved with Egyptian hieroglyphic figures over the main entrance.

We pulled around to the back, where a ramp led to a door set into an ivy-covered wall. A light burned next to the door, which was unlocked. Sara went inside alone and a few minutes later returned with a man over six feet tall, wearing a short-sleeved shirt and an old pair of paint-splattered trousers; a pair of reading glasses dangled from a cord around his neck. His boyish face and crewcut made him look younger than his age, which was in the late fifties.

When Edwards saw me standing by the truck with May, he looked momentarily caught off guard, but the introductions were friendly enough.

"Let me help you with that," he volunteered when May opened the rear door and started to slide out the casket.

We climbed a short flight of steps. May and Edwards had the casket. Sara helped me carry the smaller box that contained the skeleton; the scrolls were in a briefcase.

I looked down the hallway.

"My god, what's that," I said with a start.

Hidden in shadows, a figure in stone—half animal, half man—covered an entire wall.

"The Assyrian winged bull," Edwards said. He was a little winded. "It once guarded the palace of King Sargon in Khorsabad."

"You must have had a hell of a job getting it here," I said in amazement.

"We did. It weighs 40 tons."

The first floor of the institute served as a museum with connecting galleries devoted to the antiquities of Egypt, Persia and Mesopotamia. Classrooms were located on the second floor, the offices and laboratories on the third.

"You're sure we're alone here tonight?" May asked as we ascended the stairway.

Edwards nodded. "Most of the faculty is out of the country on digs. We're quite alone." He looked at Sara. "All this insistence on privacy... my curiosity has had the better of me ever since you called this morning."

Reaching his office, we put down the caskets and locked the door. The windows of the room overlooked a courtyard; the walls were lined with bookcases. An oscillating fan perched on one of the shelves provided a breeze.

"They're too light for pottery," Edwards said with a puzzled smile, studying the cases. He sat down at his desk and folded his hands. "What kind of surprise do you have for me, Sara?"

"We've found a body that looks partially mummified. It was buried near the shore of the Dead Sea in the Trans-Jordan. We've just returned from there."

"The smaller box contains a skeleton from the same location," May said.

"How old?" All business now, Edwards spoke almost brusquely.

"Perhaps 2,000 years," Sara said. "At least that's what the evidence suggests."

"From Palestine? I can't believe it." He looked skeptical.

Sara began to explain. Even in abbreviated form, her story had a marked effect on Edwards. At its conclusion, he had shed most of his professional reserve.

"Parchments in ancient Hebrew," he said slowly. "A corpse, which you say is well preserved.... I've never heard of such discoveries coming out of the Holy Land."

He wanted to know as much as she could tell him about the body and the tomb.

Sara described the shroud and the tightly sealed sarcophagus. She also mentioned the X-ray that had been taken in Jerusalem.

"What did Parker have to say about all this?" Edwards asked.

He knew the professor well. They had been colleagues at the institute before Parker had left for Jerusalem to take charge of the American School of Oriental Research.

Sara said that Parker thought, as she did, that the body might have been mummified. She mentioned that the sarcophagus had been filled with blocks of natron.

"That hardly sounds possible," Edwards said.

"We were there," May said. "We saw it."

"But the classical Egyptian embalming techniques were rarely used in Palestine. Even during the Roman occupation."

The Romans, he said, were familiar with these burial methods and sometimes practiced them. Edwards mentioned other forms of mummification, a word he broadly used to mean any natural or artificial process to preserve a body.

"The Incas wrapped their dead kings in linen bundles called 'fardos' and sealed them in mountain caves. The Aleuts and Alaskans also had mummies. So did the Indian tribes of the American southwest. There was no evisceration or embalming; the bodies were simply left to dry in the sun."

Then there were the so-called "bog bodies" of Denmark, he went on. These perfectly preserved corpses, which had been found when several deep marshes were drained, dated to the late Bronze Age.

"Some of them had ropes tied around their necks," he said. "They were apparently sacrifice victims."

He started to enlarge on the subject when May interrupted him.

"Will you help us examine the remains?"

"I would have used force to stop you if you had tried to leave," Edwards said, smiling. "When would you like to begin?"

"What about right now."

May asked the professor for his word that what he saw would remain a secret.

"You have it, of course," Edwards said testily. His integrity had been called in question and he didn't like it.

"I don't know you, Doctor," May said, sensing what had happened. "We wouldn't be here tonight if it wasn't for Sara. She trusts you, so that's good enough for me. If I upset you, I apologize. Once you see what we have here, you'll understand why I had to say what I did."

Edwards looked unsure of himself. He finally said, "Let me show you where I spend my days—and nights."

His office opened onto a laboratory equipped with two work tables with metal tops. The walls were lined with specimen cases, cabinets, and book shelves. A sink was built into a corner. A bench was fitted with a microscope and other instruments. There were also an X-ray machine and a camera mounted on a tripod. Two stainless steel fans circulated the air.

We placed the casket on one of the tables and removed the lid. Before doing anything else, Edwards took several full-length photographs of the burial shroud.

"The linen is in superb condition," he noted. He looked surprised as he gently ran his fingers over the cloth. "You were right about the tomb and sarcophagus. They were incredibly well sealed."

The stains on the shroud puzzled him.

Sara explained that the doctor who had taken the X-ray in Jerusalem thought they might be blood marks.

Edwards hadn't expected anything like that and it momentarily threw him. He may have had his first glimmer of an idea that this wasn't going to be just another mummy.

"Were there any wounds?"

"Nothing immediately apparent. The right wrist was broken. So was a finger on the right hand."

Edwards wanted to take another X-ray before going further.

With Sara's help, he adjusted the machine and positioned the lense so that it was directly over the corpse. He shot several pictures.

Developing the film took half an hour, but the results were worth the wait. Edwards explained what showed up like a surgeon preparing for an operation: the body was that of a male, probably no older than forty or younger than twenty; the teeth were in good condition; the brain, still intact, was roughly one-third its original size. The cerebral hemispheres showed clearly; they were lying in the base of the skull.

Edwards said, "If this body had been mummified in the Egyptian way, the brain would have been removed by the embalmers, usually through a hole punched into the base of the skull. They used a special instrument with a hook at the end." He continued studying the film. "There's nothing on the X-ray to suggest the skull was trepanned."

The presence of the brain surprised May. He thought, as I did, that it would have decomposed long ago.

"Brain tissue usually retains its general shape," Edwards said. "It simply shrinks."

The X-ray revealed a strange mass just to the right of the thorax. It was too large for a heart. Edwards thought that over time the heart and liver may have adhered.

"This corpse desiccated naturally," he said. "There's no evidence of evisceration or even embalming although the natron you mentioned certainly would have served as a preservative."

The fracture in the right wrist showed on the films as did the broken finger on the same hand. The knee joint of the right leg also suggested an injury.

"From the looks of this, he may have broken his leg shortly before he died," Edwards said. "Or it might have happened during the handling of the remains. Who can tell?"

There was evidence that the sixth rib on the left side had been fractured.

By then my shirt was soaked through. We had just begun and the tension was already heavy in the room, which smelled faintly of formaldehyde.

Edwards held another X-ray up to an illuminated display panel attached to the wall.

"This is curious," he said. "The heel bones are broken."

The damage showed in sharp detail on the film. The calcineus of each foot was split open.

The only sound in the room now was from the fans. Edwards continued to pore over the X-ray. He looked at us and said, "Was this man crucified?"

"We're not sure," Sara said. "That's one of the things we're trying to find out."

"The X-rays don't indicate any conclusive cause of death," Edwards said. "But the stains on the shroud at the feet and hands, the damage to the wrist and heel bones. I might be wrong, but it all seems to suggest death by... crucifixion."

He took more photographs before we opened the shroud.

Edwards winced when the corner of the cloth was lifted. "I never dreamed...."

I took a long look at the face, studying the features that were already fixed in my memory. The jaw was strong, the cheekbones prominent. The temples were hollowed; the chin was high and the eyebrows jutted out over the forehead. The mouth was pressed shut.

The total effect was powerful enough; but the lidded, almond-shaped eye sockets still made the greatest impact on me. They dominated the face.

"The preservation here is extraordinary."

"It looks as if it's changed color," May said.

I saw it, too. The skin appeared to have darkened slightly.

"Exposure to the air might account for that," Edwards said. "It frequently happens with mummies."

The hair that remained on the skull was thicker at the sides and temples and fell in a short lock behind the head. I mentioned this to Sara. The braid reminded me of a pigtail.

"That was a characteristic hair style for Jewish males."

The black hair had turned powdery yellow near the crown.

Edwards thought that might have been caused by burial perfumes. "The chemical," he said, "may have acted like a dye."

The neck had withered to the point that it was no thicker than the spinal column. The thin, slightly hooked nose, almost classically Roman in shape, was flattened at the tip, probably from the weight of the burial wrappings.

"There's been trauma to the face," Edwards said.

The right cheekbone looked broken; the face was swollen there and discolored. The deep gash plunged from the scalp to the eyes.

The forked beard and mustache were ragged in appearance. The facial hair, Edwards said, had probably continued growing after death, if only briefly.

The thorn that protruded through the upper lid of the right eye socket had always been one of the most ghastly components of the face. The part of the puzzle that had led Parker to think the unthinkable about the dead man's identity. If Edwards had made the same association, he didn't show it. My guess was that the professor wasn't saying everything on his mind.

When he examined the thorn with a magnifying lens, he said only that it had been driven through the temporal bone of the skull.

That would have taken a hell of a lot of pounding, I thought.

Edwards suggested making an incision in the eyelid to examine the socket.

"You don't expect the eyes to be intact," May said.

"It's possible. The eyes are frequently overlooked. The assumption is they couldn't possibly survive. But it often happens; the globe simply contracts."

With May's approval, he made a narrow opening in the left eyelid with a scalpel. He adjusted the movable fluorescent lamp attached to the worktable so that he could see better. Something translucent glinted deep in the socket, he said.

"It's what I thought. The globe has collapsed." He shined a penlight into the socket. "The retina's gone, but you can still make out part of the cornea."

"What about the other eye?" May asked.

Edwards was reluctant to try. He thought the thorn would present problems.

Sara asked whether he could remove it.

"Not without cutting, I'm afraid. It might be best to let that go for a while."

The next step was to remove the rest of the shroud and wrappings. Using surgical scissors, Edwards and Sara cut away the linen strips that criss-crossed the shroud; the bindings consisted of finely woven linen. The upper end of the shroud rolled back easily.

"That's a break," Edwards said. "I was worried the cloth may have stuck to the body."

The shrouds of many Egyptian mummies were far more difficult to handle, he said. The unguents and resins poured over the corpse during embalming often carbonized.

Sara folded the shroud back an inch at a time until the upper part of the chest and arms were exposed. The thin arms, crossed at the pectorals, were badly shriveled. The skin had the same black-brown tint as the face.

"Look at the wrists," May said.

The wrist of each hand had a dark depression—the telltale mark of a wound.

Edwards probed one of them with a scalpel.

"There's been some closing, but the wound appears clean enough. It passes through the opening in the wrist bones." He put down the scalpel. "Whoever made these wounds knew something about anatomy. That small opening in the wrist, it's called the space of Destot. It had to be searched for—probably by a skilled executioner. They would have driven the nail there instead of into the palm."

"Why's that?" May asked.

"It would have torn loose under the weight of the body," Edwards said. "The best place to drive a nail would be into the wrist, between the bones where it wouldn't pull away from the flesh. Look here." He pointed to the right hand. "You can even see how the thumb is curled back. The median nerve was nicked by the nail. I don't think there's any question now—this man was crucified."

189

CHAPTER 29

"THERE'S SOMETHING I still don't understand," Edwards said. "How did you find the body? What led you to the grave?"

Sara had deliberately passed over that part of the story. She looked at May.

"I think we should tell him."

May agreed and Sara described the copper scroll, explaining where we had found it and how the scroll had provided directions to the tomb in the Qumran cemetery. She laid the tarnished pieces of copper on the table. I watched the trace of astonishment form at Edwards' mouth corners.

"It names someone called the Teacher of Righteousness. We only know that he must have been recognized as a holy man or prophet."

"And you have no idea who this man was, this teacher as you call him?"

Edwards asked the question as he threw himself into an examination of the fragments of copper.

May's answer, delivered matter-of-factly and without hesitation, made him look up.

"For a while there back in Jerusalem, Parker wondered if it couldn't be Jesus of Nazareth. I'm starting to wonder if he wasn't on to something."

An awkward silence followed. We hadn't spent much time discussing Parker's theory. In all the excitement of leaving the Holy Land and returning to the States, we'd had too much else on our minds. Now that it had been brought out into the open again, the idea sounded even more implausible to me than it had in Jerusalem. May's comment had surprised all of us.

"That's a poor joke," Edwards said finally. His expression made it clear he didn't believe Parker would have suggested anything so absurd.

"It was just a thought he had," Sara said. "He admitted the evidence was purely circumstantial. There's the crucified body and the thorn. And the fact the scroll says the Teacher was put to death by a Wicked Priest, who isn't named. He wondered if that might have been a veiled reference to one of the Pharisees."

"Parker made his comment without really seeing all of this," May said. There was a hard, aggressive edge to his voice. "If he were here right now, I'll bet he'd be even more willing to believe this might be the body of Christ."

"You're not serious," Sara said.

"I'm damned serious. You've got the wounds in the wrists and feet, not to mention that thorn through the eye. And we already know the body's old enough."

"That's hardly enough proof to suggest that these are the remains of Jesus of Nazareth," Edwards said impatiently.

"Crucifixion was a common form of execution," Sara said, staring at May. "What happened to Christ probably happened to hundreds, thousands of others. Maybe some of them died with a crown of thorns on their heads. Professor Parker said he regretted even raising the idea."

"We're forgetting what we came here for," I said. "This isn't helping anything."

May wasn't ready to drop the subject.

"Do you think Christ rose from the dead?" he asked Edwards.

"Of course not. But I'm an archeologist, not a theologian."

"Then why not assume his body might still be buried somewhere?"

"This whole discussion is preposterous," Edwards snapped.

"It may be, but I don't hear anyone coming up with any better ideas," May said.

When Edwards objected again, Sara tried to defuse the argument, which was threatening to get out of hand.

"I don't believe this is Christ any more than you do," she told the professor. "The only thing we can say with certainty is that we've got the body of someone who was crucified. Maybe he was a religious leader or a self-proclaimed prophet, but we don't know that. We don't know who he is, or was. We hoped you could help us with that question. That's why we came here tonight."

May for the moment had apparently decided to go along in silence.

Edwards stared at both of them. "All right," he said slowly. "Why don't we take it from the beginning again."

A little later Sara rolled back more of the shroud.

An angular wound in the left side extended from the top of the ribcage almost down to the pelvis.

In spite of myself, I remembered the Bible verses about the soldier who broke the legs of two men, but cut open the side of the third.

May looked as if he had half expected it.

"I guess this is just some more circumstantial evidence," he said sarcastically.

"How many more times do I have to say it," Sara said angrily. "Nail marks, even a wound in the side. They wouldn't have been out of the ordinary during a Roman crucifixion."

"Could a spear have caused that?" May asked.

"A spear, possibly a knife," Edwards said. "That's precisely the spot where an embalmer would have made his incision in the abdomen."

"But it might also be where a soldier jammed a lance into his side," May said.

"That still doesn't prove a thing," Edwards said.

"We're not going to get anywhere," I said in frustration. "Let's stop this."

May was in no mood to back off, but he wasn't willing to push Sara or Edwards too far. "All right," he said finally. "Have it your own way. Maybe I was out of line."

The body, we knew from the X-rays, hadn't been eviscerated. Using a lancet, Edwards felt resistance inside the wound.

"That might be part of the liver."

He asked whether we wanted to begin the autopsy. The procedure would require making several incisions in the chest cavity.

May asked about the chances of damage.

"The chest will be opened," Edwards said, explaining what would happen. "When it's sutured, it should look almost as it does now. I've done operations like this maybe a dozen times, but never on a body in such excellent condition. The risks, I would say, are minimal."

May wanted to know Sara's opinion. She told him she thought an autopsy was a necessity; a complete analysis of the corpse required it.

"I don't like the idea of this any more than you do," she said. "But I think we should go ahead."

The final decision was May's. I think he may have been bothered by a concern he didn't mention—the overtones of desecration in what we were doing.

"Okay," he said. "Let's get started."

The remainder of the shroud was removed. The legs were badly emaciated. The heel bones, as the X-rays indicated, bore the imprint of wounds. The scrotum had almost disappeared.

"It looks as if a single nail were used," Edwards said. "The feet must have been crossed, one over the other. My guess is the executioner probably drove the nail between the metatarsal bones."

The man, as we already knew, had been fairly tall—just under five feet nine, according to Edwards' measurements. He would have been a few inches taller in life; the body had contracted slightly during its long centuries in the ground. The chest was full, the shoulders square and well rounded. Despite the mutilations, an impressive looking man.

And someone, we all realized, who had died an undeniably horrible death.

The pressure on the wrists could not have been relieved without paying the price of another jolt of excruciating pain in the feet. Pinned there like an insect on a board, he would have rocked up and down until the end came, probably by asphyxiation. I wondered how long it had taken—several hours, an entire afternoon?

Edwards began the autopsy by cutting open the thorax with an electric saw with a circular blade. The work was easily done—just as he had predicted. The opening in the chest wall showed that most of the internal organs were intact, but greatly reduced in size.

The lungs, which had collapsed, were a powdery gray; the heart, by contrast, resembled a piece of dried leather. The liver and bladder, both considerably shriveled, were also easily identifiable.

May and Sara decided against having the skull opened—at least for the time being. More photographs were taken. All that remained was for Edwards to sew up the chest. The incision was barely visible when he finished—a thin, slightly crooked line running down the center of the chest and crossing the shoulders in a T.

The time was just past four in the morning.

Sara made the final discovery. She noticed them first on the shoulders—small, pitted imprints that resembled scars. Almost invisible against the withered, darkened skin, they also covered the thighs and legs. She thought they were the marks of a scourging.

CHAPTER 30

SARA AND Edwards managed to get the body turned over on its side. There was hardly any weight to it, they said. The strange marks also covered the back and legs; every square inch of skin, it seemed, was peppered with small welts.

"What the hell is that?" May said.

"It looks like a perfect example of a Roman flagellation," Sara said. "The whips were made of leather and tipped with metal or pieces of lead. Two men usually did the scourging. Twenty blows could kill."

May brought up the subject again as we stared at the corpse.

"If this isn't Christ, you've got to admit there are some pretty strong similarities..."

"That's not good enough," Sara said sharply.

"Similarities don't mean a thing. When the Romans condemned someone to death, he was often scourged first. All we know is that this man was apparently executed in the Roman fashion."

Edwards leaned against the laboratory table. He looked exhausted.

"It may be you won't learn his identity," he said. "I'd frankly say the odds of that are a longshot at best. But even if you never pin it down, you've still made a wonderful discovery. Was he a rebel, one of Bar Kokhba's freedom fighters? Was he an Essene holy man, someone we've never heard of before? The possibilities are endless."

"Unless something turns up in the scrolls, we only have a historic curiosity," Sara said. "That could be all we'll ever have."

She said she'd make some calls later to the university to see if she could find a metallurgist. We all agreed we had to get that copper scroll opened—even at the risk of damaging it in the process. She also wanted to keep trying to unravel the scroll from Bethlehem, the one that seemed to describe a monastic community like the Essenes.

195

"There might be a clue, anything," Sara said. "A couple of words...a phrase. We need something concrete."

We still hadn't told Edwards about the skeleton. When Sara finally opened the other casket and showed him the remains, it was almost an anti-climax.

Edwards closely examined the shattered neck. The cuts in the bone were clean and deep. He agreed that they had probably been caused by a sharp instrument that had severed the head.

"Who do you think it is? Do you have any ideas?"

May was watching Sara. I knew what was running through his mind.

"I wish I'd never said anything about that," she said.

"You sound just like Parker," May said irritably. "Go on and tell him. What harm can it do?"

She reluctantly explained her theory about John the Baptist, saying the thought had occurred to her after Professor Parker had made his comment about Christ. The prophet and the messiah, both buried together in a wind-blown cemetery by the Dead Sea; each had paid the same price for their preaching and each had gone to the same resting place.

"I know that sounds absurd," Sara said, finishing.

"It was just something that occurred to me at the moment. I usually try to be more professional than that."

Edwards said, "I've spent nearly thirty years trying to understand ancient history—to make some small sense of it. But right now I'm at a total loss about what to say or think."

Not long afterward, we left his office. Daylight was coming. Edwards helped us wrap the body in the burial shroud and carry the casket downstairs. It was hot and muggy, but I was relieved to be outside again.

We got into the truck. Edwards walked around to the driver's window; his face was haggard, the cheeks stubbled. He stood there a few moments before speaking.

"I hope you'll let me help you," he said. "After what I've seen here, I don't think I could stand not being involved in trying to sort all this out."

Despite his fatigue, there was no mistaking Edwards' excitement. Sara promised to call him soon. We left him standing by the back of the building; he watched us until we turned the corner.

May drove up the deserted streets. Sagging back into the seat, I closed my eyes, grateful it was over.

"What were you trying to do back there," Sara asked May after we went a few blocks. She was still upset.

"Let me ask you something first." He'd been ready for the question. "If this isn't Christ, then who is it?"

"A man who was crucified. That's absolutely all we can say."

"Dammit, he was scourged and crucified and he's got that thorn driven into his head. I'm not a scholar like your friend Edwards, but that sounds a lot like that guy who's mentioned in the Bible."

"How many times do I have to keep saying it—that proves nothing. If you keep jumping to conclusions..."

"Isn't that what Parker did—jump to a conclusion."

"Stop it, both of you," I said wearily. "We've gone over all this."

When we got back to May's townhouse, he put on a pot of coffee. The sun was already up, but we were much too keyed up to think about sleeping.

As we sat there in the kitchen, each of us absorbed by private thoughts, May asked me what religion I'd been raised in.

The question caught me off guard. "Catholic. But I haven't been to mass since I was a kid."

Just saying the words brought the memories streaming back like water from a tap. An elementary school in south Pittsburgh. Mass every morning, confessions on Friday, the obligatory daily religion classes, nuns in black habits with belted rosaries and white headgear that always reminded me of sails. Then sometime in my teens I gradually stopped going to church. Perhaps believing got too difficult or I got too lazy to make the effort. The truth was I hadn't missed it.

May said his parents had been Methodists. He'd tried several religions as a young man, but had quit each of them after a few months.

He looked at me attentively.

197

"Do you believe that Jesus Christ rose from the dead?"

It was the same question he'd put to Professor Edwards. He was starting again. Sara threw up her hands.

"Not if you mean the physical rising of a corpse," I heard myself say.

May hadn't taken his eyes off me. "Then you don't believe in miracles?"

"Not in that one."

"Or that Christ was the son of God?"

"What in hell are you driving at?" I asked.

"I wish I knew," May said. He noticed how Sara and I were watching him. "I'm sorry," he said. "I know I've been off the deep end tonight. After what we've gone through to find that body and bring it back here, I guess I can't keep myself from hoping it's someone important."

Sara started to say something.

"Don't worry, I'm not turning religious on you," May said, stopping her. "I'll watch myself. My problem is that I keep getting hung up on what Parker blurted out in Jerusalem."

"My advice is to forget what was said then," Sara said, letting him know with her eyes how much she was relieved to hear him talk like that. "It was just conjecture. Thinking about it will only make our job more difficult. We can't go into this with any preconceived ideas, no matter how tempting they are."

May smiled and said, "I guess we could all use some sleep."

I couldn't have agreed more. I was glad to see that peace had been restored.

A little later, up in our room, I recalled my exchange with May. It reminded me of my old Baltimore catechism drills as a schoolboy. Hurried questions followed by hurried answers delivered from rote memory before an attentive priest or a nun. I'd been expert at the ritual. It was like rattling off the vital statistics of a baseball or football player; you didn't have to think, just repeat the right words.

Too tired to sleep, I lay close to Sara and thought about the man whose scourged, broken remains we had brought back from the

Holy Land. The gospels were hopelessly sanitized when it came to describing the crucifixion; they didn't go far enough at getting across the butchery of a death like that. I'd seen the results and knew that I'd never forget. I didn't believe for a minute it was Christ's body. The sooner we got over that crazy idea the better. But if that's how he died, nailed to a cross for the sake of an idea, he deserved to be called one of God's children. A son of God.

CHAPTER 31

A FEW DAYS LATER, Sara found a professor of mechanical engineering who agreed to take a look at the copper scroll. Sara and I met him at the university in the afternoon. May promised to stop by later after taking care of some business at his bank. The professor's name was Roger Gilcrest. Despite the heat, he wore a sweater and a loose fitting linen suit, which lay on his slender frame like a sack.

"Since we spoke on the telephone, I've given your problem a great deal of thought," he said, rising from his cluttered desk to greet us.

Sara took the scroll from her briefcase.

"The outer layer of copper was already removed," she said.

"Yes, I can see where it's been cut," Gilcrest said, gently handling the scroll. He had put on a pair of cloth gloves.

Sara described what Professor Parker had done in Jerusalem. Gilcrest shook his head and said, "I had hoped the metal wouldn't be so badly oxidized. It's completely corroded. I'm afraid that will make things more difficult."

The scroll, Sara said, had been written by an ancient Jewish sect roughly 2,000 years ago. She was deliberately vague about the contents or where it had been found. I don't think the professor was even listening as he examined the copper under a magnifying lens.

He eventually gave us the bad news: there was no chance at all of restoring the metal's flexibility so that it could be unwound..

"Can it be cut open without damaging the inscriptions," Sara asked.

"I should say you've already tried that," Gilcrest said.

"Yes, but can you do a better job?"

Gilcrest continued to study the copper in silence.

"There's a possibility," he said finally. "But I should warn you that any value you place on this scroll as a rare artifact will be quite lost. I'm afraid it's the only way."

"We understand that," Sara said. "Will you do it?"

"I hesitate to take the responsibility, but I'll try," he said.

He proposed using a high speed saw to slice the scroll into strips. The work would be done with a precision instrument in his laboratory.

While Sara helped him set up his equipment, May arrived. He asked me to step into the hallway. I knew something was on his mind from the way he'd been pacing.

"A few days ago I wired some money to Professor Parker," he said. "I thought a donation to his school would help show my appreciation for everything he did for us."

I sensed immediately that something was badly wrong.

"This came this morning. It was sent from Jerusalem."

He handed me the telegram. I started reading and looked up at him hopelessly. Parker was dead. Nearly a week earlier, during a skirmish in the Musrara Quarter, he'd been killed on the street by a stray bullet. The telegram had been signed by someone who apparently had taken charge of the school. I didn't recognize the name.

"I've already checked with the State Department," May said. "His body will be shipped to Milwaukee. He's got some family there, a sister."

He was watching me closely. I knew what must have been going through his mind. Another man dead, a very good man. First Benteen and now Parker. And that wasn't even counting the Arabs who had been killed—men that I had watched die up close. You could only think about it, wonder, and then try to let loose fast.

May kept standing there. I knew he had liked Parker. Finally he said, "I didn't want to tell Sara. I didn't think this was a good time for her."

When we went into his laboratory, Gilcrest had already begun working on the scroll. He had mounted the copper cylinder so that it could be moved back and forth on rollers set into wooden grooves. A suction device removed dust from the center of the scroll and its exterior surface. He then had inserted a spindle through the hollow section and tightened it down with dental plaster. Before he began he had coated the scroll with a chemical mixture to try to strengthen the corroded metal. The saw was attached by a clamp to a movable arm. The blade, fixed in place and operated by a hand control, was about the size of a quarter. The copper cut easily with only a minimum of disintegration.

It took him just over two hours to finish the job, which required considerable delicacy as he sawed between the lines of inscriptions. Only a few letters were lost. The strips, each less than an inch in width, were cleaned of dust and dipped in a preservative, a solution of diluted acid.

Sara sat there reading them. They were laid out on a table.

May and I had agreed not to mention Parker. Not for a while at least. I still didn't know when or how I was going to break the news.

"How's it going?" May asked.

"I'm not sure," she said. But her face suggested she meant more than she was letting on.

If Gilcrest was curious about what was written on the copper, he didn't show it. This was strictly an unusual technical challenge for him. A pleasant diversion from his daily work as a metallurgist.

When May offered to pay him for his trouble, he put up a hand and smiled. "I wouldn't think of it," he said. "I only regret we weren't able to treat the oxidation. The metal was just too far gone."

But not far enough gone to offer some remarkable passages. Sara began an excited description as soon as we got into May's car for the trip back to his house. The scroll, at least what she had read so far, mentioned a martyred prophet whose followers were called "the New Covenant." There were also more references to buried treasure.

May asked whether there was any more about the Teacher of Righteousness.

Sara continued examining the copper when we arrived at May's home. The lines that referred to the teacher and his tomb were among those most heavily damaged.

She translated one of the inscriptions as "he and the men of his counsel formed a New Covenant."

May started to say something.

"There's more," Sara went on. "The teacher, and I'm quoting now, 'a suffering, righteous man, was delivered into the hands of his enemies, who have revolted in their pride and vanity against God.'"

Another phrase, she said, described the teacher as "a man of God" who will one day "return in glory to bring his community into light."

I asked whether there were any additional references to the Wicked Priest, the other name prominently mentioned in the scroll.

Sara said, "There's really very little here about these men—who they were, what they taught, what they were trying to accomplish."

As for buried objects, the scroll's composition, she said, had a distinctive pattern—a terse description followed by directions that included the depth of the treasure below the ground.

"There must be hundreds of talents of gold and silver referred to here."

Studying the copper fragments, she said, "Twenty-four talents of silver in the hollow of a tree; another 60 talents in a tomb... it goes on and on. Most of these places would be very close to the monastery."

"Where would they get wealth like that?" I asked.

"The members may have sold their property and turned the money over to the community when they joined," Sara said. "The monastic orders did the same thing during the Middle Ages."

The scroll certainly appeared to be some kind of inventory, which prompted Sara to wonder whether it dated to the Roman invasion of Palestine in 70 A.D. "With the Romans approaching, the Essenes would have wanted to hide and keep a record of their treasure."

She noted that was the period when the monastery was most likely abandoned.

"The body might have been moved out there around this same time," she speculated.

"But why would someone go to all that trouble?" I asked.

Sara said, "The scroll may have been meant for his followers, or at least for a trusted few who may have planned to recover the body later."

The questions continued piling up, among them the mystery of the dead man's identity.

"It might be a good time to call in some other people and get a few more opinions," Sara said. "We've taken this about as far as we can. I could use some help."

"Who do you have in mind?" May asked.

Sara suggested inviting several experts to examine the body and scrolls and offer their theories. She'd been thinking along those lines for some time now. The group would include biblical archeologists as well as theologians—Christian and Jewish scholars alike.

"They should be as interested in getting to the bottom of this as we are," she said.

May had reservations. "If we get too many involved, the cat's out of the bag. There's no way we'll be able to keep them from talking. I don't think it's a good idea to let a lot of people know what we've got here—at least not right now."

I agreed with him. "Why not start with, say, one person and see what happens? We can always call in some other people later if it doesn't work out."

Sara had no objections. She still thought that eventually we'd need to share our finds with the top experts in the field.

"So who gets the call?" May asked.

"There's a good man right here in Chicago," Sara said. "His name is Martin Rothwell. He's a professor of archeology at Loyola, a Jesuit. He's probably the leading American authority on ancient Palestine."

May liked the idea and said that he knew the archbishop of Chicago, Thomas McGuire. Over the years he had made several large contributions to the archdiocese's building fund. The archbishop considered him a friend.

"McGuire's always kidded me about my art collecting," he said. "I think I'll ask him to take a look at what we found. It might change his opinion."

"I thought you wanted to keep down the number of people who know," Sara said.

In spite of what he had said earlier, I got the impression May couldn't resist showing off his prizes.

"McGuire's going to find out sooner or later anyway," he said. He was already smiling in anticipation. "No, I want Tom to see this. I wouldn't miss it."

CHAPTER 32

THE NEXT MORNING Sara called Reverend Rothwell. She invited the Jesuit to visit her that evening for a look at what she described only as a "rare artifact" that she had found on a recent dig in the Holy Land. During their conversation, it turned out that Rothwell was a good friend of Professor Parker's. They also had several other mutual acquaintances. Rothwell said he'd be happy to drive out to Hyde Park to meet her. He promised to be there around seven o'clock. For his part, May telephoned Archbishop McGuire, who also agreed to come.

The rest of the day passed quickly enough. I worked for several hours in the study. Late in the afternoon, Sara came in to show me a folio-sized art book that she'd found lying on a table in May's library.

"What do you think this is all about?" she asked.

The volume had been opened to a color reproduction of Breughel's painting—the Crucifixion and Carrying of the Cross. The scene suggsted it might have been painted by a casual onlooker at Golgotha on that spring morning in A.D.33. Two crosses with thieves fastened to them were depicted on top of a hill; there was a hole in the ground where the third cross would soon be erected. All that was traditional enough, but in the foreground, a group of spectators with picnic baskets had turned out for the show. The holiday atmosphere reminded me of the descriptions of Wild West hangings, where the whole town showed up for the fun.

"I hope he isn't going to start again," she said.

I knew what she meant. We didn't need a repetition of our earlier arguments.

Huxley, Sara said, had written an essay on the painting by the Flemish master. "He said that when you look at a tragedy like this impassively and from the outside, there's nothing uplifting or inspiring about it, nothing to hold you in awe. It isn't noble at all."

206

Later, when the priests came, I remembered the Breughel.

Rothwell arrived punctually by car. He came with McGuire, who had apparently called him for a ride. Rothwell appeared to be in his early fifties; he was much taller and heavier than his companion—almost as big as May. McGuire, a much older man, peered through thick wire-rimmed glasses. Rotund and white-haired, he wore a black, ankle-length cassock with scarlet piping.

"It's been a long time, Tom," May said, greeting the archbishop at the front door and offering his hand.

McGuire smiled. "Too long," he said. "I've been meaning for weeks now to talk to you about my plans for a new church in South Chicago. Not far from here actually, on the edge of Hyde Park." He smiled again. "Once I hook a benefactor, I never let him wiggle loose. I sometimes think that's what Our Lord really meant about being a fisher of men."

The archbishop struck me as an easygoing man who enjoyed seeing people. He appeared on first impression to wear his high office in the church lightly.

May introduced everyone. We shook hands and spent a few minutes talking casually in the living room. McGuire was inter-ested to find out that I was a writer and asked a few polite questions about my work.

"Sara tells me you know Professor Parker," May said to Rothwell.

The priest said, "We had some fine days together about five years ago photographing the mosaics at the Khirbet Mafjir." The ruins, he explained, were near Jericho, the remains of an eighth-century winter palace built by one of the caliphs.

"I hope he's all right." Rothwell went on. "I worry about him over there in the middle of all that fighting. I wish he wouldn't have stayed, but I know him well enough to realize he'd never leave—at least not willingly. A very stubborn man."

I glanced uneasily at May. I still hadn't told Sara that the professor had been killed.

The talk turned to what was happening in Palestine. McGuire praised President Truman's recent diplomatic recognition of Israel. "The Jews are only claiming their ancient homeland—the land promised to them by God himself," he said with undisguised feeling.

"I had planned to visit Jerusalem earlier this summer," Rothwell said. "Unfortunately, that was out of the question."

"Surely the war will end soon and the holy places will be reopened to pilgrims and scholars," McGuire said. "I pray often for that day. It's already overdue."

After discussing Israel awhile longer, Rothwell was ready to settle down to business.

"That discovery you mentioned has intrigued both of us," he said. "Don't leave us hanging here in any more suspense."

Sara began by asking how much he knew about the Essenes.

"They're not exactly a household word," Rothwell said. "The group isn't mentioned anywhere in the New Testament. Except for a few passages in Josephus and Pliny, any reference to them at all is rare."

At May's suggestion, Sara described the sect and what she believed was their extinct community on the western shore of the Dead Sea. She mentioned the three scrolls in our possession, the two in leather May had bought from the dealer in Bethlehem and the copper scroll we had found hidden in the cave near Qumran. One of the leather scrolls, she explained, appeared to be a complete copy of the Book of Kings; the other a kind of rulebook for members of a monastic sect. Her brief lecture was detailed, eloquent and concise. I was as impressed as the priests, who hung on every word.

Rothwell was especially taken by her description of the settlement. "Anything that elaborate would certainly indicate the place was inhabited a long time."

Sara said, "We think the scrolls were written at the Qumran monastery. If that's the case, their age suggests the community may date at least to the first century before Christ."

"Could I take a look at one of them?" Rothwell asked, his interest growing by the second.

May opened a metal box that contained the pieces of the copper scroll.

"But it's been mutilated!" Rothwell said in alarm. "What's happened here?"

Sara explained that when the scroll was found it couldn't be opened. She could read only a few passages on the exterior of the rolled surface. It was necessary to cut the copper into thin strips so that the writing on the inner folds could be deciphered.

"Can I examine this," the Jesuit said.

"Of course," May said.

When Sara handed him a magnifying lens, he almost snatched it in his eagerness.

"The Hebrew is remarkable," he said, looking perplexed after just a few minutes of reading the copper fragments. "I've never seen anything like it in my life."

"The writing on the outside of the scroll led us to a grave at the Essene settlement," Sara said.

The mention of a grave took the Jesuit by surprise.

Sara pointed out the relevant words that had been incised into the copper.

"Can we assume this grave contained burial artifacts?" McGuire's lips parted in a smile of anticipation.

"Perhaps we ought to step into the study," May said. He ushered the priests into the adjoining room. They looked confused when they saw the casket.

"I want to tell you up front that this won't be what you think," May said. "We have a body here."

McGuire stared at Rothwell as if he didn't understand. The friendly smile he had worn through much of the evening abruptly faded.

"The body was covered with natron, which we've removed," Sara said. "With that exception, the remains are just as we found them in the cemetery."

"The Egyptians used natron salts to mummify their dead," Rothwell said.

"Have you found a mummy?" McGuire asked, seizing on the observation. "How extraordinary."

He sounded relieved.

"Maybe it would be better if we let you see for yourselves," May said.

I was almost sorry for the priests when May and Sara opened the casket.

The wound in the left side; the withered legs bent slightly at the knee; the wounds in the wrists and ankles. I took it all in again and felt the same sensation of pity I experienced whenever I looked at the remains.

"Who is this?" McGuire said, stepping back.

"We don't know," Sara said. "It's the body of a man who was crucified. The remains were buried in a tomb in the desert. We think it might be the body of an Essene religious leader, someone lost to history."

Rothwell, who looked as startled as his companion, couldn't take his eyes off the corpse.

"Tell me again where you found this," he said. He spoke slowly, deliberately.

Sara began a long, painstaking description of the tomb and how we had uncovered it in the desert cemetery. As she spoke, I took a look at May. At first he'd been enjoying himself, especially when we showed the priests the copper scroll and the body. I could tell from the unpleasant set of his mouth that he was starting to get impatient.

Every few moments, Rothwell interrupted to ask another question. He wanted to know as much as she could tell him about the scroll and her translation, especially the passages that referred to the Teacher of Righteousness. While he listened, he continued studying the words with a magnifying lens.

He asked whether Professor Parker had seen the corpse.

"In Jerusalem," Sara said.

"What did he think? What was his opinion?"

Rothwell asked the questions breathlessly.

"He wasn't sure..." Sara had just begun her answer when May interrupted.

"We're wasting time here," he blurted out. "I know what I promised, but he's got to know, so let's tell him now and get it over with."

"I thought we'd settled this," Sara said, struggling to mask her irritation.

Rothwell and McGuire stood there, not understanding.

"It's only conjecture and probably crazy conjecture at that, but I want these people to hear it anyway," May said. "What's the harm of getting another opinion? I've got too much tied up in this not to lay all the cards on the table."

"I'd hardly call unfounded speculation a card," Sara said sharply.

"I wish I knew what you were talking about," Rothwell said.

"I can't believe you're doing this." Sara was as angry as I'd ever seen her.

May squared around to face Rothwell. "You wanted to know what Parker thought? For a couple minutes back there in Jerusalem he wondered if this could be the body of Jesus Christ."

A lingering stillness followed as the words sank in.

"This must be some kind of joke," Rothwell said with a nervous smile.

"Does that look like a joke," May said, pointing to the body.

"Doctor Parker said he was sorry he ever mentioned the idea," Sara said. "It was only a momentary thought. I regret it was repeated here now."

"Well, dammit, I don't regret it," May said.

"We wanted you to see this because we need your help," Sara said, ignoring his outburst. She was speaking to Rothwell, but her eyes coldly focused on May. "We have no idea who this is, none. We only know the man was crucified. Our hope was you could give us some background on what was happening in the Holy Land at the time of the Essenes. Were there any recognized holy men we don't know about? What were the religious groups and sects and who were the leaders? If we knew enough history, it might suggest something about his identity."

"Jesus Christ rose from the dead," McGuire said to May, his voice trembling. "John, what you're saying is scandalous."

Rothwell appeared as shaken and confused as McGuire.

"The scrolls you found, do they actually mention our Lord's name?" he asked, recovering his voice.

"No, they don't, " Sara said.

"And there's no way of knowing precisely when they were composed."

Sara repeated that her analysis of the script led her to conclude the writing dated to at least the first century before Christ.

"But it could be older or even more recent?"

"That's certainly a possibility."

"Then there's no way of knowing conclusively that these scrolls refer to the crucified Christ," Rothwell continued. "You've already suggested it might have been some spiritual leader connected with the Essenes."

McGuire took courage from this. Regaining his composure, he said, "So you really have no proof at all."

"I didn't say anything about proof," May said. "I just said that Parker thought it might be the remains of Jesus. We wouldn't be going through this with you now if there was any proof."

"We've only begun our inquiry," Sara said apologetically. She continued staring icily at May.

"Nothing you say will convince me even for a second that this is the Son of God," McGuire said. "If we weren't old friends..." He looked at May. "Don't you realize that what you're saying comes close to blasphemy?"

He spoke without arrogance or anger. Deeply sincere, he was acknowledging his faith in one of the great mysteries of his religion.

"I'm not trying to convince you of anything," May said. "I just want you to know everything that's been discussed. The only thing I'm interested in is finding out who we've got here. I want to find that out a great deal."

At my suggestion, we went into the living room. McGuire sat there, the large gold pectoral cross that hung from his neck rising and falling rhythmically as he breathed.

"I don't know what to say," he said after a few moments. "I don't even pretend to grasp what you've just told us. A crucified body you say was buried in an ancient cemetery. You're sure you have no idea who it could be?"

I had to admire his coolness. He had been shocked, but had quickly recovered his equilibrium.

"That's why we wanted to talk to Profesor Rothwell," Sara said. "We hoped he could help us. Right now, I'm afraid we're lost in the dark."

"I'm sure father can be of some help," McGuire said. "There's no question this man was an important figure. To have been executed and then have his body hidden away...I want to learn his identity as much as you do."

"Let's forget the argument," Sara said. "The only thing that matters now is finding out who this man is—if that's possible."

"I couldn't agree more," May said, sounding contrite.

McGuire took comfort when Sara asked Rothwell for a historical perspective on what was happening in the Holy Land during the years the Essene monastery was most likely inhabited. For the next hour or so, Rothwell discussed in fascinating detail the principal Jewish sects, mainly the Sadducees, Pharisees and Zealots and their often tense relationship with the Romans.

"All that can be said with certainty," he said, finishing, "is that it was a period of chaos and instability. Josephus probably put it best when he said that Judea was full of robbers and plagued by disorders. There were constant revolts against the Romans or their puppets. In one uprising alone, two thousand rebels were crucified. It happened under Varus, the Roman governor of Syria shortly after Herod the Great died in 4 B.C."

"Is there any chance the body could have dated from that mass execution?" McGuire asked.

"That's impossible to say," Rothwell said. "The most interesting possibility here, it seems to me, is whether the dead man had any direct connection with the Essenes. Unfortunately, there's virtually no record at all of who their leaders or priests were, what they believed, what manner of lives they led. That's why your discoveries are so important."

"You mentioned the Zealots," Sara said. "Is there any indication they had dealings with the sect at Qumran?"

"The ground's a little firmer when it comes to the Zealots," Rothwell said. "It's known that a man named Sadduk, a Pharisee, led a violent protest against the Roman census around A.D. 6. Several other leaders are mentioned, but as far as I know, there's no written proof they were involved with the Essenes. It's fair to say they had great influence among the Jews until the Roman legions crushed them during the first revolt."

"By more executions, no doubt," McGuire said.

"The sight of men nailed to crosses along the roads of the Holy Land was all too common," Rothwell said.

He noted that Herod the Great excluded the Essenes from swearing allegiance to him as he did with the other religious groups. "That makes me think he didn't consider them a threat. If that's true and if the dead man actually was an Essene, it seems to me that he was probably put to death either before or after Herod's rule, which ended in 4 B.C."

"When I think that the body could date almost to the dawn of our religion...It leaves me speechless," McGuire said. "The historical significance of what you've discovered can't be denied. The church has people who could help in this, men like Reverend Rothwell. Experts in archeology and the Holy Land. There's so much we could do, so many resources we could offer. I don't have to tell you again that we're all as interested as you are in solving this mystery."

"Where are these people, here in Chicago?" May asked.

"In Rome. It might surprise you how much the Vatican resembles a large university. I know I'm biased, but the scholars there are some of the best in the world."

Sara looked as if she wasn't sure how to react to the archbishop's proposal. But May was taken by the idea. He asked who McGuire had in mind.

"Father Bourgonne is at the Vatican," Rothwell said. "He's really our best authority on the Middle East. A superb archeologist. I can't think of anyone more qualified to bring in on this."

I remember the name. Professor Parker had mentioned Bourgonne back in Jerusalem.

Rothwell said that Gabriel-Marie Bourgonne worked in the Vatican's Lateran Museum. He had recently returned to Rome after an extended stay in Paris.

"I met him once," he said. "A fine man. His books are lucid, even beautifully written. I should also mention that he has his critics."

I asked why, sensing that he immediately regretted the remark.

"His scholarship is sometimes clouded by, ah, certain controversial views," Rothwell said, choosing his words with care. "There are some in the Vatican who find that disquieting. His career, it's fair to say, has suffered from it."

"I'd be happy to call Rome to make some inquiries," McGuire offered.

"Don't you think we should talk this over first," Sara said to May.

"Why waste any more time?" he said, sensing her uncertainty. "You already said you were at a dead end. If this guy Bourgonne can help, why not talk to him? What do we have to lose?"

"Our only interest would be to assist you," McGuire said. "I can't help but believe you did the right thing in calling Reverend Rothwell. It was an excellent start, but I wouldn't want to go beyond that if you don't think it would be useful."

"I say let's do it,"May said. "Call your people and see what they suggest. We've got to get this moving."

Sara said nothing. I knew she was irritated.

"I'll cable the Vatican for instructions as soon as I can return to the chancellery," McGuire said. "The message will be in code. I know how important secrecy is in this matter."

The session had ended. McGuire got up stiffly; the movement pained him in the hips. I wondered if he suffered from arthritis.

On his way out, he paused by the door to the study and looked in again at the casket.

"Whoever this poor man is, my heart goes out to him," he said in a soft, low voice. "I hope he found his peace with God."

CHAPTER 33

SARA, I want to do this," May said.

"How do we know we can even trust them?"

"My god, you heard him. They want to find out whose body that is as much as you or I do. Why shouldn't we trust them?"

The argument had started moments after McGuire and Rothwell had left.

"We shouldn't rush into anything," Sara insisted. "If the church gets too deeply involved at this point, we could lose some control. There might also be a lack of balance. We need as many different points of view as possible."

She repeated her earlier idea—to invite a panel of experts to examine the corpse and scrolls.

May kept pressing to see what the church could come up with, especially Bourgonne. If it didn't work out, we'd try something else—whatever she thought best.

When Sara still had reservations, he lost his temper.

"I know you've paid for all this," Sara said steadily. "But I have a responsibility to tell you what I think. I'm pretty good at what I do. I've had to be—it isn't easy to be a woman in my field, to be taken seriously. If you don't want to listen to me, why keep going on?"

May pretended not to have heard what she had said. They continued going back and forth over McGuire's proposal.

"What's the matter?" May finally said in exasperation. "Is it because you're Jewish and you don't want the Catholics to help?"

"That's the best one yet," Sara said, her face reddening. "You just can't forget what Professor Parker said, can you? You're going to keep pushing it, no matter how absurd..."

She turned her back on him.

Finally she said, "I wish I could call him in Jerusalem and have him talk some sense into your head."

"You better tell her," May said.

I couldn't believe he'd say it now.

"Tell me what?"

She realized something was wrong.

"Sara, let's forget it," I said.

"What are you talking about? I want to know."

May left the room.

"Paul, what is it?

She stood close to me, trembling, her voice a whisper.

"Parker's dead," I said slowly. "He was shot. It happened a couple of weeks ago. There was a crossfire and he..."

Frozen rigid, she looked at me. "You should have told me earlier. You had no right not to tell me."

I tried to explain but she ran out of the room sobbing.

I found May. He was in the kitchen, sitting at the table. A bottle of bourbon was in front of him.

"I know I'm a bastard, but you know as well as I do she had to find out," he said.

"You've got part of it right. You're a bastard."

May poured a glass. I refused when he offered me one.

"Tell me this," I said angrily. "Just what do you want to do with the body? What are you trying to prove? I really want to know."

"I'm going to do whatever it takes to find out who it is we've got lying in that casket. He has to have a name."

"And why is that so important? Isn't just having it enough?"

May smiled. "It's only half the prize. I want all of it."

In the morning, May fumbled through an apology about how he had broken the news of Parker's death.

"I shouldn't have told you, not last night. It makes me ashamed to know that I..."

Sara stopped him. She didn't want to talk about it. Maybe later, she said, but not now. She hadn't slept well; the color was drawn from her face. When we finished breakfast, I suggested a walk. The old feeling of something gone wrong had returned. I thought a walk along Lake Michigan might lift some of the gloom.

Sara put on a sweater and we went down to the shore. May's recent behavior worried her; it worried me as well. He'd been great during the trip to Qumran and afterward when we had to get out of the Holy Land. He seemed different now—harder to deal with, more opinionated. The tough, self-made millionaire used to getting his way was coming through loud and clear.

"If he keeps this up, we could be in for trouble," she said. "We're not going to get anywhere if he insists on blurting out that business about Jesus Christ. You saw how Rothwell and McGuire reacted when he mentioned it. They thought he was crazy."

"The guy's an art collector," I said. "He's got a sensational find on his hands and he wants people to know about it. It's that simple.

"But he could damage our credibility. He can't go on saying the things he's saying. After a while no one will take us seriously. Once something like that starts you can't stop it. Archeologists live and work in a small world. The word gets around quickly."

"No, he won't ruin it. It'll be all right because he's not going to forget the bottom line. May's a businessman, a shrewd one. He's got too much money riding on this to screw it up."

"My god, the man doesn't need any more money."

"It's not just that," I reflected. "He wants recognition as much as dollars. That's probably where I fit in. I'm the guy who's supposed to write the story that will make him famous."

Sara wasn't convinced. She was still uneasy about him.

"There've been moments these last few days when I almost wish I hadn't spoken to him when he introduced himself in Jerusalem," she said. "I almost didn't. I thought he was trying to pick me up."

"You couldn't blame him for trying to do that."

I wanted to make her smile, but it didn't work.

We walked for a while, not speaking. The city's soaring skyline, several miles to the north, curved gracefully around the rim of the lake. The tall buildings, their windows glowing red in the sunlight, almost looked like stage props.

Chicago had always been a raw, boisterous place to me, a city that floated raft-like on the plains under a depressive, annihilating sky. Lake Michigan, magnificent on any day and in any weather, made up for all that; it made up for a great deal.

Distracted, Sara was facing the lake. "I wonder what Josef would have thought about all this," she said. She had spoken only once before about her dead lover—the young Haganah soldier from Poland who'd been killed in a parachuting accident.

For whatever reason, she began to talk to me about him.

"Sara, you don't have to tell me this," I said.

"No, I want to. It will help me."

Josef had been a medical student at Krakow when the war broke out. She said he was immediately interned with other Jews following the Nazi invasion. His skill had saved his life in the camps, where he had spent three years working in a dispensary that treated wounded German soldiers. After the Nazis retreated from Russia and Poland, he was sent to another camp in Bremen. It was late in the war. The camp housed several thousand POWs— most of them captured allied servicemen. One night after a heavy air raid on a nearby factory district, they were packed into boxcars and sent south toward Bonn. Strafed several times with terrible results, the train finally halted on a remote siding in a forest. The SS guards ordered everyone out—one car at a time—and began to machinegun the prisoners on the graveled trackbed.

He told Sara much later how he and about thirty others were lined up by the freight cars. Some of them fell on their knees to pray. Josef, she said, stood there staring over the trees; the sun was starting to come up and the sky was clearing. He wasn't aware that the guns had jammed, or that the Germans had run away. He didn't realize what had happened until a woman next to him fainted into his arms.

"He was the most deeply religious man I've ever known," Sara said. "I used to be jealous that God had given him something he had denied to me."

"He was lucky."

"He knew that. He told me each of us are given at least one chance in life to know God—one time when the door swings open."

"And you think the door has opened a crack now?"

"I don't know. Sometimes I wish it would." She turned to me, her face fresh and lovely in the light. "What about you, Mister Davoren? Do you believe in God?"

"You're starting to sound like May," I said, smiling.

I could tell that she was serious, so I mentioned a young French woman I'd met shortly after Paris had been liberated. I'd thought about her often since then. A dark haired teenager, she'd been convicted of being a collaborationist. The charges said she had given aid and comfort to the enemy, but the real reason was that she had taken a German lover. They had already beaten her in the street and shaved her head when I met her. I had covered the trial and managed to interview her a few times. She wasn't bitter; she wasn't even frightened. Her faith in God was all she wanted to talk about. She hadn't changed on the day they shot her. I was there with a few other reporters early in the morning when they led her out into a courtyard behind the Palais de Justice. She was wearing a gray prison smock, wooden clogs and carrying a rosary. She looked happy—there was no other word for it. They marched her to a wall, tied her hands behind her back, and put a black cloth over her head. The firing squad—ten sleepy looking soldiers— stood less than five yards away. She was still holding her rosary and praying out loud when the volley nearly cut her in two. An officer hurried over and fired another bullet into her head. It wasn't necessary. They carried her body away on a stretcher and led out another woman, but I didn't stick around to see any more.

"I can believe in the God that girl called out to for help," I said. "The God for the dying."

Sara kissed me on the cheek. "I feel so close to you right now," she said. "Thank you for telling me that."

We stood there on the windy beach, holding one another. The astonishment that I'd found a woman like her had never left me.

"Sara, you make me very proud to be with you."

That night when we lay together in bed, there was a new bond between us. Something spiritual had been added, making our love stronger, deeper. We couldn't explain it, but we'd been changed. We were happy, so unexpectedly happy that we were almost afraid to enjoy it.

CHAPTER 34

GABRIEL-Marie Bourgonne arrived in Chicago just over a week after our conversation with Archbishop McGuire and Reverend Rothwell. He was met at O'Hare airport by the two priests, who drove him straight to May's home in Hyde Park.

Bourgonne was forty-nine-years old—a tall, big-boned man with long arms, large hands and large feet. His thick black hair was cut short. He had a narrow face with a hawk nose, high cheekbones, and watchful brown eyes; his large ears were flattened to the sides of his head. He spoke fluent English but with a pronounced French accent. His expression was one of worried amiability.

He began by thanking May for allowing the visit on such short notice.

"From what I have been told, you have made a great find in the Holy Land," he said. "I want to thank you for letting me come here. It is an honor."

He made a short bow when he was introduced to Sara.

"We have met before, have we not?" he said.

"In Jericho. You were directing a dig for the École Biblique. I didn't think you'd remember."

"I could never forget such an attractive young woman, especially one who asked so many intelligent questions."

"You were dressed differently," Sara said.

"Ah, the beret and country boots," he said, rolling his head back. "And I am sure I had not shaved. It amazes me how much I miss all that. I become another person when I work outdoors in the sun."

Bourgonne's politeness was disarming. Part of it, I was sure, was the polish of a man trained to handle problems no matter how major or minor with good-natured restraint.

"We do wish to speak freely," he said, promising that the discussions would be held in strictest confidence. "I am sure you would agree that is crucial."

Only a few members in the Curia knew of his trip to Chicago, McGuire said.

"That they made the decision to send me here so quickly is still astonishing," Bourgonne added. "The law's delays are nothing compared to the delays of the Curia."

"We've already gone over in a general way what you've told us about the scrolls," McGuire said. He made no mention of the body.

"Yes," Bourgonne said eagerly. "Perhaps we could begin with that."

Sara showed them the two leather parchments May had purchased in Bethlehem as well as the inscribed pieces of copper. She mentioned the difficulty she had had trying to open the scroll she called the Manual of Discipline.

"These are extraordinary," Bourgonne said after only a brief examination. "The orthography is remarkable."

The writing on the copper fragments, which he read slowly, threw him completely.

"I have spent most of twenty years in the Holy Land," he said finally. "If I should spend another century there, I would never hope to find anything like this."

The discussion soon focused on the Essenes. From his comments it was apparent that Bourgonne knew a great deal about the sect. At one point during the conversation, Sara asked him whether he thought there might be a connection between John the Baptist and the monks of the desert.

"Do you think he was familiar with them?"

"It would not be an unreasonable assumption. There is a tradition that the Baptist was born in Hebron, which is not that far from the ruins you explored at Wadi Qumran."

One could make an argument, he thought, that John might have had some dealings with such an important sect, especially if he grew up near their settlement.

"There are, of course, all manner of theories regarding the Baptist," he cautioned. "Even to the speculation that John and Christ were brothers—or homosexual lovers. The idea has been suggested in literature by writers like Christopher Marlowe."

I began to understand why Bourgonne's reputation as a free thinker must have caused him some difficult moments in the

222

church. The comment about homosexuality hadn't pleased Rothwell.

"I think we ought to show you something," Sara said. "I wanted to do it later, but considering what we've been talking about this might be a better time."

With May's help, she carried the headless skeleton into the room. McGuire and Rothwell hadn't seen this before. Their expressions betrayed their discomfort.

"The copper scroll mentioned the tomb where these bones were found," Sara said. "No name was given, or at least nothing I could decipher. Some passages, as you've seen, are missing."

She noted the evidence of beheading and also displayed the soapstone cup that had been found in the grave. Drawing attention to its smooth, flanged edges, she said, "I keep asking myself if this might have been used for pouring water."

Bourgonne recognized the significance before it dawned on the others.

"Are you suggesting this could be the remains of the Baptist?

His companions looked dumbfounded.

"The location of the other body was given in reference to the grave that contained this skeleton," Sara said. "That's all we can say with any certainty...But I think it's likely some connection must have existed between them."

She was being deliberately guarded. The whole idea, after all, was to present the evidence and let the visitors draw their own conclusions.

"But that's hardly reason to assume this is the skeleton of John the Baptist," Rothwell said, controlling himself with considerable effort.

"I thought I had got used to being surprised," McGuire said softly. "I see now that I was mistaken."

May suggested that they examine the other corpse. With Bourgonne in front, the priests lined up around the casket as May and I opened it.

Bourgonne stood there, unable to turn away.

Slowly, with difficulty, McGuire knelt down and began to pray. Rothwell also dropped to the floor and folded his hands. They prayed quietly with their heads bowed. They must have knelt there for five minutes before McGuire finally got up; he moved heavily and was helped to his feet by Rothwell and May.

In a barely audible voice, Bourgonne whispered, "Ecce Homo."

He turned to Sara. "Is this," he asked, "your Teacher of Righteousness?"

"It certainly isn't Christ," Rothwell said mechanically.

Bourgonne's troubled gaze remained fixed on the corpse. It was obvious that he had been thoroughly briefed on the speculation about Christ.

Rothwell had stepped away from the casket and now avoided looking at the corpse. "These are mortal remains," he continued. "To indulge in any fantasy that this might be the body of the Son of God would be unfortunate."

Bourgonne, who had not taken his eyes off the battered face, now said, "I do not mean to be difficult, but some problems are presented in the use of titles like Son of God."

"We're all familiar with your views," Rothwell said impatiently. "This isn't the time or place to discuss them."

"It does seem a little off the mark," McGuire agreed, sensing Rothwell's irritation. "Perhaps we could come back to it later."

"I wouldn't mind hearing what you're talking about," May said to Bourgonne.

The priest glanced at McGuire as if seeking permission to answer. The archbishop nodded.

"I mean," he said, "there is no evidence in the gospels that Jesus referred to himself as the Son of God. The one title he did use, and only a few times, was Son of Man, which is extremely vague."

Rothwell again objected. Further discussion of the subject, he said, would serve no purpose.

Lingering at the casket, Bourgonne took another look at the body. "You have made a profoundly important discovery, no matter who this is."

"That's just the question," McGuire said. "Who is it?"

"I quite agree that is the dominant issue to be resolved," Bourgonne said. Smiling faintly, he added, "If we can establish who it is, we will also know who it isn't."

We returned to the study. Bourgonne asked Sara to tell him as much as she could about the expedition to the Dead Sea. He wanted details, anecdotes, whatever any of us could remember about the trip. He also took another look at the scrolls. The examination and discussion lasted well into the night.

Bourgonne was especially interested in the unopened leather scroll. Sara had been trying to soften the brittle leather, which slowly was becoming more pliable.

She asked Bourgonne if he would help her try to unroll it.

"It would be a great favor."

"That is very generous of you—and very kind," he said, delighted at the offer. "We can begin at once if you like."

Rothwell asked who else knew about the existence of the corpse.

"A few people," May said. "No more than that." When Rothwell asked for names, he declined.

The priest persisted.

"It might be useful if I knew what others thought about this."

"I already told you what Parker said back in Jerusalem," May said a little testily. "That's what caused all of our problems in the first place."

"I agree that nothing useful would be served by discussing that subject again," McGuire said, deftly trying to defuse any trouble. He looked at his watch. "Father, it's already past ten o'clock. Perhaps we could start again tomorrow."

The priests, following the archbishop's lead, got up to leave.

"If you have no objection, I would also like to reexamine the body," Bourgonne said to Sara and May. Reluctant to go, he delayed at the door. "There is one additional procedure I would suggest," he said. "It might be useful to reconstruct the face of the dead man."

The process, he explained, involved making a plaster impression of the face, fitting the pieces into a mold and then filling it with plaster to form a cast. The rest of the work was done with modeling clay carefully sculpted to fit the contours of the cast. The final steps included applying skin color and facial hair. Bourgonne said he had already used the technique in fashioning the busts of three Egyptian mummies that were badly decomposed.

If all went well, he hoped to recreate a reasonable likeness of the face.

"I can assure you there will be no risk to the body," Bourgonne said. "It could help to see what the man looked like in real life... The effect can sometimes be surprising."

CHAPTER 35

AFTER THE PRIESTS LEFT, May said he was willing to let Bourgonne make a cast of the face provided the work could be done in absolute safety. Sara was also curious to see the procedure.

We discussed it a while longer and then she stood up. She looked tired.

"We can talk this over again in the morning," May said. "It could be a busy day."

I followed Sara upstairs. When I closed the door, she put her arms around my shoulders and kissed me. "I do love you," she said, smiling. "If you weren't here I don't know how I would get through this."

I heard myself say, "Sara, I want to marry you. Let's get married tomorrow."

"You heard John. Tomorrow might be a busy day," she said playfully. "What about the day after tomorrow?"

I kissed her, her lips holding mine as she clung to me. I had always wondered how it would happen, if it ever happened, and now here it was—a beautiful woman had agreed to marry me.

"I know you've loved someone else," I said, struggling with the words, knowing I didn't want to say them, but couldn't help not saying them. "I'd never expect you to forget. I don't..."

She touched my lips. "You're the man I love, the man I need."

In that single wonderful moment I saw myself married to this woman, living with her, growing old with her, supporting her with all my heart and soul.

"We can find a justice of the peace tomorrow," I said.

"No, I want to marry you properly—after all this has been settled. I want to celebrate our wedding. I want our friends to be there."

"I don't have any friends." I meant it as a joke but the words were almost true. I had a few friends, real friends, who were

226

reporters. I had no idea where they were. Probably scattered all over the globe. I realized again how glad I was to be out of that rat race.

She smiled.

"I have enough for both of us."

"You've got a large family, I guess."

"Huge. Aunts, uncles, nieces, a dozen nephews. Most of them are still in Brooklyn. We make the Italians look like they practice birth control."

"Brooklyn! Then I'm in real trouble," I said. "I don't speak the language."

"I'll teach you. It's simple. You practice by pinching your nose and swallowing your words."

"How do you think I'm going to go over with all those aunts and uncles?"

Sara laughed. "That's going to be interesting. I've got a seventy-year old aunt, Aunt Stella, who's been writing me letters for a year now, telling me she's found three or four good Jewish men she wants me to meet when I get back home. One of them's an accountant who owns his own car. You could be in real trouble with Aunt Stella." She lay down on the bed. "What about me? How will a Jewish girl make out with the Davorens?"

"I've got that figured out. I'm going to tell them you're a divorced Catholic."

We hadn't talked much about my parents. They still went to mass regularly every Sunday, Mom to listen to the sermons, Dad to sleep. There would be no problem at all with Sara's religion; it wouldn't even come up. The last letter from home said my father was thinking of retiring from the insurance company where he had sold policies for over forty years. They owned a two-story flat and had just made the last payment on an aging Plymouth. They had given me everything and asked for nothing.

I tried to tell Sara this.

"I already like them," she said.

I cradled her in my arms. "I wish my father could have known you," she said.

"What do you think he would have thought?"

"He'd be happy I found such a fine fellow."

227

I asked about her mother.

"I'll write her tomorrow," Sara said, frowning. "I should have done that sooner. I'm afraid I haven't been a very good daughter. I haven't sent her a letter in weeks. Mom must still think I'm in the Holy Land."

"Sara, I want to spend a lot of time with you," I said, feeling the warmth of her body as she curled her legs against mine. "I want to find a nice clean hotel room with a wide bed and not leave for a month."

She laughed.

"Would you read to me?"

"I never read in bed with a woman. It's a real problem. I just can't seem to do two things at the same time."

She brushed the hair back from my eyes. "I want to have children."

I'd never really thought about that before. I had always viewed children as the price you paid for sleeping with a woman. They had never held much of an attraction for me; parenthood, if you were going to do the job properly, demanded all the time, care and devotion you could muster, and I had never thought I was cut out for that particular brand of sacrifice. But if that's what she wanted, all right. I'd give her anything I could.

"You look so serious," Sara said, still smiling. "Have I said something that frightened you?"

"You bet you did. How many do you want?"

"Four or five."

I groaned.

"Now I have frightened you, haven't I?"

"What makes you think that? Just because my hands are shaking and I'm breaking out in a sweat doesn't mean a thing."

"You'd be a wonderful father," she said.

"With four or five kids I wouldn't be a father. I'd be a zoo keeper."

"I'd want to raise them so they'll know that believing in yourself and having the courage to love and take risks are what sets a life apart." She looked up at me. "I don't think I would have said that a year ago. Some things have become clearer to me since we left the Holy Land."

I knew what she meant. My experience had been the same. But I was still too close to it to try to explain to myself or anyone else what had happened or how deeply the feeling had taken hold of me. All that would have to sort itself out later.

"What do you think's happening back there?" I asked.

"I'd like to go back someday and find out. I wasn't there very long, but I almost feel as if it's my home now."

"The promised land."

Sara came to me then, making the first soft move of her hips against mine as she slipped off her blouse. I was quickly lost in wanting her, wanting her as I had never wanted a woman in my life and knowing there could be no other and that she would always be a part of me.

She straddled my waist and leaned forward so that my cheek touched her shoulders. I could smell her fragrant hair. The clock ticked on the mantel, ticking away the long minutes of gratitude and joy.

Then, because I had said nothing, telling her, "Thank you for loving me."

CHAPTER 36

MAY WAS READING the morning *Tribune* when we came downstairs. Sara told him about our plans. He stood up and took her in his arms. "I knew that one of these days you two would come to your senses," he said, taking my hand and pumping it hard.

"Where will it happen?".

"We haven't decided."

"Why not right here? This house would be a perfect place. I don't think it's ever had a wedding. A couple of funerals back in the Twenties, but no weddings."

He hurried down to the cellar for a bottle of champagne.

"I haven't opened one of these since my divorce," he said, returning with a vintage brut.

He'd never mentioned his marriage. Sensing our interest he explained that he had been married ten years earlier to a young society woman. They hadn't had any children; the woman had since remarried and moved to California.

"She didn't like art," he said, smiling. "And I didn't like horses. We lasted just over a year."

It was good to see him loosen up; there had been some strained moments between Sara and him the past few days. Our announcement restored the old mood.

May was still pushing us to set a date when Bourgonne called. He wanted to know whether he could make a cast of the face of the corpse. After discussing it again with Sara, May invited him to come over.

"You're sure about this?" I asked when he hung up the telephone.

"I'd kind of like to see what he'll come up with," May said.

Sara would have preferred to postpone the experiment for a while, but made no objection. She admitted she was as curious as May.

Bourgonne arrived alone in a taxi within an hour. He was

carrying a small suitcase, which he said contained the materials he needed.

May inquired about Archbishop McGuire.

The priest said, "The archbishop wanted me to tell you again that he will help you however he can—in any way you suggest. He wants you to know how much he appreciates your willingness to let us assist in your research. I can only add that I share his sentiments."

It looked for a moment as if he wanted to go beyond that, but had second thoughts.

"How much time will it take to reconstruct the face?" Sara asked.

"I need to do a mold, then make a plaster cast." He thought it would take about two days to get a reasonable likeness.

"If I had to piece together and refashion the bones of the skull, the process would take considerably longer."

Before we got started, May told Bourgonne that he would stop him if he suspected even for a moment that he was damaging the body.

The priest looked hurt. "I know you are only saying what had to be said, but I am sorry that it must be so."

We went into the study and Bourgonne got to work, taking several cans of modeling clay and a small package of plaster of Paris from his case. He also had an assortment of paint brushes and what looked like putty knives. His first step was to coat the face of the dead man as well as the wispy beard and eyebrows with a thin layer of petroleum jelly to prevent the mold from adhering to the hair and withered tissue. He worked slowly, delicately, applying the coating with cotton swabs.

At his request I brought him a pan of water; he added a few cupfuls of a powdered compound, slowly stirring the mixture until he was satisfied with its pasty consistency. He explained that the compound was the same kind used to make dental impressions. When it hardened, it would form a flexible mask that he could lift off and use as a mold to pour the plaster cast.

"The important thing," he said, "is to move quickly, but with care. You have to pour in the plaster before the mold loses its shape."

May, who stood next to him, quietly repeated his warning.

231

"I trust you. But please... be careful."

Bending over the open casket, Bourgonne expertly applied the dental mixture to the upper part of the face, using a small brush.

I wasn't sure what May would do if something went wrong, but I hoped I wouldn't have to find out.

Bourgonne covered a section of the face at a time, first the forehead, then the cheeks and lower chin and finally the ears. When the compound hardened—it only took ten or twelve minutes—he gently peeled it off. The face, undamaged, was later swabbed with alcohol and tissue paper to remove the petroleum jelly. When the casket lid was closed again, everyone was relieved.

After inspecting his mold, Bourgonne coated the inside with a clear shellac to seal the surface; the coating, he explained, also would serve as a separator to keep the mold from adhering to the fresh plaster he would pour inside to form his cast.

"Now what?" I asked.

"At this stage one must be very careful," Bourgonne said.

He slowly poured a small amount of liquid plaster, no more than a cupful, into the mold and sloshed the mixture around until the insides were coated.

"If you do not do this, bubbles could form in the surface. They would leave pit marks."

Satisfied with his preparation, he filled the mold with a thicker mixture of plaster.

"Now it is a matter of letting it set until morning," he said, positioning the mold on a wooden box on the table. "Then I will begin working with the clay."

As they had agreed earlier, Sara and Bourgonne turned their attention to trying to unravel and decipher the unopened scroll— the Manual of Discipline. The leather had become more flexible after several treatments in a bell jar that contained a damp sponge—a crude humidifier. Sara had been trying to loosen and roll back the edges of the tightly wound parchment.

With Bourgonne's help, she opened two more folds. The coffee-colored leather was stained and torn. Working with brushes, they cleaned the parchment with a mixture of alcohol and castor oil. The larger of the tears were patched with clear adhesive tape. More supple now, the leather still required careful manipulation.

Translating while they worked, they were able to read several passages. The writing reinforced Sara's earlier opinion that the scroll resembled a kind of Benedictine Rule. Candidates for the order had a two-year probation period after which they had to swear to "terrible oaths." Members, as she had deduced from the quantities of precious metals described in the document, were expected to turn over their possessions to the order; they could leave, but if they wanted to rejoin there was another tough initiation. These and other details were spelled out in the scroll.

"All this agrees with what Josephus has written about the Essenes," Bourgonne said.

When they began working on the third fold, the picture changed dramatically.

Sara slowly read one of the passages aloud: "And when they shall gather at the common table to eat and drink wine and bread . . . let no man extend his hand over the bread and wine before the Priest . . ." She looked at Bourgonne who sat next to her. "What is this?"

The priest took up the translation himself. "Thereafter, the master of Israel shall break the bread and all the congregation of the community shall utter a blessing."

He fell silent. Then he said, still reading, "They shall take of the common meal when at least ten men are gathered together."

Another passage described how members of the sect were to avoid the "temptations of the flesh" and love all men as brothers. One section in particular caught their attention. Bourgonne read out the words: "A member will enter the water and be touched by the hands of the priest. For no one will be cleansed until they are immersed in the water and have repented of their wickedness."

"What's all that supposed to mean?" May asked.

Bourgonne sat there, staring at the parchment. He looked shaken; the stamp of it lingered in his eyes.

"You have a sacred meal celebrated in common with bread and wine," he said. "You have the doctrine of love of neighbor and the practice of baptism by water . . . Does any of that sound familiar?"

"It sounds like Christianity," I said.

The priest's eyes bore into me.

"Christianity before Christ."

I realized that we had considerably more than a list of regulations for a religious group that had disappeared 2,000 years ago.

Sara mentioned the cisterns we had found among the ruins at Qumran.

"I wondered about the steps that led down into them," she said. "They must have been used for ritual immersions."

"Some of the similarities between the sect and the early Christians are striking," Bourgonne said, hurrying on. "Their faith almost appears as a prototype."

"Hold it now," May said. "I'm not following this. What do you mean, prototype?"

"The beliefs and practices the Essenes lived by could have been a model for the Christians," Sara said, offering an explanation. "They might have borrowed them." She was becoming as excited as Bourgonne.

"In these writings we may have reached the bedrock of the gospels," the priest said. He appeared distracted, uncertain of himself. "It is simply unbelievable."

Sara said, "Doesn't this suggest that the birth of Christianity was the result of an evolutionary process? That it didn't just happen? The seeds may have been planted long before Jesus of Nazareth came on the scene."

Bourgonne added. "One could ask whether Christ incorporated elements of the sect's doctrine and enlarged on them, refined them to suit his own purposes. Think what that could mean."

"A lot of Christians won't be happy to hear news like that," I said. All this was way out of my line, but I knew they were walking onto a mine field.

May began to catch on to the the implications of what they were talking about. He was smiling as he stared down at the scroll, which lay partly opened on the table in front of him. "If what you say is true, how much is something like this worth?"

Bourgonne swiveled around in his chair to face him. "I can not answer a question like that. Matters of value do not concern me."

He stood up and walked away from the table. It was nearing midnight; we'd been working steadily since the early afternoon.

"I am almost afraid to suggest this," he said. His back was to us as he faced the plaster cast. He stood there a long time.

"This scroll could challenge the uniqueness of Christ."

CHAPTER 37

BOURGONNE SPENT THE NIGHT. He and Sara had continued to work on the scroll until well after two in the morning. As tired as I was, I didn't sleep well or long. Sara was still in bed when I went downstairs. Already up, Bourgonne was in the study examining the cast. It was just after seven.

"I'm glad I wasn't the only one who couldn't sleep," I said.

"I was able to rest a few hours," he said. "I am quite refreshed."

He didn't look it; his eyes were rimmed and bloodshot.

I asked how the cast had turned out. It was a fine reproduction of the dead man's face; the plaster was hard and smooth. The priest had been cleaning the surface with a damp cloth when I came downstairs."

"It set wonderfully," he said. "Better than I had hoped. There is always the chance of a serious flaw when you pour a cast. We were fortunate."

"What's next?"

May asked the question as he walked down the stairway in the hall. He was still buttoning his shirt. Like me, he hadn't shaved.

"Now the work becomes more difficult," Bourgonne said. "We have to turn the cast into a face."

I could tell from the moment he entered the study that May wanted to get something off his chest. He immediately asked about the scroll.

"I have not been able to get it out of my mind," Bourgonne said. "Your scroll could compel the Christian churches to reevaluate their common history. It could be of revolutionary importance. There is no other way to describe it. I cannot begin to imagine the confusion this will cause—the anguish."

When Sara joined us, Bourgonne got started again on the cast. He began by cutting a dozen or so strips of rubber into small pegs of different lengths; the longest looked no more than half an inch.

Attaching the segments so they stood on end, he glued them to the forehead of the cast as well as to the cheeks, brow and chin. The pegs, he explained, represented the varying thickness of the skin tissue and would serve as landmarks. The clay was applied directly over them. If everything worked, the finished product would follow the original contours of the face.

"The technique was first used in Germany in 1895," he said. "Measurements of the skin depth were taken on dozens of cadavers. The results were compiled in a table which is still used today. I consulted it earlier this morning. I wanted to be sure I made no mistake."

"What did the Germans do with all that information?" I asked.

"They reconstructed the face of Johann Sebastian Bach," Bourgonne said. "I have seen the original. A superb likeness."

When the pegs were firmly attached, he took tape measurements of the mouth, eyes, and ears to make sure they were precisely positioned. He also glued two plastic eyes into the open sockets.

Using clay mixed with a trace of terra cotta for color, he began filling in the cheeks and other facial hollows to the height of the pegs, covering them over. He stopped often to smooth out the clay to the proper thickness and texture with his moistened fingers and a flat-bladed knife.

"You would have made a fine sculptor," May said, watching quietly.

"One learns with practice," Bourgonne said, applying more clay. "If you get a good cast, the rest comes easily. I am merely using the clay as a substitute for the dried skin."

Wetting his hands frequently, he worked with the clay for several hours until he was satisfied. The priest was doing a wonderful job; slowly, almost magically, the face of a man dead for nearly 2,000 years was taking shape before us.

"He will not be, how should I say, handsome to look at," Bourgonne said. "The wound over the eye badly marred the symmetry of the face."

As he worked, he mentioned the scroll again. He admitted he was still having trouble coming to grips with what he had seen and read the night before.

"First we have the Teacher of Righteousness, a person whose name and life are a mystery, who died violently. That, in itself, is a discovery of the first rank. But now your scroll suggests some of the essential Christian beliefs may have originated with an obscure Jewish sect. After all these centuries of darkness, of historical uncertainty, a light has been turned on. Things unseen, unimagined, begin to emerge from the shadows."

"You don't sound very happy about it," I said. He had spoken somberly.

"It is a strange feeling," Bourgonne admitted. "I cannot help but be excited, overwhelmed by what you have found in the Judean desert. And yet I must tell you...it leaves me uneasy."

Late in the afternoon, Archbishop McGuire arrived. His driver, a young priest from the chancellery, waited in the car.

"I couldn't stay away any longer," McGuire told May, apologizing for the unannounced visit. "I had to see how you were doing."

When Bourgonne stopped his work to greet him, McGuire hastily told him to continue with what he was doing. He held back in the doorway before approaching the table for a look at the cast. He spoke in awe when he said, "I wouldn't have thought it possible. It's almost human."

The effect was already striking; the face was that of a middle-aged man with large, deep-set eyes, prominent cheekbones and a long, graceful nose. Despite Bourgonne's attempt to smooth it out, the scar had left a deep welt across the forehead.

McGuire edged nearer. An invisible barrier seemed to keep him from the cast. He murmured something under his breath which I didn't understand, a few disjointed phrases. His face had darkened.

Bourgonne began applying flesh-colored paint to the clay with an artist's brush. He used a pointed instrument to etch hairlines into the plaster beard and eyebrows.

This done, he stood there gazing at the face, carefully turning it.

I couldn't take my eyes off McGuire. His expression had been transformed from cautious, uncertain interest into what looked to me like frightened recognition. His hands fell to his sides.

"I must," he said slowly. "I must not..."

"What's wrong," Sara said.

"I thought I saw it earlier, but I didn't believe it," McGuire said with a restrained cry. "I can't believe I was so blind."

"What are you talking about?" May asked, going over to him. "You better sit down."

"This looks like the face of the man in the shroud," McGuire said. "I'm sure of it. The same face.

"What shroud?" May asked. "Tom, are you all right?"

"The Shroud of Turin."

Sara looked at May. They didn't understand. But Bourgonne and I did. We knew what he meant.

I remembered once again how I had felt at the tomb after we had opened the sarcophagus. The same oppressive uncertainty weighed down on me now. McGuire was talking about the shroud that bore the mysterious image of a dead man. A relic that some believed to be the burial cloth of Christ.

I stared at the cast again. I didn't believe it was the face of Christ. There would probably never be any definitive proof. But if he had looked like this then I could understand why so many men had willingly given up their wives, families and homes to follow him—follow him even to death.

Whoever he was, he had the face of a man who could command. The face of a king.

CHAPTER 38

MCGUIRE HAD VENERATED the shroud ever since he was a young man. He had seen it for the first time in his early twenties when, fresh out of the seminary, he was studying canon law at the Gregorian in Rome. Fifty years later he still recalled the emotional impact of his visit to Turin.

"I was certain that I was looking at the face of Our Lord, that I was in his presence," he said when he had begun recovering from his shock. "I have never experienced a deeper sense of peace in my life. It strengthens my faith, even today."

"I still don't know what you're talking about," May said peevishly. "I've never heard of the Shroud of Turin."

McGuire provided some details. The shroud's first recorded appearance dated to the late 14th century when it was acquired by a French nobleman. Eventually purchased by the Duke of Savoy, the strange relic was kept in a locked iron grille behind the high altar in the Cathedral of St. John the Baptist in Turin. A church fire during the 16th century almost destroyed the shroud; it was pulled smouldering from its silver casket and doused with water; the singe marks and water stains were still visible. On rare occasions through the centuries, the Santa Sindone, as it was called, was displayed with great pageantry to the public.

The elusively faint, brownish-yellow image on the linen cloth had always been subject to violent controversy, McGuire admitted. It showed the life-sized imprint of the front and dorsal view of a bearded man with shoulder-length hair. Many skeptics regarded the likeness as a cunning fake.

Although he made no attempt to interrupt McGuire's narrative, I suspected from Bourgonne's blank, tight-lipped expression that he was among the nonbelievers.

The controversy, the archbishop went on, broke out most recently when negatives of photographs taken of the shroud in 1931 revealed the gray-white picture of a recumbent man. The detail was incredibly sharp and completely unexpected.

"But couldn't the photographs have been doctored?" Sara asked.

"That isn't likely," McGuire said. "Observers were present at every step during the photographic process. Notarized statements were taken, declaring that the pictures were free of any tampering or touchup."

"I don't understand," I said. "How could a negative offer more detail than the original photograph?"

"So far that question has defied scientific explanation," McGuire said. "I'm not expert in such matters, but I've been told that this image emerges only when the light values are reversed by a photographic negative. This has led some to argue that the shroud figure itself may actually be a negative."

"There's no chance the image could have been painted on the cloth?" May asked, frowning. His skepticism hadn't helped his irritability.

"Many have long insisted that is precisely what happened," Bourgonne put in.

It was my impression that he was similarly upset by the diversion but was doing his best to mask what he thought.

Approaching the cast again, McGuire didn't appear to hear the comment. "I haven't seen the shroud or studied the photographs in years," he said. "But I'll never forget it." He ran a hand over the reconstructed face. "My eyes tell me that this is the same as the sacred impression on the shroud, and yet my faith tells me that is impossible."

"So what's the problem," May said. "What difference does it make if they're the same.?"

McGuire looked unsettled to the point of confusion but managed to say, "It would mean the shroud is the burial cloth of a man who was not Christ. For the millions of faithful who venerate it as a relic, it would be a shattering blow, especially now when it's already so easy not to believe in God."

He stood in the center of the room, his bowed head hanging forward over his white collar. Later I tried to recall how long the silence lasted, five minutes, ten? He finally said he wanted to have photographs of the shroud and copies of the negatives sent to Chicago to compare with the body and Bourgonne's cast.

"It's the only way."

Considering the intensity of his feeling about the shroud, the decision was all the more remarkable.

"Are you sure you want to know?" I asked.

"It will come out sooner or later," McGuire said. "That will be unavoidable. If the shroud isn't authentic it will be a great misfortune, but the truth must be faced no matter how difficult or painful."

"What makes you think they'll send the photographs?" Sara asked. "They might not be willing to take a chance like that."

"They won't have a choice," McGuire said with subdued, almost mournful emphasis. "I'll explain what I've seen here today. I'll make the request personally. They'll have to respond. When they realize what's at stake, they won't be able to do otherwise." He kept his eyes focused on the cast. "There may be another explanation. I only pray we'll be able to find it."

CHAPTER 39

WITH May's approval, McGuire cabled the Vatican that same evening. He didn't get the answer he expected; he was told, instead, to have Bourgonne return to Rome to make a complete report on what he had seen in Chicago. We learned this later from McGuire after Bourgonne had already taken a plane to New York. No one had any idea how long he would be gone. He wasn't sure how difficult it would be to work out the arrangements to get photographs of the shroud.

I still didn't know what to think about that. Even if the body matched the image on the shroud, that wouldn't prove we had the remains of Jesus Christ. There was no definitive proof that the Shroud of Turin was actually the burial cloth of Christ, just as we lacked definitive proof on the identity of the corpse we had found at Qumran. After Bourgonne's experiment, the mystery was almost certain to remain unanswered.

There was no denying how provocative it would be if the body and the impression looked identical. McGuire was right; it was bound to be a shocking disappointment for all those who held the shroud to be a sacred object.

"They'll have to admit it was the burial cloth of a man who wasn't Christ," Sara said. "That won't be easy to accept for a lot of people."

"This could get ugly," I agreed. "As soon as you start raising questions about the most famous relic in the world, you're asking for trouble."

While we waited for the priest's return, Sara took up a subject we'd been deliberately avoiding for days. What were we going to do with the body when all this was over?

"I'd like to know what you're planning," she said to May.

He was sitting in an easy chair in his study; his beard was showing more gray since we had left Palestine.

"We don't need to make a decision now, do we?"

He avoided a direct answer. I could tell that he had some thoughts on the matter, but was playing it cagey.

"The body belongs in the Holy Land," Sara said. "It would be unthinkable for us to try to keep it."

May wasn't about to commit himself on that; but he had already told us he wanted a return for bankrolling the expedition to Qumran. Although his motives were hard to read, at the least complex level it was still my guess that he also wanted some public recognition and acclaim. The collector who had got his hands on a masterpiece and was going to make sure people knew about it, but in his own good time, relishing every moment. I didn't expect for a minute that he would easily part with the body or the scrolls.

That's why I waited for an argument when Sara pressed him. Instead, he was unexpectedly calm. The discussion, he insisted, was premature. We were still trying to find out what we had and what it meant, so why worry about the next step before it was absolutely necessary?

I foresaw at least one difficulty with Sara's plan. We'd found the body in Trans-Jordan, territory that had belonged to the Arabs before the fighting broke out. For all we knew, that area still might be under Arab control when the war ended.

"So who do we give it back to—the Arabs or the Jews?"

"You can't be serious," Sara said. She looked at me as if unsure whether I were joking. "The body and scrolls are part of the heritage of Israel. We could never let them fall into the hands of the Arabs."

I argued that the Arabs might make a territorial claim. With a war on and the borders up for grabs, it was an open question whether any antiquity laws remained in force; but all that would change once the shooting stopped. The legality of our finds would almost certainly be challenged—perhaps from both sides.

Another, potentially more serious problem also had to be considered.

"That body could be a target for every Arab fanatic in the Middle East," I said. "What if someone tried to steal or destroy it?" I could come up with any number of bloody scenarios.

As the days passed without word from Bourgonne or McGuire, May began to get impatient. He was starting to agree with Sara that we should talk to someone else, that we had gone as far as we could with the church in trying to identify the body and solve the mystery of the scrolls. He didn't think anything would come of Bourgonne's trip to Rome. He now agreed with the idea she had proposed earlier—inviting a group of prominent biblical scholars and archeologists to Chicago to examine the remains and the scrolls. The group would include both Jews and Christians.

Bourgonne should be among them; Sara was firm about that. It was more than the priest's abilities that impressed her. She liked the man.

Sara spent most of her time during this period trying to unravel more of the Manual of Discipline. The inner folds of the scroll from Bethlehem remained resistant to unrolling; but after painstaking work softening and cleaning the leather, she managed to translate several additional sentences. They reinforced her theory that the Essenes must have practiced an early form of baptism.

"The faithful," she said, reading the section aloud to us one afternoon, "shall be plunged into the water of purification that they may be cleansed of all wickedness and escape the guilt of their sins."

There was also a phrase describing a "meal of the holy," another reference that suggested a ritual prefiguring the eucharistic celebration.

I was sure the church was going to find just short of shocking the still-accumulating evidence in the scrolls of Christian practices that predated Jesus. When Bourgonne finally returned from Rome with photographs and negatives of the shroud, he admitted as much. He'd been gone nine days.

Bourgonne was accompanied by an American bishop named Edward Gray, a distinguished-looking man in his late forties with sharp Nordic features and fine blue eyes. He was a member of the Curia's staff and also served as one of the Pope's personal secretaries. Their plane had landed late in the evening, so they had spent the night at the chancellery. They arrived at May's house early the next morning.

Archbishop McGuire was with them. He looked in a mist, his face dead cold and distracted. He hesitated to sit down, dreading no doubt what was coming.

The decision to send the negatives of the shroud had been made at the highest level in the Vatican, Bourgonne said.

"By the Pope?" May asked.

"The Holy Father has not been told," the bishop said pleasantly. "I know that may sound strange, but if you knew anything at all of the Curia, perhaps you'd understand. The pontiff likes to joke that he's often the last person to find out anything."

"What do your people think of all this?" May asked.

Bourgonne glanced at Gray.

"Naturally they do not believe you've found the remains of Our Lord," the bishop said. "But they're extremely interested in trying to help you solve the mystery of the dead man's identity. I should also tell you in candor that there was some resistance to proceed with this . . . experiment."

"Father Bourgonne convinced them to do it," McGuire said with a forced smile. "I've already told him how grateful I am for that."

Gray mentioned the scrolls.

"Father's description of their contents made a strong impression and that's putting it mildly. To be honest, there was more discussion about the scrolls than about the body. His analysis of the Essenes and of their possible influence on early Christianity was intriguing. I've never heard anything like it."

I wondered how it had gone over when Bourgonne brought up some of the uncomfortable, almost uncanny similarities between the desert sect and the Christians. I also wondered what lay concealed behind the bishop's charming affability.

Plenty, I was willing to bet; you didn't make it to the Curia on an engaging smile, especially if you were an American. With an Italian hierarchy that would be like trying to swim with a stone tied around your neck. The bishop was nobody's fool. He'd been sent to Chicago for a reason.

"I understand you have two bodies," Gray said.

"One of them is a skeleton," Sara said.

"Without a head, I'm told. Perhaps I could examine it later if you have no objections."

Gray then asked to see the cast. "I've been looking forward to this ever since Father Bourgonne told me what he had done here."

We went into the study. May removed a dust cover from the cast.

I was struck again by the impact of the profile, the strong features and commanding eyes, the entire face dominated by the wicked scar that ran down the center of the forehead.

Bishop Gray examined the reconstructed face as if it were just another curious museum piece. He noncommittally confessed how much he admired the work, but gave no hint as to what he really thought.

McGuire exchanged glances with all of us, his small eyes bright with fear. "I haven't stopped praying that I'm wrong. These last few days have been very hard for me." He faltered helplessly. "Please, I must see the negatives."

"Perhaps that might be a good idea," Gray said.

I had been watching Bourgonne for any sign he already knew how this was going to turn out; I couldn't detect a thing from his preoccupied, business-like expression.

Opening a bulky valise carried from Rome, he laid a large color photograph of the Shroud of Turin on the table. There was also a thick stack of negatives, each enlarged to correspond to the actual size of a section of the shroud. He carefully arranged them on the floor. The shroud, he said, was 14 feet long and just under four feet wide. The cloth would have wrapped the body on both sides, folding over the head. When the shroud was spread out flat, the result was a double, head-to-head image of the front and back. The assembled negatives showed both views.

The sight was arresting. There on the floor was the unmistakable likeness of a tall, well-developed man whose strange, almost three-dimensional shape was lightly shaded in white and gray against a dark background. The image on the negatives was much clearer and sharper than the faint outline of a corpse, which showed up as a blurred, straw-yellow silhouette on the photograph. The body lay on its back, hands folded across the pelvis. The bearded face appeared in fine detail. The eyes were closed; the nose and cheeks looked slightly swollen.

At Bourgonne's suggestion, we opened the casket. Displaying icy control, Bishop Gray stared down at the corpse in silence. He finally said to Bourgonne, "When I listened to you describe this in Rome, I'll confess I didn't believe you. I realize now I owe you an apology."

It was at once apparent to all of us that the image on the shroud couldn't have been made by the dead man from Qumran. Even McGuire could see the pronounced differences. A drawn-out gasp escaped him then as he brought a white-knuckled fist to his mouth.

"I was so sure, so certain," he said as he leaned against a table, no longer able to support his weight. "I thank God. I thank Him with all my heart."

He spoke with the exhausted gratitude of a man just awakened from the ether after a successful, near fatal operation. His face began to regain color. Believing as he did that the shroud was Christ's burial cloth, his joyful, near overwhelming relief had pushed him almost to tears.

"My faith," he said, "has never depended on the shroud, but it would have been such a misfortune if the image had resembled the man in the casket. It would have meant the shroud wasn't a sacred relic of Our Lord's death." Another deep sigh passed his lips. "A nightmare has just ended for me."

Bourgonne and Gray, by contrast, studied the negatives and body in dispassionate silence. They didn't look in the least surprised. My guess was that Gray shared Bourgonne's skepticism about the shroud.

"There are some similarities," Bourgonne said finally. "I can understand how his excellency might have been mistaken."

But the slight resemblance in facial structure, the shape of the beard and slender body type were more than overcome by glaring differences.

The expression portrayed on the cloth was of a man peacefully at rest; it depicted none of the agony that contorted the face of the dead man. That was the most pronounced difference. The lips of the corpse in the casket were fuller, the eyes larger and more widely spaced; he was also nearly three inches shorter than the man depicted on the shroud, who measured five-feet-eleven.

"Even taking into account that the body would have contracted during the centuries, that's a significant disparity," Sara said.

She also pointed out how the face on the shroud seemed to show different areas of physical damage.

"The swelling below the right eye isn't visible on the body. Neither is the puffiness on the left side of the chin."

The apparent bloodstains were also dissimilar. The stains on the Turin shroud showed as white shadings around the forehead and forearms.

"Notice how precise and sharply outlined these tracings are," Bourgonne said. "Even if we assume they are bloodstains—and we have no way of proving that—would it not be more logical to assume that after the body was wrapped with burial spices and positioned in the tomb the blood would have smeared?"

The stains on the shroud that wrapped the dead man from Qumran, he observed, were smeared.

"It also seems curious that the genitals are not visible," Bourgonne went on. "You would expect that part of the anatomy to show up as vividly as the face and hands."

"The feet and chest aren't that clear either," May said, studying the negatives. "You can barely make them out."

"Perhaps the shroud didn't lay completely flat," McGuire said.

"That is possible," Bourgonne answered, "but one could also argue that an artist would have concentrated precisely on the areas that stand out, the face and hands. Artistic modesty might have kept him from painting the genitals."

McGuire smiled. "An interesting interpretation, father. The fact remains that no one has ever proven that the shroud was painted."

"While I was in Rome, I did some research on the subject," Bourgonne said. "Several painted shrouds were known to exist in the 14th century, the same time this one made its first recorded appearance. There is even a record that during its first exhibition in France an influential bishop argued quite forcefully that it was the work of an artist. Similar complaints were made."

As skeptical as anyone about the shroud, I nevertheless was struck by the three-dimensional image that had been unlocked in the photographic negatives.

"If it were painted," I asked, "who could have done something like that? The work is ingenious."

"It has been suggested that Leonardo da Vinci might have been the artist," Bourgonne said. "We know that he loved to do counterfeits. He would have been perhaps the only man with the necessary knowledge of anatomy to achieve such an effect."

"So you think it's a fraud?" Sara asked Bourgonne.

"I'm afraid I must. I am sure the image is an example of devotional art from the early Renaissance."

"What about you," she asked Gray.

"The church has never insisted on the authenticity of the shroud for the very good reason it can't be proved," he said carefully. "To be honest, I'm more concerned about the identity of the man lying there in the casket."

"I see that I'm outnumbered," McGuire said. "That's all right. I don't mind. My faith in the shroud is unshaken." The crisis passed, he had regained his composure.

At May's suggestion, we went into the living room. All three priests seemed relieved to get away from the negatives and body.

In his methodical, precise way, Gray steered the conversation back to the scrolls and the Qumran community.

"It wasn't easy for the church to send the negatives here," he said. "The decision was unprecedented. Certain members of the Curia who wouldn't have approved had to be circumvented, one of them the archbishop of Turin. I only mention this in the hope you can see how serious we are in wanting to help you. There's so much we're prepared to do. I think we could begin by..."

"You could begin by telling us why they sent you all the way from Rome," May said, stopping him.

Gray smiled. "You're very direct, Mister May," he said. "I was asked to come to Chicago for a simple reason. The body you found is of special concern to the church. We know that it isn't the remains of Jesus Christ just as we know that the bones you dug up can't possibly be the skeleton of John the Baptist. But we're prepared to admit that your Teacher of Righteousness was a man of importance—not just to the history of the Jews, but also quite possibly to our own religion. Your remarkable scroll suggests as much. There have never been finds like these. I was directed by the highest authority to offer our help in trying to resolve the enigma of these discoveries. The Vatican is prepared to place all of its resources at your disposal. All of our archives, our archeologists, specialists like Father Bourgonne, our church historians...whatever and whoever could be of help."

He paused, leaning forward in his chair.

"If you would agree, we'd like to take the body to Rome. We have the facilities there, the experts to do a thorough investigation. Expense is no consideration. You can..."

The suggestion caught us off guard. Sara recovered first.

"That's out of the question," she said. "There's no way we'd agree to that."

"If you're worried about the objectivity of such an inquiry, you needn't be. It's our intention that you would direct the proceedings yourself."

"The research can be done right here in Chicago," Sara said firmly. "We don't have to cart everything to Rome. That's the last thing we need to do now."

"Couldn't we at least discuss the matter? You might find some advantages with such an arrangement."

May shook his head. "I don't like the idea either. So let's drop it."

McGuire spoke up. "John, just let us try to explain. I ask you as a friend to hear us out. As a favor."

"The church can be very generous," Gray said.

How generous became apparent moments later when the bishop asked whether we would consider selling the body and skeleton as well as the scrolls to the Vatican.

"The Holy See," he said, "is prepared to pay one million dollars."

The proposition, coming on the heels of the other one, stunned us. I felt myself pushed back deep into my chair as if an invisible fist had been driven into the pit of my stomach.

Sara shot to her feet, her face coloring. "I can't believe this!" she said, her voice harsh and corrosive in her anger. "First you want us to ship the body to Rome and now you have the audacity to try to buy it as if it were a painting in a gallery. Is that supposed to be your idea of 'helping us'? What do you take us for?"

May said nothing. He stared straight at Gray, who went on patiently. "I'm sure this must come as a shock. As I said, we would be willing to let you take charge of the work, whatever has to be done. In fact, we'd encourage it."

"Don't give me that," Sara countered. "You'd never let us near the Vatican. If you ask me, you want to make sure all of this is covered up."

Addressing May, Gray said, "If you don't think the price is fair, we could possibly increase it."

"I'm listening," May said.

"John, my god. You can't go on with this."

"Maybe I can't, but I want to hear what they've got to say."

I couldn't tell whether he was really interested or just playing along. It was possibly a little of each.

Sara brushed past the priests and walked to the far end of the room. She stood there with her back to us.

"We'd only ask you to withhold any public comment until after the inquiry has been concluded," McGuire said. "A premature announcement would only cause unnecessary confusion among the faithful. I think you'd agree that the immediate assumption will be that you've discovered the remains of Our Lord. We know that isn't the case, but the world press would be quick to draw that conclusion and spread it across the front pages. Or if not the Lord then someone very much like him—an unknown prophet. A Teacher of Righteousness—a Second Christ. I'm sure you can see the serious difficulties that sort of thing might cause."

McGuire was pleading with us and making no apologies for it.

"This isn't easy for me to say, but even the best of men are often shaken in their religious convictions," Gray said, "The spark of faith is so incredibly faint; the slightest breeze and it's snuffed out forever. We're only asking you to help us eliminate any risk of..." He was weighing every word. "...of misunderstanding."

"What would you do with the body once you finished with it?" May finally asked. I sensed that he was stalling.

"It would be treated with the greatest respect and care," Gray went on. "No harm would come to it. You have my word on that. It's our hope you will agree that the church really would be the most qualified to conduct such an examination. As for the scrolls, they would give us a chance to learn something about how our religion, how Christianity started. It's an incredible opportunity."

After a long silence, May said, "You've sure as hell given us a lot to think about."

Gray smiled. "I know we've offered you a great deal of money, but then you've taken considerable risks and gone to much expense. The church only wishes to be fair. The money has already been arranged. You may be paid in any manner you wish. At any time."

"We'll need to talk this over," May said.

"By all means, take as long as necessary," the bishop said, brightening at the hint of interest he caught in May's voice. "I hope I'll be able to report favorably to my superiors in Rome as soon as possible. They're anxious to conclude this matter to everyone's satisfaction."

The priests stood up to leave. On his way out, Bourgonne, who hadn't said much since we finished with the shroud, shook my hand. At the same time, he pressed a small, tightly folded piece of paper in my palm. He looked straight into my eyes and said, "I hope we can meet again. That would be a great privilege."

When they were gone, I opened the note. It said: "I must talk to you. I will call tonight. There are things you do not know."

CHAPTER 40

BOURGONNE CALLED in the late evening. I spoke to him. He said he was at a drugstore pay phone on North Superior Street a few blocks from the chancellery. He didn't have much time to talk.

"I must see you, soon" he said. "Now if possible."

A bad connection made it difficult to understand him, but there was no mistaking his agitation.

"Is anything wrong?"

The line went silent for a moment. Then he said softly, "There are powerful men in Rome who may try to stop you if you do not do what they want. I must talk to you."

I put my hand over the mouthpiece of the phone and repeated this for May. He looked puzzled.

"We can meet him wherever he likes," he said.

Bourgonne said that he would wait for us at the drugstore. We would pick him up at a news kiosk outside. I wrote down the address.

"I hope that I can get away without being seen," Bourgonne said. "It will be a risk, but I have no choice. You must come." He hung up abruptly.

"What's that all about?" May asked.

"Whatever it is, we better show up," I said. I didn't understand what was going on, but Bourgonne's urgency had left me troubled. He sounded frightened.

We left Hyde Park a few minutes later. May drove. On the way we discussed the church's offer to buy the body and scrolls. We had spoken of little else. May had made it clear he wasn't about to give up control of the discoveries.

"You sure had me fooled," Sara said. "I didn't know what to think when you encourage Gray to go on about the money."

She had lashed out at him as soon as the priests had left. Even now, after he had reassured her, a residue of anger remained in her voice.

May had his own temper under control for a change. "Sara, there's a little rule I have," he said patiently. "When someone offers you a million bucks, you better listen."

It didn't take long to get uptown; we crossed the drawbridge over the Chicago River at Michigan Avenue and a few blocks later turned onto North Superior. Bourgonne was standing at the kiosk, watching for us; he was wearing a hat and a raincoat with the collar turned up. I opened the door and he slid into the back seat.

"I do not have much time," Bourgonne said as we drove toward the lake. "I might be missed. I am so glad you could come, all of you. I know this is an inconvenience."

He looked and sounded anxious.

"You said someone might try to stop us," I said.

"I find this difficult to explain," the priest said slowly. "You are dealing with something that I do not understand—even now after all these years." His face was in shadows, but we passed under a street light and I saw that he was staring straight at me. "There are men in the Vatican who might be willing to take...drastic steps if you do not sell them the body from Qumran and the scrolls."

"What do you mean, drastic steps," May said, glancing back at him over his shoulder.

"You must forgive me if I cannot answer with precision," Bourgonne said with the same hesitancy of speech. "It is only a feeling I have."

We drove along the deserted streets and turned onto Lake Shore Drive. The Gold Coast with its high-priced apartment buildings and townhouses was behind us now; we were heading toward Evanston. Bourgonne sat there in silence, leaning back in the seat; he stared out at the black curtain that was Lake Michigan.

Finally, May said, "I think maybe you better try to explain all this a little better. If we're in some kind of jam, I'd like to know where we stand."

Bourgonne rubbed his temples as if the blood were throbbing there. "Do you know what the Italian expression 'senza paura' means?"

"It's been a while since I studied Italian, but doesn't senza mean 'without,'" Sara said. Sitting next to May, she turned in her seat so that she faced Bourgonne.

"Without fear," the priest said. "It is the name of a secret group within the Curia that has been talked of quietly for years, since before the war. A prudent man did not ask questions."

He came to a full stop as if uncertain whether to continue.

"What does this have to do with us?" May asked.

Bourgonne, still struggling with himself, took a while to calm down.

"I need not tell you how certain members of the Curia were shaken by my report," he said. "Great care is being taken to keep this affair secret. Only a handful of men know."

"Whose idea was it to buy the body?" May asked.

"Cardinal Marco Frilandini made the decision. I am certain of that. Frilandini and two, possibly three others. A small group of men—the Senza Paura."

"Tell me about this Frilandini," May said, keeping his eyes on the road.

"He is the eminence grise of the Curia. A remarkable man and very powerful. Perhaps the only one who can truly be said to have the pontiff's ear."

During his short trip to Rome, he'd asked a good friend of his at the Lateran Museum, a man he trusted completely, to check out his suspicions.

"He knows nothing of the body or of my work here. He did not ask questions. He has taken a great risk."

This friend, Bourgonne went on, had recently sent him a telegram about mutual friends; its real meaning was that Frilandini had been meeting with two other influential cardinals, whose names had been linked to the group.

"And this Frilandini has enough influence to pay us one million dollars without consulting the Pope?" Sara asked doubtfully.

Bourgonne nodded. "You must understand that he is a key member of the Secretariat of State for the Vatican. He is also consultor to the Congregation for the Doctrine of the Faith—the modern successor to the Inquisition. The Pope has honored him

255

repeatedly with high office. No one has more influence and power with the Curia. Not even the Pope himself. The pontiff is so very isolated. By tradition he is not even permitted to dine with others."

"I still don't see why you're worried," May said. "What's the problem?"

Bourgonne smiled. "Let me tell you about these men," he said. "Since the conclusion of the war, this cabal has become more active. Its purpose is to preserve the authority of Holy Mother church in times of crisis. Most recently it has tried to counter the criticism that the Holy Father did not do enough to protest the slaughter of six million Jews by a nation in large part Catholic. That he failed to use his influence to stop the killing. I think history will show that the Pope took many risks to help the Jews— more than is known. But Senza Paura has worked constantly behind the scenes to stifle such attacks. You can see the effects in your own country. How much moral indignation to the massacre of the Jews has been expressed from the pulpits or in pastoral letters? The Catholic church in America has said little about the Holocaust. Frilandini has done his work very well. A few letters, a few private visits. The word eventually gets out...I have no proof, of course. Just as I have no proof that it was Frilandini who advised the Pope not to speak out publicly when it was well known the Jews were dying by the thousands. Dear God, I can imagine what he would have said." His voice rose in sarcastic anger. "This is a political affair, Holy Father. There is nothing we can do. Our hands are tied. Italy is a Fascist state after all. We are an occupied country. You would do better to wait for the right moment and try to mediate. It is better now to be silent and pray."

Bourgonne pounded a fist against the door. "They will have to explain this before God himself some day! Just as I will have to explain my own cowardice during those awful years. We will all be judged for what we didn't do or say. Thank God, some of us had more courage. Many Catholic priests and nuns died in the concentration camps. Others risked their lives to help Jews escape from Europe. Many were provided with forged passports that said they were Catholic."

"The church did as much as anyone," Sara said softly.

"But it could have done so much more."

We drove a long time before anyone spoke again. When we passed under a street light, I saw that the priest's eyes were teary.

May finally asked him whether he knew the other members of Senza Paura.

"Cardinals Andamo Viti of Florence and Giovanni Maspero of Turin are most frequently mentioned. Both are close to Frilandini. Maspero is a wealthy man, who raises horses. He has several large estates in Parma and a villa outside Rome. Frilandini and Viti have visited his villa often in recent days. My friend has passed this information on to me. I am sure these meetings are not a coincidence. Bishop Gray must be aware of them."

"Surely he can't have anything to do with this," Sara said, resisting the thought.

"The bishop was a special assistant to Cardinal Frilandini in the secretariat," Bourgonne said. "His administrative skills were greatly appreciated by the cardinal. It is no secret that he owes his position as a papal secretary to Frilandini's influence."

"Then you think he knows about this group you've mentioned, Senza Paura," I asked.

"I am certain of it."

May asked about Archbishop McGuire.

Bourgonne shook his head. "He would not be included in such discussions."

"You said they might try to stop us," May said. "What did you mean?"

"You do not intend to accept their money?"

"Of course not," May said.

Sara explained our plan to let a panel of scholars examine the body and scrolls. May had finally agreed it was time to go ahead with that.

"Professor Edwards might be able to help," she said.

"A fine man," Bourgonne said. "I am familiar with his writings. The University of Chicago is fortunate to have him."

"We'd like you to join us," Sara said.

"That would be impossible. They would never grant permission... You must be very careful." Bourgonne started to say more but broke off.

"But why?" May said angrily. "What could they do?"

"*Il faut que ils vouz arretent!*" the priest cried out, slipping into French. "They will try to stop you. They do not want a public discussion of your discoveries. That is what they wish to avoid at all costs."

"But how—how could they stop us," I said.

"I must tell you again that these men are not afraid to take risks. They are methodical and efficient and they believe they are doing God's will, which makes them dangerous."

Sagging forward in the driver's seat, May said, "I don't believe this."

"You must believe it!" Bourgonne shot back. "You must believe exactly what I am telling you. In times of crisis, the church has never lacked strong, ruthless men willing to take matters into their own hands. The history of the Borgias is only one example. Torquemada is another. Frilandini believes your discoveries constitute the most serious crisis the church has faced in centuries. If he suspects that you do not intend to sell, he will move against you. I am sure of that."

"But how?" I asked again. "What could he possibly hope to do? We're in Chicago. This isn't Madrid or Rome during the Inquisition. We're five thousand miles away. We don't have autos da fé here."

Bourgonne smiled. "It would not be difficult. Have you heard of Opus Die?"

The words, he said, meant the "Work of God" and referred to a reactionary group of ultra-conservative Catholics that was worldwide in its organization. Many of those who belonged, he said, were wealthy and well connected.

"Opus Die has influential members in the United States, possibly even here in Chicago. Yes, Cardinal Frilandini would be able to get whatever help he needs. He is not a man for equivocation. If the time should come, he will act quickly. Make no mistake on that."

May stopped at a red light.

"Well, that's one bitch of a story," he said.

Sara and I looked at one another.

"Whatever we do, we aren't going to sell to them," she said.

"Then you must announce your discoveries as soon as possible," Bourgonne insisted. "Before they learn of your intentions. They might hesitate then. It could be...a protection."

"You're really sure they'll try something?" May asked, still skeptical.

"They already have," the priest said slowly. "They have sent Bishop Gray to Chicago and offered you one million dollars. The more important question is what will they do next."

CHAPTER 41

WE DROPPED Bourgonne off two blocks from the chancellery in a pelting rain. He pulled his hat low over his eyes and raised the collar of his coat before he got out of the car.

"You're sure you don't want us to get closer?" May said. He had parked at a deserted intersection on North Superior. The green light of a traffic signal reflected on the wet pavement.

"No, this will be better. I do not want anyone to see your car."

Bourgonne put his hand on the door handle. "I owe you so much," he said, not moving. "Your discoveries are a great gift. I am afraid we may never know what they mean, not completely. I keep asking myself whose body that could be, whose face on the shroud? I think of it every hour. If those questions could be answered, it would be a wonderful advance. It might give Christians a new understanding of their religion."

"What if some people don't like that?" May asked.

"It will happen anyway, and if we are luckier than we deserve it will strengthen our faith." He sounded tired as he said this. "You have been very kind." He smiled and started to get out of the car. Turning once, he said, "Please be careful."

When we got back to Hyde Park, we had a long talk. The plan that evolved was to delay for time—at least until Sara could make the arrangements to assemble the group of experts she wanted to examine the discoveries. Unsure of how the church might react, May didn't want to tip his hand.

"How long will it take to get set up and down to work?" he asked. "The sooner the better."

Sara thought that Edwards could help her come up with a list of names.

"I'll talk to him tomorrow," she said. "We should have a good idea who to invite by then."

It was nearly two in the morning before Sara and I went up to our room. The storm had continued and the rain was beating against the windows. Neither of us was tired; lying in bed, we were still trying to digest everything that Bourgonne had told us.

"This isn't the Middle Ages," Sara said. "You said so yourself. What could they do?"

"I'm not sure, and that's what bothers me."

"In a few days everything will be over. As soon as we make our announcement that will be the end to it. He admitted as much himself."

Bourgonne hadn't gone quite that far.

"We'll have our meeting and then we'll get married," Sara said. "I hope you haven't forgotten about that." She was pretending to look serious—and failing. "I intend to hold you to your promise."

I drew her to me. There was no longer any need to worry, not about cardinals or the Curia or even about the dead man—who he was, who he wasn't. That wasn't necessary anymore. I was about to make love to the woman I was going to marry.

CHAPTER 42

BISHOP Gray called early in the morning. May spoke to him on the telephone. Sara and I were still in bed. When we got up, he told us that the bishop wanted to know whether we'd made a decision yet.

"I told him we needed more time to talk it over. I tried to sound like I was interested."

"How did he take that?" I asked.

"He promised to call again. He said he didn't want to rush us."

Later that morning, Sara called Professor Edwards. Not wanting to explain what she had in mind over the telephone, she asked him to come out to Hyde Park. Edwards, who didn't have to be coaxed, drove out immediately. After listening to her plan to assemble a team of scholars to examine the body and scrolls, he quickly agreed to help. The only problem was that he didn't have time to discuss the idea in detail; he had an appointment to meet a student at the university. He also wanted to develop the film he had taken during the autopsy.

"Why don't you stop by my office this evening and we can talk about it some more," he suggested. "I can have the film ready by then. We can look at it together."

Sara promised to come at seven o'clock. Edwards also took along the film we had shot at Qumran. May didn't want a commercial studio to do the processing, and the professor readily agreed to handle it himself.

I used the rest of the day to polish the articles I'd been working on. I thought I'd done a fair job of getting the story down in a couple thousand words. There was a good deal that I had deliberately left out. For one thing, I didn't mention the killings— the Bedouin at Qumran; the young Arab we'd buried in the garden in Jerusalem; Benteen shot dead by Jewish soldiers at the airstrip. I also left out that hard to describe, harder to explain feeling of apprehension that had dogged me for weeks now.

After dinner Sara and I left for the institute. May stayed behind. I drove his big Hudson. The evening was clear and cool, and a lot of people were out walking in Hyde Park, enjoying the weather.

"When do you think we should tell Edwards about the church?" Sara asked.

"Let's leave that up to May."

"Paul, I'm still not sure how to read him. I don't understand what he wants in all this."

"I doubt he knows himself."

"I'm afraid of what might happen when we've finished with the body," Sara said. "What will he do then?" She looked over at me. "It has to go back to the Holy Land. If I have to, I'll fight him hard on that."

As soon as I turned onto 57th Street, I saw the squad cars, at least six black and whites. They were pulled over to the curb in front of the institute. A few more were across the street. Fifteen or twenty people, their faces hushed and intent, were standing on the sidewalk under the canopy of trees.

"Something's up," I said. I pulled into a space and got out with Sara.

The crowd was knotted up near the curb, small groups talking among themselves. Most of them looked like students. But there were a few well-dressed men holding newspapers and briefcases, faculty members obviously. Police were mingled among them; some had pads out and were taking down names in notebooks.

When we were closer, I saw two cops bent over on their knees in the street, making a chalk sketch on the pavement a few yards from the curb. A beefy man in a soiled laboratory coat walked over, pointed a bulky camera at what they were drawing, and took a photograph. Rising up on tiptoes, I looked over the heads of the spectators and peered down at the two cops. They were sketching the outline of a man, the arms thrust out straight from the sides like a stick figure. A dark, wide stain seemed to flow out from the middle of the sketch. Two books were lying in the gutter; the man in the lab coat took a picture of them as well.

I became aware now of a moaning sound, low and intermittent. A woman's voice, it was coming from inside the opened front doors of the institute. Some police were standing there. A young woman in a blue skirt was sitting on a chair just inside the building's vestibule. She was sobbing. A cop was sitting next to her with a yellow pad on his lap. An elderly woman stood nearby holding a glass of water.

Two cops stopped us as we tried to walk through the entrance.

"Go on, keep moving," one of them said with a frown. I knew the look: it meant get lost if you don't want trouble.

"What's going on?" I held out my press card and explained that we had business there.

The cop wasn't pleased, but his expression changed. He was going to cooperate, but only as far as the ritual required. "A car nailed a guy," he said reluctantly. "Lady saw the whole thing." He nodded toward the young woman.

"Is he all right?"

"He's dead. He was crossing the street out front there..." He pointed to the two cops who were still hunched over on their knees. "Guy comes around the corner and clipped him with the bumper. Car ain't damaged at all, not even a dent."

The accident, he said, had occurred thirty minutes earlier. The ambulance had already taken the body to the morgue.

The driver of the car had stopped and tried to help the man, the cop went on.

"How did it happen?" I asked.

"That's the problem. The driver don't speak much English. The best we can make out, he didn't see the poor bastard. He's standing over there across the street. They're still trying to get something out of him before he goes downtown."

I had noticed him earlier, a blond, anemic looking man with a light beard, smoking a cigarette. He was about forty and had a dazed expression. Three cops were standing with him. The car he was driving was parked nearby, a blue sedan.

"The guy's a Pole," the cop told me.

"Will he be charged?"

"Man he hit was right in the crosswalk," the cop said, nodding. "The woman who saw it says the car came around the corner and plowed right into him. The hell of it is he wasn't going more than twenty, twenty-five. He shoulda been able to get that car stopped."

"Could have been the brakes," said another cop, who stood nearby. He snickered. "Be just like a Polack to have a car with bad brakes."

Almost as an afterthought I asked the dead man's name as we were getting ready to continue into the institute's lobby.

"Guy named Edwards," the cop said. "He was a teacher here."

Sara made an unsteady movement and slumped against me. I could feel her go limp. I put an arm around her and half carrying her, started back to the car.

"Hey, you know him?" the cop asked.

"She was a student of his," I said. "I think I better get her out of here."

I drove down the street, made a turn and headed back to May's house following the university midway. Sara was leaning forward in the seat. She'd been crying.

"He was such a good man," she said. "How could it happen? How can he be dead?"

"Sara, come on, you're going to be fine," I said, taking her hand. I was worried she was going to pass out.

When we got back to the house, I told May.

"Sara, I'm so sorry," he said, coming to her at once. He took her by the shoulders and looked hard into her eyes. "How do you feel?"

"I'm all right," she said slowly, "I'm better. It's just so horrible. I know his wife. I've been to dinner at their home. I've met their daughter. I feel like I should go over there. Maybe there's something I can do . . . Something."

I remembered what it had been like when she found out that Professor Parker had been shot in Jerusalem. She'd been closer to Edwards. May brought her a glass of brandy.

After giving her a few moments, he asked what she wanted to do next. He thought we should move ahead with the plans to assemble a panel. The problem now was we needed a new sponsor.

"I don't think this is the time for that," I said angrily. "My god, she hasn't even had a chance to pull herself together."

"No, I don't mind," Sara said. "It'll help me get my mind off what happened."

We had only begun discussing the options when Bourgonne called. He was using a pay phone again. As before, he sounded agitated. May got on an extension in the kitchen while I took the call in the study.

Before he went too far, I told him about Edwards.

There was a long pause before he said, "I am so sorry. I regret I knew him only by reputation." He inquired about Sara. "This must be a great sadness for her."

"She's OK," May said brusquely, cutting in on the extension. "We've got a lot going on here. What do you want?"

"Something is happening," Bourgonne said. "Bishop Gray has been in communication with the Vatican all day. I am afraid they have decided you are not going to cooperate. You must make an announcement. You cannot wait any longer."

"But we still don't know they're going to do anything at all," May said irritably. The pressure and doubts of the last few days welled up in his voice. "We just have your suspicions. And Father, don't take me wrong, but that's not much to go on."

"What I told you last night was not a suspicion," Bourgonne said. "These men believe they must save the church. I am afraid of what might happen. You must believe me."

He let that sink in, then said, "I have been ordered back to Rome. I am to leave tomorrow."

Before we could respond, the priest went on, "I have made a decision. I will not go." What he said next was as startling as what had preceeded it. "Can you meet me tomorrow at the airport? I will come with you. I will bring the negatives of the shroud. They will have a great effect. Please, you must let me help in this. To be silent now would be a greater sin than disobedience."

The words tumbled out as if he were afraid he'd lose his nerve.

May put down the telephone and came back into the study. "What do you think?" he asked, after explaining to Sara what had been said.

"Those negatives would be a big help," she said at once. "So would Bourgonne. He could be invaluable to us."

Especially now with Edwards dead, I thought.

May got back on the line and asked the priest when he was scheduled to leave.

"At nine-ten in the morning. We are to go to New York and get another plane to Rome. I will be accompanied, but I will get away. Somehow I will get away."

"All right, listen. This is what you do," May said. "We'll be waiting at the main entrance to the terminal. We'll be in a green car, the same one we picked you up in the other night. Do you want us to come in after you?"

"No, that won't be necessary. I must get back. God bless you."
He hung up.

"Can we trust him?" May asked quickly.

"We can't afford not to," I said.

CHAPTER 43

MAY HAD A SUMMER HOUSE on Lake Michigan about an hour's drive up the shore. He still thought the priest was overly worried, but suggested moving out there as a precaution, at least until we could get a better read on everything Bourgonne had told us.

We decided to leave that same evening. In the morning, we'd drive back in and pick up Bourgonne at O'Hare. The panel truck we had brought in Mississippi was leaking oil by the quart; so we took the rear seat out of the Hudson and removed the partition that separated the passenger compartment from the trunk. The casket with the body just fit inside, but there wasn't room for the one with the skeleton. We left it locked in the storage room in the basement; none of us liked that but we didn't have any choice.

Sara got the metal strongbox that contained the fragments of the copper scroll; she also brought the two scrolls from Bethlehem, which she had carefully wrapped and placed in cardboard boxes.

A short time later, we were on Lake Shore Drive, heading north. it was just after ten o'clock. May said it was about thirty miles to his home, which was in Lake Forest.

We passed Grant Park and the high walls of Soldiers Field. Despite the late hour, Michigan Avenue was jammed with traffic. There was a tieup at the drawbridge over the Chicago River; the span had been raised for an ore boat. As we waited, we saw the stacks glide by festooned with red and white lights like a Christmas tree. When the bridge was lowered, May punched the accelerator.

He turned at Fullerton Avenue, drove north a few miles, and then picked up Lake Shore Drive again. He wanted to avoid some road construction.

Once or twice I thought I saw something out the rear window. Headlights that seemed to be hanging back behind us, but which always disappeared when we passed someone.

Then we turned again and this time the lights were still there, a couple hundred yards behind us. May slowed for a traffic signal. We made it to the end of the block and started around another corner when I saw the car sail through a red light to keep up with us.

"Someone's back there," I said.

"I know," May said. "I wasn't sure at first." He made a turn, then another sharper turn, changing streets quickly.

The headlights stayed with us, two amber discs boring into the darkness.

May sped down a deserted street, the tires squealing as the heavy car slid around the corner with the back end pulling hard.

"Where are we?" Sara said.

"Division Street!" May snapped. He was concentrating on the road, arms stiff as he grasped the wheel. We leaned around another corner. I got a better look as the car turned behind us. Still a good block away, they weren't trying to overtake us, just keep us in view.

"It's a big four-door," I said.

We hurtled across a narrow bridge that spanned a canal.

"The body won't take this kind of jarring!" Sara warned.

"There's not much I can do about that," May shouted. "I'm not going to slow down for these guys."

We'd covered the casket with a tarp and padded it all around with blankets. Crouched over, I was holding it down with my hands, trying to keep it from bouncing.

May turned onto a one-way street that ran like a tunnel between a long row of warehouses; I caught a glimpse of a grain elevator towering up against the black sky.

"Railroad tracks!" May yelled. "Hang on!"

The Hudson banged over a crossing. The impact threw my head against the roof, but I kept my grip around the casket. It was some ride.

We cut onto a brightly-lit street, where there was more traffic. The lights formed a tapering line that seemed to touch in the distance. We raced alongside a trolley and then swerved in front as its bell clanged angrily. May hit the gas, passed two or three cars on the inside, and made another turn. We were in Evanston, somewhere near Northwestern University, a quiet residential neighborhood with large homes and broad lawns. We turned onto a dark street and pulled over to the curb. A dog was barking nearby.

"I think we've lost them," May said. He'd driven beautifully.

"Who were they?" Sara asked.

"I don't know, but it looks like Bourgonne was giving it to us straight all along," I said, aiming the comment at May. "He knew something was up."

There was no doubt in my mind that the chase and the priest's warning were related.

"I should have seen it coming," May agreed. "I just didn't believe the guy." He sat there thinking. "Those boys were after the body. They were probably watching the house and decided to make their move when they saw us leave."

"The question now is what will they try next?" I said.

"Shake us down," May said. "They want the body and scrolls. But they'll have to find us first." He rapped his hands on the steering wheel. "I wish Benteen were still alive. I'd have a job for him right now."

We waited an hour before we got started again. It was well past midnight when we finally reached Lake Forest. May turned off on a gravel road that wound through a pine forest.

"The lake's just over that ridge in front of us," he said.

Made of rough stone with a timbered front, the house was set away from the road, screened by a row of trees. May parked and we unloaded the casket. When we got out I noticed my shirt was soaking wet.

The place smelled stale and musty when we opened the back door. May said he hadn't paid a visit in over a year. We put the casket in the living room.

I parted the curtains of a picture window; the lake was just beyond the treetops. The moon was reflected on the water like a china plate.

May had a pump-action .12-gauge shotgun locked in a cabinet. He took it from its rack and shoved six red shells into its breech.

I was relieved to hear the dial tone when I checked the telephone.

May got a bottle of bourbon and poured out three stiff drinks. Sara looked pale and upset. It had been a hard few hours on her; the freak accident that had killed Professor Edwards was still fresh in her memory, and now this.

"We better make an announcement about our discoveries," she said.

It's what Bourgonne had been urging all along. I seconded the idea and suggested talking to a reporter.

"Let's get the story out now, in case something happens," I said. "It might make whoever's after the body and scrolls a little more reluctant to try something. I could call the Associated Press and set it up."

May balked. "If they want them bad enough, that's not going to stop them."

"Maybe it won't, but if they're stolen, at least there'll be a record we had them. We'll have some witnesses."

May's moody silence told me he wasn't happy at the prospect of being forced to go public before he was ready. It fit the pattern. He'd been reluctant for the same reason to have some experts to examine the finds from Qumran. He didn't want to lose control over treasures he still regarded as his personal possessions.

"John, I want to call some reporters," Sara insisted. "If you won't, I'll do it myself."

If May thought of arguing it out, he quickly gave up the idea.

"When could you arrange that?" he asked me finally.

"We'll have to wait until morning," I said. "If I call the AP bureau now, I'll just get the night rewrite man and he won't be able to do a damn thing."

"I'd pay money to talk to Bourgonne right now," May said. "I wonder if he knows anything about this?"

"They could be watching him," I said. "It may not be easy tomorrow." I thought about the chase again. "I'd still like to know who was driving that car."

"In a town like this, it wouldn't be hard to hire guys who'd do anything you want," May said. "What about that conservative

271

group Bourgonne mentioned? What was it called? Something in Latin."

"'Opus Die.' The work of God." Sara spoke the name with biting irony.

We made some plans. In the morning, Sara and May would drive to the airport and get Bourgonne, a calculated risk, but one we felt we had to take. They would also stop by the Oriental Institute; we wanted to get those photographs that Edwards had planned to develop. If someone else found them and started asking questions, there might be trouble. Sara was known around the school; she thought she could get into his office without raising anyone's suspicions. I didn't like the idea of her leaving, but knew there'd be no stopping her.

While they were gone, I'd call the Associated Press and make arrangements to have someone come out here for an interview. I figured there was a good chance the bureau chief would recognize my name, especially when I mentioned Jerusalem. I'd filed a lot of copy out of there with my by-line; I didn't think I'd have much trouble convincing him I was on the level.

May and I stayed up the rest of the night with the shotgun close by. Sara fell asleep on the sofa. I couldn't sleep, not even after two glasses of bourbon. I kept thinking about what we were caught up in.

CHAPTER 44

IF EVERYTHING WENT SMOOTHLY, May thought it would take three or four hours to pick up Bourgonne at O'Hare Airport, stop at the Oriental Institute for the photographs and return to Lake Forest. There would be some traffic to fight but they would be well ahead of the rush hour.

They left just after dawn. Before Sara got into the car, I took her in my arms. She shivered in the cold wind blowing off the lake.

"I love you so much," she said, smiling at me.

"Get back here soon and be careful," I said, unable to say more as she put her hand on my cheek.

Before he left, May handed me a piece of paper. Penciled on it were the numbers to a combination safe hidden behind the medicine cabinet in the bathroom. He explained how to remove the glass shelves; the back of the cabinet would then be sprung open with the blade of a knife.

"It's been a couple years since I checked, but there should be over $50,000 in there," May said, grinning. "I guess I haven't got over the Depression." The grin vanished. "In case something happens, don't be afraid to use it," he said.

"I'm not going to need any money," I said. "You already paid me ten grand. I haven't even cashed the check yet."

He had given me the money—what he had offered to pay in Jerusalem—shortly after we arrived in Chicago.

"I just want you to know it's there."

There was no point in trying to argue with him. "I'll have a reporter here when you get back," I promised.

A few minutes later, I watched May drive down the graveled road. Sara waved from the window and then I could only see the red glow of the brakelights as the car was swallowed up in the morning mist that covered the ground.

I waited nervously until eight o'clock when I called the Associated Press. I didn't like giving them the story, but it was the best way to get it out quickly. It might even help; the advance publicity was sure to kick up some interest when I followed later with my exclusive.

The bureau chief's name was Pete Robinson. He'd just checked into the office, which was down in the Loop. As I had hoped, he knew me from my work overseas. But when I told him I'd quit the AP and wanted to talk to him about a story, he immediately went on guard. I understood the reaction. I'd had the same experience myself, unexpected calls from former reporters who usually wanted a favor. He probably thought I was a public relations flak cashing in on the old school tie to try to hustle an item for a client.

Robinson's attitude changed when I explained why I was calling. I didn't give him all of it—just enough to whet his curiosity. I told him that some ancient artifacts had been found in a cemetery near the Dead Sea, and that I was offering him the story as an exclusive. I didn't mention the body, but I described the scrolls. That was all I needed; he said he'd come himself. I gave him directions to Lake Forest. He wanted to drive out in the early afternoon, but I convinced him to make it sooner. He told me he'd try to leave his office before noon.

While I waited, I found a can of stale coffee in a kitchen cabinet and brewed a pot. The sun had already climbed over the trees; the sky was high and blue. The lake sparkled in the hazy distance. I kept checking the clock on the mantel. May and Sara had been gone just over two hours.

They should be out at the airport by now, I thought. I hoped the rendezvous with Bourgonne would come off; we needed him, and he was taking a tremendous risk to help us. It was going to be tricky, especially if someone was with him. He had been confident he could get away, but things had come unraveled since we last spoke.

Just let it work, I said to myself. Nice and easy and no problems.

I thought again about the car chase.

Whoever was after us had the advantage; they knew who we were and could take their sweet time tracking us down. Luck had been with us the night before. If they had overtaken us on one of those back streets, it could have been rough.

I toyed with calling Archbishop McGuire to tell him what had happened. The fact was I liked McGuire. He and the other priests who had seen the body had been just as confused as the rest of us. It wasn't the church that was responsible for what had happened. I didn't want to make any mistake about that; I didn't want to let the truth slip away from me in anger. Only a few individuals were to blame. That's why I wanted to talk to McGuire, to put him on notice that someone back in Rome, men who worshipped the same God and shared the same faith were trying to strong-arm us. I was under no illusions. I knew that even if I spoke to him, the archbishop wasn't likely to do anything. He wouldn't even believe me.

Neither would the police. Not even if we gave them all the details on a serving tray. We didn't have any hard proof that someone was trying to steal the body and scrolls. So who would listen to us? The answer was simple: until we got the story out—no one.

I was still sitting there, staring at the lake when Robinson called. As soon as he opened his mouth I could tell that something had happened.

A report, he said, had just come over the police radio. It was about a traffic accident, a bad one on a service road near O'Hare. A car and a heavy truck. The AP bureau monitored the radio around the clock.

"I started paying attention when they gave the names," Robinson said. "I even double checked to make sure. One of the victims was identified as John May. The car was a Hudson. I thought you ought to know this...Is that the guy you were talking about?"

I heard myself say it was.

There was a long pause before he said, "I don't know how to tell you this..."

I didn't say anything. I felt as if a vise had squeezed shut around my throat.

"He was killed..."

Choking out the words, I said, "And the woman? What about the woman who was with him? Her name was Sara Garner."

"She was taken to Billings Hospital." Robinson hesitated, unsure whether to go on. I knew he was holding back.

"Come on dammit! Tell me the rest of it."

"She was seriously injured. They had to cut both of them out of the car . . . Say, are you okay?"

I was leaning against the wall, gripping the telephone. I didn't answer. Then I asked some more questions in a strange half-dead voice that didn't sound like me talking. I heard him describe how a truck, a flatbed, had rolled through a red light and smashed head-on into their car. May had been killed instantly. The truck driver told the cops his brakes had failed. His head had hit the windshield; they thought he had a concussion. He must have been really moving; the car's engine had been pushed into the front seat.

"Was there anything about a priest," I asked. "His name was Bourgonne." I was getting sick now.

"No, just May and the woman. What was her name again?"

"Sara. Sara Garner."

I mumbled the words in a daze. I had to swallow hard to say anything at all.

"This is terrible. I'm so sorry."

He wanted to know whether he should still come out to Lake Forest.

"I'll call you later," I said slowly. He started to ask another question and I hung up.

So they had found out and were waiting near the airport. It was a professional job right down to the driver getting himself injured; no one would think it wasn't an accident. They had probably fixed the brakes. Who sold us out? Bourgonne? I couldn't believe that. But he was the only one who knew. How else would they have known what car to look for, or when May would arrive?

I staggered to the sink and splashed water on my face. I had started crying; I was crying hard. It took awhile before I had enough control to call the hospital. I told the nursing supervisor I was a reporter and asked about a young woman who'd been injured in an accident.

The nurse sounded old and officious. She made it clear that she was busy and that I was inconveniencing her. I heard her flipping through the pages of the admissions register.

"A truck hit their car," I said, forcing myself to speak calmly. But I was thinking, You bitch. God damn you to hell. Find the name or I'll come down there and beat it out of you. "They just brought her in."

"You already told me that," the woman said curtly.

"I'm telling you again."

Finally the nurse said, "She's in intensive care. She has internal injuries."

"She's still alive?"

The words dropped from my mouth like pellets of hot lead.

"You must not hear well," the nurse said. "I can't waste time repeating myself."

I slammed down the receiver. I made my decision quickly; I was going to the hospital. I started for the door and stopped—I didn't have a car. I called a cab; they would meet me in Lake Forest in front of a post office I remembered passing the night before. I'd have to walk there; it wasn't far, maybe two miles. On the way to the door I passed the casket. That's when I screamed. I fell to my knees and screamed and pounded my fists against the floor, screaming and crying until the tears blinded me.

I was still crying when I started walking. I followed the gravel road out to the highway and walked into town. I was supposed to meet the cab but had another idea. There was a used car lot across the street; the cars were parked under strings of red and yellow pennants that fluttered in the breeze. I looked at a late model Ford. The price was marked in soap on the windshield. Two hundred dollars. I checked my wallet. I had a little over that. I went into the one-room building that served as the sales office and paid a young man. He looked surprised when I dropped the money on his desk and told him I'd buy the Ford. He reached into a drawer for the papers.

"Mind if I take it for a test drive?" I asked. "I can fill all that out as soon as I get back."

I asked whether there was any gas in the car.

The salesman—he had a pink, sunburnt face and oily hair—smiled and said it had a full tank. "You're gonna like that baby," he said. "She's got a lot of life in her yet."

"Maybe if you give me the keys I can find out for myself."

He took the ring off the hook on the wall and handed them over. Still talking, he followed me onto the lot, carrying a dealer's plate, which he taped to the inside of the rear windshield. I got into the Ford and pulled onto the highway, spraying gravel and dust behind me.

I drove south for the city. I was going much too fast. Someone cut me off and I slammed on the brakes; they didn't hold well. My hands were shaking.

I tried to pull myself together. I had to be ready for whatever was coming. I knew it might be a set up. There was a good chance they'd be watching the hospital. That's what I would have done in their place.

Trying not to speed, I thought about Sara. I remembered her face, every detail. The wonderful hair and dark green eyes and the lovely smile when she was with me in bed.

As I drove, I realized how far south I had to go. Billings Hospital was in Hyde Park, part of the University of Chicago complex.

I prayed to God not to let her die. I prayed and kept praying as I drove in the fast-moving traffic with the lake right up against the highway. I told God that she didn't deserve to die. I tried to talk to God and not feel foolish or ashamed or hypocritical.

Just don't let her die, I told Him. She wasn't trying to harm anyone when she found the body; it was there in that cemetery at Qumran and she found it and if you hadn't wanted it to work out that way, it wouldn't have happened. There must have been a good reason why we stumbled onto that tomb. What possible reason could there be for letting her die? I don't believe You want that to happen. Please let her live, please.

I tried to pray for May, but I kept thinking about Sara. She needed it more than he did. He was already gone.

When I finally got to Hyde Park, I stopped and asked someone for directions to the hospital; it was on Ellis Avenue right by the university. I'd worked out a plan to get inside without being observed. I found the campus bookstore and bought a white jacket, the kind interns and medical students wore. I put it on in a restroom and went around to the back of the hospital and came in a service entrance. I checked the building directory; the intensive care unit was on the second floor.

The place smelled antiseptic and dead. I walked up a flight of steps, following two interns with stethoscopes dangling from their necks. They looked at me, but said nothing. I entered a dim hallway on the second floor. Intensive care was behind a pair of double doors. I pushed open the doors and stepped into a small, brightly lit room with white tile walls and a tiled floor. There were only a few beds, each surrounded by a curtain, oxygen tanks and other equipment. Two doctors and a nurse were standing by one of the beds.

They watched with puzzled expressions as I approached them. The doctors wore green surgical gowns and green cloth caps; their gauze masks were pulled down around their necks. The nurse had red hair and looked about fifty.

The doctors were surprised to see me there.

"You can't come in here," one of them said curtly. He had probably mistaken me for a student.

"Yes I can."

I walked to the bed and the nurse tried to stand in my way. I gently but firmly moved her to the side.

Sara lay in the bed. Half of her face was bandaged and the bandages ran down to her neck. Her left eye was swollen and puffy. They hadn't covered her face yet, but she was dead. She looked small, lying under a sepulcher of white covers. I wanted to gather her up in my arms.

The nurse hurried out of the ward.

I asked when she had died. My insides were already ash by then.

The doctors didn't answer. They stepped back to get out of the way.

"I asked you when she died," I said. I grabbed one of them, a middle-aged man with glasses.

"A few minutes ago," he said quickly. "Are you a relative?" His partner started inching toward the door.

I didn't say anything. I was trying to talk to her, trying to break through before she was gone. She couldn't be that far away; she had just left me.

"If it's any help, she didn't suffer," the doctor said. "She never regained consciousness."

"How do you know that?" I said bitterly. "Is that just some crap to make me feel better because you don't want to tell me she was all broken up inside and died in agony?"

The doctor looked at me. The other one had already left the ward.

"You better go. The nurse will be sending for a guard."

I stood there at the bedside. Sara's face—the part I could see through the cocoon of bandages—was paste white. Wisps of her long black hair showed under the wrappings.

"You really should leave," the doctor repeated. "There's nothing you can do for her."

"No, you get out! Get out now!"

He started to say that I was making a mistake, but he must have noticed what was happening to me because he quickly turned and left.

He was wrong about there not being anything for me to do. I could tell her again how much I loved her and how much I had wanted to spend all of my days with her and, now that she was gone, how I dreaded the thought of living. "Sara, you shouldn't have left me like this," I said, staring down at her face. She looked like a broken statue. "How could you leave me? What kind of life do you want me to have? Did you even stop to think about that? How am I supposed to get through it without you? Sara, oh why, why?"

The doors swung open. The nurse came in with a Security guard. The two doctors were behind them.

"That's him," the nurse said.

Adjusting his gunbelt, the guard started in my direction. He wore a blue uniform and was stocky and self-confident.

"Buddy, you better come with me."

As he reached for my arm, I hit him hard and felt his jaw shatter. He slumped down between the beds and I stepped over him and started for the hallway. The doctors and nurse got out of my way. The nurse screamed. I hurried for the stairwell, wondering if anyone was watching me but not caring. If they had staked out the hospital, fine. I hoped they'd try to stop me. I went out of the building through a fire door, crossed the street and walked into the university quadrangle. I passed under a stone archway. I was crying now. Two young women carrying books looked at me and turned away.

I was still trying to tell her good-bye.

CHAPTER 45

I DROVE TO MAY'S TOWNHOUSE. I realized I had left my notes and papers there the night before, something I had overlooked in the excitement of trying to move the body. I didn't like the idea of going back; the house was the one place they almost certainly would have under surveillance, but I didn't dare leave that material behind. I knew I would need it later. My best chance would be to come in through the garden, where the trees and thick banks of high shrubbery would offer some cover. The double doors to May's study would be easy to force open.

My plan was to park a few blocks away and circle back on foot. But I stopped suddenly as soon as I passed the entrance to May's cul-de-sac. Fire trucks and police cars, their lights flashing, were pulled up in front of what was left of the house. I had to take a deep breath. The place looked like one of the bombed out ruins I'd seen in London during the blitz. Only the façade stood, along with the stumps of charred walls. Firemen were hosing streams of water on the smoking rubble.

I got out of the car and joined the crowd that had gathered in the street. Some reporters had a police captain hemmed in against an ambulance.

"We think the house was empty, but we're still looking for bodies," I heard him say. I edged closer. "That's probably going to take the rest of the day."

He thought a gas leak or possibly dynamite might have caused the blast, which had shattered windows several blocks away. It had apparently gone off in the basement.

"You can see how the walls caved in on themselves," he explained. "The place folded up like a card castle. The explosion must have knocked out the support beams."

Several reporters shouted questions at once. One of them mentioned that the owner of the house had just been killed in a car accident. He wanted to know whether the police thought there was any connection.

"Give me a break, boys," the captain said wearily. "We don't know any more than you do right now."

Sure, that's what they'd do, I thought, staring at the debris. They needed to get rid of the evidence, which meant eliminating the body, and so they had blown up the house. They probably figured we had moved it, but weren't taking any chances.

I wondered if they had found the remains of the skeleton from Qumran, which we had locked away in the storage room. They would have searched the house thoroughly before they set off the explosion. I was sure the skeleton had either been destroyed or stolen. I knew the impact of this would hit me later. A treasure had been found and now was lost again, lost forever just like Sara. That was all I could think about, the only reality I could grasp. Sara was dead. Whatever else had happened no longer had significance.

"Can you give us any more on this guy May?" one of the reporters asked. "He was supposed to be some kind of art collector. Any idea what he had in the house?"

"I don't know anything about that," the captain said. "If there was any art in there, it's lost art." He started to say more but was called away by a detective.

I drove back to Lake Forest, worried all the way that someone might have tried to follow me even though I doubted they knew what kind of car I was driving. Lacerating, body wracking anguish came in waves that almost lifted me out of my seat. The woman I loved was dead, and I was going to have to spend the rest of my life without her in a world that was no longer worth the price of admission.

Somehow I made it back to May's summer house, a trip I wouldn't even remember later. I parked the car and went inside.

The body had always made me uneasy. But this was different; I was almost consoled to be alone with it.

I still don't even know who it is, I thought. A prophet? One of those crazy ascetics who wrestled with God in their desert caves? Whoever it was, they killed him because he was a threat to the peace. He became a public enemy and so he had to go, just like Sara and May. Just like I'll have to go if they find me.

I turned away from the casket. I realized I had to get moving. I'd told the AP bureau chief about the house; he already might have gone to the police with the information. Or, more likely, driven out on the chance I'd still be here. I needed to hide until I could figure out what to do. Even if I showed some reporters the body, there was no guarantee the killers wouldn't find out and pay their respects. A bomb would take care of everything, and what would it matter if a few newsmen died? I had to consider that possibility; they had already proven they were capable of anything. There was no point in going to the police; I had no proof, only a wild story that would never be believed. It would be easy to hold me for questioning about Sara and May's deaths or about the explosion. In the meantime, what would happen to the body? I had to make sure it was safe. My life depended on that; I didn't think they would try to kill me until they had what they wanted, wanted so badly they had murdered two people.

I decided to leave at once and try to find a place to hide the corpse before someone tracked me down.

First I checked the wall safe behind the bathroom medicine cabinet. The combination May had given me worked perfectly. The safe contained just under $50,000, most of it in 100 and 1,000 dollar bills. I folded the money inside a pouch, which I fashioned out of a pillow case and tied under my shirt.

It took awhile to fix the car so the casket would fit inside. I made enough room by removing the rear seat as we had done the day before with May's Hudson and knocking out the flimsy panel that separated the trunk from the passenger compartment. Covering the casket with a blanket, I put the metal box with the scrolls on the front seat and started driving. I had no idea where I was going. I headed west and got as far as Joliet. I couldn't keep it up anymore; the wires had snapped. I found a motel—six or seven cabins arranged like over-sized doll houses around a barren patch of lawn. I took one of them for the night and lay on a torn mattress in a room that smelled of cigarette smoke; darkness was coming when I passed out.

In the morning, I walked to a grocery store and made a telephone call to O'Hare. I had to find out about Bourgonne. I got an airline clerk who remembered seeing two priests in the terminal the previous morning. He thought, but wasn't sure, that they had boarded a TWA flight for New York. They were carrying suitcases.

I kept asking myself what had happened. I couldn't believe that Bourgonne had been part of a doublecross, but it was the only logical explanation. Somehow they knew we were going to be at the airport. Bourgonne must have told them, but why? The question tore at me.

The newspapers had the story of the explosion and fire on the front page. There was a photo of May—an old one taken before he grew his beard. Younger and wearing a suit and tie, he looked like a different man.

The police were quoted as saying they believed May had stored explosives in his house and that the blast may have occurred accidently. They knew he was involved in the oil business. Years earlier, the story went on, May had handled some of the field work himself, even the rough stuff like blasting, something he had never told us. He might have put some unused explosives in the house and forgotten about them, a detective stated. They'd found evidence that a mixture of ammonia-nitrate and fuel oil—a commonly used blasting compound—had been involved. Usually stored in bags, the mixture might have become dangerously unstable over the years, according to a member of the department's bomb and arson squad.

I'd covered police beats long enough to know where things stood. When they said the investigation was continuing, they really meant it had been shelved.

Sara was prominently mentioned in the article, which ran a full column and jumped to an inside page. Police were uncertain about her connection to May, but they believed she had accompanied him on a recent trip to the Holy Land to collect art work. The story said that she had lived in Jerusalem and was survived by a mother in New York City.

The driver of the truck—a young man with a strange looking name—had been charged with driving while intoxicated. The story said he was from Hungary and had recently immigrated to the United States.

I read the story over again before it hit me. The man whose car had killed Professor Edwards outside the Oriental Institute had a similar East European nationality. The circumstances were strikingly similar; both were unfortunate, explainable accidents. It was all very neat and well packaged. A numbing coldness spread through me as I realized they had killed Edwards as well as May and Sara.

Somehow, in some way, they had found out the professor was helping us. Maybe they'd been watching the morning he stopped at May's house to discuss who should examine the body and scrolls. It would have been easy enough to follow him. Their plan was as simple to understand as death itself; they wanted everyone who knew.

Later that day, I called Lawrence. I tracked him down to Biloxi, where he had set up his air cargo service. He was out at the hangar, working on his plane and they had to send for him to come to the telephone.

I told him that May and Sara were dead. I said they had been murdered and that I was on the run and needed his help. I said it had to do with the bodies we had brought back from the Holy Land and promised to explain the rest later, that I couldn't tell him the details over the telephone.

Lawrence didn't ask any questions. He said that he'd fly up to Joliet that same day. He would leave in the afternoon.

There was something else I had to do. I called the hospital where Sara had died. Her body already had been sent to a funeral home. Her mother was handling the arrangements, I was told. She planned to come to Chicago and take the body back to New York by train. I made some half-hearted attempts to find her, without any success. It was just as well; I wouldn't have known what to say.

I ordered some white roses from a florist and had them sent to the mortuary. I'd never bought her flowers.

CHAPTER 46

THE AIRFIELD was a few miles outside Joliet. A herd of white-faced herefords grazed in tall grass across from its single runway.

During the drive from the motel, I had kept checking the rearview mirror to see whether anyone was tailing me. I couldn't shake the feeling that a car was back there, just out of sight. But every time I looked in the mirror, the road was empty. I was getting a lesson in what it meant to live on the run.

I had another, less irrational fear. I realized I was putting Lawrence's neck in the same noose.

His plane got in early in the evening. I recognized the DC-3 immediately as it made its landing approach, the sunlight glinting on the wings. I drove out to the runway as Lawrence parked the plane to the side of the runway and cut the engines. He saw me standing by the car and waved from the cockpit. The plane had been painted a new color—sky blue. The words "Gulf Stream Air Freight" were painted in slanting white letters across the fuselage.

He stepped out on the wing and jumped to the ground.

"What the hell happened?" he asked, shaking my hand. He hadn't shaved and looked tired.

"They're dead," I said. "Somebody rammed a truck into their car so it would look like an accident."

Lawrence studied my face. "You know who did it?"

"Whoever it was, they're still looking for me."

"When did it happen?"

"Yesterday morning out at O'Hare. They were on their way to pick up a priest."

Lawrence stood with his hands deep in his pockets.

"Where do you want to go?"

"I don't care. Anywhere. I think I've lost them, but I don't know how much longer that's going to last."

I kept expecting a car to pull up by the runway.

286

"We'll head back to Mississippi," Lawrence said, making his decision. "We can figure out the next step down in Biloxi."

"There's something in the car that needs to go with us."

I opened the trunk. As soon as he saw the casket, Lawrence said, "Man, I was thinking it might have something to do with this."

We tied the casket down in the cargo bay. I had put the scrolls in a suitcase, which we also brought on board.

"What happend to the other coffin you folks were carrying?" he asked.

"I'll tell you about that later."

"We need to get some fuel," Lawrence said.

I wanted to take off immediately, but there was no choice. Lawrence was able to refuel at the airfield's solitary hangar.

Half an hour later, we were banking through a light cloud cover that partially obscured the lights of Joliet. The sun set as we flew over the black and green fields that lay like a patchwork quilt across the Illinois prairie.

I started to tell him as much as I knew.

"May was killed at the scene," I said, fighting to get the words out. "Sara died later in a hospital."

I looked at him. He leaned back in his seat and rubbed his tired eyes. I was conscious only of the pounding engines.

"You don't have any idea who did it?" Lawrence asked.

"There are some things you need to know first."

I started at the beginning, telling him about the scrolls. I tried to put all the details in the right sequence, but it didn't work out that way; I quickly lost the thread.

After a long silence, Lawrence said, "Are you telling me you got the body of Jesus Christ back there?"

"I'm telling you that we dug up the body of a man who was crucified."

"But you think it's Christ, don't you?" He turned slightly in his seat, watching me out of the corner of his eyes.

"I don't know who it is," I said. "I swear that to you. We found something I don't understand and can't explain. You've got to believe that."

Finally, Lawrence said, "If I had known what you were carrying that day in Jerusalem, I would have asked for a whole lot more money."

He smiled.

"I'm sorry we didn't tell you the truth then," I said. "We wanted to. You had a right to know."

I told him about Bourgonne and his warning. I also explained about the skeleton with the severed head—how it had either been destroyed or stolen when May's house was bombed.

"That French priest..." He fumbled with the name. "I know how you say he helped you and all, but do you think he might have had something to do with this?"

"I don't know anymore."

I still couldn't believe Bourgonne was involved. Yet I had to admit it was at least a plausible explanation; too much had happened to discount anything. Someday I'd find out—even if I had to go to Rome. I promised myself that.

"I want you to know I'll pay for this trip," I said. "I'll make it worth your while."

I asked whether he thought $1,000 would cover all his expenses and trouble.

"Hold on, pal. That's way too much," he said.

I insisted.

"Forget it, we can talk about money some other time."

He held out his hand, reaching over the controls. I shook it and blurted out my thanks.

"I just need some time to think—a few weeks, a month."

I already knew I was going to have to make all this public. The question, as always, was when and how. They would do whatever was necessary to stop me. I'd been a reporter long enough to know that anything could be covered up. I was going to have to be cautious about picking the right moment.

Lawrence said, "You can stay at my place. It's out in the country. No neighbors, no one close anyway. I got me a nice little business started down on the Gulf. I couldn't have done that without the money I got from Mister May. Whatever you want to do, count me in." Smiling, he said, "You ever been to New Orleans?"

I shook my head.

"We'll drive down and take us a little vacation."

I told him that Sara and I had planned to get married.

After letting that sink in, Lawrence said, "I'm sorry, so damn sorry. She was a fine human being and one beautiful lady."

"Yes, she was." I carried that thought with me like a candle into the dark night.

On the way south, we ran into some storms, towering, anvil-flat thunderheads too high to climb over. The sky was ripped apart by lightning; I thought the same thing was going to happen to the plane. Lawrence didn't seem to notice the pounding.

"I'd like to see it."

He'd been fighting the controls for nearly an hour, dropping as low as he dared to get out of the turbulence.

I knew what he was talking about.

"It's not pretty," I said.

Five hours later, we were on the ground in a damp fog at an airport outside Biloxi. There wasn't much to look at, just a few hangars with a couple of light planes parked in front. We loaded the casket into the back of Lawrence's old station wagon and drove to a rundown farmhouse that he rented a few miles from town. The place was set back in some hills off a rural road.

"You're sure you still want to do this?" I said after we carried the casket inside.

Lawrence nodded. But he didn't look convincing.

He helped me unfasten the lid. I removed the burial shroud, revealing the face and upper torso of the dead man. Lawrence stood there, his face hardset. I'd seen that look before—disbelief, the shock of seeing something so grotesque and yet so pitifully moving that the impact struck you like a blow.

"He was a big man...bigger than I would have thought," Lawrence said finally. "Whoever he was, he must have been something to see, hanging up on that cross."

I let him take a good look; then I re-covered the body and closed the casket. I never wanted to see it again.

CHAPTER 47

ONE WEEK after we got to Biloxi, I started flying with Lawrence on his daily trips up and down the Gulf Coast. He delivered supplies to oil companies scattered from Apalachicola, Florida, to Port Arthur, Texas. We spent a couple of nights in Lafayette, a small town in the middle of the Louisiana bayou country. The state's coastal marshes floated on oil and Lafayette had become a backcountry Dallas. A nice town with plenty of cajun restaurants and color, but it didn't help me snap out of it. I couldn't get my mind off what had happened, or off the more pressing worry that I had to find a place to hide the body and scrolls until I could figure out my next move. For the present the casket lay under a stack of packing crates in a backroom in Lawrence's house. I started drinking too much. By then I was just trying to hang on and not smash up.

At Lawrence's insistence, we drove into New Orleans on a hot muggy weekend late in the summer. He thought we, or at least I, needed a break. Having already told me about his girlfriend—he had brought up the subject as delicately as he could—we met her in Jackson Square, a good-looking brunette in tight slacks and a halter blouse. She took us to her apartment, which had a balcony fronting Royal Street. She had a friend she wanted me to meet and offered to call her up, but I gracefully declined. After a couple of gin and tonics, I left them there.

I spent the rest of the day drinking Sazeracs in a decrepit bar on Chartres Street, a three-storied ruin called the Napoleon House. There was nothing decrepit about the booze or the service; the waiters wore ankle-length white aprons and served stiff drinks at cheap prices. I paid the owner to let me sleep it off in a back room. The next day, I repeated the performance.

Lawrence rejoined me early Monday morning. He was in a fine mood. On the way back to Biloxi, he turned off the main highway to show me some of the Mississippi countryside. It was yet another step in his continuing program to help me loosen up and get back in control. My head was throbbing with a hangover, but I tried to pretend I was interested as we passed a succession of hard-scrabble farms and tin-roofed shanties.

"What's that?" I asked, pointing to a row of telephone poles. They were buried beneath a matted covering of what looked like ivy.

Lawrence laughed. "Kudzu. That stuff's gonna cover the South one of these days. They say if you watch close, you can see it grow. No joke."

Fence posts were draped, highway signs—anything the leafy vine could throw a tendril over. This virulent greening of the countryside only added to the mixed impression I'd already formed of Mississippi—a land both beautiful and foreboding.

We'd driven on the steamy blacktop for over an hour when we came up on a cemetery that was surrounded by a stone wall and shaded by oak trees. The flat roofs of whitewashed mausoleums, dozens of them, projected above the wall.

I asked Lawrence to stop. I wondered if it could be the place to put the body.

"I want to take a look at this."

A small church was across the road from the cemetery. Badly rundown, its white paint faded and peeling, the building still showed traces of an earlier elegance; the stained-glass windows sparkled like precious stones in the sunlight. But part of the roof was sagging; and a cross erected on the uncut lawn tilted precariously. A sign over the padlocked door said, "Primitive Gospel Church—Faith, Healing, and Deliverance."

"That used to be a Presbyterian church," Lawrence said, pulling over to the side of the road. "Goes back way before the war. Times have sure changed. I hear a Negro congregation bought the place."

I got out of the car and walked to the cemetery. No one was around. I pushed open the iron gate and stepped inside.

"This is it," I said at once. "I'm going to hide the body here."

Just what I was looking for, the cemetery was remote enough and less than thirty miles from Biloxi; we could get there in an hour. I'd never seen anything like it. With its rows of tightly packed mausoleums, all of them in varying stages of decay, the cemetery resembled a macabre city of the dead. The paths that wound between the tombs were covered with powdered shell. Many of the tombs had doors with elaborate grillwork, marble steps—even patches of weedy lawn.

"Don't they bury anyone in these parts?" I asked.

Lawrence shook his head. "We're too far below sea level. The water table's too high. You get a good rain and a casket would push up through the ground. They run these pumps round the clock down in New Orleans just to keep the streets dry."

The mortar that sealed the entrances to the tombs had often split open. Green lizards scurried in and out of the cracks, sunning themselves on the crumbling brickwork.

The thick, mildew-stained wall that enclosed the cemetery was galleried with burial vaults shaped like ovens—row upon row of them. The bronze memorial plates that covered these niches were often inscribed with more than one name; I counted eight on one of the plates, the names of the dead beautifully etched into the metal. The writing was often in German or French.

I asked Lawrence how they could have crammed so many bodies into such a small space.

The practice was common in southern Louisiana and Mississippi, he explained. The law required a one-year waiting period between burials—long enough for the body to decompose before another was inserted into the tomb. When the time came to reuse the vault, the remains of the last family member to die were simply pushed to the rear, where they fell into a common chamber in which the bones of generations were mingled. The system worked fairly well as long as two people didn't die within a year of each other.

"The problems started when there was an epidemic—yellow fever or cholera. They ran out of room plenty fast then. Only thing you could do was cover the bodies with lime."

We walked down one of the paths that crisscrossed the cemetery. "Looks like some of the tombs are being used by black folk," Lawrence said, frowning. "I guess no white people come back this way any more. It's a good thing. Otherwise, there'd be a lynching."

With burial space at a premium, I could understand why poor blacks might be willing to run a risk like that. It was nothing more than squatter's rights for the dead.

Lawrence pointed out a row of wall vaults. Several of the plastered openings were freshly sealed; dozens of red Xs had been chalked onto the stone.

"That's for good luck," he said. "It's some voodoo foolishness. People make their X and mumble some hocus pocus and walk away backward. You do that and the evil spirits are supposed to stay clear of you. The trick's to make sure you use red chalk."

A piece of chalk rested within convenient reach on a brick ledge.

The most elaborate of the tombs was in the middle of the cemetery. All the paths converged there. Over a story high, the large, vaulted mausoleum had an ornate facade decorated with carved angels.

I climbed the steps and put my shoulder to the iron door, which creaked open on rusted hinges. The narrow entranceway led into a burial chamber. I waited until my eyes adjusted to the darkness. The main chamber was connected to a smaller one by another passageway; an empty sarcophagus made of marble had been built in the center of this inner chamber.

"What about putting it right here?" I asked.

"It might work," Lawrence agreed.

"Who do you think owns this place?"

"Let's see if we can track down the preacher who uses that old church. Anybody knows, he will."

We went back to the main gate. A pickup truck came rattling up the road. An elderly Negro was hunched over the wheel. Waving for him to stop, Lawrence asked if he knew where the pastor lived. The man's face, creased with deep furrows, was beaded with sweat. Sacks of flour lay stacked in the bed of his battered truck.

He said he wasn't sure.

Lawrence handed him a five dollar bill. "We're not aiming to cause him any trouble."

The man smiled. His memory had suddenly improved. The pastor's name was Jason—he lived half a mile up the road.

We thanked him and drove to the house. An old hound the color of milky coffee barked halfheartedly and limped off the porch as soon as we got out of the car. A faded card that bore the hand-lettered words "Bishop Timothy Jason" was taped to the mail box.

I knocked on the front door.

A middle-aged Negro with a narrow face and closely cropped hair answered. He wore bib overalls and a denim shirt rolled up at the sleeves. I let Lawrence do the talking. We had worked out a plan during the drive from the cemetery.

The Negro, tight-lipped and solemn, started at us suspiciously. I didn't blame him. He wasn't used to casual visits from whites.

Lawrence said his brother had just died and that he wanted to bury him someplace near the old family homestead.

"And where's that?" the minister asked.

"Bonne Terre." The town was five miles away.

"They got themselves cemeteries over at Bonne Terre," the minister said skeptically.

"But ain't none of them as pretty as the one out by your church," Lawrence said. "Bob always said if the time came, that's where he wanted to be laid out."

He asked the minister who owned the property.

"That place ain't been used in years," the Negro said. "I don't rightly know if anybody own it."

He asked about Lawrence's "people." He obviously didn't believe the story. But Lawrence's answers seemed to reassure him; he knew he wasn't an outsider and even recognized the family name.

Lawrence said I was a good friend of his brother.

"What did you say the boy died of," the Negro asked.

"I didn't say," Lawrence said. "But I'll tell you this—it wasn't old age."

The pastor almost smiled. Then Lawrence asked about the mausoleum with the vaulted roof.

The Negro said there was a story that the tomb had been built back at the turn of the century by the owner of a logging mill whose wife had died in childbirth. No costs were spared by the grief-stricken husband, who even imported a stone mason from Italy. But the woman's parents wanted her buried in Georgia, her home state; and that's what happened. As far as the pastor knew, the vault had never been used.

While he spoke, his wife stuck her head out the door for a look and ducked back inside again. She didn't say a word, but from the frowning glance she gave her husband, she didn't like any of this. I figured she had listened to every word. A heavy, large breasted woman, she was a foot taller than the pastor.

Taking care not to rush anything or to appear too eager, Lawrence slowly got down to business again. He said he was going to put his brother's body in the tomb and then try to find the owner, so that he could properly bury it. In the meantime, he wanted to know whether the pastor would accept $500 a year to cut the grass in front of the mausoleum and make sure no one tampered with the lock.

I could tell the Negro didn't buy any of this. He stood there with his mouth clamped shut. I took out my wallet and handed him just over $200 most of it in twenties and tens.

"We'll send you the rest in the mail," I said.

Lawrence leaned forward and said, "I don't guess there's any reason for us to tell the sheriff about those chalk marks."

"Don't know nothin' 'bout that," the pastor said quickly. From the skittery way he peered at Lawrence, he had got the message loud and clear.

"I'll keep my eye on that grave right proper," he promised.

"I'm in your debt," Lawrence said. "My brother sure did love this part of the country."

We came back to the cemetery two days later late at night. In the meantime, I had bought an expensive new casket, one made of bronze that was airtight and damp proof. I made the purchase from an undertaker in Biloxi who accepted $300 more than the coffin was worth but didn't ask any questions. It was the best I could find; until I figured out what to do with the body, I wanted to reduce the possibility of damage in the humid Mississippi weather. The original wooden casket fit inside the larger metal one.

We drove to the cemetery on pitch-dark country roads. A half moon cast its light on the mausoleums. Rats scurried through the grass when we opened the gate. Using a wooden dolly that Lawrence had picked up at the airport, we were able to push the casket up the shell path to the tomb without much trouble.

It was much harder to wrestle it into the burial chamber. Lawrence did most of the lifting as cobwebs brushed our faces. I hadn't realized how strong he was; his thin, wiry arms were deceptively powerful.

As a final step, we placed the metal box that contained the scrolls into the crypt with the casket and then nailed some boards down over the opening.

"Maybe we ought to say a prayer or something," Lawrence said, straightening up. "It don't seem right just leaving it here without saying some words." He held a flashlight on the sarcophagus.

At that moment I thought of Sara. She was never far from my mind. It occurred to me as I stood in the darkness of the tomb that I didn't even remember her age. Was she twenty-eight or twenty-seven? I tried to recall her face. I could do that all right: the green eyes and high cheekbones and the thick, lovely hair she liked to pull tight to the side of her head when she was working outdoors. I didn't have a picture of her. But I wouldn't need one.

What would she say now if she knew what I was doing, I wondered. What kind of prayer would she want me to whisper over his body? What kind of apology would she want me to offer?

Lawrence repeated his question.

I shook my head. "Let's get out of here," I said. "I wouldn't know what to say."

CHAPTER 48

I LEFT Biloxi a few days later for Chicago. Lawrence thought I was crazy to even consider returning. I knew he was right, but I couldn't help myself. I had to go back. I couldn't stay in Mississippi anymore; I felt in exile there. Maybe the real reason had to do with Sara. Somehow, in ways more imagined than real, I thought I'd be closer to her.

So one morning after a bad night's sleep, I took off in an aging Chevrolet that I'd bought soon after we locked up the mausoleum. I had a couple thousand dollars with me and left the rest of my money in a Biloxi savings and loan.

"Don't do anything stupid," Lawrence said. We were lingering over a cup of coffee. "They're still looking for you. And they're not going to give up. Be damn careful, you hear?"

He told me not to worry about the body. He promised to check regularly on the tomb.

"When will you be coming back?"

"I don't know," I said, and I didn't. "I can't think that far ahead any more."

Lawrence walked to a window. He stood there a few minutes before he said, "We've chewed all this over before, but why don't you stay? You can help me down here. I'll teach you how to fly. We can make some good money and enjoy ourselves."

"You keep that offer open," I said, shaking his hand. "We'll see what happens."

He slapped me on the back and said, "Be sure to call me as soon as you get there. If I don't hear from you, I'm going to fly up and find out what's going on. You remember that."

The drive took two days. I found a furnished apartment not far from the University of Chicago that rented by the week. When I was settled in, I called Lawrence and gave him my address and telephone number.

Shortly after I arrived, I visited the cemetery where May was buried. I didn't get out of the car; I was afraid someone might have staked out the grave on the off-chance that sooner or later I'd show up. A hearse was parked just inside the main gate. The mourners were gathered there around the freshly dug grave. I stopped at a traffic light and watched them, the men bareheaded, the women all in black awkwardly clutching their husbands' arms as a minister said some inaudible words.

The casket was small and white—it was a funeral for a child.

I tried to say a prayer for May, but it wasn't any good. How do you pray for dead children or a murdered friend? How could you do that sincerely without ruining your goodwill with a curse? It was easier just to tell him good-bye and promise I'd try to find out who killed him.

That same day I wrote to Sara's mother. I told her I'd met her daughter in the Holy Land. I wanted her to know that she had raised a lovely, intelligent woman and that she had reason to be proud of her; I didn't tell her that we had planned to get married or that Sara had been murdered. I didn't sign the letter.

There was another piece of unfinished business I needed to take care of. I wanted to get back the photographs Professor Edwards had taken during the autopsy as well as the film May had given him—the pictures from Qumran.

I waited until late one afternoon and enterd the Oriental Institute when I was reasonably certain there wouldn't be too many professors or students around. The door to Edwards' third-floor office was open; the place was a mess—books and papers were scattered everywhere. I figured his wife or some of his colleagues had started removing his personal effects, and hadn't finished yet. I was there nearly an hour, rifling through the clutter, but I never found the film. A watchman making his rounds finally scared me out of the building.

The next morning, I telephoned the chancellery and asked to talk to Bishop Gray.

That, after all, was one of the main reasons I'd returned to Chicago. I'd been afraid to admit it to myself for fear of losing my nerve. I had a pistol with me—a parting gift from Lawrence—and the vague idea of forcing the bishop if he was still in town to tell me what he knew about the deaths of Sara and May. I still wasn't sure whether he and Bourgonne had flown out of the city the morning of the murders.

As it was, I never found out what I might have done even if he was there. A bad case of jittery second thoughts made me hang up as soon as a secretary asked for my name.

I considered trying to see Archbishop McGuire, but gave that idea up as well. I didn't know what I would have told him. McGuire was a good man. Principled and devout. But I knew that if I spoke to him, he would immediately report the conversation to Bishop Gray or to Rome. It was another risk I didn't need to run.

Not long after that, a Sunday, I went on impulse to the Cathedral of the Holy Name while the eleven o'clock mass was being celebrated. The white-stoned church was at the intersection of State and North Superior a few blocks from the chancellery. McGuire was at the high altar. I stood with the crowd in the vestibule, late comers who hadn't been able to find room in a pew. A huge, larger than life crucifix suspended from the nave hung right over McGuire's head. Shafts of colored light poured through the windows to the sides of the altar. The archbishop held a wafer of bread over his head at the moment of consecration. A bell tinkled, the tone as high pitched and pure as crystal.

It was all I could do to keep from crying out. I leaned against the wall. An elderly woman wearing a lace veil and holding a missal stood next to me. Her glance fell soft and kind upon mine. "Can I help you," she said. I shook my head and hurried out of the church into the sunshine.

The nights were very bad after that. I had never believed in heaven; but I now believed in hell, the kind of hell we build ourselves. Hell in neat packages of our own design—hell on earth.

I made up my mind to drive out West. Maybe to California. I had no plans. I didn't know what to do, but then the decision was made for me. The night before I was going to leave, Lawrence called; he said that someone had been asking questions about him at the airport. Two or three men. They had tracked us to Biloxi. I left for Mississippi that same afternoon.

CHAPTER 49

I HAD DRIVEN through the long day and into the longer night by the time I crossed the Mississippi line. I stopped and ate a plate of fried catfish and hushpuppies at a lunchcounter in Corinth. The food and a few cups of vitriolic coffee helped; so did the benzedrine tablets. I was wide awake when I got back into the car.

Before I left town, I found a hardware store and bought a flashlight and an extra box of shells for the long-barreled .38-caliber revolver I had with me.

Lawrence and I had agreed to meet at the cemetery. I told him I'd be there around eight in the evening. But even after the hard drive south, pushing way over the speed limits on the rural blacktops, I realized I wasn't going to make it. I hoped he would wait—that he could wait.

How had they managed to find him?

I kept asking myself the question. I'd been thinking about it ever since Chicago. For all I knew, they might have started backtracking in Jerusalem. They certainly would have had contacts there, even with a war on. I couldn't believe they wouldn't have checked all the freelance pilots who'd signed up with the Jews, especially those who had made unannounced departures; they might have got a lead on Lawrence's name that way and made the right assumptions.

It wouldn't have been that difficult, considering the virtual impossibility of leaving the country by ship or car. The easiest way out was by air. Then, too, there'd been those customs checks in Tunis, Port au Prince and the other places where we had stopped during the flight back to the States. There was bound to be a written record of our arrival—a record with his name and ours as well as the number of his DC-3. I didn't have trouble believing that some good detective work on the plane might have led them on a trail straight to Mississippi.

That was the only scenario that added up. Not that it mattered.

The water was already way over the dam; they had found him, and that was all that counted. I doubted they knew about the body—at least not yet. The thing to do now was get it out of that cemetery and keep moving.

I arrived shortly after eleven. I parked well off the road behind some trees and got out of the car. When I didn't see Lawrence's station wagon, I almost lost my nerve. He wasn't here. That meant I was going to have to start looking for him, and if someone else was doing the same, our paths eventually were bound to cross. I just hoped I saw them before they saw me.

My only certainty then was that if there'd been any way at all, he would have waited for me. I wondered what had happened to him.

The branches of the trees swayed in the wind. A storm was coming. I played the flashlight beam on the cemetery wall. I didn't want to go in there.

Stop stalling, you bastard.

I waited outside the entrance for my eyes to adjust to the darkness. I carried the pistol. A bat shot through the open gate, wings flapping. I ducked down, dropping the flashlight as it flew by my face.

You're not so good at this, Davoren, I said to myself, sweat breaking out on my forehead. Not so good at all.

Rats were moving in the grass; I could hear them all around me. My shoes crunched on the broken shells as I walked along the rows of tombs.

The mausoleum was just ahead. I shined the light on the entrance—it was still locked. I opened the padlock and pushed back the door. The stale air of the closed tomb hit me full in the face.

I took a deep breath and went inside. My flashlight caught two beetles scuttling across the floor. Something else moved in a corner. I pivoted with the light—a rat the size of a cat froze in the beam; rising up on its haunches, it sniffed the air like a squirrel before disappearing down a hole in the base of the wall.

I stepped through the narrow passageway into the inner vault.

My heart was pounding. I could almost hear it beating in my chest like a muffled drum. I leaned against the wall for a few moments, feeling the cool stones through my shirt.

Using the flashlight, I saw that the boards had been pried off the top of the marble sarcophagus, which resembled a low altar. Swallowing, I looked inside. The metal casket was still there; but the lid was ajar. The inner casket that contained the body was missing.

Lawrence must have taken it, I thought. But why? And had he come alone, or had someone made him open the crypt?

I didn't have any anwers. If he'd been forced to enter the tomb, why had they gone to the trouble of relocking the outer door? I had to assume that Lawrence, for whatever reason, had removed the body himself. But where had he gone? And how long ago?

Staggering outside, I sat down on the broken steps of the mausoleum. It's gone, I told myself, sinking quickly into depression. The only thing you can do is sit here now and deal with it and try to figure out what to do next. You've got to find Lawrence and there's a chance somebody from Chicago may be hoping you'll do just that.

Thunder rumbled in the distance; a storm was moving in off the Gulf. I walked back to the car and had a pull from a bottle of bourbon I'd brought along with me. The liquor burned all the way down. I took another drink and threw the bottle away.

I decided to talk to the minister we had done business with only a couple of weeks earlier. I drove up the dark road and parked well away from the house. I didn't want them to know I was paying a visit.

I kept waiting for their dog to bark as I crossed the front lawn. But nothing happened; the only sound was the drone of the locusts and the rising wind. I knocked on the door. After a few moments it opened a crack; in the sliver of yellow light I saw the minister's wary face. He tried to slam the door, but I pushed it open.

The room, cluttered with old, thickly upholstered furniture, was very warm. A ceiling fan slowly rotated, barely moving the still air. The minister stood in his stocking feet in the middle of the room. His wife was sitting on the sofa that sagged under her weight. They stared at me with wide, fearful eyes.

"You got no right to burst into a man's house," the minister said. "I'm gonna call the sheriff."

His wife started shuffling toward the kitchen. I told her to sit back down.

"Have you seen the man I was with," I said.

The minister looked at his wife, who continued to glare at me. "I ain't seen no one."

"The body's gone," I said. "You know anything about that?"

The minister shook his head.

The woman was frightened but defiant. Her sheer bulk, wrapped in the loose folds of a faded cotten dress, was an imposing sight.

"Where's Lawrence?" I asked again.

"He been here," the minister said, faltering.

"When?"

"Yesterday. I told him to take that body away. I told him I'd call someone he didn't do that. Said I wanted to give back the money."

Fear still glinted in his eyes. He had spoken rapidly, almost incoherently.

"You called him?"

"Didn't have to. He come out to look at the tomb."

"When was that?"

"I done told you. Yesterday."

"When yesterday?"

"Round eight o'clock in the evening. I was in the church and he wanted to know if I seen anybody out at the cemetery, pryin' around. I told him I ain't seen nobody."

"And that's when you said you wanted him to remove the body?"

I was running out of patience. I didn't have time for much more of this.

"It don't belong here," the woman said suddenly. Her voice was deep, resonant. She was bent over in the chair, her big hands folded on her lap.

"Who you bury in that tomb?" the minister asked. "I ain't no fool. I know it ain't the body of no brother of your friend."

His lips trembled.

"I been out there," his wife said sharply. "I felt somethin'. You go out there at night. You know what I talkin' about."

I figured her superstition must have got the better of her.

"Woman, you shut up now," the minister said angrily.

"What were you doing in the cemetery at night?" I asked.

The pastor shot another disapproving look at his wife. My guess was they were holding services out there—the kind of services they didn't want to talk about.

I mentioned this, but neither of them answered. The woman clenched her teeth; she had said as much as she was going to.

If they were telling the truth, Lawrence had been to the cemetery yesterday evening. I was certain now that he'd taken the body with him as a precaution. He wouldn't have done that or risked being followed if he hadn't expected trouble. He had probably moved it after the minister threatened to talk.

"Was he alone when he came here?" I asked.

"He was by himself. I told him I didn't want that body out by my church. Gave him all that money back."

I left them sitting next to each other in the dim light and oppressive heat and went gloomily back to my car. I tried to think; nothing that came to mind was reassuring. Lawrence definitely had to be in some kind of jam, a bad one, or else he would have met me.

The rain started falling. I sat in the car and listened to it beat on the roof. After a few minutes, I drove back down the road and passed the cemetery, but didn't stop. It rained more heavily, the thunder crashing over me.

I didn't want to go straight to Lawrence's house. If they were looking for him that was one of the first places they'd check. I wasn't sure who I'd find waiting there.

I decided to drive out to the airfield. He might have flown somewhere. That's what I would have done in his place; I would have forgotten about the body and cleared out as fast as I could. But I wasn't Lawrence; he had more guts than that. Instead of running, he had warned me; he had stuck around and gone back to the cemetery. I hoped I could find him—and soon.

When I got out to the airport, the rain had turned to drizzle, but lightning still flashed across the horizon. Both hangars were closed. I didn't see anyone. A few planes were parked on the edge of the runway. I drove over for a closer look. One of them was Lawrence's DC-3. A tarp covered the engine cowling on the port side; my guess was he'd been tuning it.

Unsure what to do next, I was getting ready to leave when I saw a light coming from the rear window of the machine shop next to the main hangar, a small brick building with a tarpaper roof. I thought I heard a radio playing. I got out of the car and pounded on the door.

A man wearing a dirty pair of coveralls came to the door. He looked at me suspiciously through the glass.

"I'm a friend of Tom Lawrence," I said. "I'm trying to find him."

The man motioned for me to come inside. He was about fifty— potbellied, burly, and thick across the shoulders. His forearms and cheeks were stained with oil and grease. He was wiping his hands on a dirty towel. I had seen him around the airport when I was flying with Lawrence. His name, I recalled, was Dyer.

"I ain't seen Tom since yesterday," he said. "He might have gone off somewhere. He'll go and do that every now and then when he takes a notion. Usually he drives over to New Orleans for a day or two. He's got a girl down there. I know he'll be back here before morning. He's got to run some drilling equipment down to Port Arthur."

I casually mentioned that Lawrence had told me two men had been asking questions about him at the airfield.

"I was the guy who let Tom in on that," Dyer said. "They came snooping around here, asking questions about who flew DC-3s. I told them to beat it."

"Can you tell me what they looked like?"

"I'd say they were in their late thirties. Average height. One did most of the talking. Other guy just stood around. They come in a Buick."

"Did either of them have an accent?"

I remembered the two men, both apparently imported from Eastern Europe, who had killed Sara, May and Edwards.

"No, nothing like that," Dyer said. Still trying to describe them, he said, "Both had dark hair. They were wearing regular work clothes. Said they might have some business for Tom." He grinned and wiped a smudge of oil from his cheek with the towel. "That's why I told them to get lost. Looked like bill collectors. They came back again this afternoon. I gave them the same brush off."

In that one moment, I felt the abyss swing open under me like a trapdoor. I leaned against the wall and rubbed my eyes. So they were still here. I prayed I could find Lawrence before they did. But I knew I was running out of time.

"Say, pal. You okay?" Dyer asked. "You look like you need to sit down."

"I'm fine."

"You like a drink? I got a bottle of mash around here someplace."

"No thanks."

I asked whether he had a telephone.

"There's one over in the terminal. Come on, I'll show you."

We walked across an expanse of wet asphalt to a frame building with large windows that faced the runway. Dyer unlocked the door. "Phone's by the counter there," he said pointing.

I called Lawrence's number, but couldn't get through. I dialed the operator, and let her try. The line was dead.

"Probably that storm we had," Dyer said. "Happens a lot around here this time of year. Tree falls on a line and it takes a repair crew a week to get out and fix it."

"You know a good hotel in Biloxi?" I asked. "I'll get some sleep and come back in the morning and catch him before he leaves. Be a nice surprise."

I didn't want Dyer to know where I was going next. I had decided to drive to Lawrence's house.

"Might try the Pontchartrain. It's a little on the high side but they change the sheets every day and they got a nice bar."

I thanked him and went back to my car. As I walked away, Dyer said, "You better be out here early—before eight. Tom ain't one to be late taking off." He looked at the clearing sky. "Gonna be a good day for flying tomorrow."

I drove a few miles down the highway and pulled over under some trees. I realized that someone might be watching Lawrence's house. I didn't think the storm had knocked out the telephone.

I snapped opened the cylinder of my revolver and made sure it was loaded.

If they got him, they'll try to make him talk, I thought. It won't be easy to get him though. He's tough enough to take care of himself, and he knew someone was after him. At least he had that much of an edge. It wasn't much, but maybe just enough to make a difference. He's probably hiding.

Sure, I said, still talking to myself, but he also might be at his home. You can't rule that out. Or if he's gone, maybe he left his car behind, or something else that could tip you off to what happened. You've got to go there—you've got to do that or you'll never be able to live with yourself. It's going to be enough of a bitch living as it is.

I tried to think of a good excuse to run. There wasn't any. I started the engine and pulled back onto the road.

CHAPTER 50

THE HOUSE was set back in some trees with a steep hill behind and another hill in front, both of them overgrown with woods and brush. Wedged in between, the two-story home was on a sloping gravel road that ran about 50 yards to the blacktop. It was hidden from the road. The nearest neighbor was over a mile away.

The best plan would be to hide the car and hike in from the back. That way I figured I might have a chance of getting close without being seen.

I drove with my headlights out. The sky was clearing fast and I could see stars through the broken clouds. I pulled off the road well before the turnoff to the house and parked the car in a shallow ditch behind a hedgerow. After a short walk, I was behind the higher of the two hills that flanked Lawrence's house. I started climbing. The ground was wet from the storm and when the wind blew, drops of water pelted down on me from the tree branches. I tried to move as quietly as I could, stopping suddenly and cursing under my breath whenever I stepped on a twig. Even the faintest noise seemed to carry like a shot.

When I got to the crest of the hill, I crouched behind a tree and looked down at the house; it was at the bottom of the slope, a good 40 yards below me. A light burned in one of the back rooms. A car was parked in the driveway, a sedan with a dark paint job. Lawrence's station wagon was nowhere in sight.

I strained to see whether anyone was outside. As far as I could tell, no one was down there, but I couldn't be sure. In the darkness, a man could be easily missed.

Who's in the house, I asked myself.

Go take a look. You're just wasting time.

No, why not wait a couple minutes and see who comes out.

I don't have any idea how long I knelt there in the wet carpet of fallen leaves, trying to work up my nerve before I finally started down the hill. I walked in a crouch like a soldier under fire, moving cautiously from tree to tree. When I was within ten yards of the house, I started crawling, holding the pistol in my right hand. The farm house, which lacked a basement and foundation, rested on stone pilings. I crawled beneath it; there was almost a three-foot clearance between the ground and the floor joists. The space was cluttered with piles of wood, boxes, stacks of bricks, and other debris; I wondered whether any rats or snakes made their home there. I heard footsteps and froze. The floorboards creaked above me.

How many were there? One? No, maybe two. I pressed my ear to the floor—the footsteps were louder. Someone was walking from the front of the house to the rear where I was hiding, knees bent, almost too afraid to breath.

I crawled toward the front porch. Cobwebs brushed my face, the strands sticky like cotton candy. I wanted to see whether anyone was waiting by the car. I was sure they'd have a lookout watching the road. But when I'd inched forward as far as I dared, I couldn't see a thing. There was no one by the car. I could make out the emblem on the hood. It was a Buick.

Moving on my knees and hands, I made my way to the side of the house, where I knew there was a window. I felt a sharp pain in my right palm; I'd cut it open on a piece of glass.

Taking a breath, I rolled from under the crawlspace and peered through a crack in the curtains. The room was dark, but there was a light on in the hallway. I heard movement inside and ducked under the house again.

Maybe there's only one of them, I thought. He's searching the place. I wondered if Lawrence had hidden the casket in there.

I hoped he'd given them the slip. He might have gone to New Orleans. Maybe he was staying with his girlfriend in the Quarter, hiding out until things blew over. Yeah, sure. Maybe that's where he went. I should have considered that possibility earlier.

No, he didn't do that, I told myself. He wouldn't have left, not without his plane. He's still around here, waiting for you.

Now I heard footsteps on gravel; the sound came from far up the driveway. A man was out there after all. I started backing up; I wanted to move to the rear of the house again, the side closest to the hill in case I had to clear out. Hurrying, I kicked something over. It sounded metallic. I'd bumped into an empty paint can. A dog barked. Someone was running inside the house. The front door slammed open.

"He's got something!" a man shouted.

"Where at?" another voice yelled.

"Check around back!"

I didn't see or hear the dog until it was on top of me. It had run around to the back wall and charged in straight at me. I turned just in time to see a black shape hurtling out of the darkness, jaws gaping, teeth gleaming white. I threw up my left arm. The dog bit down hard and held on, jerking its wedge-shaped head, the fangs digging in to the bone; hot wires of pain shot up my shoulder. It was a big solid animal with a thick, flat skull. The ears were pointed like a doberman's. I swung sideways with the pistol, hitting it in the head. The blow had no effect. The dog tightened its grip, tearing deep into my forearm. I put the pistol barrel against the head and pulled the trigger. There was a flash and explosion. Something wet and warm splashed against my face. The dog rolled across me and lay still.

I crawled away from it, wincing at the searing pain in my arm. My back was against one of the stone pilings. I saw legs running alongside the house. A man crouched down and looked into the crawlspace. I couldn't see the face; he was turned away from me and in shadows. He held a rifle or shotgun. He still hadn't seen me. He was wearing a jacket and gloves. Straightening up, he sprinted to the back. When he bent down for another look, I braced the pistol against the piling and fired. There was another flashing explosion, the sound echoing under the house. The man screamed and pitched backward. I fired two more shots. He flopped on the ground, gripping his stomach.

Someone else was out there. I couldn't see him. I lay flat and still. My left arm felt as if it was on fire. I rolled over, desperately searching for him. Then I heard him running. A car door opened and slammed shut; the engine started. I saw the car back up, loose gravel flying from the rear wheels. It swung around sharply and still throwing gravel, sped up the driveway with its lights out. I didn't get a look at the driver or the license plate.

I got up and walked to the rear of the house. The man I had shot was lying on his back, mouth open, breathing hard; the sucking gurgle deep in his throat sounded like a wet sponge when it's squeezed. A wave of dizziness almost made me black out. I fell against the wall, my left arm hanging by my side. I looked at it and bit down—the flesh was raked open in two deep wounds. Blood was dripping down on my trousers and shoes. I wiped my right hand across my wet face; it was splattered with the blood and brains of the dog.

Picking up the man's rifle, I went to the front of the house. The door was open wide. I glanced inside, my back pressed against the wall, chest heaving. I shouted for Lawrence. No one answered. Moving quickly, I went inside holding the rifle up with my damaged arm.

The place had been torn apart. The contents of drawers were scattered on the floor, tables were overturned, chairs. I looked in the kitchen. The same mess there. And again in the front bedroom. There was no casket. I staggered down the hallway to the rear bedroom, where I had slept. It was dark and the door was open. I switched on the lights.

Lawrence was sitting in a chair, his hands tied to the arms with extension cords. His head was tilted forward. I took one look at his raw, oozing face and closed my eyes. I went down on my knees and put my ear to his lips. He wasn't breathing.

Oh, no! I thought, biting my lip. Not this!

They had beat him to death, trying to make him talk. The fact they were still there when I arrived meant he hadn't told them what they wanted to hear. He had moved the casket somewhere and held on to the secret to the end.

How long had it gone on? His mouth was ripped at the corners and teeth were missing. Blood had splattered the front of his shirt.

I got up slowly, bracing myself for another wave of shuddering dizziness. I was cold and dead inside. Maybe if I had moved faster, I could have got there in time. He hadn't been dead long; I might have saved him. He hadn't talked, and I hadn't helped him and now there was nothing left but self-disgust and emptiness.

This was how it had to end, I thought, cursing myself. I think I had known that from the first moment we'd found the lost grave at

Qumran. So many dead, so many friends. The woman I had loved, murdered. And for what? For what purpose? For the body of a man, whose identity I would never be sure of. Someone who'd been lost to the world for centuries and now was lost again.

I went outside. The wounded man was still lying in back of the house, gasping for air. I had shot him in the stomach. Another bullet had clipped off the top of his right knee.

I knelt at his side and turned his face toward me. He was younger than I thought. The brown hair lay in damp strands across his forehead; his eyes were closed. I jammed open his eyelids with my fingers and cupped his face in my hands.

"Who sent you!"

The mouth opened and a trickle of blood spurted out.

"Who sent you down here, you bastard? You killed them, didn't you? You killed them in Chicago and then you came down here and you killed Lawrence."

I slammed the head down again and again, pounding it into the muddy ground, trying to smash it to jelly until I was out of strength. When I stood up, sobbing and coughing, I knew he was dead.

CHAPTER 51

I LEFT Biloxi that same night and was still driving when the early morning sky started to change color. My left arm had stiffened. I had to stop to see a doctor in Tupelo to have it stitched up. He didn't like what he saw and, after giving me a tetanus shot, started asking a lot of questions. I made up a thin story that a stray dog had attacked me while I was changing a tire by the side of the road. A few minutes later he excused himself and went into his private office. I put my ear to the door and heard him call the sheriff. I left twenty bucks on a table and cleared out; he hadn't even finished the bandaging. There was some nerve damage and I still have the scar and a slight tremor in the left hand.

When I got as far north as Memphis, I called the Biloxi police department. I told the desk sergeant to send a car to a farmhouse just outside town and described how to get there. I hung up when he started to ask his first question.

I never found out what Lawrence had done with the body. I was sure he'd moved the casket. He'd had some time before those two caught up with him—maybe as much as a day; that would have given him a chance to hide it somewhere. I went back to Biloxi six or seven months later when I thought it would be safe enough to do some quiet checking, but nothing turned up, not even the slimmest lead. Dozens of old cemeteries were scattered along the Gulf Coast; he could have used any one of them, or then again, maybe he had discovered a better place.

In either case, the final secret was his, and he had taken it with him to the grave. After twenty centuries hidden near the Dead Sea, the body was lost again.

I needed years to get used to the idea. But I eventually accepted it just as I accepted the fact that I had to live on the run and change my name just to make sure I'd stay alive. I knew they would keep hunting for me, but I became skilled at being a fugitive. The technique is surprisingly simple—you learn to live like a frightened animal and keep moving. I didn't go anywhere without a pistol.

I spoke to Bourgonne once. The occasion was shortly after the pope had died. I read a piece in the *Times* that he was teaching at the University of Paris and had just written a new book, which had created a stir. The subject had to do with the archeology of the Old Testament and the continuing research into what had come to be called the Dead Sea Scrolls. In the early 1950s, dozens of scrolls and fragments of ancient Hebrew writings similar to those May and Sara had bought in Bethlehem were found in the caves that scarred the cliffs near the Essene monastery at Qumran. They had caused a sensation; an international team of archeologists had begun excavating the ruins and cemetery. Bourgonne's book suggested, as he had earlier in Chicago, that the Essene monks helped shape Christianity.

I was living in Southern California then. I called Bourgonne long distance.

We didn't talk long. I told him how Sara and May had been murdered. I didn't tell him what had happened to the body.

"I swear that I did not know," he said, choking out the words. "I had no idea."

His story was short and simple. After talking to us that last time in Chicago, he had lost his nerve; in a moment of fear he told Bishop Gray that he was to meet May and Sara at the airport. He also told him why. The bishop was understanding; he promised that the church would continue to negotiate with May. The morning of the accident, the two of them flew back to Rome together. The bishop, Bourgonne said, later told him that May had agreed to sell the body for $1.5 million dollars.

"And you believed that?"

"I wanted to...believe him," Bourgonne said slowly. "I never made any inquiries. I did not want to know. I was afraid...afraid I was losing my faith."

"Why, because of the body?" I asked.

He paused and said, "Because I was not strong enough to live with my doubts."

He asked me whether I could forgive him. "You must, if you have any mercy," he begged. "I can never forgive myself."

I don't remember which of us hung up first.

He died a few years before the results of the carbon dating tests on the Shroud of Turin were released, showing it to be a fake. I've always thought about what he might have done during the surge of publicity that followed the long-awaited announcement. Would he have dared to say anything? Would they have let him even if he had wanted to?

Maybe the body's disappearance was for the best—the implications would have been too unsettling. It's been a rough century and the next one promises to be even rougher, so why make things any more difficult for the poor bastards who have to live through it. The price of religious disillusionment comes high.

At least that's what I told myself when the hard times came and they came often. The memory of Sara was the only thing that helped me get through the succession of nights when I thought the door was going to slam shut and I'd find myself out in the darkness forever. The recollection of her love brought me back from the dead more often than I can remember. I knew she was still with me. That a light was still burning out there.

I've never tried to read too much into that—there weren't any visions or apparitions, just a strange, comforting peace that gave me the strength to keep going. Love that survives death—it's the only resurrection I can believe in.